HOMECOMING QUEEN

by
Linda Hughes

CeShore

Pittsburgh, PA

ISBN 1-58501-057-X

Paperback Fiction
© Copyright 2000 Linda Hughes
All rights reserved
First Printing—2000
Library of Congress #99-65234

Request for information should be addressed to:

CeShore Publishing Company
The Sterling Building
440 Friday Road
Pittsburgh, PA 15209
www.ceshore.com

Cover Design: AJ Rodgers - SterlingHouse Publisher
Typesetting: McBeth Typesetting and Design
Photographer: Michael Bain
Model: Jennifer Bennett
CeShore is an imprint of SterlingHouse Publisher, Inc.

Printed in Canada

Dedication

In memory of
Richard "Killer" Kilbourn

and in honor of all the men who served in Vietnam.

Acknowledgements

Thanks to Laura Brott and David Sinclair for their good editing, Bob Fenton for his good agenting, Steve Robbins for allowing me to use his lovely poem, my husband Joe for his unending support, and my kitty Rosie for warming the pages with lots of long snoozes.

CHAPTER 1

June, 1970

The beautiful young woman, drenched in sweat, writhed on the delivery room table.

"There we go. It's done," the obstetrician spoke softly as he handed the bloody bundle over to a nurse, allowing the limp mother only a glimpse before it was whisked away. A cackle of a sound - was it a cry? - echoed through the sterile white room as the burly nurse hurried out the stainless steel door.

"Can't I see it?" the girl rasped, so exhausted she could hardly speak.

"Now, now," the doctor soothed. "It's like I told you. I was afraid it wouldn't survive. Things haven't been good recently with your pregnancy. I'm so sorry, but it didn't make it. You were thinking of giving it up for adoption anyway."

"But I changed my mind," she protested with as much strength as possible.

"Don't talk," he advised, stroking her matted, long, ash blond hair. "I'm so sorry."

"But, but ... I thought I heard ...," she disputed, trying to lift her lead head. But, a needle was poked into her arm and her head fell back with a thud as she drifted into oblivion.

♦ ♦ ♦ ♦ ♦ ♦ ♦ ♦

Brandy Oakley performed rakehellishly in the middle of the dance floor at Bronco Buck's House of Burlesque. With a flurry of cap gun shooting, sparks and smoke spewing from the toy gun in one hand while she cracked a whip with the other, she hooted and hollered to "Mule Skinner Blues." Suddenly the music changed as the spotlight came up. Brandy handed her weapons over to a man in the audience, throwing him a suggestive look inviting him to use them. Then, while Jerry Lee Lewis' "Whole Lotta Shakin' Goin' On" wailed, she shimmied her provocative breasts as they peeked out from beneath her beaded and fringed red leather vest, which she summarily wiggled out of, twirled above her head, and cast to the floor. From the waist down she was decked out in black net hose held up by a black satin garter belt, under which she wore black lacy bikini panties. Her fancy red leather cowgirl boots came high up her shapely calves. The tassels on the red, sequined pasties covering her nipples danced merrily as she jiggled her enormous boobs. The sexually charged frenzy amidst the horde of men escalated with every move.

Llayne Robertson stood like a bad statue at the end of the bar waiting for a drink order to be filled by the 55-year-old rhinoceros hide of a bartender. She stared at the risqué stripper and then at the laughing, groping throngs of schnokkered-up men. Clearly, her life had reached an all-time low, she concluded. Here she was, a Golden Saddle Gal waitress in a strip joint, watching a floozy whose bowling-ball-sized bare breasts bounced around taunting a roomful of horny men. The DJ had just announced that Brandy would soon do her "amazing blazing tit routine" and Llayne didn't even want to venture a guess as to what in the hell that meant. Her feet hurt from running around in three-inch heels all night, and her minuscule red and black brocade costume was so tight she couldn't breathe, her post-pregnancy paunch not helping matters. A mere month ago she gave birth to a stillborn child, conceived during an ill-fated affair with a raffish professor who, when she informed him of her pregnancy, said, "I can't relate to that." To hide her condition, she quit her job at a restaurant and dropped out of the last couple of months of the spring semester at college. Now she had to take extra credits to get her degree on time. Consequently, she was so desperately broke she had to resort to living in a ratty camper so she could work this sleazy summer job, where a drunk guy now yelled at her. *Could life possibly get any more grim?* she brooded.

"Baby, baby, where's my bee-er?" the drunk guy hollered.

Llayne took the frosty mug the bartender set up and headed for the pit, as she thought of those tables full of boozed-up men where endless streams of cigarette smoke slowly meandered toward the lofty ceiling.

"Hey, hey, solider boy, paws off!" she admonished, swatting the lush's clumsy hand away as he groped for the red garterband encircling her black-netted thigh. The guy already had three dainty garters decorating his hulky body, one hanging from a Dumbo ear, another around a bulging tattooed bicep, and one around the thick ankle of his dirty army boot.

"Here," Llayne commanded, "drink your beer." She plunked the mug down in front of him.

"Shanks," he slurred with a cock of his head which made the garter on his ear fall and plop into his beer.

Llayne shook her head as she walked away, fanning the plume of red and black feathers ascending from a big bow on the top of her head, feeling like a junkyard attached to her scalp. She knew being a waitress in a strip club would be wild, especially with all these guys coming home from Nam, but she couldn't afford to castigate, since she so desperately needed money to finish her last year of college. She may have totally screwed up her life in the last year but she was determined to unscrew it by finishing her degree in psychology.

The one bright spot in her life right now was that in the last week she'd made as much as she normally made in a month at the restaurant in her college town. At this rate, she'd have enough money saved by the end of the summer to finish school without having to work her last year. And there was the bonus that this place was in a remote vacation town, Harbor Springs, in the northwest tip of the state on Lake Michigan. No one from her college, Central Michigan University in Mt. Pleasant in the middle of the state, would ever know.

"Llayne!" She heard a shout."You're Llayne, aren't you?" a preppy, good-looking, young man walked up and asked."You were in my drama class at CMU last fall!"

"N-no," she stammered,"you must be mistaken." Hell, she did remember him and hoped he was too pie-eyed to catch on to her lie.

"Llayne!" Buck, her burly boss, called from behind her.

"Damn," she said through clenched teeth as she threw Buck a forced smile.

"Hey, you are Llayne!" the young man stated, trying to protest as she scurried away. Her boss motioned to a table that needed attention and she rushed over to it, glancing back in time to see her former classmate pointing her out to his friends, gawking as they left the building. Yes, life could get worse, she realized. She could only pray he graduated and wouldn't be back at school to gossip about her.

Thankfully, all attention reverted to center stage as the music abruptly stopped and the lights went out in a theatrical flare. The dark room became silent.

A match scratched and lit in the middle of the dance floor. Brandy hissed, then moved the match to her left pasty, which flashed in a little ball of flame. The audience gasped. Brandy struck a second match and lit her right side. They gasped again.

Brandy had lit her tits.

Well, technically, she'd lit the wicks on her fireproof pasties and her chest was covered with fireproof ointment. But no such technicalities concerned that crowd. All that those grunting cavemen knew was that Brandy's amazing boobs were ablaze and they loved it!

Llayne was mesmerized at what the dancer did next: As "Great Balls of Fire" played, Brandy rocked her ribs until her breasts began to swing. She rocked faster and harder, making complete syncopated circles, each boob rotating in a different direction like gears. As one fire ball went under and outside, the flame of the other was in the center. Llayne shook her head as she grabbed empty glasses and bottles off of a couple of tables.

The audience was agog, heads rotating in time to the mammoth burning breasts. Those two flames just kept going round and round.... Even the women in the audience, who'd come with "dates" and "husbands," cheered and clapped along with the men.

No one would order more drinks until Brandy was done, so Llayne was headed for the bar when she bumped into another waitress, butting headdresses as each bent to catch the clinking, empty bottles on their trays."Sorry," Llayne apologized.

"Yeah, yeah. New, ain't ya?" the woman asked in a gravely voice.

"Yeah. One week. You new, too?"

"Ha! Been here three years. Seems like forever. But, hey, got three kids to support. Where else can a girl like me make money like this?"

Llayne glanced her over. She was probably in her late 20s but the heavy makeup made her look older. And tough. Indeed, where else?

"Name's Janice," the woman continued."Off last week. Had to take the little brats to see their dads. Vulgar, adolescent cretins! The men, not the kids!" This Janice's nonchalance about exposing family secrets to a stranger was a little shocking, and Llayne caught the reference to "dads." Families are getting more and more complicated in these wild '70s, she thought.

With that thought she hitched up the garter around her thigh and strode together with Janice to the bar, then reached behind with one hand to adjust the big bow of a tail on her brief costume while balancing her tray with the other.

Janice noticed, commenting, "Damned costumes. That Chicago designer who rigged 'em up is a sadomasochist who hates women, if ya ask me. Same one who done the Playboy Bunnies, the boss man is proud to say."

"Really?" Llayne said. "No wonder they're so painful!" She took a breath, no mean feat with rigid stays constricting her sides.

Janice scoffed, "Feel like a sardine in a can, don't ya? And this stupid Kleenex the dresser, also a sadomasochist if ya ask me, this Kleenex she sticks under our boobs fer cleavage makes me feel like a stuffed crab!"

Llayne added, "Yeah, it's all pretty fishy. I hate the chest makeup she makes me wear."

"Ha! These idiots don't have a clue what they're really lookin' at!" Janice scoffed, gesturing to indicate the customers.

Llayne checked her own cleavage for reassurance. A waitress the night before had a wad of Kleenex hanging out the side of her get-up. The tissues filling the bottom half of the built-in underwire bra and a streak of dark blush between Llayne's breasts were in place, causing her to appear to be much bustier than she really was without such assistance. She looked at the clock over the bar. Midnight. Two more hours and the damned getup would be off. She would breathe once more!

They turned their attention back to the show when the room burst out with laughter as Brandy shoved a burning nipple near a man's face. He flinched so convulsively he almost tumbled over backwards in his chair.

"How do they keep those things on, those pasties?" Llayne asked her self-appointed mentor.

"Bubble gum. Oh, there's a special gummy glue, but most a' the girls like gum. An' did ya know that after the show men buy those damned pasties fer 20 and 50 and sometimes even a hunderd greenbacks a pop?"

"No!" Llayne exclaimed as Janice vigorously nodded her head.

"Yeah, it's amazing how bone stupid men can be after a few beers. But ya know what's most insane? Last week Ginger Snapper was here, right?"

Llayne nodded. How could she ever forget the stunning woman, or the name?

"Ginger won a gold metal in track at the last Olympics."

"No woman won in track last time."

"Exactly! Soon as them games was over, Ginger, Gene back then, headed fer Sweden fer the operation he'd, she'd, always wanted!"

"No!" Llayne had thought she was beyond shock, but she was shocked now.

"Yeah, an' these dumb dicks don't even know it!" Janice snorted a laugh. Calculating the impact of her next words, she continued, "Most a' these guys've seen Brandy before and they know she's available after the show, fer the right price!" She chortled, having dropped her bomb, and sauntered away.

Llayne hadn't known that. So, this wasn't just a strip joint. It was a pimp parlor, too. Yes, she'd plummeted to the depths of depraved hell.

Brandy Oakley concluded her performance by blowing out the great balls of fire, licking her finger, placing it between her breasts, and hissing loudly. The message was clear: Brandy was hot! She grabbed her gun and whip, and galloped out of the room, tapping her butt with the whip like a rider would a horse.

The crowd went ape shit, as the saying went, but the din receded as Llayne's mind wandered, unbidden as it had want to do, to its solitary place, the place where the excru-ciating pain over the loss of her baby existed. Her child, a corpse, dead? Had she heard a cry? No, it'd just been her mind playing tricks on her. Her baby had died and the body had been "properly disposed of," she was told the morning after the birth when a nurse shuffled her out of the hospital.

Llayne shook herself from the waking nightmare. Life moved on. In a mere eight weeks she would begin her senior year at Central Michigan University. After that she'd have to figure out what to do with the rest of her life, on one hand terrifying in its inher-ent responsibility and on the other hand exhilarating in its potential freedom.

She blinked her eyes, probing herself back to the moment at hand, and looked around the saloon at the various groups of drinkers. Some old, some young, but all with the same idea. They wanted to forget their problems by drinking booze and watching a hot, young woman strut her stuff. Serve and strut, serve and strut. She needed to work hard to keep her mind off the vicissitudes of life.

That's when she noticed the young man at the end of the bar. He looked so sad, all alone, bringing the old phrase "crying in your beer" to life. *No!* she said to herself. *Don't say hello. Don't get involved. Men are nothing but trouble.* She didn't even glance his way as she went up for a Coke for herself.

"Excuse me," he said, his voice hoarse from crying. "Would you please pass me some matches?"

She handed him a pack of matches from the box beside her on the bar, put the Coke on her tray, and turned her back to walk away. That's when she heard him gasp back a sob.

No, don't do it! She turned around and asked, "You okay?"

The pause was definitely pregnant as he mulled that over. "Yeah, I'm okay," he lied. "Thanks for asking, though." She smiled slightly and turned away. "My girlfriend just left me, that's all," he added with a melancholy sigh.

"I'm sorry," Llayne offered, reluctantly turning his way again. "I doubt that getting drunk is going to make you feel much better, though."

5

He conjured up a weak grin. "It will tonight. I'll deal with the hangover tomorrow." He tossed back a double shot of whiskey.

Llayne nodded and walked away as the bartender poured him another double shot of Jack Daniels and a frothy beer from the tap to provide him with another boilermaker which he obviously didn't need.

The next time she went to the bar he said, "I love her so much. How can someone you love do that to you?"

"Beats me," she stated, determined to harden her heart to this man's plight. She couldn't handle her own plights.

On her next trip to the bar he let his new confidante know that Karen had been the only woman he'd ever really loved. Each time he was more drunk. Each time Llayne encouraged him to go home. Finally he headed out the door.

"Oh, cripes!" Llayne murmured under her breath, noticing his uneven stagger. "He can't drive." She dumped her tray, ran out the door after him, and found him standing at a shiny, brand-spanking-new, canary yellow Corvette, ironically parked next to her '62 Beetle, dull white in the spots that hadn't yet been eaten away by rust, which she'd bought two years hence for 75 dollars. He was obviously one of the rich vacationers who frequented the area from Detroit or Chicago. Wrapping her arms around her waist to protect herself from the slight evening chill, dressed scantily as she was, she approached him with caution. He stood with his hands on the hood, crying. "Hey, hey," she said gently. "I know I said you should go home, but you need someone to drive you. Come back inside and call a friend."

"I don't have any friends. Not now that Karen's gone. She was my best friend," he lamented.

With a stiff, gawky move he grabbed Llayne in a smothering bear hug. He smelled like booze as only someone who's been drinking all day can smell, so she turned her head in avoidance as he clung to her like a child clings to his mother upon realizing he's about to get a shot. Reluctantly, because she knew better than to get involved, she put her arms around the poor dope and patted his back. It was a combination of comforting him and simply holding him up.

But then his hand slipped down her back and found her bottom, so she grabbed his arm to stop him. They arm wrestled for a moment as he said, "Why don't you drive me home. Then we could ..."

An abrupt explosion of light from the bright headlights of a cherry red Fiat convertible struck them and almost toppled them over. They let go of one another and shaded their eyes. Gravel spit in every direction as the sports car screeched to a halt. The engine shut off and the lights went out.

Stunned, Llayne and the man watched as a striking debutante in a short, mint green, silk dress, more expensive than Llayne's entire wardrobe, exited the vehicle with calculated moves. Lanky bare legs stretched out and onto the ground; long blond hair swished from shoulder to shoulder; a small pink tongue wetted pink bow lips. With a

6

broad, dramatic gesture, she slammed shut her car door, then placed her delicate hands atop her slim hips.

"Well, well, well, Charles," she greeted the man sarcastically, striding toward them with measured steps. In her astonishment, Llayne still managed to notice the woman's high fashion, ankle-strap, leather shoes. Italian, no doubt, the kind called oat coat-tour for some reason Llayne didn't understand. "So, this is what you've descended to," the woman spat as she pointed at Llayne.

Suddenly Llayne realized she was the object of the woman's derisive ire. "Hey, wait a minute!" she protested. "What do you mean, 'descended to?'" The woman really pissed her off, reminding her of the snobby sorority girls at college who'd refused her admittance into their elite groups, treating her like a plebeian because she needed to work her way through school. Maybe she was standing in the middle of a raucous strip joint parking lot dressed in a ridiculous dollop of a tawdry costume, but she was still as good as anybody else. It just didn't show. That is, except for her good figure.

"I saw you two groping each other!" the woman snarled in disgust. "What were you going to do next, Charles? Take this little whore home? How could you even think of sleeping with something like this?"

Llayne didn't mean to. It just sort of happened. With all her might she swung her leg to kick gravel at the hooty-snooty bitch's shoes. She'd always had bad aim, though, and missed, careening herself into the side of the Fiat. No one noticed her spangles scratch the surface as she scampered for balance. There may have been a no-holds-barred brawl if a suddenly sobered Charles hadn't stepped in.

Placing his body between the two women and holding them apart, he warned, "Hey! Let's calm down here. She was just telling me I shouldn't drive because I've been drinking, and I gave her a thank you hug," he explained, pointing at Llayne. He had to be given credit for cleaning up the story. "And you!" he exclaimed, now pointing at the woman, "I can't believe you're here. I thought I'd never see you again."

The woman considered his story and decided not to lock horns. At least not now. She was ready to get out of there and barked, "Get in, Charles." He got in the passenger side of her car and dropped his throbbing head into his hands.

Don't do it. Llayne knew there was no good reason to help this conceited harpy. It may have been a pang of guilt over the kick or a power play because she knew something the elitist didn't know, but she felt propelled to whisper, "He's been crying in his beer all night because you left him. Said he couldn't live without his Karen."

The woman's expertly kohl-lined eyes widened, then narrowed to slits as she looked over at the heap of a man in her car. "Really?" she quarried in a low, growly voice. "So, that bitch finally left him. I came here because a friend said he was here without her. I'm Mary Alice, the one he left for Karen. I was hoping to get an edge, but it looks like I've got a big one."

Llayne couldn't believe it. She couldn't even help a poor slop without handing him over to the wrong damned dame!

7

As she got into her car and started the engine, Mary Alice yelled, "I sure as hell am glad I got here before the likes of you got your claws into him!" With that she sped away.

Llayne kicked dirt and gravel in the direction of the clearing dust, but it didn't help. People like that just didn't see people like her as people.

Buck's big form appeared at the door, his booming voice commanding, "Get in here! You can't help every stupid drunk in the state!"

Work, that was the way. Work to keep from thinking. Work to keep from crying. Work to keep from laughing at the absurdity of it all. Llayne went inside and attacked her tables with a vengeance, cleaning, wiping, emptying ashtrays, providing napkins, filling pretzel bowls and serving drinks.

Hustling up to one of her tables, she asked one of the five men who were chuckling over a lewd joke one of them had just finished telling, "Can I get you another beer?" Although in civilian clothes, the guy was obviously on leave from or just out of the army. That buzzed crew cut always gave them away in this age when hair over the ears was the rage for men.

"Yes-sir-ee," he said, eyeing her up and down. "That ain't all you can get me," he said as he patted his crotch. He thought he was so clever, saying the same thing she heard every night.

"Beer is it," she said without expression. "Take it or leave it."

"How about your garter, for my next tour in country?" he winked, using the slang soldiers used to refer to Vietnam.

"Sure. Ten bucks. I take it off."

He agreed, so Llayne yanked the garter off her leg without the sensual ceremony some gals gave the gesture. The guy shoved a 10 across the table and boastfully laid the lacy leg band down to frame the large hard-on begging to escape from his pants.

Llayne scooped up the 10-dollar bill and walked away shaking her head as she asked no one in particular, "Do all you guys come home from Nam so horny?"

♦ ♦ ♦ ♦ ♦ ♦ ♦ ♦

The casket was dull gray steel under a steely gray September sky. Hard. Cold. Dead. The American flag draped across the top laid lifeless.

"He came home a hero. Benny Shawl's loved ones can be comforted knowing he died for the freedom he believed in ..." The preacher droned on.

About 50 people gathered around the moribund grave. Llayne looked at Priscilla, her best friend and roommate, standing beside her. In her mourning the 21-year-old looked a thousand.

The line of seven soldiers were finally given the signal and in unison they hoisted their rifles. Shot one, shot two, shot three-ee. One was off beat. An almost 21-gun salute.

A shoddy ceremony.

◆ ◆ ◆ ◆ ◆ ◆ ◆ ◆

"What a crock of shit! A hero? The motherfucking bastards didn't give him a chance. Benny died because he was scared shitless." Priscilla dragged on a Winston between words. Back in their college apartment she looked more like the pretty young woman that she was, and although Llayne was accustomed to her quick comebacks and playful use of vulgarities, she'd never heard her friend use fowl language with such venom.

"He wouldn't marry me before he went. Did you know that?" Priscilla asked.

Llayne shook her head.

"I wanted to. But he said it'd be harder for me to start over as a widow than as a former fiancee." She fondled the tiny diamond ring on her finger. "Christ, Llayne, he was the most gentle kid alive. He knew he'd never make it back. Those fucking bastards!"

Her voice cracked, and once again tears rolled down her alluring face. Llayne had always thought she looked like a diminutive Sophia Loren, her Italian descent etched into her face and evident in her lush, dark hair, burnished with deep auburn highlights. Now she just looked tormented.

"Life's been a bitch for us," Priscilla noted, looking intently at her friend as if making a decision, sucking on the cigarette as if it gave her oxygen. As smoke drew a scrim up over her face, she said, "Don't ever tell anyone this. Promise?"

"Promise."

"I did the most awful thing. It's against the law, I think. Benny's casket was sent back sealed, never to be opened. I told the funeral director I wanted to be alone with him, and I opened it. It was hard, the top was heavy. But I got it open." Another drag. Another tear. "The fucker was empty. Except for some goddamned dog tags, which looked brand new. Empty." Her dark eyes glazed over as she spastically smoked.

Llayne had never felt so useless in her life. She had no idea what to say.

Priscilla looked off into space, her eyes covered in mist, and said, "So, who in hell knows what the fuck they're doing over there?"

"All we are saying ... is give peace a chance ..."

She felt out of place, singing and carrying a candle in a peace march. Sad and aimless, she joined on a whim. But here, in the dark of night amidst strangers, the tears finally came. Tears for Benny, the boy who'd been her childhood friend, the boy who betrothed her best friend, the boy who was killed in that strange, foreign, Asian land only two weeks after landing there.

And tears for the child who was lost to her.

Llayne huffed out her candle and flung it to the street, freeing her hands to swipe at the relentless flood from her eyes. Unexpectedly, a tall, lean man came to her and enwrapped her in his strong arms, holding her tight while she cried into his broad shoulder. He wore a black, balloon-sleeved shirt open half-way down his chest displaying a gold peace pendant on a chain. His eyes were piercing brown; his facial features were large; and, his shiny, black hair was shaggy and shoulder-length. It was abundant, healthy hair which was accentuated by his sideburns and mustache. He ran his thumb down the bleached pale streak on one side of Llayne's long, straight, ash blond hair, saying nothing as his testostero-warmth soothed her and, she had to admit, relit her dormant sexual desires. After a time he left her and only then did she realize that the hippy was Peter Smith, the leader of the protest. He reminded Llayne of the do-gooder caballero Tyrone Power played in *The Mark of Zorro*. She saw the old movie at a campus film festival and fell in love with Zorro, the fox, the swashbuckling Spaniard of chivalrous valor. Although Peter was what some might call homely, Llayne understood this modern hero's charismatic appeal.

"Phantasmagorical!" a hippy raved, his pukka shell necklace rising and falling on his Adam's apple. "Groovy," "Outta sight" and "Right on," the marchers blurted out as they entered Peter's living room through a door hung with strings of multi-colored love beads. The lavender Victorian house with the orange and yellow and pink gingerbread trim had been easy to target from the street as Peter's. The hit song "War" could be heard half a block away blaring from the stereo. "War ... What is it good for ..? Absolutely nothin' ..!" But it was the eerie, luminescent glow of psychedelic posters under a black light inside the home which caused the stir. Cryptic, phosphorescent images papered the walls with peace signs, Sly and the Family Stone, The Doors, The Rolling Stones, Sharon Tate, moon and stars, Buzz Aldrin and Neil Armstrong landing on the moon, Edwin Star, Janis Joplin, Tom Petty, The Beetles, Creedence Clearwater Revival, The Temptations, Mickey Mouse. Mickey Mouse? That one made Llayne look twice. Peter must be a complicated man. Most of these types of college kids, the ones like her who either couldn't afford to or didn't want to go the traditional Greek route, could buy a couple of posters and a black light if they pooled their funds. And they couldn't even wish for an eight-track stereo set-up like this one, and furniture that looked relatively new, and what appeared to be an honest-to-god wool rug, woven with multi-colored art deco designs. No thrift shop junk here.

The group Peter invited over after the peace march was varied, students, professors, misfits. There were even a few Afro-Americans, which was unusual because there were so few of them on campus. Llayne didn't know what surprised her most, the posters, furnishings, stereo, 15-inch television set (she couldn't remember the last time she'd watched one bigger than the size of a cracker box), the underground pawn shop Peter ran out of his basement, or his "harem" of three bare-breasted women. Even if there had been a flash of sexual attraction during those comforting moments in his arms, this all told her he lived in a weird world which was beyond her. Three women at once! Bronco

Buck's had liberated her, but not this far. She may accept it for others but would never want to be one of a gaggle of women herself.

She did realize, however, that prior to last summer she would've been horrified being in a group where half-naked women roamed around. After the strip joint it seemed as ordinary as nails.

Others, however, were clearly shocked. A shy, elderly professor sitting next to Llayne was stunned when one groupie girl dressed in hip-hugger bell bottom jeans that were decorated with enough patches to serve as a personal billboard, clunky earth shoes, a bandanna around her neck, and earrings so big they could substitute for tambourines, but with her torso buff-bare, leaned over his shoulder to hand him a glass of wine and her taut nipple casually grazed his arm. He choked back a cough, caught his breath, mumbled "thank you" as he took the glass, and stared off into space.

From across the room Peter saw Llayne observing the goings on and cast her a wide smile. She smiled back.

The lifestyle might be rather barbaric, but it was obvious Peter treated his followers well. He had charisma, power over people which he thankfully seemed to use positively. Not like that crazy Manson out West. This man appeared to be a kind prophet, not an evil devil.

There was pot and wine. No hard drugs or hard booze, which surprised Llayne because she'd stereotyped hippies, "freaks" as some people called them, as all being into hard stuff, drug-of-the- day stuff. She noticed Peter drank slowly from a glass of white wine and puffed on a sweet, pungent joint each time it was passed around. One of the bare-chested women asked Llayne what she wanted, and brought her a Coke. Llayne, too, puffed on a joint when one came her way.

Settling back into a bean bag chair, she decided she liked Peter's place. It was comfortably strange. This was better than those ignorant frat parties with garbage pail drugs where kids dumped whatever drugs they had on them into a garbage pail, stirred them up, grabbed a handful, and popped them without knowing what the results might be. It was considered cool to be able to handle whatever befell you. Fried brains is what a lot of them got, if all the zombies on campus were any evidence, in Llayne's opinion. And there was the obligatory athlete asshole with his mouth permanently affixed to the tap on a keg, with others slapping him on the back for being the life of the party. Here everything seemed more honest, even the nudity. Not a bunch of bozos trying to get their "brothers" dates into a bedroom to screw, only to brag about it later.

After an impromptu lesson from a professor about the history of marijuana; in which he taught that the weed's original name, hashishin, is where the word "assassin" came from because of the pack of Middle Eastern mercenary warriors during the Dark Ages who would get high on the stuff before setting out on their killing missions; someone turned down the music, allowing the Stones to recede into the background. A hush fell over the gathering as Peter sat cross-legged on the floor in the middle of the room.

The discussion about Vietnam began ....

11

CHAPTER 2

"Ah, excuse me, miss." The man rolled his cigarette from one side of his lips to the other as he looked down at her with a cocky grin.

Llayne glanced up from her fixed gaze at the clean glass ashtray on her small table and saw Paul Newman. Well, that was her first impression of him, whoever he was. A rugged Paul Newman in *Butch Cassidy and the Sundance Kid*. Of fair height and excellent slim build, with the scent of Old Spice wafting around his hard body, he had the most vivid pale blue eyes to ever look at her. She actually thought she might swoon.

"Wow, you have beautiful eyes," he said, echoing her thoughts about him. "I never noticed before, because I've obviously never been this close, but they're deep sea blue."

Shaking herself from the trance of attraction and come-on, she said, "Thanks, but you didn't come over here to discuss my peepers."

"Oh, yeah, well, me and the guys were just wondering ...." He took the cigarette out of his mouth and pointed it at the group whose feet were planted as if in cement in the same place every night at the bar. Llayne recognized them as Nam vets. "We were just wondering ...," he repeated, lightly touching her shoulder, then pulling the other chair out from her table-for-two.

Llayne remembered that even Mr. Newman needed to be put in his place sometimes. "Sorry, soldier," she said, having learned how to deal with forward men like this at Bronco Buck's. "I don't recall asking you to talk to me, let alone touch me."

Instead of being offended, he let out a howl of a laugh and hollered over to his buddies as he pointed at the top of her head, "She's the one!"

"Excuse me, miss," he began again, dropping his cigarette onto the peanut-shell-covered floor, stomping it out with the heel of his boot, and shifting his bottle of Strohs into his left hand from his right. He rubbed his right up and down his pressed jeans to dry it off then thrust it forward, saying, "My name's Mack O'Brien. May I please have the honor of discussing something with you that I do believe you'll want to hear?"

Llayne looked him over, intrigued by those stone-washed-denim-blue eyes, and relented. She shook his hand and said, "I'm Llayne Robertson."

Politely he asked, "May I please sit down, Miss Robertson?"

She nodded, actually rather glad for the intrusion. She'd been sitting here alone at The Cabin bar, the college hang-out which sat on the outskirts of town, waiting for Priscilla who was 20 minutes late. Oh, she wasn't embarrassed to be alone, the atmosphere was so homey, just bored because the band hadn't started yet. The Cabin really was a big old cabin with a small stage for the band and a dance floor on one end and the bar on the other end, with tables in between.

"You know," he informed her, "the Vets' Club - we're a campus version of the VFW, the Veterans of Foreign Wars - well, our Vets' Club has over 2000 members because so many guys are going to school on the G.I. Bill..."

"Wait a minute," she interrupted. "C.M.U. only has 9000 students. You're telling me 2000 are vets?"

"There're 9000 full-time students. Most of the vets are part-time. But that doesn't matter because they can still vote for Homecoming Queen. And that's why I'm talking to you. We've seen you in here a lot, dancing." He fondled the pack of Camels in his breast pocket but thought better of lighting up and finished off his beer instead, grinning at her askance over the bottle. "The guys like the way you dance," he chided. "In fact, I've heard the word 'fox' thrown around a lot." Llayne had the decency to blush. "Now, we want somebody to run for Homecoming Queen for us. We need somebody who's not only pretty, which you are, but somebody who can put up with us rascals. That's you. You know what I mean?"

No, she wasn't sure what he meant, so she studied this brutally handsome man as he yakked at her. He was one of those males who oozed sex appeal without effort. His lush but trimmed, wavy, brown hair didn't quite cover his ears, but he had a habit of running his fingers through it to shove it out of his face, an inviting, nonchalant gesture which tempted a woman to run her fingers through it, too. He was older than most students, probably in his early 30s, and was much neater than typical college kids, a throwback to the '60s. He even wore a moderately starched, pin-striped shirt with his jeans. Most other vets had adjusted to the fads of the day by dressing like third-rate military men in worn fatigues, scuffed boots, and an array of gaily colored shirts and bandannas, just like other college kids who acquired their army clothes at the Salvation Army store. She gandered a look over at the motley crew of vets at the bar. Every girl wanted to run for Homecoming Queen. But like this?

Yes, like this! She suddenly decided she wanted this desperately. Her life had been so strange for so long. This was the kind of thing that was supposed to happen to a young woman. Maybe a homecoming campaign would help her forget her past. Her excitement dissipated, however, as quickly as it had arisen.

"Thanks, Mack," she said. "I'm truly flattered by your offer. But, you see, there might be a problem. I've been a war protester. It's nothing against you guys. I think a lot of vets don't understand that. In fact, I respect you for having done what you think is right. I believe in that; I just don't believe in that war."

Mack chawed on that. "Shit! Oh pardon the language ...," he apologized, not realizing, as most men didn't, that when alone many females are capable of matching truckers in heat word for word. "I'm not sure I believe in that war, either," he leaned forward and whispered candidly. "Just have to tell myself I do to justify having spent a year of my life in that hellhole, you know? Let me talk to the gang."

He walked to the bar, lighting a cigarette along the way, and Llayne watched his bad boy swagger. His firm buttocks sensuously stroked the inside of his tight jeans, causing Llayne to experience a flash of a vision of that butt naked, rhythmically pumping up and down. She shook the apparition and whispered to herself, "Yup, he's trouble." At the bar he ordered a fresh beer before turning his persuasive powers on his club members.

14

Llayne sat alone and waited as he gestured broadly while talking to his comrades. He laughed loudly and slapped a huge man on the back. They looked over their shoulders at her. She felt like a cow at auction and nervously gulped a swig of her Coke. Mack talked some more and eventually the other guys seemed more interested in their beer than in what he was saying. He smiled and yelled "Thanks!" as he strode back to Llayne.

He turned the chair backwards and straddled his legs on either side to sit down facing her, and announced, "We don't need to worry about them. They'll vote for anything with round eyes."

Llayne wasn't sure if she was offended or charmed, but it didn't matter. She was running for Homecoming Queen!

The band started up with the Beatles hit, "Let It Be."

"That'll be our campaign slogan!" Mack declared. "Let It Be, Llayne Robertson!"

If he touched her one more time she would surely lose control and grab his hand to rub it around her breasts.

He did it again! It was all she could do to keep her composure while Mack smoothed a wrinkle near the waist of her tight, red sweater. His touch sent shockwaves of excitement through her body. Did he see her shudder with desire? His insouciant look said no. Obviously this was just entertainment, a diversion from The Cabin, for him and his buddies.

"Okay, Neckbreaker, you can start shooting."

A dozen vets and a number of others hung around while the behemoth man, nicknamed Neckbreaker for reasons she didn't want to know, shot picture after picture so one could be used for homecoming buttons and posters.

Unlike most campaign photographs, this wasn't staged in a studio with a fancy satin or fur wrap demurely draping the candidate's shoulders. No, their campaign strategy was nontraditional in every respect. At Mack's suggestion, they were in the campus park and Llayne wore tight jeans and the sweater, making no attempt to hide her appealing figure.

She turned sideways and reached for a leaf on a tree, smiling provocatively into the camera as her long, straight hair with the bleached streak down one side, fell seductively over one side of her face.

"That's the one!" Mack announced. "Good job, kiddo," he complimented as he laid his hand for a brief moment on her back.

His handprint singed the sensitive skin on her hindside, but she was surprised he didn't pat her on the top of her head, he'd been treating her like such a child.

Her preoccupation with Mack caused her to miss seeing Professor Rex Bates in the crowd of onlookers. Although with a pert, adoring, blond coed, he blatantly ogled Llayne as he stroked his neatly trimmed, dark beard. Mack didn't miss it, and used his body to stand in the way and fuss over her to protect her from the gawker's salacious glare. He didn't like it and he didn't like that asshole drama instructor. He'd seen him before, squiring girls around campus, taking advantage of their naiveté and vulnerability. Somebody should put the cocksucker in his place. He'd damned well better stay away from Llayne.

Mack invited Peter and his hippy followers to a campaign meeting, which surprised Llayne and disgruntled some of the vets. True to their military training, however, the men didn't buck their leader's decision. A dozen vets were in their usual places in The Cabin and blinked at the intrusion of bright afternoon sun when Peter and his entourage entered. The door closed behind them and the windowless place dimmed again. The vets relaxed.

"Hey, I'm Mack O'Brien, President of the Vets' Club." Mack introduced himself as he and Peter shook hands.

"Glad to meet you, and help with the campaign. We think a lot of your candidate," Peter said, smiling at Llayne over Mack's shoulder.

She stepped forward and offered a soft "Hi," suddenly overcome with shyness. She hadn't known that Peter thought a lot of her and wondered why.

"Listen," Mack addressed his guest. "I know this might seem odd, you being war protesters and us putting our asses on the line over there and all, but I've been thinking it over and figured, you know, in the end we all want the same thing. No more war."

Everyone listened intently. The hippies registered no expression. Some of the vets nodded assent. Some seemed pissed, as if maybe they liked war.

Peter flashed Mack his biggest smile, which was considerable. "You're right," he concurred. "Our methods may be different but our goal is the same. This should be a very interesting meeting."

Llayne then understood that this homecoming campaign had come to mean more than whether or not she became a queen. In fact, she felt rather inconsequential as she watched the scene unfold before her. Peter's followers moved flanks out and into the room analyzing this alien place. They seldom went to bars, preferring their own places where they could smoke some good dope. The vets blatantly stared at them, so the hippies returned the visual interrogation. The two leaders talked at the door, so alike in leadership ability but so different otherwise. One had the face of an all-American Irish boy, open, energetic, wavy-haired, blue-eyed, scrappy Mack O'Brien. The other was mysteriously extrinsic, tall, and foreign. Enigmatic Peter Smith with the dark, soulful eyes.

Llayne felt an attraction for both men. But, she had to admit, she felt attracted to most men. The other day she'd drooled over an older gas station attendant's hinder in greasy jeans as he'd pumped her gas. She was obsessed! Of course, that bedevilment had landed her in trouble last year. She wondered if she'd still be possessed if she ever actually had sex again. She wondered what sex was like with different men. Could it possibly ever be as good physically with anyone else as it'd been with Rex? It certainly hadn't been with her two high school boyfriends, one as bumbling as the other. Her 11th grade beau had convinced her to make love with him in his old jalopy convertible and had taken her to the woods on a pleasant summer's day. They parked at the end of a dirt path at the bottom of a hill. Very secluded, he reassured her to salve her frazzled nerves. It worked, too, until a Cub Scout troop appeared at the top of the hill, looking down at them in all their nude, copulating glory. Then there was her 12th grade boyfriend who'd spent weeks convincing her to skip school so they could have sex in his bedroom while his parents were at work. Stupid as only 17-year-olds at the height of hormonal poisoning can be, they left their clothes in the living room and pawed their naked way to his room. Five minutes later they'd heard the front door slam. His father had come home! The lamebrain kid didn't know that his dad came home for lunch everyday. Both of those brief encounters had ended abruptly from sheer embarrassment.

Neither had it been what one could ever even remotely call romantic or satisfying with two sexual liaisons, well sort of liaisons, in college before Rex. During her first year at CMU there was a singular, 15-minute slam-bam-thank-you-ma'am with Brady Thomas, a boy she'd had a crush on since ninth grade. He'd been drafted into the army and, after totally ignoring her in high school, came on to her for a "quickie" before going overseas. She'd been so ecstatic that he'd finally come to his senses and realized she was worthy of his everlasting love, she hadn't realized he meant quickie literally, ejaculating prematurely and leaving her before she had time to so much as spell orgasm. She hadn't heard from him since. Then during her second year there'd been a vapid collision with a student who'd changed his mind at the last minute, saying "no" he didn't want to have sex with her after all because he was saving it for marriage. When Llayne had told Priscilla, she'd wondered, "Marriage to whom, a woman or a man?" No, Llayne's physical exploits with boys hadn't even begun to satiate her lusty desires. That didn't happen until she met Rex.

Professor Rex Bates had shown her what it was like to find sexual pleasure with a real man and she'd never want a boy again. Could there possibly be another man as good in bed as Rex? Would she ever find out?

Mack or Peter? Which would she want? Which would she want first? She practically hyperventilated at the thought. The thrill of being in Peter's strapping arms during those few minutes when she'd cried at the peace march and the stimulation of Mack's electrifying touch when the campaign pictures were being taken lingered and aroused her still. No matter. At the moment, neither knew she lived.

The two men had gone to a corner table and fallen into deep conversation. Mack gulped a Strohs and Peter sipped a white wine spritzer.

The others found mingling more difficult until someone passed out campaign poster and button materials. With a common goal, everyone went to work.

Llayne mused at what the frat rats would say about this! They were already upset she canvassed campus in her jeans instead of dressing up like the Greek candidates. A number of these posters had already gone up and the Panhellenic Council had expressed their dismay over the informality of the pose. That made Llayne gloat. She liked dismaying some of those people; they were so smug they deserved it. They would go bonkers over this scene!

These two disparaging groups, vets and hippies, were dressed in an assortment of old army clothes splotched with festive adornments like bandannas, hats, pins, fringed boots, gaudy earrings, and hair worn frizzed, straight, shaggy, Afroed, braided with beads and feathers, or any combination thereof. Ironically, the three harem women were the most conservatively dressed of all, in jeans and plain sweaters. Even they, whom Llayne would have guessed to be totally disinterested, worked diligently on the posters.

The week before when Llayne had stumped with a nice married vet named Dennis, they'd found that most of her posters had disappeared, which was why they already needed more. At first they suspected opponents had torn them down, but as they distributed fliers door-to-door in the men's dorms, they saw the posters on guys' walls, most often over the bed. Dennis suggested they let them be, saying they'd get more votes that way, anyway.

Now the group at The Cabin glued small prints of her picture onto buttons. When they finished, everyone put one on. Unlike the tradition of wearing a campaign button on one's lapel, these supporters had to be creative because they didn't have lapels. One went into an Afro, another on a head rag, a few on boots, one on a purple sock, and one on a denimed rear end.

Llayne started to complain to Neckbreaker that he should move his, but when she looked up into that massive moon-cratered face and gap-toothed smile wide enough to harbor a ship, so proud of himself for his ingenuity, she decided that if he wanted to wear her picture over his pecker on his fly it was okay with her.

Eventually, she sauntered over to the corner where Mack and Peter were so engrossed in conversation, with the intention of joining in. But, as she neared their table, it was evident that they'd forgotten everyone else in the room. There were tears brimming in Peter's eyes as Mack told him about Dennis, the married vet who'd campaigned a week earlier with Llayne. She stood pressed against the wall in a shadow where they didn't notice her, and listened to Mack explain that Dennis had succumbed to nightmares that were so bad his wife had called for help. Just yesterday Mack and Neckbreaker had taken Dennis to the Veterans' Hospital in Ann Arbor, and admitted him into the psychiatric ward. The war had driven him crazy.

Llayne thought of her own father and of all the nights he awoke the entire household with horrifying screams of terror from his World War II nightmares. She looked at Mack and Peter, and felt a ray of hope. Hope that there were people who could work together for peace. She left them to talk and slipped back into the group.

Wishing that Priscilla was there, she ambled from table to table, trying to make polite conversation with each group as she helped work on the buttons. Her roommate would have enjoyed all of these weird people, but worked at the pizza joint next door to their apartment on Saturdays.

Somebody put the Beatles tune "Let It Be" on the jukebox and the meeting started to come to a close. The song roused the two leaders, and they rejoined the group.

Peter raised his hands for silence and addressed them. "Some of my people were against our coming here today. Some because we protest the war, and some because they don't believe in what they call 'meat market' pageants involving women. But I reminded them that firstly, we all have a goal of peace in mind, and secondly, a person should be free to do her own thing. If Llayne wants to run for Homecoming Queen, that's her thing and we have no right to deny that. She doesn't hurt anybody else by doing it. Plus, she's the kind of person who'll use that forum well. You have our support!"

Llayne had never thought of any of that. It sounded good.

Some of his followers clapped; a few vets did, too. Clearly there was not total support but both groups were willing to follow their leaders. That fascinated Llayne most of all.

Now Mack took a turn. "I thank all of you for your help here today. Our winning won't just be a victory for our candidate," he said, smiling at Llayne, "it'll show this campus that the vets are a group to be reckoned with! We're back and we won't be ignored anymore! It's been hard coming home knowing there are groups protesting all we did in Nam. But this, our joint effort, is proof that all of us can get past that. We shall, as you are so fond of saying, overcome! I don't mind telling you it was hell over there, and most of our men would have chosen to be anyplace but there. We believed we didn't have a choice; we were doing what our country told us to do. Don't blame us for being loyal. Respect us for being brave. Let this, finally, be a homecoming for us all!"

Hoots of assent scattered about the room; Mack and Peter shook hands; and, with a flip of his long, black, wool cape, Peter and his devotees vanished out the door.

Some of the vets went back to their beer, some argued football with Mack and some danced to the jukebox with their wives and girlfriends. Llayne went on home.

19

Chapter 3

His big brown eyes bore through her as she ignored his glare. He played with his thin, black mustache incessantly and she noticed it twitch ever so slightly in discomfort over the silence screaming through the stagnant little room.

She hated it here. She hated him. Why had she come? she berated herself.

This was the last fall she would be a student at Central Michigan University, the autumn of her college life, supposedly a sentimental time always to be remembered. This situation would never qualify for waxing nostalgic.

The brush of vivid fall hues outside the smudged window behind him invited her to escape to its bright life. For lack of anything better to do and because to look out the window made her feel more claustrophobic, she scrutinized the room, carefully avoiding the piercing stare of the man. A coat rack considered tumbling over with the weight of too many well-worn sweaters. A child's Crayon drawing of a purple cow seemed morose as it hung sideways from a misplaced tack in the drab olive green wall. Papers were in piles everywhere she looked.

It occurred to her that perhaps she would suffocate and die right here in this awful place. She imagined the scene one year hence when a perky work-study student's nosiness would get the best of her and she would decide to snoop beyond the "Do Not Disturb" sign hanging outside on the doorknob. This clinical psych student with frizz hair, braces, a sack dress, clogs and granny glasses would peek into the room only to find two seated skeletons, one a male behind the desk with its hand bones melded to its upper jaw bone, the other a female facing the wall. The only connection would be the cobwebs between their skulls. Later the newspaper would list the causes of death: She "died of boredom and lack of direction in life" and he "died in pursuit of fulfillment of his clinical psychology professorial duties."

The mustache jerked her attention back to it by speaking. "You must feel something, Llayne. Here you are, one of the most popular young women on campus. You've just been elected Homecoming Queen ..."

She didn't bother pointing out that she couldn't have lost, with the Vets' Club having 2000 members compared to the traditional club or fraternity or sorority which had about a hundred. All Mack had to do on voting day was place sentries outside the doors of classrooms filled with vets to remind them to vote. Most hadn't even seen their candidate's picture, but they didn't care. After so many horrendous losses in Nam, they just wanted to win something.

"You test out at a high intelligence quotient," the mustache continued, "but your grades are slipping drastically. And you say you don't feel anything."

"That's right," Llayne said. "I'm dead inside." It was true. Even though she was thrilled to be Homecoming Queen, she'd fallen into a real funk since the election and didn't know why.

Linda Hughes

Again she questioned herself about why she'd come. This conservative-over-30-thus-not-to-be-trusted-adult professor, Dr. Raymond Lichenger, of her clinical psychology class took his job much too seriously by insisting she see him privately. She was suspicious. He might be another man/child attracted to a college girl, like so many of them, like Rex. Or, he truly could be into his shrink role. Probably the latter, she surmised.

He was Jewish. A classmate told her Lichenger was a Jewish name, although she herself had no idea how one could tell. And he was from New York. A New York Jew shrink. She'd never met a Jewish person before, that she knew of. Never met a shrink, either. Or someone from New York, for that matter.

"I'm very concerned about your grades," he said.

Tough padoobies, she thought, *if I fail that's my business.* Besides, she knew she'd never let it get that bad. She desperately wanted a degree, even if acquiring it was turning out to be a royal pain in the ass.

"You don't need to worry," she said.

In class this guy taught that silence in a therapy session can be productive if used properly. Here it was dreadfully boring. After a long spell the doctor of psychology finally spoke again.

"You said you feel dead. I'm not sure dead is the word you want. Dormant may be more appropriate. I think you've been so overwhelmed with feelings you don't know how to handle them. You know how some people explode, get angry a lot? Well, some 'implode.' Instead of going out the feelings get buried inside, under the rubble of life. I think that's what's happened to you, and I want to help you sort through that rubble and find your feelings and therefore enjoy your life."

"No, Dr. Lichenger, not dormant," she corrected him. "Dead." *Crimony!* She hated meeting with him. Or having a "session" as he insisted on calling it. He aggravated her no end, telling her how she felt.

He sighed. Irritatingly so. She could see his brain rudder turning to try a new tack.

"Tell me about how you grew up," was what he came up with.

Ah, she thought, *a piece of cake.* She could easily take up the rest of the hour with this kind of bullshit.

"I was born in West Branch," her saga began. "It's on the west branch of the Rifle River. Small town, 90 miles northeast of here. Mt. Pleasant seems like a big town to me, about 20,000 people not even counting the college, because West Branch only has about 2000. We were kinda poor, I guess, but so were most other folks in town, so it didn't make much difference. Don't even have dial phones up there. I never dialed a phone until I got to college!"

He remained expressionless. Usually that phone story evoked interest.

"Yeah," she forged ahead, "in West Branch you just pick up the receiver and wait for Elizabeth or Edna to come on and say 'Number pa-leese.' Not only can they tell you if the line's busy, they can tell you who the person's talking to. It's cool."

Cool didn't impress him.

"The radio station," she rambled, "is WBBM, for West Branch Bob Marshall, the owner. But of course, all the kids call it West Branch BM. You know, shit." She chuckled.

He did not.

"Not much to do up there," she pressed on, "except go to the show every week. The Midstate Theater has one show a week, on weekends. We bowled during the week at Ogemaw Lanes. I went to one show a week all my life except the first week. My mom wasn't ready yet. But by week two we went. There's a cry room for women to take their babies. My mom told me about it a thousand times; we saw *Joan of Arc*. She loves Ingrid Bergman."

Ingrid didn't move him. She wondered if anything did.

"Do you have any brothers or sisters?" he asked.

"A brother, two years younger," she said. "He's in the army in Germany. I never see him."

The professor didn't seem to care much about Germany.

"I have to admit I never paid much attention to him," she prattled. "By the time I got to high school I guess I was pretty boy crazy and that was all I cared about. Had a crush on Brady Thomas from ninth grade on. He was two years older. I had a couple of other boyfriends, though, because he wouldn't go out with me. Said I was too nice for a hood like him. I haven't heard anything about him since he left for the army." No way was she about to tell this man about her brief, unsatisfactory sexual encounter with Brady, so she continued with, "He broke my heart when I was 15, at Benny Shawl's birthday party. Candice Canton ..." She hesitated as this promised to shock the stodgy professor. Maybe if he were offended it would keep him from wanting to talk to her again, so she continued, "The guys called her Candy, you know, Cunt." She flushed at saying the dirty word in front of an adult male. It was too late to stop now, so she herded ahead, "C.C. for short. Well, C.C. was offering her services out back in the cornfield between Golden Bantam and Field. Brady was the first in line."

Ah ha! A twitch of the mustache.

"Do you have a boyfriend here?" Dr. Lichenger asked.

"No!" Immediately she knew she'd answered too vehemently, too quickly. It was true. She had no one. Not since Rex last year.

"I, well, I," she stammered, "I date a lot. Just no one special. But it's better to go out than stay home alone, I guess." She attempted lightness, smiling grandly, showcasing her dimples and broad white teeth.

Unsmiling, he said, "Are you saying it's easier to go out with just anybody than to stay home alone and face yourself?"

An invisible two-by-four whacked Llayne in the gut, knocking the wind out of her. Turning away from him, she tried to hide the pesky tears which had suddenly come to her eyes.

Staring at the bleak wall, she knew there was no way to explain to anyone, especially this strange man, that there was nothing to face in herself. She truly felt empty, dead, inside.

Her discombobulated mind scrambled to try to piece together whether or not she should tell him, *"The empty hole in my heart filled with love for Rex last year only to be blasted away when he left, then filled with love again for his child during my pregnancy only to be sucked dry with the stillbirth. It's eaten me away. I'm maimed, wounded, unable to function normally. I don't feel anything, don't belong anywhere. Oh, yes, I'm happy to be Homecoming Queen. But I expected too much from it, as if it could magically transform my life.*

"I don't even know why I'm in college majoring in psychology. It's interesting studying human behavior, but what will I ever do with a degree in it? I can't even figure out why I behave like I do. The academic advisor told me I had to be a teacher, insisting it's the best career for a woman. I don't want to be a teacher. I have no idea what to do after graduation! I want an exciting and meaningful career, but don't know what. I want adventure and romance and love and marriage and children. How can a woman possibly have all that?

"I don't understand girls who get married and think that'll take care of their lives. I don't understand marriage, especially seeing that my one attempt at love was a colossal flop. If I married it would be for sex and a child. Maybe another child would make me forget the first one. Other peoples' babies always seem so adorable. I can never help wanting to touch their bird-like tufts of hair. But the truth is maybe a child would give me a purpose in life and maybe that would be unfair to the child. I wanted to keep my baby, but have no idea how I would have taken care of it.

"Besides, I couldn't have taken care of a baby and seen the world, too. I have a burning desire to see it all! I couldn't wait to leave my hometown, to be free of my family, to meet new kinds of people. But I don't know how to make my dreams come true. Life is so confusing!"

"What are you thinking?" Dr. Lichenger asked, his voice gentle.

"Nothing," she stated flatly.

"You told me a lot about growing up but didn't say much about your parents. What are they like? Are they involved in your education?"

Her eyes became glassy, her pupils pin-pointed, blocking out the exterior world, as she pondered the question. "My mom's really passive and my dad's a drunk," she said, coming back to the present, her candor surprising her as much as him. She continued, "They're always broke. Oh, she slips me a 20 whenever she can, but basically, I've been paying for school on my own."

He smiled a little and looked at her intently.

She panicked, her thoughts running wild! *He's flirting! Damn it! I knew it. He wants to jump my bones. Prick! He would be so boring in bed. Anybody who always wears a brown suit and bow tie has to be boring in bed. Wait, maybe he's just being nice. Why?*

His smile faded. Relief.

He said, "Tell me what you're thinking right now."

Damn! He can read my mind, she feared. He knows I just pictured him in bed!

"Nothing," she repeated. "Dead brain. Remember?"

"Ah, yes. Plato once said we dance with the shadows on the wall of our cave, believing they're real, when all we have to do is leave the cave to find reality."

"Huh?"

He sighed. "Well," he said, looking at his watch, "our hour is up. You must have a busy week-and-a-half ahead. Lots of homecoming activities."

"Yeah!" she said. She had no plans whatsoever until homecoming day a week from Saturday.

"Are you excited to be Homecoming Queen?"

"Sure," she said honestly.

"That's nice. I hope you enjoy it. But, as I was saying earlier, I think you're overwhelmed right now and I'd like to help you." His voice soothed, even with that weird New York accent. "I know you're busy, but will you come back next week, same time?"

Damn! she thought. *Do this again? Never! I can't believe he has the gall to ask.*

"Sure," she said.

She fled across the campus yard in front of the typical ivy-covered, weathered red brick building that housed Dr. Lichenger's awful office, cursing herself for setting another appointment. It'd been a quick escape. How in hell was she going to get that self-imposed savior off her back? She knew she'd never go back. She'd have to dodge him after class. Damn!

The crisp fall leaves crackled under her feet as she strolled through the peaceful campus park. Sitting on her favorite wooden bench under a huge old maple tree, she sucked in the air of freedom. That room had been suffocating.

She perused Warriner Hall at the end of the park. Another ivied brick building, three stories high with a bell tower, it was the kind of antiquated structure that makes a college look authentic. That hall symbolized Central Michigan University and therefore her college life, the only life with which she could grasp a bit of identity.

It was a glorious afternoon! The clouds overhead were wistful wisps called cirrus clouds, according to her meteorology professor. The air was moderate, so her beige suede jacket, which matched the suede boots which rose over her jeans to her knees, was warm enough.

All was quiet until a class on military instruction let out of the ROTC, Reserve Officer Training Corps, Building at the other end of the park. Llayne examined from afar the young men as they left, uniforms perfectly pressed, boots spit-shined, bodies erect. She wondered what made them, in this time of war, want to serve their country. A country that wasn't serving them with anything but an invitation to unjustifiable death.

25

She'd learned enough in history classes to know the United States of America was founded on a premise of justice. Getting involved in Southeast Asia wasn't justice. It was just dumb.

And profitable, if Peter was right. He said the whole damned war was about making money, speculating that it may not have started out that way but had deteriorated to that point.

Llayne looked at the last of the ROTC boy soldiers as they walked toward various dorms, knowing they believed in what they did in preparing for war as strongly as she believed in what she did in protesting it. She felt no resentment, only remorse.

Suddenly she was tired of pondering the plunder of war, so she spread her arms across the back of her bench and closed her eyes, breathing in clean air. The breeze played with her silky hair and it tickled her face, forcing a grin. Her unbound breasts reveled in the unladylike unrestraint of wide-spread arms, feeling sensuous against the underside of her soft sweater. She stretched her legs to either side in front of her and they felt long and slim in her tight, worn jeans. She hung her head back and inhaled deeply.

There were some things in life to be thankful for, she decided. There was the air and the sky and the trees and there was herself. It was a great place to start.

Life was simple after all.

That Dr. Lichenger wanted to complicate it unnecessarily. He made everything so confusing! It boggled her mind, so she decided not to think about it and laid down on her bench to close her eyes for a minute.

A young, red-haired marine ran down a long tropical beach as palm trees lolled in the breeze and gentle waves licked at his muddy boots. This place of earthly peace was disturbed. Something was wrong. The leatherneck fell to the sand; the gentle surf painted that sand; he picked himself up and ran harder, faster. Tears streamed down his bold, chiseled face. He was wretched. Finally he made his way to a stand of boulders, sinking listlessly to dry beach behind the massive shelter. He sobbed.

Eventually he took something out of his pocket. Pictures. Pictures of pretty dark-haired oriental women with innocent smiles, their slanted eyes bright with hope and love. And children, bouncing, laughing, velvety-skinned babies, with those adorable, big, black, almond-shaped eyes that look straight into the heart, piercing it with their life.

The marine wept more convulsively. Moments earlier he'd knelt before their dead fathers, ransacking their pockets for military messages. The only message was that they'd loved and lived just like him.

Llayne roused herself from the twilight zone of light sleep in which she'd dreamt. She napped to escape but the disturbing memory had invaded her slumber. It'd been a Saturday when she was 12 when her dad had come home and instead of going to bed like usual to sleep off his Friday night binge, he'd sat down beside her at the kitchen table where she'd worked on her scrapbook, gluing in pictures of the seventh grade

Snow Dance from two weeks earlier. The photos showed that she'd been Snow Queen and had worn a glitter snowflake in her hair. She remembered that on that Saturday morning she'd had pink rollers flopping in her hair, having just learned how to put them in, and not having been very adept at it.

Her dad had started to cry. "I know I drink too much," he'd told her. "And I know you hate me."

Llayne had felt trapped. It'd been uncomfortable enough to be sitting next to her dad, but to have a conversation, a crying conversation, had been terrifying. She'd wanted to get up and walk away but feared he might become enraged and call her a goddamned no-good-brat, his favorite name for his kids when he was mad, drunk, or both. One thing she'd learned well was never make him mad. It happened enough without provocation.

She'd sat as still as granite.

"You hate me, don't you?" he'd asked, blubbering like a baby.

Yes, I hate you, she'd wanted to admit. Of course admission would have incurred his wrath. She had said nothing.

He hadn't waited for her response. "Well, I don't blame you. I haven't been a very good dad."

She'd been stunned that he'd realized he was a dad at all.

"It was horrible, Llayne. I joined right out of high school, all fiery and ready to go kill Japs."

His abrupt transition had lost her for a moment, but then she'd realized he was talking about World War II, the one they called The Big One. She'd heard about it all of her life but found it hard to comprehend, as it'd ended prior to her 1948 birth.

"Huh! What a damned joke!" he'd spat out. "Oh, everybody thought I was brave. A hero. Hell. I was scared to death. Here I was on some of the most peaceful, beautiful islands in the world, killing people. A mighty Marine. God, I was scared." Sobs had interspersed his speech as he'd clawed at the tears falling down his face.

Llayne had wanted desperately to run away. For the first time she saw her father as human rather than as a mere inconvenience in her life.

"I was in the 3rd Division," he'd said, more to himself than to his daughter. "We were always the first ones to hit the beach, never knew what we were walking into. Guam, Guadalcanal, Okinawa, Iwo Jima. If it was in the Pacific, we were there first.

"Everybody looked up to me. I could be trusted to make snap decisions under paralyzing pressure. It was my idea when we hid in tombs in a hillside one night, right with the skeletons. God, I'll never forget that skull right next to my face all night long! Some of my men almost went insane, bunking with the dead. But we all lived through the night. At least that night.

"Nobody knew that brave Gunnery Sergeant Red Robertson, their Gunny, was scared to death! No matter what seemingly insignificant speck of land we thrashed with bombs and bullets and our own bodies, no matter how many thousands on both sides died ....." He'd run out of air and gulped for more. "So many of my men died," he'd sobbed. "And we killed so many men. We were made to do unspeakable things to other human beings. Unspeakable! And they did those things to us, too." His eyes flared with a wild, far-off gaze as he totally lost himself in flashbacks. The words shot out like the rat-a-tat of a gun. "One morning we woke up to a woman's shrill scream. We ran into the village to see what was wrong. The heads of marines surrounded the ledge around the town well, dripping fresh blood into the water. Some of those guys were my buddies ...."

His eyes had flared with sudden recognition as his muddled brain somehow returned to the present and recognized the fact that he spoke the unspeakable to his daughter, something no man should ever do. He dropped his head into his hands and his shoulders quaked as he wept.

Llayne had looked around the room, thinking this the time to escape; but, she hadn't moved fast enough. He looked at her, locking her eyes into his own and for the first time she noticed that his eyes were the same deep blue as hers. But his were blue and bloodshot.

Then he described finding the pictures and running down the beach to cry. "Hell," he said, "we didn't need to be slaughtering each other. We needed to be in a bar comparing pictures of our kids and buying each other beer."

She'd seen lots of pictures of him in his uniform, a fiercely handsome face with bright eyes, freckles, and a crooked grin that displayed perfect white teeth. He was a slight but muscular man, adding even more power to the stark black and navy Marine Corps dress uniform. The hat had a design on it, the "noble anchor and eagle insignia," her mother had told her. Her mother often talked about his hair when she reminisced to ease the pain of reality. She would say, "The first time I ever laid eyes on him he whipped off that hat and there was all that curly red hair on top. Made me wonder how he got it all under the hat." Her mother also kept a bunch of metals in a purple velvet-lined wood box. She got them out sometimes like they were the family jewels. Llayne never understood what they were for. You couldn't wear them or anything. In the old pictures her dad looked like a movie star. Sitting next to her on that Saturday when she'd been 12, he'd looked like a bum.

"The worst part," he'd whined, "is that in my sleep I still see those children's eyes, those children in the Japanese soldiers' pictures. I close my eyes and theirs are there. Those big, dark eyes are etched into my soul. That's why I don't sleep and I go drink."

She'd thought it unwise to point out that instead of dwelling on those children he could turn his attention to his own. It had occurred to her that he might have been a different dad without that war.

"War makes no sense," he'd moaned. "Oh, yeah, I'd do it again to save my country and my family. But that still doesn't mean it makes any sense. It's not us, the little people who make war. It's petty men in positions of power who want more power."

The racking sobs had subsided as he'd calmed down and taken on an almost tender look. Llayne had been gripped by an urge to reach out and touch him. But she couldn't. He was still a stranger.

He stood up as abruptly as he sat down and staggered off to bed. He never mentioned that conversation again and she didn't either. Neither knew what to say.

A chill struck Llayne as she shook herself from her long reverie. She'd lain on the bench in the park for almost an hour, trying to fit together the puzzle pieces of her life. They didn't fit.

Rising, she stretched toward the gloaming sunset. A shadow of gloom swept through her as she wondered why she was suddenly so absorbed in those disjointed thoughts about her dad.

It was that damned Dr. Lichenger. He started all this tumultuous soul-searching by dredging up her past. She hated thinking about it!

"Hell," she said to a squirrel who stared at her from a few feet away, "on top of everything else, I'm going crazy!" Chattering in agreement, it scampered off.

Stuffing her hands into her jacket pockets to wrap it snugly around her body for reinforcement against the impending evening chill, she started to shuffle through the leaves in the direction of her apartment but went only a few yards before spotting a flicker of a figure in the shadows by the ROTC Building. Then another, and another, all darting about in the quickly approaching dusk. Then there was an unmistakable silhouette in a flowing, ebony, wool cape which caught a sliver of twilight and shone for a fraction of a second before disappearing behind the building.

Llayne walked straight to the building and into the bushes where she saw the evening visions vanish. " Peter!" she exclaimed.

All four of them jumped and the girl who was with them screamed, so Peter clapped his hand over her mouth.

"Peter!" was all Llayne could think of to repeat at the strange sight of the hippies huddled together in the bushes.

"Shh-h-h-hh!" Peter shushed her emphatically, staring at her like a kid caught looking at nudey magazines behind the garage.

"Well," she implored with as much whisper as curiosity would allow, "did you come into the bushes for a group whiz or what? What the hell are you doing here?"

The others looked at Peter. The males were dressed in black but the harem girl appeared to have come as an afterthought, obviously not dressed to hide in the darkness. She wore a neon pink and blue paisley print midi-skirt with a yellow gauze blouse, under which her breasts stood visible. She also had on a white knit shawl, cast down to her elbows, and white lace-up boots and a floppy denim hat with an orange peace patch on it.

"We're taking over the ROTC Building tonight," Peter informed Llayne, using the slang pronunciation "rot'-cee." "Want to come?" Now he sounded like a little kid mischievously asking if she wanted to steal a smoke behind the barn.

"Oh, Peter," Llayne said. "What for? What good will it do?"

"Honey, I can't stop to explain it all now, but a bunch of us decided it's time to move again. We can't let our protest die. We can't cop out now."

"I know; I agree. But why this? There are better ways. Aren't there?"

"Hey, man, like what?"

She looked at him, then at his cadre of faithful followers, then at the monolithic brick structure at their side. They waited for an answer. She couldn't think of "what."

"We've gotta move," Peter announced. "You coming?"

"Oh, why not?" she relented. "May as well. I was just sitting over there going crazy anyway."

"I know what you mean," he said as he handed a list to his comrade. "I go crazy when I don't have enough to do."

That wasn't what she'd meant, but she let it ride. She didn't want to tell him she was off the deep end, insane, bats, berserk, tetched, whacko, loco, crackers, bananas, nuts ....

Peter grinned with that huge smacker of his and bussed her on the cheek, his thick mustache tickling her tender skin. Someone whistled from the other side of the building and they were off. Without hesitation Llayne followed.

Chapter 4

It only took 10 minutes to takeover the ROTC Building. There were about 16 rebel students originally, with sentries at the two entrances allowing someone new to enter every few minutes. The occupation had been much easier than anticipated. The only person in the place had been an old janitor who said he didn't get paid enough to put up with this kind of shit, and he left.

Peter called everyone together in the smelly, dilapidated gym, which had clearly sheltered far too many grimy sweat sox and stale jock straps. Llayne examined her friend as he stood on a desk hauled in from an adjoining classroom. He was indeed an imposing figure, about six feet tall, slender, and dressed in his black shirt with balloon sleeves, tight jeans, and knee-high suede moccasins that were intricately embroidered with black, red and white beads. The footwear had been given to him by the local Chippewa tribe at a peace powwow. He'd given them a stereo in return.

Everything about the guy loomed bigger than life. His nose, his mouth. His presence. Character. Intelligence. Those eyes. Llayne wondered about his heritage. He'd told her he was from Portland, Michigan, a relatively small town not far from the capitol, Lansing. With the last name Smith it sounded as if some ancestor, or he, didn't want others to know from where they had originally come.

Peter allowed a moment of silence for effect before addressing the group. When all eyes were upon him he began, "Welcome, my friends. Let me clarify our purpose here. We come for peace. We will never, never," his voice rose to a timber, "resort to violence. Let it be understood that no matter what goes down here, we shall remain shining examples of peace!"

The crowd stood as if in a trance, all eyes focused on this man. There were lots of student hippies; his housemates, the women wearing blouses, be they a little sheer; two business-type men in dark suits; a student Llayne recognized as having recently been ostracized by his fraternity for objecting to drug parties; a sorority girl who vowed to give up shaving her legs for the cause; and others.

Peter continued. "We will not condone the actions of the SDS, Students for a Democratic Society, who infringe upon the rights of others with bombs. Neither will we allow this to turn into another Kent State." There was a group shudder as everyone recalled the National Guard killing of protesting students on the Kent State campus in Ohio the prior spring. "We will not tolerate the blasphemy of the 'conflict' in Vietnam. Innocent, well-intentioned, brave, red-blooded American men, boys really, are being sent to slaughter so a select herd of fat cat corporate swine can continue to fill their bellies, and their pocketbooks. Well, our bellies are full, too," his voice reached a fevered evangelical pitch. "Full of this garbage!

"Therefore, we have sent a message to the president of the college, demanding control of this military building. We will no longer stand idly by while young men are trained to be sent to their deaths." He paused, then continued in a more conversational tone. "Our own fathers and mothers lived through World War II. Our fathers killed to save us. That didn't make it a good war, there is no such thing. But it made it a necessary war."

Llayne's thoughts reeled. It seemed as if he'd read her mind.

"Many say Vietnam is the same thing," he went on. "Not so. That is a war which has gone on for hundreds of years and is none of our business. It's time the United States of America got out of the business of war!"

His audience whistled and applauded. Peter was at peak performance, at this moment rivaling the best of tent evangelists; his fervent believers surely would have felt healed of any malady had he deigned to touch the afflicted spot. He was indeed Elmer Gantry!

"Stay with us; pray with us in this humble place for this night." He now preached in a hushed voice, causing the entire crowd to lean forward, straining to hear. "When the president denies us the building, he'll call the police. Our messenger, Alex, is with him now. It shouldn't take too long. The police will come, you will leave, I will stay. They'll read me the Riot Act and I'll be arrested. It'll receive media coverage and our point will be made.

"And we, my friends, will never stop finding ways to make that point!" Once again he worked himself up into a frenzied shout, gesturing broadly. "Not until every single American is home where he belongs, from Canada, from Vietnam. Not until everybody and every body has been returned from that hell! Not until we are all once again safe in a once again free and righteous America!"

He raised a clenched fist and expelled from his large mouth a clear, though not quite on key, voice, singing, "We shall overco-o-ome .... We shall overco-o-ome .... We shall overcome some day ...."

His followers joined in. By the end of the song, a tear streamed down the leader's face and a girl handed him a white linen handkerchief. Having unashamedly wiped his eyes, Peter spoke again.

"We welcome all to stay who agree by these principles and ask only that you have consideration for your fellow friends. Thank you." He jumped off the desk like a gallant caballero who surely would have marked a "Z" for Zorro had he but wielded a sword.

Once again the crowd broke into applause. He was immediately surrounded by admirers and well-wishers, slapped on the back, hand shook and cheek kissed.

Eventually he made it over to the two businessmen. He introduced himself and they told him they were Vietnam veterans. Llayne watched with interest until her attention was diverted by Mack, who'd come in with a woman she recognized as a cashier at the book store. The woman was probably in her early thirties and was pretty in a rough sort of way. A pang of jealously stabbed at Llayne's gut. *Ridiculous! I have no hold on him. Especially since I'm just a "kiddo" to him.*

Mack didn't see her sitting on a bench at the side of the room as he ushered the woman over to Peter and the professional men. Glad to see his new amigo, Peter made introductions. One businessman said he owned the Mt. Pleasant Country Store; the other was a lawyer. They said they'd come over to the ROTC Building because they'd heard that Peter was different, a war protester who wasn't antagonistic toward vets. Peter hugged each man. The store owner hugged back; the lawyer developed temporary rigor mortis which prevented him from responding. Mack stifled a chuckle behind his hand, and his companion looked confused as she twirled a lock of hair with one hand and inspected her orange nail polish on the other.

"We're skeptical about what you're doing," the lawyer admitted. "We've been there. We've operated on orders from the Big Machine. We'd like to think you, or anybody, can make a difference. But we know better. They're just bigger than we are. Bigger than God."

Peter, for the first time, seemed to be at a loss for words, so Mack stepped in. "It's true, that's how it seems," he agreed. "On the other hand, we've experienced the power of a group of men pulling together to help each other survive. We lived it every day in Nam. No one of us could've made it without the others. It's a bond between human beings like no other. Just think if we used that power for peace instead of war!

"We've been born to a free country. With flaws, granted. But freedom gives us opportunities and I believe those opportunities give us an obligation to make this a better country. I know it seems like a losing battle and I understand your pessimism, but we can't give up. We're all in this together, and our futures and that of our country are at stake."

"Right on!" Peter agreed, slapping his cohort on the back.

The cashier's attention had long since wandered and she gnawed on her gum while her vacant eyes scanned the gym; but, the vets seemed to seriously consider Mack's plea.

Then the store owner asked Peter, "Why weren't you drafted?"

"I'm lucky. My lottery number is 303," Peter answered, referring to the drawing of dates and how men were drafted in the order in which their birth dates were picked. The draft board was only half way through the 365, so men with high numbers wouldn't be called for a long time, if at all.

"Wow, that's great. Don't knock luck," the lawman advised. "Mine was three, or they never would've got me over there."

"Three," Peter empathized. "Shit!"

"Well, good luck," the store owner said, attempting to bring the conversation to a close. "I'm a doubter but I'll stay on the outside chance this may help keep one guy, just one kid, from living in the pisspot I lived in for a year."

"Good luck," said the other, and they mingled with the crowd that had now grown to about 200 people.

Llayne watched as Mack's date tugged at the sleeve of his brown leather bomber jacket and whispered into his ear. She was ready to leave. Probably to go have sex,

Llayne sighed. With a hasty good-bye to Peter, Mack and the lucky lady left. He never even noticed Llayne, and she hadn't had the energy to approach him and go through the formality of being cordial to his date.

Well, there was still Peter, who's harem was nowhere in sight at the moment. Llayne sidled up to him and casually put her arm around his waist. "Peter, we've got to get this over with fast. I'm not crazy about sleeping on this scuzzy floor," she razzed while flirting with him.

He said, "I know. Fighting capitalist pigs destroys my basement business!"

He'd opened the subject so she asked, "About your business ... is it legal?"

"If you mean is the stuff stolen, no. I buy stuff from kids who need money, usually for tuition. I keep it for awhile and if they can't buy it back, I sell it. It's a pawn shop. I suppose the government would think there's something illegal in that, but I don't have a whole lot of respect for the government right now."

Other people besieged him again, so Llayne called Pris from the pay phone to let her know where she was. Then she borrowed paper and a pencil, and found a quiet corner on the floor to do her homework. She'd written one word when a cute, chubby coed scooted up beside her.

"Excuse me," the girl said. "I hate to interrupt but I just wanted you to know I'm real glad you made it for Homecoming Queen."

"Thanks," Llayne said.

"You see, I'm an Alpha Delta Pi, and a couple of the girls in our sorority are kinda snobby, but most of them are really nice. The snobs are the ones who usually seem to get elected for that kind of thing, so some of us are glad you got it instead. We're happy for the vets and we think you make a good queen. Congratulations."

Surprised, Llayne thanked her again, and the girl scootched away to rejoin members of the Art Club as they sat cross-legged in a circle making peace signs. So, Llayne thought, she might have to break down and modify her opinion of sorority girls. Maybe she'd been as wrong about some of them as some of them were about her. She'd thought most of them were brats and, after her freshman year when she'd rushed and been denied, she'd decided she was glad not to be associated with them. She had to admit, however, that the girl who'd just talked to her was the kind of person she'd like as a friend and maybe she'd missed something after all by not being part of a group.

But she had to put that thought aside to concentrate on her creative writing homework for the next day's class. She blocked out the room as best she could and wrote, in what she fancied to be the style of e. e. cummings:

> *don't worry little girl   you'll find your thing*
> *to love*
> *it won't hit you like a homecoming parade*
> *or movie production*
> *it'll slither into your overanxious heart*

unnoticed
then someday when your silly mind moves from mindless
and meaningless things
it will come home and discover
that which has long been there
a grown love
a warmth
itself

She read over the work which had tumbled out of her mind and spilled so easily onto the paper. Like maybe the crazies had crept through. So heavy. Forcing herself to sweep all serious thought from her mind, she wrote again:

Gitty Ditty Ditty
   Gitty Ditty Da;
Bitty Witty Witty
   Bitty Witty Wa;
Kitty Mitty Mitty
   Kitty Mitty Ma;
Now I know my laugh's alive!
   Nitty Gritty Ha!!

Much better, she determined. If she was going nuts she may as well enjoy doing it.

The class assignment done, her attention reverted back to the crowd around her, who seemed bored. Overhearing bits of conversations Llayne learned that Alex, the emissary sent to the college president, had returned bearing news that the man hadn't been home yet. His wife had informed the young Paul Revere that her husband wouldn't be home until 10 o'clock, one hour away. He owned a farm somewhere outside of town and went there every night to ride his horse and clean the stable. Alex could come back later, she'd told him, because she had absolutely no intention of telling her husband about the ROTC Building takeover. Then she'd invited Alex in to have a reheated, twice-baked, cheese potato, a piece of fresh baked apple pie, and a glass of milk. Alex said it was real good.

The hour dawdled on until it was time for Alex to go back to the president's house. Another hour passed. The old traditional clock on the gym wall ticked each minute at the end of what seemed like 10, just like school clocks do during class. Peter became concerned that their messenger was behind bars.

When Alex returned at midnight, it was obvious the news wasn't good. Shoulders slunk, head down, shuffling along, he seemed embarrassed to approach his stolid leader. Slowly, he went to Peter and whispered at length into his ear. Peter shook his head and asked a question. Alex whispered back. Peter pulled his shaggy hair away from his ear as if to hear better. The anticipation in the room rose to its apex as their chief mounted the desk. Peter showed no emotion as he peered at the gathering through hooded eyes. He let a few moments pass to create even more suspense, then spoke.

"The president was late getting home. Said he had an extra large haul of manure tonight. Said he shovels manure around his desk all day then goes out to his farm to shovel more at night." That evoked titters. "The president's wife insisted that Alex come in again while he waited and have another piece of pie. He had it with ice cream this time." Peter raised his eyebrows in mild disapproval, but every struggling student knew they would never pass up homemade pie. "Anyway," Peter continued, "when the president finally came home Alex stated our demands and the president gave him an immediate reply."

Anticipation festered with the dramatic pause. He let the silence hang, then told them, "The president said we can have the building."

A stillness filled the air, then there were hearty shouts of "All right!" Some, however, maintained their cool and muttered "What?"

"Quiet, quiet, please!" clamored Peter. "The president said he doesn't understand why anybody would want this old rat trap anyway and we can stay as long as we want. He's going to let the ROTC classes meet in the new gym across campus."

Some of the more hard-core revolutionaries shouted profanities but were subdued when Peter raised his arms and let out a long laugh. Some of the others joined him. Llayne remained silent, intrigued by what his conniving mind might do next.

"We should've known we were dealing with a smart cat. He's been cool through all of our marches. He called our bluff. So, he knows how to win a battle," he said, eking every possible bit of theatrical play out of this, "but, not this war! We cannot and will not give up! Now, we'll call his bluff. We'll make certain our statement is made to the press tomorrow morning. A statement against that atrocious war perpetrated only to finance the insipid lives of greedy capitalist pigs!"

There was thunderous applause and hooting assents. The two businessmen vets smirked and shook their heads in disbelief, enjoying how Peter worked at getting himself out of this dilemma. Peter held one hand up with the other across his waist and took a deep bow before jumping off the desk.

Llayne joined him. "Peter, what'll happen next?"

"Hell! Pardon my language, but I wish I knew." A genuine grin struck his face. "Man, I'm telling you, I've got to meet that president. He's one far out dude!" He shook his head and snickered, scratching his scalp in the typical gesture of a person caught in a bind. "Well, we'll do something to say this is a success. If the public believes it about Nam I guess they'll buy this, too."

Others surrounded them and queried what to do next. Some wanted to take over the new gym; some insisted they move into this one to live; another suggested they call Domino's Pizza and have them deliver several large pizzas; three roommates, one woman and two men, invited the whole group over to their pad for a party; and the final agreement was made. If the police weren't going to come to attract media attention, they themselves would call *Central Michigan Life,* the student newspaper; *The Daily Times News,* the Mt. Pleasant newspaper; and WNEM, the TV station in Bay City, the nearest town big enough to have its own television station. If Peter could generate enough interest to get them to show up, he'd make a statement declaring that he was giving the building back to the university in the name of peace; then, everyone would go home. They hoped the president would never tell anyone he'd called their bluff in the first place, making this an entirely unnewsworthy event.

Llayne returned to the quiet corner, rolled her jacket up for a pillow and eventually dozed. A couple of hours later she awoke with a start, having dreamt of men's severed heads bleeding into a town well, the nightmare that had so often terrified her as a teenager. The vision still chilled her to her very core. But now she had enough adult wisdom to realize that she was only experiencing a minute fraction of what her father had endured for so many years. With wide eyes, she laid still in the darkened gym for a long time, then eventually nodded off again.

By 7:30 the next morning about five hundred additional students and professors, bundled up in warm coats, looked up at the hostaged building from the campus park outside, having heard about the takeover through the proverbial grapevine. Several hundred people had amassed in the building throughout the night and many of them now spilled out the doors, with an estimated 1000 on the scene. Two newspaper reporters and one television reporter and a cameraman were allowed in and Peter talked to them in the musty locker room. Afterward, he went to a second-story window, opened it to the brisk fall air and put his hands on top of a peace sign hanging from the sill, its bright orange inverted Y surrounded by a purple circle.

In a clear voice that rang over the grounds, Peter announced to the crowd below that a statement in protest of the war had been made and now the building would be returned to all of the good people of C.M.U. He raised his arms and sang, swaying with his song ....

"All we are saying ... is give peace a chance ...."

Many joined in, their breath visible in the chilled morning air. When the song ended, Peter waved majestically. The onlookers clapped, the sound muffled by their warm gloves.

Peter's interviews came out the next day in the Mt. Pleasant and campus papers, accompanied by an impressive picture of the dark-haired man at the massive Gothic window, flashing a peace sign with his fingers as a lively poster of a peace sign billowed in the breeze from the sill. The TV station covered it as well. Peter came off as the intelligent, charismatic, strange young man that he was.

Through it all, the president refused public comment and as far as anyone ever knew the man never mentioned the entire incident to anyone. Except maybe to his horse.

◆ ◆ ◆ ◆ ◆ ◆ ◆ ◆

She yawned a cavernous yawn, stretched her neck from side to side, and unlocked the door to her apartment. Totally tuckered out and stiff as a board after the night of sleeping on a hard gym floor, Llayne couldn't wait to hit the rack for 20 minutes before having to head out for class. So she became discombobulated when she opened the door and found a sleepy Priscilla, donned in a worn-out bathrobe and scruffy slipper-socks, playing hostess to a neatly dressed, vaguely familiar young man in the living room.

"Hey, Pris, what's up?" she asked.

"Am I glad you're back!" her roommate rejoined, stretching her arms out and yawning, too. Lowering her voice she pulled Llayne aside and said, "He's all yours. Dragged my ass out of bed at 7:30 to talk to you about homecoming. Jammed the crapper of my day! I sure as hell hope it's important!" She disappeared into the bedroom and could be heard falling onto her squeaky twin bed.

Llayne said hello congenially as she took off her jacket, to no response from the sour-looking, preppie-type person sitting on the lumpy, gray couch. He wore tan chino pants with a fastidious razor-sharp crease down each leg, a white button-down shirt, a maroon tie with CMU embroidered in gold, and a maroon sports coat. And he leered at her from cold eyes that couldn't hide their malice behind thick, horn-rimmed glasses. Why did he hate her?

In a split second, she ascertained that his discomfort might be due to the decor of the apartment. He appeared to be such a straight arrow, the place might have shocked him. It was a ratty little hole, the only place the two young women could afford, on the bottom floor of an apartment building that was in such disrepair that on the day they'd moved in the front door had come off its rotted frame when they'd opened it, and there had been mushrooms growing along the walls in the moldy, green, shag carpet. The manager had fixed the door, and they picked the mushrooms, but it was still a rat trap. Upon entering from the dingy, brown hallway, the first thing one noticed were the double glass doors at the opposite end of the small, combination kitchenette/living area, which opened out onto a tiny pit of a "patio," edged by the tires of cars parked in the lot. The view was of a dirty cement retainer wall with a rim of tires on top. Real attractive.

But it usually wasn't just the apartment itself that bowled people over, it was Priscilla's art work. An art major, she'd been recognized by her instructors as having amazing talent. To please those beatnik profs, she painted in an incredibly ingenious and shocking, manner. On the wall beside the door was a life-sized rear-view painting of a nude hippy girl with long, black hair cascading down her back. Her bare derriere was the most prominent feature of the piece as she peered over her shoulder with what Pris called a "come-hither" look on her face. Over the couch on the side wall was an extremely impressive, meticulously wrought reproduction of a medieval Madonna, gold gilt halo and all. The only difference was that in this version the savior's mother was bare-breasted with gold gilt nipples. Priscilla said that "gilt nipples" made as much sense as "virgin mother." Then there was the half-finished beach scene of a group of frolicking, half-clad people, propped up against the wall on the kitchenette counter.

Llayne instantly scanned the room and the young man's darting eyes followed. Yes, she felt certain, he was appalled by the place. But, why was he even here? Like a blast of foul air, recollection returned to her depleted brain and she recalled that this was the frat cat who was chairman of the Panhellenic Council's Homecoming Committee. Although they had to allow participants from other groups in the homecoming election, the select group of Greeks still organized the event. Ever since election day this creep had made it clear he was "displeased" that a non-Greek sponsored candidate had won the honor of representing their school. He'd demanded a recount of the votes, insisting no one could win by such a margin but was dissuaded when statistics were brought forth showing the number of vets on campus. Llayne had dismissed him as a geek and surmised his father had money connections that got him into a fraternity and the members made him their lackey on committees to keep him occupied while they screwed off.

"What can I do for you, Howard?" she inquired.

"It's Harold! Harold Hackleberry! It seems you could at least manage to remember the name of the person in charge of the greatest honor of your life!" He spat the words in disgust, his terse squeaky voice cracking with tension.

Llayne couldn't help herself. She said, "Well, Harold, Harold Hackleberry, I remember the greatest honor of my life. And believe me, honey, you didn't have a damned thing to do with it."

Lurching off the couch, he stood up and marched toward her with a raised chin, standing a good four inches shorter than her five feet seven inches.

"Listen here, you tramp!" he yelled. "I know how you won that election! You slept with those vets. Everybody knows what those guys are like. They're animals! There's no other way they would've chosen you, and no other way you could've won over one of our fine sorority girls! And look at this whorehouse you live in! You're nothing but a whore!"

"What? I am not!" Llayne shouted, her face turning beet red with the insult as surely as if she'd been slapped. She raised her hand in a clenched fist in defense.

"Oh, please! Don't try to act innocent with me!" he shot back. "I know you're a stripper!"

"What?" Llayne and Priscilla both yelped, incredulous. Priscilla had bolted out of the bedroom, furious. Like her roommate, she was ready to deck the jerk.

"You heard me! A stripper!" Harold squealed. "One of the Tekes told me all about it. He saw you at a club in Harbor Springs last summer, and he says you're not even that good."

"He's a liar!" Priscilla defended her friend.

"Oh, of course," Harold simpered indignantly, "you would think she's good!"

"No, not that ...!" Priscilla started to argue, but Llayne held up her hand in a gesture to stop.

"Don't bother, Pris," she said, having taken a long deep breath to collect her composure. "This guy isn't interested in the truth. It doesn't serve his petty little needs."

Priscilla folded her arms and leaned against the wall in a protective gesture beside her friend.

Her temper now under control, Llayne decided there was a better way to handle this clown of a chairman. Nonchalantly she fell into a chair and lifted one leg over the arm. "Oh, Harold darling," she feigned affection. "Grow up. Anybody could've beat your girls. At least I have better sense than to get the clap and spread it around like the gal your fraternity sponsored."

His skin tone had been so pasty it was a surprise to see his face become even whiter, and she thought he might have a stroke and die right there on the spot. Too messy, she decided.

"Harold," she said, "just tell me what in hell you're doing here. What do you want?" She swung the other leg over the first one up on the arm of the chair, watching him become even more uneasy as the lank of denimed thigh confronted him. She was starting to enjoy this.

He raised his head and howled, his spittle showering the air, "You were in the ROTC Building last night, all night! It's bad enough that we have a stripper tramp representing our school, but now you have to hang out with those free-love hippies! Is that any way for a Homecoming Queen to act? Huh? Just what do you have to say for yourself? Well?" His chin thrust towards her in self-righteous indignation, his hands defiantly atop his scrawny hips.

Llayne may have felt sorry for him if he weren't so hateful. She wondered if he'd be this pathetic all of his life.

"We-e-l-ll?" He was furious now, shaking and staring at her with bulging fish eyes magnified by the thick spectacles.

Llayne looked back at Priscilla who gave her a mock 'Well?' gesture. "Well," Llayne said flatly as she swung her legs about dramatically and rose, walking straight at Harold as he backed away and stumbled over an end table. "I think it's time for you to get the hell out of our apartment."

"Here, here!" Priscilla chimed in, going over and opening the door to the hallway.

"You don't have anything to say for yourself?" he catechized, refusing to forfeit the match. "First stripping, then fornicating with the vets and now spending the night at a hippy orgy in the ROTC Building?"

Both females' jaws dropped. They looked at one another and couldn't help but laugh.

"Harold, leave," Llayne stated adamantly, walking to the door to stand beside her friend. "I'm exhausted. You know, after the big orgy and all."

The little twerp poked a long, bony finger at her as he stomped to the door, stopping in front of her to jab at the air in front of her face. "I'm warning you, 'lady!' Don't you dare besmirch the title you hold! You're supposed to be a shining example for all the women on our campus. You do anything like this again, and I'll have the Panhellenic Council strip you of your title. Do you hear me? Have you got that?"

His pointing finger was so close to her face she just couldn't resist. She bit it.

Harold yanked his finger back as his mouth gaped open and he stumbled backwards across the threshold in disbelief. Priscilla seized the opportunity to slam the door in his face, locking it quickly. They listened to him storming around outside their apartment until the noise finally faded away, and they laughed so hard their sides ached.

"Damn! I have to get to class!" Llayne remembered suddenly as she looked at the clock on the stove.

"And I gotta find me some food," Priscilla said, loping back into the bedroom.

Llayne rushed into the bathroom for a quick cleanup job and when she came out Priscilla was buttoning a coat over her big bosom. She'd changed into jeans and a sweatshirt, both speckled with many colors of paint. She hadn't bothered to brush her hair. "God, I'm sorry," she said. "I never would've let him in if I would've known what he wanted. I thought it had to be important for him to be here so early. What a turdball! But, tell me Llayne, if you slept with all those guys, how come you didn't invite me? I could of got you a coupla extra votes." She strutted around the room, wiggling her rounded ass in a provocative manner, making her friend giggle. Playfully she poked Llayne in the arm, but then became serious and asked, "Hey, how was last night?" They both knew she still had a hard time dealing with Benny's death but was glad Llayne protested the war.

"It was good, Pris. I think a point was made."

"Yeah, but what about the orgy?" Priscilla chided again, as Llayne scrounged through the refrigerator looking for something to eat.

Llayne gobbled down half a piece of cold pizza and licked her fingers as she retorted, "Oh that was great! I fornicated with 10, no, 12 guys last night!"

"You know what I think?" Priscilla asked, her voice edged with mirth. "I think Harold's jealous because he knows a girl like you would never look at a wuss like him."

"Pris, he knows that no girl would look at him, period."

"Tell me one more thing. Did their candidate really have the clap?"

"Rumor has it her nickname is Patty Applause."

Priscilla could be heard laughing all the way down the hall on her way to go get some breakfast at Falsetta's restaurant and pizza parlor next door.

"Don't forget The Cabin tonight," Llayne hollered after her. She heard a faint, "I won't."

Besides Falsetta's, where she worked five nights a week, The Cabin was the social place Priscilla most liked to go to. She didn't drink much, or dance much, or even talk all that much once they got there. She just watched. Very different from the days when she and Benny had been the best dancers on the floor. Readjusting to a Bennyless world would take time.

41

Time. Llayne looked around the apartment, the place where Rex used to come to pick her up for dates. Getting over him sure was taking plenty of time. She knew she couldn't feel precisely Priscilla's pain over the death of the man she loved, but thought it must be something akin to what she felt over the loss of her baby. At least Professor Rex Bates, her child's father, was alive, although with other women. Why couldn't an asshole like him croak instead of a gem like Benny?

Thinking about her former lover made her want to re-read the heavy poem she'd written the night before, the one about "finding your thing to love." She dumped her books on the kitchenette counter and pulled it out.

It made her sad, bringing back images of how intensely she felt about Rex, the memories painfully rich and melancholy. She felt more fulfilled and alive and vital with him than ever before. Then all of a sudden he was off to another girl before she even knew she was pregnant. That poem he inspired wasn't worth handing in, she decided, so she found some matches and burned it in the kitchen sink.

She looked into the flames as it burned and recalled the first time she'd seen his naked body. It'd been by candlelight in his bedroom. She envisioned again his rippled, glistening thighs as they strode to her where she laid across the chocolate brown, satin sheets on his big bed ... his tousled, dark brown hair as it reflected the flickering light ... the erotic sheen of slightly sweaty muscles on his sleek form as it wrapped itself around her smaller, hungry body ... those steely gray eyes piercing her soul ... the long Roman nose and soft, short beard ... his warm molded lips kissing her eyelids closed ... her heart pounding with anticipation while her body ached for him ... his lingering tongue licking her soft breasts and then tracing the hardened rosy nipples, sucking any semblance of resistance right out of her ... love-making that sent her into arched spasms of ecstasy beyond belief ... heaven, the stars, the universe ... the warmth of gently touching flesh as they lay together when it was over ... the tickle of his sweet breath on her neck as he turned to her and in his deep resonant voice whispered, "Oh, baby, I love you."

Gone.

The affair ended abruptly when he quit calling and wouldn't return her calls. A week after their last date she saw him at a drama department play with the girl for whom he presumably dumped her. They looked good together. He'd been so smitten by her he hadn't even noticed his former lover standing nearby. Llayne had eventually caught on that he was smitten with a new female every week or two. When she finally tracked him down in his office to tell him about her condition, he just plumb hadn't cared.

The flames died in the kitchen sink, her heart had long since died inside of her, and she couldn't waste any more time. "Damn!" she said to herself as picked up her books and went to the door. "I'm late! I'll have to skip clinical psych and hang out in the union until writing class. Then I'll hand in the funny poem. Have to keep up the appearance of a happy-go-lucky, well-adjusted Homecoming Queen. Nitty gritty ha!"

She slammed the door behind her.

CHAPTER 5

Mack spoke loudly, in order to be heard over the blare of the band, to Llayne. "Listen, kiddo," he started, "I've hashed it over in my mind, you know, and I think you should ask this decorated vet just back from Nam to be your homecoming escort for the ball. You know, kind of a homecoming for him, too. He's a real hero, kiddo, if you know what I mean!"

Llayne swatted the air as if fending off the annoying nickname, "kiddo," and to mask her disappointment that Mack didn't offer himself as her escort to the ball. She and Priscilla sat on barstools at the bar in The Cabin where Mack, Neckbreaker, and some of the other vets stood huddled around them. The girls were in high spirits. They'd cast off their long, wool coats and draped them over the backs of their barstools, and were reveling in the knowledge that they looked good. Llayne was dressed in her favorite outfit of blue simulated leather hot pants with a polyester pink and blue flowered blouse. And, of course, her blue simulated leather platform boots. Her makeup was perfect, not overdone but enhancing, with a thin line of navy blue eyeliner around her blue eyes, a hint of pastel blue eye shadow arching across each lid, navy mascara on her thick lashes, and shiny pale pink lipstick on her generous lips. She held her body erect in total confidence that she looked sexy as hell. She even convinced Priscilla, who was starting to ease out of her grief-stricken shell, to wear a snazzy number she hadn't put on since Benny's death, consisting of a purple and white herringbone mini skirt, a white blouse and a purple suede vest with fringe that hung to her knees. She wore her white boots with the zip-up sides to complete the ensemble. She looked adorable with her continental features, big dark eyes outlined in black eye liner, black-auburn hair cut shoulder-length, full lips enhanced with shiny light coral lipstick, and glossy olive skin, all accentuating the trendy, mod attire. They were real hip for Mt. Pleasant and they knew it. Especially Llayne in her hot pants, a style which was new to this conservative Midwest area. As Priscilla had said approvingly as they left the apartment, "It takes balls to wear those little pants!"

The two young women looked like an attractive female version of Mutt and Jeff; the fair one five feet seven inches tall, the dark one just a hair's breath over five foot. Both elicited second looks from just about every guy who passed by in the packed, smoke-filled bar.

"Hey, how come you ain't gonna take her to the ball?" Neckbreaker asked Mack, echoing Llayne's thoughts. "You're a goddamned hero, too!"

Mack shot him a look that fairly roared "shut your trap!" "I'm too old for these girls," was his defensive reply. His adamant facial expression belied his jumbled thoughts: He was too old; he'd already lost at love; he didn't want to hurt another woman; he didn't want to get hurt himself. He already been through that scene, had fallen madly in love with a 24-year-old Pan Am stewardess named Jillie, had fantasized about this goddess of a woman all through Nam, had taken R&R with her in Hawaii where he'd enjoyed what he thought was unparalleled sexual bliss, and had come home to learn she married a dentist. He quit the Army after a 10 year career, which he loved until being sent to Nam. He quit because he wanted to give a family stability, although he'd always enjoy traveling for pleasure. He'd grown weary of the constant mobility of the service and was ready for a new life, with Jillie, he thought. But when he surprised her by arriving unannounced at her apartment in San Francisco, prepared to pop the question, he'd been the one to get a heart-stopping jolt. A man, the dentist who was her new husband as it turned out, had answered the door. Mack had been caught totally off guard, baffled and embarrassed. Jillie had granted him a quick five minutes in the hallway where she informed him that the dentist was nice and stable, and only 25, while he was too wild sexually and too old to be a good husband for her. Mack hadn't bothered to try to come up with a rebuttal. After all, she was already married.

I left my heart ... in San Francisco ....

No, he couldn't go out with Llayne, he thought. He was the wrong man for any woman, let alone someone like her. Now he only played it safe with grown women who understood this wild man's needs for sex and fun. The commitment thing obviously was not for him.

"Now," he said, raising his voice another notch over the racket, "you aren't going with anybody in particular, unless you've got a body stashed on the side we don't know about." He gave her a playful wink. "And I just thought maybe you wouldn't mind doing this for us, you know what I mean?"

When Mack got loud and excited, like now, his Midwest accent became so prominent he sounded almost Canadian. She asked him where he was from.

"Escanaba. Yup, I'm a yupper," he fessed up, using the slang for the upper peninsula of the state. "I know, we sound like Canucks. I think it's being socked in there with mounds of snow every winter for 18 years that made me such a wanderer. I want to take vacations someday to see it all! Every terrain, every season, every kind of person in the world!"

Llayne's heart skipped a beat. Her desires, exactly.

"Hell," Neckbreaker chimed in, "you saw monsoon season and Charlie in Nam. You sure you wanna see anymore?"

"Who's Charlie?" Priscilla asked.

"Ah, that's just a little nickname American soldiers use for the Commies," Neckbreaker told her.

The guys laughed and Mack shook his head. "It's not all like that. There's more of this world for a kid from the U.P. to see."

"Yeah," one of the other vets interjected, "when you start out a yupper, way up there in the woods, you've got a lot of catching up to do!" He exaggerated the pronunciation, 'yoo-oo-per,' emphasizing the age-old jibe about the upper peninsula being so isolated its inhabitants were primitives "in the woods," cut off from the civilized world.

"Hey, don't forget, he's a goddamned war hero!" Neckbreaker good-naturedly stuck up for his friend, slapping Mack on the back. "Green Beret, Silver Star, working on a Master's degree in poli sci, and lots of other good shit, too."

"Wow! That is lotsa good shit! I'm impressed!" Priscilla teased. "Really, though, that's neat, that you were a Green Beret, with a Silver Star, no less, and survived." Llayne focused her attention as this was the first time Priscilla had spoken about the war in casual conversation. "My fiancé didn't make it home," she confided in a hushed voice. Each man leaned toward her as if to make certain he'd heard her correctly.

Silence amidst the babble and band playing the Beatles song "Come Together" enveloped the small covey of acquaintances as those words sunk in. That one sentence instantly cemented a bond that was like a protective shelter encasing these diverse people in common experience, an experience so outside the realm of normal existence that those who didn't have first hand knowledge just couldn't, no matter how much they wanted, to be a part of the fellowship.

Mack reached out and gave Priscilla a big brotherly hug, and Llayne experienced an involuntary stab of jealousy over her friend's opportunity to press her body up against his. Then each ex-soldier did the same. Llayne was surprised at how well Priscilla took the gestures of support. Instead of tears, which she would have expected, there was a big smile, an acceptance of the comfort. The healing process, thankfully, had finally begun.

"You ever need anything," Neckbreaker said to Priscilla while she caught her breath after his overpowering body squeeze, "you come to us. We'll take care of you. For our buddy who didn't come home."

"Thanks," Priscilla said. She started telling them more about Benny and Llayne's mind wandered to thoughts about what a great sex life Pris and Benny must have enjoyed, if her friend's funny and touching stories were any indication. That thought opened the door to worries about her own sex life, a door which seemed forever ajar, inviting her mind to enter the tumulary space. She hoped that one day the right man would close that door forever. Too bad Mack didn't want to do it.

He'd been a Green Beret and earned a medal; she hadn't known that. And he was so damned sexy that every time she got near him like this it caused a brazen yet glorious tingle between her thighs, a blatant declaration of her womanhood. Oh, most college girls wouldn't "get wet," as coeds liked to say, over Mack, he was too ruggedly mature for them. But that's what Llayne liked. No matter how well groomed, no matter how precise his behavior, there was an undercurrent of wild abandonment. Probably with his sexual proclivities, as well, no doubt. It wasn't just the glimmer in his eyes or the catch in his voice that gave him away. It was his thick, wavy, dark brown hair. He combed it, but it just kept busting out of place and wayward curls poked winsomely about his face. He had a habit of running his fingers through it to push it back. It would stay for a few seconds, then tumble down again due to his animated movements as he talked passionately. God, what she wouldn't do to run her fingers through that hair, to weave her fingers through it and grab hold to pull him down to her!

Tonight he had on new jeans and a beautiful teal turtleneck sweater. He looked so good. So very good! She had an urge to ask him to take her to bed. He'd be so much fun; he'd know all kinds of kinky things to do. She wondered what he'd think of her if she asked. But, of course, she couldn't. She couldn't make Harold's accusations come true.

She watched his gestures as he talked to Pris and the guys, and was drawn to his wonderful mouth. The dangling cigarette attached to his lips, were it but her tongue.

Tongues, talking, he was saying something and she should pay attention. She pried her mind away from her lurid sexual fantasies to listen.

"By the way," Mack switched gears in mid-conversation as was his habit, "I heard you were in the ROTC Building last night," he said to Llayne. "Me too, for a few minutes. Sorry I missed you. But hey, don't worry about us." He cocked his head toward the other vets. "It doesn't bother us you stayed there all night. We know you're okay."

"I'm glad," Llayne said, "because I ain't okay by Harold Hackleberry, the Chairman of the Homecoming Committee. He visited me early this morning. Seems I've embarrassed him."

Mack slapped the bar and howled with glee, "Ooo-eee! That's great!"

"Har-old Hack-le-ber-ree-ee!" Neckbreaker purposely slaughtered the pronunciation of the nomenclature. "Shit, I hate that kid. Mean little son-of-a-bitch. We'll just hafta think a' how we can help him outta bein' such a li'l weasel."

"Yeah," Mack agreed, a gleam in his eyes. "Because, you know, he's embarrassed."

"Now guys, don't get yourselves in trouble over him," Llayne remanded.

"Oh, no. No trouble at all." Mack's cunning smirk revealed a mischievous mind already in motion.

"Okay, okay," Llayne said, attempting to take his mind off trouble. "Who's this guy you want to be my escort for the ball?"

Mack searched the room, then pointed. "There he is. Tommy Tanner. 'Tank,' he's called. Big, good-looking dude on the dance floor."

Llayne looked but there were lots of big dudes, only parts of which were visible in the tangle of bodies as they jerked around the floor to the rhythm of the blaring rock beat. Giving up trying to disentangle the enmeshed mass, she looked back at Mack as he talked to the others. His energy and verve were infectious; everyone was laughing and not paying any attention to the bodily gyrations on the dance floor. Finally he told her not to worry, he'd send the dude over, and he immersed himself into middle of the mob.

The crowd thickened. Llayne was asked to dance and soon forgot all about Tank Tanner. She came back to the bar, ordered another Coke and peanuts, and joked with Priscilla about some of the characters who ask a girl to dance in a place like this. A friend of theirs had been asked by a real scumbag once, to whom she politely said no. The boy had grabbed her purse and run into the john. By the time the bartender had been frantically summoned and rushed into the men's room, the guy held the purse open with his pecker pointing into it, ready to pee. The bartender retrieved the bag just in the nick of time. Or as Priscilla pointed out, "in the dick of time." Thankfully, Llayne and Priscilla never carried purses. They just stuffed their keys and the few bucks they had into their pockets.

The group was laughing over the story when a man they'd never seen before came up and asked Llayne to dance. She hesitated because he had such a short, brush hair-cut and looked strange. This guy was obviously just home from Nam.

Her hesitation made him hem and haw, and he said, "Come on, Jane. Mack wanted us to meet."

"Oh, yeah, well, you're off to a great start, soldier," she snapped. "My name is Llayne."

"Sorry. I've been in Nam for the last 14 months. Guess all you American girls look alike to me." He grinned, pleased with himself for his wit. Neither of the girls saw the humor and stared at him blankly.

But, because Mack had asked, Llayne agreed to dance with him. On the way to the dance floor she decided to be civil by asking, "What's your name again?"

"Tank."

Not so civil!

They danced to the band's rendition of "I Heard It Through the Grapevine." This Tank was a fabulous dancer.

He was tall, about six foot two. Not bad looking. Snappy, hazel eyes. His hair might be sandy brown. It was so short it was hard to tell.

The band moved on to a bad version of "Proud Mary," then did a little better with "Louie, Louie." Then they slowed it down with "Close to You," sounding nothing like the Carpenters and, at the prospect of getting close, the couple automatically returned to the bar. He awkwardly said hello as she introduced Priscilla and a few vets he didn't know. Then, try as they might, Tank and Llayne didn't have a single thing to talk about. She turned to watch the dancers and when she looked his way again, he was gone.

A few minutes later she spotted him on the dance floor with a strawberry blonde who had a reputation, a "rep," as being easy. Earned or lustfully imagined by horny young men because she was wildly sensuous, Llayne didn't know, but she was a gorgeous, long-legged creature named Rosie Saleman. The joke was that she was on sale for any man. Sometimes she bartended here at The Cabin but tonight was obviously her night to play! Llayne flinched as Rosie swung her long, light reddish mane in Tank's face, gyrating madly to a facsimile of Mick Jagger screaming, "I can't get no-o ...sat-is-fac-tion ..." *I'll bet,* Llayne thought. Tank was loving it, apparently wanted to make up for lost time overseas, although she doubted he missed much. Now Rosie shimmied at his knees. How tacky!

Priscilla followed Llayne's glare and her thoughts, saying, "A guy really gets his money's worth at that sale!" Llayne wadded up a napkin and threw it at her in jest as Mack rejoined them, tripping over a barstool while staring at "Sale" advertising her wares.

47

Llayne asked him, "Why on earth do you want that Tank to be my escort?"

"Because," he said. "He's a real nice guy, you know what I mean?"

She rolled her eyes and said, "Yeah, we can tell."

"Nice guy. Sure," Priscilla jibed. "He and Rosie probably read to each other from the Bible in bed at night. Oh, wait, they probably don't go to bed together. I bet she's a virgin. Well, hell, I'm sure he is, too. Think so, Macky?"

Prying his eyes off Rosie and back to them, Mack said, "Ah, come on you guys. He's a nice stable guy. Already got a Master's degree. Just taking a couple of classes at night."

"So we can see," Llayne drolled.

"He's got a real good job," Mack countered. "He's a counselor at the high school. Just started this week."

"Oo-oo-ooo," the girls chortled, looking wide-eyed at one another, feigning awe.

"Oh, you guys. Just wait until you get out of here and try to find a job. That is if you graduate," he teased right back. "I'm telling you, this guy is a gentleman."

The two young women looked back at the dance floor. Tank and Rosie were epoxied together for "Venus." "Mack, I suspect your definition of 'gen-tle-man' and mine come from different dictionaries," Llayne retorted.

The twitter was lost, however, as Mack's attention was riveted on Rosie once again, his eyes bugging out of his head as he ogled her wiggling hips. They all gawked, seeing that Rosie was in full bloom now, swaying as the sheen of her poured-on, red, velveteen, capri pants glimmered in the light of the rotating mirrored ball above the dance floor.

Llayne wondered why she hadn't noticed when she was dancing with him what a great body this Tank had. He was muscular, strong. His butt, tight under tight black pants. His shiny red and black flowered shirt was open at the neck and a heavy gold chain nestled in the thick hair on his chest. He was sweaty from dancing. Just like he'd sweat during sex, Llayne imagined.

The song ended and Rosie froze in a marble goddess pose for the few seconds it took the band to strike up an imitation of the Temps: "Get ready, 'cuz here I come ..." With the first beat of a chord Rosie turned and shimmied to the floor with primeval body thrusts, her outstretched arms revealing a boastful hint of bare breasts under the spaghetti-strapped, gold lame' top. She was definitely ready.

Stretching out on the floor in push-up fashion, she did the alligator. Tank joined her, his version of the 'gator more athletic than hers. They pumped themselves up and down, butts high then low, turning for backwards push-ups, legs kicking right then left. When Rosie jumped up, he once again followed her lead. She swished her hair in his face. Her languorous hips swayed, then jutted back and forth, back and forth. Tank aped the gesture.

Now playing lewdly to the crowd as well as to her man, long talon nails, painted crimson, reached up and pulled his head to hers. Seductively she licked her lips before planting a full kiss on his lips as a long lower limb wrapped itself around his leg. Then in a flash she threw him from her and thrust her arms in the air, throwing her head back for a deep laugh.

Heads popped all over the room when she flung hers back.

Llayne felt dizzy. She looked down at her own body. Earlier she felt particularly sexy in this blue, simulated leather hot pants outfit, but compared to Rosie she felt like a nun. A dumpy earth mother nun. Maybe she should join the Peace Corps.

"Geez!" Llayne exclaimed. "Is she out to get laid or what?"

"Yeah," Priscilla answered through puffs on her Winston, "she wants the Big 'O' bad." She blew a perfect "O" smoke ring. "That broad wouldn't hesitate one minute to take it right there on the dance floor in front of everybody. In fact, the more peepers the bigger the 'O,' I suspect."

"Just think of the diseases she could have," Llayne noted.

The look of pure lust in Tank's eyes belied his desirous delectation.

Mack dragged his attention away from the spectacle on the dance floor and said, "Ah, he's just fooling around. No harm done. He's been in Nam a long time, you know? He's really a nice guy. I don't know him real well myself, but I've been hearing about him ever since coming to school here. He has quite a reputation as an athlete. He was a lifeguard in the summers; he's an avid skier; and he was a pitcher for the baseball team the year they won the championship. Might of even turned pro if Uncle Sam hadn't drafted him first. His parents were both professors here before they died. I wouldn't set you up with anybody I didn't think was a good guy. Besides, he's the only one we can count on to stay sober through the whole schpeel because he doesn't drink much. But he'd still be our representative. These other guys are so excited about winning the election, they're already drunk and they're going to stay that way until a week from now when homecoming is all over."

"Mack," Llayne reminded him, "they're always drunk anyway."

"I know, kiddo. But, he won't be. What do you say?" His plea was salubrious, protective, and mighty persuasive.

Llayne said, "Mack, I do know guys. I date. I can find someone. That Tank doesn't want to be my escort."

"Sure he does."

His argument she could resist, but his crooked grin won her over.

"Will he have more hair by then?" she asked.

The winning grin broadened. "Thanks." He patted her on the side of the head as had become his habit, nodded to the others, and was gone.

"That Macky! A real enchanter," observed Priscilla. "Could charm the socks off a rattle snake."

"Yeah," Llayne had to agree, noticing that Tank and Rosie were at the bar having a drink. "But I wonder why he was so insistent on setting me up with that guy."

"Probably didn't want anybody to know their queen couldn't get a date," Priscilla said, blowing a whimsical smoke ring in her friend's face.

This time Llayne threw the peanuts.

♦ ♦ ♦ ♦ ♦ ♦ ♦ ♦

Mack hadn't meant to confront the drama professor. After all, it was an accident that he got lost in Warriner Hall while trying to find Velma, the secretary to the Dean, to break their date for Friday night. (He was going to tell her he had to go to a vet's meeting, although he was actually going to a party at The Bird bar downtown and thought she would be a drag to take along.) It was sheer coincidence that Professor Rex Bates happened to have an office in the building where he was looking for Velma. But as long as he was there, Mack decided to have a man-to-man talk with the guy. They were both in their thirties, older than these kids, and surely he could drill some sense into the man, lecherous as he was.

The professor was obviously a male with primitive desires that had caused hurt to many a young female, including Llayne, according to Priscilla. Mack didn't know exactly what the prof had done to her, but last night at The Cabin while Llayne was dancing with Tommy Tanner, that Tank fellow, Priscilla had alluded to her roommate's heartbreak over Professor Rex Bates. Mack couldn't stand the thought of that lizard touching Llayne. It made his skin crawl!

He shook off the rain from his hair and his hands as he looked up Rex Bates, Ph.D., on the directory by the main entrance, turned and took the stairs two at a time, and strode across the hall to room 221. He would have been okay if the instructor had been working in there alone. But that wasn't the case, and what he saw was the trigger for Mack.

In his small cubicle of an office, the lights dim, Professor Bates sat knee-to-knee with yet another pretty coed, this one Asian with bobbed ebony hair, his hand under her plaid, pleated skirt, resting gently on her thigh. He whispered sweet nothings, in this case, Mack scoffed, truly nothings, as she leaned into him, looking up with reverence at his handsome face. His dark hair tumbling across his brow, cutting Mack out of his peripheral view. It was the girl who looked up first and saw the imposing, roughly hewn man standing in the doorway.

"You need to leave," Mack ordered her as the professor looked up quizzically.

"What?" she asked at the same time Rex Bates said, "What the hell?"

"I have urgent business to discuss with, ah, Professor Bates." The name burned Mack's tongue, so badly did he want to resort to profane name-calling to expose the rake as the unconscionable, slick pervert that he was. His Green Beret training ran deep, however, and he knew how to keep his cool and work it to his own advantage.

Sensing a fight, the girl quickly rose and headed for the door, fearfully saying, "I'll see you later."

"No," Mack ordered, "don't ever come back, miss. He's not the right man for you, or any of the other young women he has a hankering for."

With a confused furrow of her delicate brow, she left.

Rex Bates was on his feet, confronting the intruder. "What in hell is going on?" he barked.

"I've come to talk to you mano-a-mano, two grown men, facing a problem and solving it," Mack informed him.

"I don't have any problems and if you do, they're yours, not mine, whoever in hell you are. Now get the fuck out of my office!" he seethed, stepping up to thrust his face into Mack's.

The trained soldier didn't jump for the bait, even though his opponent nauseatingly smelled like the men's cologne shelf at the drug store. Mack took a deep breath and calmly said, "The problem is that you exploit young coeds and somebody needs to put a stop to it."

"Who in chrissake do you think you are, coming into my office like this? Get the out fuck out!" Rex repeated, pointing a furious finger at the door.

"No, I can't do that. Not until we've solved this problem. You see, it is your problem, because if you don't leave the young women alone I'll report you to the Dean, and to whomever else I need to to get you sacked."

The drama instructor struck an authoritative pose. "Ha! Fat chance! The Dean loves me, the girls love me, and nobody's going to make me go anywhere." Lowering his voice to a mocking conspiratorial tone, he said, "You know, you should lose the hero act and try a little of that young nookie yourself. It's good stuff; might improve your attitude."

The highly trained special forces officer hadn't planned on his next move, but when confronted with the enemy, and his enmity toward this bastard was now complete, one must strike first. Mack slugged the guy with a left hook that sent him sprawling across his office floor.

"Well, you flaming asshole, I don't love you, and I'll get rid of you any way I have to," Mack left his parting shot. Bounding out of the office, down the stairs, and out the door into a rainy fall day, he felt better. He'd done his duty. He'd saved people, women in this case, who needed saving. But then a cloud befell him as he walked in the drizzle across the street to his red Chevy truck. Was that really it? he wondered as he lit up a Camel. Had it really been an altruistic gesture for the betterment of womankind? Or had he done it because the guy had taken advantage of Llayne? He didn't even want to contemplate the answer to that question, so headed to The Cabin for a Strohs.

All the way there he talked to himself in his head, convincing himself it was a good thing he set Llayne up with that younger dude, that Tommy "Tank" Tanner, for the homecoming ball. He wouldn't lose his cool and beat anybody up; he'd show her a real nice time.

◆ ◆ ◆ ◆ ◆ ◆ ◆ ◆

Thirty minutes. The "nice dude" was 30 minutes late. They were supposed to have arrived at the Homecoming Ball half an hour earlier. Llayne paced the floor in her white satin gown, ruby and pink, paisley print, velvet robe with white faux fur trim, and a rhine-stone crown atop a bevy of recently coifed curls.

The Homecoming Queen had a no-show date. Priscilla had left 15 minutes earlier for work at Falsetta's restaurant and pizza parlor, protesting that the queen should be at the ball.

"It's not right," Priscilla had complained, "I mean, the Homecoming Queen should be there!"

"I will be. He'll come. Now go. Scat!"

Her phony smile had vanished the moment the door had closed behind her friend. She stalked to the center of the living room floor, raised her arms to the gods of dating, and shouted, "Where in hell is that frigging creep?"

It'd been a wonderful weekend up to that point. She enjoyed it much more than she anticipated. The night before there had been a concert with the fabulous Temptations, one of her all-time favorite groups. She sat with Priscilla in the front row and they had sung, and danced, and screamed to songs like "My Girl" and "I Can't Get Next to You" until they were totally beat. Dragging out of the gymnasium when it had ended, they ran into a football player who'd been serving as a security guard, and Priscilla had begged him to get them backstage, saying surely the Temps would want to meet the Homecoming Queen. When he'd gone to ask, she'd admitted to Llayne, "Okay, maybe the Temps won't give a rat's ass about the queen of a hoe-dunk college, but I had to use all the leverage I could get!"

After they'd been escorted into the dressing room, both had stood frozen just inside the door. There had stood their Motown idols, still decked-out in flamboyant stage dress, with women, beautiful Afro-American women, dressed to kill, or at least maim, hanging onto their arms. None of those people had been from around there. *They jus' don't grow 'em like this down on the farm!* Llayne thought. Neither she nor Priscilla had been able to speak.

"Well," Eddie Kendricks had said kindly in that mellifluous voice of his, "we heard that one of you girls is Homecoming Queen and wants kisses from the Temptations. Which one is it?"

"Her!" Priscilla had said, giving Llayne a shove into the room.

"Huh? Oh, yeah," Llayne had said, stumbling forward. Eddie had pointed at her with his multi-ringed fingers and come over to her, taking her face in his hands and kissing her chastely on the cheek. The others had generously done the same, except for the last, David Ruffin, who had bowed and taken her hand to kiss it as a gentlemen would to a lady.

The stunning women had stood by patiently and Llayne had been struck with an urge to ask them to sit down for a Coke so they could chat, because she'd love to know how fascinating people like them got to be so fascinating. Of course, that had been out of the question, not only because they wouldn't do it, but because right then she felt two years old, a ragtag hayseed child in the midst of sophisticated city-slicker adults who were at the height of fame and wealth. She may as well have been from Mars, so alien was their world. But she and Priscilla had been thrilled just to have met them!

And, the parade that morning had been memorable, too. It had touched her heart. There had been retarded children from a nearby home who were happy to see a queen, old folks who sat in lawn chairs with blankets across their knees while they watched from their yards as they had for years, and children of all ages who were delighted just to be alive and watching a parade with colors and movement and music and fantasy!

Then there had been the game. The only hitch had been her parents. Her dad, sober, had fidgeted to get home to West Branch, no doubt to Rau's Tavern, so her mom had compliantly agreed to leave after halftime.

Central had won the game 27 to 21 over Eastern. But the highlight had been the halftime ceremony when Llayne and the court had stood in the middle of the football field, facing the college president and Homecoming Committee Chairman, Harold Hackleberry. Llayne had been aware of Peter's entourage sitting in the expensive, reserved seats on the 50-yard line, drinking from silver flasks. Peter had been conspicuously absent. Another group of vaguely familiar, brightly bedecked hippies had sat in the cheap seats in the end zone area under the cloud of gray smoke that incessantly hovered over them. And then there had been an extremely vocal group of vets sitting near the 25, smoking, drinking, and anything else possible. Mack hadn't been in sight. Llayne had tried not to be hurt but she had been. The two men she cared about hadn't even been there.

The college president had given a brief speech into a whining microphone and placed the shiny crown on Llayne's head. Harold, with stone eyes, had shown the crowd his supposed magnanimity by handing the queen a bouquet of red roses. She'd looked at his face but in the hubbub of stadium noise she hadn't heard what he'd said under his breath as he abruptly noticed something over her shoulder. Then Llayne had turned to look.

There had been three people running across the field, one obviously a man dressed as a woman. It'd taken a moment for Llayne to realize it was Elvira Scratch, the Vets' Club mascot. She heard talk recently about "her" but had no idea what it was all about. Then she'd seen that Elvira was Neckbreaker! Balloon boobs bouncing, blond wig askew, purple house dress flying in the breeze to reveal bright yellow boxer shorts, "she" had trotted onto the field to the delight of most of the onlookers. Especially the vets. Obviously privy beforehand, they had played "Let It Be" on kazoos from the stands.

And Elvira had been escorted by Mack in Army Green Beret dress uniform and Peter in full caballero hippy regalia. Both escorts had been astonishingly striking.

Elvira had given the queen an even bigger bouquet of deeper red roses than Harold had just given her, had hugged her in an embrace that popped one boob and made the crowd squeal with joy when "she" moved the remaining balloon to the middle of her chest. Formally, Elvira had extended a hand to the president, who good-naturedly shook it. Peter had kissed Llayne's cheek, Mack had kissed her hand, and each had shaken hands with the president.

Then Elvira had turned on Harold who visibly debated about whether he should try to maintain some modicum of decorum or run. But the wry mimic was too quick for the imp. Before Harold could move, Elvira had locked him in an embrace, twirling him down to the ground for a full kiss on the lips that left gobs of red lipstick on the little guy's lifeless mouth. Elvira had held Harold's back over her knee and smiled broadly at the cheering crowd. Well, the hippies and vets had cheered maniacally, while most of the Greeks, faculty and administration had seemed to miss the humor. Harold fainted dead away.

Elvira, really Neckbreaker, had carefully lain him on the ground, reflexively checking Harold's pulse and respiration as he had done so many times in Vietnam, and upon ascertaining that all vital signs were go, had left the victim for the team trainers who were already sprinting onto the field. Elvira had thrown kisses to the crowd as she and her escorts trotted off the field. Factions of the crowd had gone wild.

The president had remained unperturbed and the ceremony continued as rehearsed. To a traditional march hammered out by the band, the queen, court, committee and president had walked off the field in formation. Well, everyone had marched off the field except for Harold. He had to be carried off on a stretcher.

But now all the homecoming activities were over except for the ball and Llayne sat on her lumpy couch in her crummy apartment waiting for her arranged date to pick her up to escort her to the ballroom - well, it was a gymnasium, but she wouldn't split hairs - and a number of parties to follow. She was waiting for Tank, the dude. Dud was more like it.

Calling Mack at the vets' VFW Hall party was the only thing she could think of to do. She dragged the phone into the bathroom, as was her habit, sat down on the closed toilet seat, and pulled the phone book from its spot on top of the tank. She looked up the unfamiliar number, dialed, and said, "Thank god," when it rang through and someone answered.

"Mack O'Brien, please. Mack O'Brien. I want to talk to Mack!" She could hardly hear whoever answered. Their party had been going on all afternoon since the game and she felt hopeless when the answerer dropped the receiver and disappeared.

Catching a glimpse of herself in the full length mirror on the back of the bathroom door, she startled herself. Pulling back the glump of hanging bathrobes, she took a better look. The irony of her reflection in the smeared glass made her shake her head. There she was, sitting on top of the can, phone to her ear, a strikingly pretty young woman in "royal" fake fur and rhinestones. Oh, she knew she wasn't flamboyantly beautiful like some women. She didn't enter a room boobs first like Raquel Welch, nor hypnotize men with inane profundity like Marilyn Monroe, nor blind them with red sparkle like Rosie Saleman. Her beauty was more subtle, more natural. She may not be the first woman a man noticed when he walked through the door, but once he noticed her, he had a hard time looking away. She had a kind of mesmerizing appeal and she knew it. Fat lot of good it did her as she waited for a no-show date while the rest of the campus celebrated her night.

"Not exactly the stuff dreams are made of, is it?" she asked the glass queen. She couldn't resist - she stuck her tongue out at herself.

"Mack?" she said when someone finally came on the line. "Oh, Neckbreaker, it's you. Doesn't anybody know where Mack is ...? Listen, I can hardly hear you .... No, the ball isn't over. The ball just started, it's only 8:30. 8:30 at night .... That's right. But, I'm not there, I'm at home, in the john as a matter of fact .... No, I'm not sick; I don't have a date. He never showed." This was hopeless, she thought, but, she pressed on. "I need another date. Know anybody who just happens to be available at this very moment ...? No, Neckbreaker, you can't come. You're engaged to that girl back home, remember? You just told me yesterday. It's bad enough the frat cats have spread the rumor I screwed all you guys; I don't need to show up at the ball with an engaged man. I just thought there might be someone there who could take me .... No! Not Creamer. The word ballroom would take on new meaning with him .... No, not him, either. He's always high. Well, never mind. Just thought I'd try. Thanks, anyway. I don't know what to do. Guess I'll go by myself and tell them my date was delayed, in the death pound, the jerk...! No, I'm just kidding. Don't go after him. It's okay. I don't even know the guy. We don't need to kill him. Yet. Well, get back to your party. By the way, Neckbreaker ... Neckbreaker? Neck ...?"

The line went dead as Neckbreaker either returned to his party or passed out. She'd wanted to tell him how much she enjoyed his Elvira Scratch show that afternoon.

Depleted, she dropped the phone onto the floor as she slumped over the sink at her side. With a sigh, she picked up the phone and hung up the buzzing receiver. So far, this was just one hell of an exciting homecoming night. She couldn't believe she'd ever thought this event would change her life. She stood, looked in the mirror, straightened her crown, flung open the bathroom door, and stalked into the living room.

Eight-thirty-five according to the clock on the kitchenette stove. Forty-five minutes late; she was to have arrived early. A rent-a-date would have been better than this. She picked up her purse and keys, and started for the door.

The hard knock on the other side just as she reached for the knob startled her. Breathing deeply so as not to scream, she slowly pulled the door open. There, melded to the frame, was the tall mass of man selected to be her escort because he'd stay sober. Drunk as a skunk. The smell of booze sent her back into the room.

"Hey, little lady," he said, "whadaya say?"

"I say we're late."

"Whoa-oa. No problem. They'll wait for Tank and The Queen."

His beer breath sent her back a few more steps. Stunned, she watched as he danced himself down the hall outside her door, singing "Get ready, 'cuz here I come," as he held an imaginary partner. It was clear he didn't need her, or anybody, to have a good time.

55

Linda Hughes

Peeking around the corner of her door she watched him entertain himself. Her decision was quick. It would take too long to try to dump him in this state of elation and inebriation. She would take him along and pray for the best.

"Hey, Queenie, I'm ready for the ball," he sang as he waltzed toward her. "You look great, by the way. Love the crown look. Um-m-m, you smell good, too!" he said, his nostrils flaring at the scent of her Shalimar perfume as he leaned in close to her. He grabbed her about the waist and swung her around.

"Let go of me!" she protested, swatting his hands away.

"Hey, just wanna do my job," he jived. "You know, escorting The Queen! Come on, let's go trip the lights fantastic!" He tripped and almost fell.

Slamming the door behind her, she swept past him and down the hall without another word. He followed, singing and dancing all the way.

Chapter 6

"Hey, Veronica!" Tank hollered. "Howarya, baby? That party last week was super. Still having another one next week? I'll be there!"

Veronica was a short, slender blonde dressed to the teeth in black. She swayed her shoulders, allowing her pearls to roll around on her bony bare sternum, and cooed up at him, "Sure, tiger. See you there."

Llayne's date, Tank the "nice dude," had been playing don Juan, Romeo and Rudolph Valentino all wrapped up into one ever since their arrival at the ball just a few minutes earlier. He already sportively asked out a 70-year-old woman, who had been delightfully flattered and playfully swatted him away; he chatted with passersby, telling everyone within earshot what a great gig this was; and, he made his arrangements with Veronica. The amazing part was that most people seemed to find him charming. What flabbergasted Llayne most was that he knew so many people after having been home from Nam for just a few short weeks. Oh, he'd known some of them before because he'd been raised in Mt. Pleasant, a relatively small town with as many college kids as local residents, so it was easy to know folks. But more importantly, he was not a shy person, seeming to make a new friend every five minutes. No, not shy, Llayne decided, insufferably egotistical!

True, he was good looking, especially dressed in a new, gray, pin-striped suit, white shirt, and burgundy tie. His hair hadn't had time to grow much, though. She felt certain that his perfectly sculpted athletic frame was what attracted most women. It couldn't possibly be his brain, because he didn't seem to have one.

And, true, he was not a dull boy. The question to her was whether or not he would be a conscious boy for much longer.

In the car on the way over he related the events of the afternoon. A few of his hometown buddies had helped him get over his nervousness about this evening - he hadn't been around this kind of thing for a long time he reminded her - by insisting he join them for drinks to take off the edge. Well, the edge certainly was off and Llayne was a nervous wreck.

She'd insisted he let her drive his car as she wasn't about to let him drive drunk. The automatic shift on his new, gold Cutlass was so different from the stick shift on her old Beetle, she caused the car to lurch after every stop. She kept using her left foot for the brake, like she was accustomed to using it for the clutch, and she pressed on the gas with her right foot at the same time, like she did in her car. With an automatic shift, however, that had caused the car to lunge forward as soon as she released the brake. Then she'd been driving just a tad fast when an officer had pulled them over. He seemed quite surprised at the crown and all, but had given her a ticket anyway. She hadn't cared; she just wanted to get to the ball.

And here they were. Hardly worth the effort, she ascertained.

"Well! Nice of you to finally show up," Carol seethed as she approached Llayne. Carol, a Sigma Sigma Sigma who was a member of the court, never had warmed to Llayne, obviously believing the coveted crown should be hers.

"We had a little trouble getting here," Llayne said feebly.

"But, hey. Am I glad we're here," Tank chimed in, eyeing Carol.

Llayne's stomach churned as Carol, obviously so stupid she didn't notice this jerk was drunk, instantly became enamored with the hunk. Realizing that he was with Llayne, Carol asserted, "I bet she wasn't ready on time, was she?"

"Well, ya know how it is with some women," Tank meowed back, leering at the two mounds under Carol's pink silk gown. Llayne almost tossed her cookies when her nemesis responded by taking a deep breath, expanding and lifting her chest to better meet his eyes.

"Come on, Tank. We have to mingle with everyone," Llayne interrupted, bumping his arm with her shoulder to spur him into motion.

"I am mingling," he said, smiling at Carol as his date grabbed his arm and dragged him away.

"How humiliating," Llayne seethed, trying to whisper so that others wouldn't hear. "I know that being civil is difficult for you, but couldn't you manage it for just one evening? As a favor to the vets? You're a cad!"

"Well, at least I'm not a little witch like you," he said to her while managing a smile to the crowd at the same time.

"What? What do you mean? How dare you say I'm a - that!"

He stopped walking and clutched her elbow, pulling her close. "Listen," he said. "We both know we don't want to be with one another. You made that clear from the very start at The Cabin when we danced, tried to dance, with one another. You walked away from me when the slow dance came on like I had the plague. You ignored me at the bar. We're both doing this as a favor to the Vets' Club. But there's no reason for me to have a rotten time just because my date hates my guts. Well, fine! I don't much like you either. I was nervous this afternoon, thinking about being with the Homecoming Queen. The queen who so obviously thinks she's too good for me. I had a beer or two, or more. So what? Let's just do this gig as best we can and ...."

She lost his last words as people in the crowd frantically motioned to her. "On the stage. You need to get on stage," they insisted.

It was time. She needed to get on stage and say a few words of thanks into the microphone. Public speaking terrified her. She'd dreaded this all day.

She was ushered up with Tank at her heels, and the court and their dates followed. They lined up across the stage. She hadn't seen Harold, and a sorority girl from the Homecoming Committee got up and made the introductions, then turned the microphone over to Llayne. She took a step toward the standing mike, but faltered. Tank inadvertently stood on her robe. She turned and yanked at it. He made a show of moving his foot and apologized loudly, beaming at the audience. They laughed. Llayne couldn't abide him! She walked to the mike. A sea of faces was all she could see. So many people. She cleared her throat. Her short, prepared speech flew from her mind. She had absolutely nothing to say. The room became restless.

"Thank you. Th-thank you," she stammered, the sound of her heart beating in her chest deafening her thoughts. Quickly she returned to the shelter of the big oaf who was her date. Feeling nauseous, she swayed. Tank steadied her with his arm around her waist. She dare not look into his face; she wouldn't be able to tolerate his smugness at her embarrassing inability to handle herself under pressure.

The sorority girl glared at Llayne as she returned to the microphone. "Thank you, Queen Llayne Robertson, for such a rousing speech."

The audience didn't know if that was a joke, and some tittered. Tank broke the tension by clapping loudly, a broad grin on his face. Others joined in. The good humor bolstered Llayne's courage slightly, and she took a good-natured bow.

"Now," said the sorority girl, hardly hiding her guile for Llayne, "it's time for the Queen's Dance."

Llayne panicked again. What was the Queen's Dance? She'd never attended one of these soirees and had no idea what else was expected of her. The band played "Some Enchanted Evening" with its big band sound, and the sorority girl gestured harshly toward the steps off the stage. A spotlight hit the center of the dance floor as sequins and suits moved aside. Tank nudged her from behind and Llayne clottered down the steps. All she could see before her was the reflection of the spotlight on the slick, wood-slat floor. She knew it may be sacrilegious, but she prayed to God that she and her drunk date wouldn't fall down.

Gallantly, Tank took her hand and led her to the center of that vast space. He bowed to her, then to the crowd with a brilliant smile and a sweeping flair of his arm. They clapped. He stumbled slightly and fell against Llayne, and some of the onlookers chuckled. He gave them a sly grin. Then, to their sheer delight and Llayne's sheer terror, he decided to put on a show, twirling his unwilling partner about in grand fashion and dipping her to the floor. Llayne felt like an amateur contestant in an Arthur Murray dance contest.

After what seemed like a lifetime later to the queen, the dance ended. People cheered and applauded. Llayne sighed deeply out of relief. Tank bowed, then pointed to his date so she could bow. After a stiff, quick curtsy for appearance's sake, Llayne walked on rubber legs straight to the john.

When she came out, Tank was in the hall talking to a doe-eyed brunette and didn't even see Rosie Saleman stampeding toward him. Rosie shouted at him, "Well, well, well! Isn't this cute! My boyfriend out with Queen Twit and flirting with another woman! Cheating on me twice at once!"

"Hey, Rosie, I've told you, I'm not your boyfriend," he protested. "Now, come on, calm down." He reached out to take her arm, but he was too late and she punched him in the gut. With that he grabbed her and turned her around, holding her arms from behind. What he couldn't see from behind her was that, with the stronghold, her breasts almost popped out of the top of her strapless, red dress. She didn't care, or was too drunk to notice, and squealed and leaned into him, kicking her feet, twisting them up inside her long chiffon skirt. Then she went limp and started to cry.

"Hey, Rosie, it's okay," Tank said. "Where's your friend, that guy who bartends with you? You said you were coming with him; he can take you home."

"I don't wanna go home. I wanna be with you. I love you," she slurred. A big guy showed up and shook his head in dismay, taking Rosie into his arms.

"I'm so sorry. I just couldn't get her to stop puttin' 'em down tonight. I'll take her home," he offered. "Come on, Rosie."

"No! No, no, no! I wanna go home with hi-im!" she wailed, pointing at Tank as the guy half-carried and half-dragged her out the door.

In the milieu Doe Eyes had disappeared and only a few people had witnessed the scene in the hall. "I'm sorry," Tank told Llayne.

"Come on, Casanova," Llayne said. "We're leaving."

"Hey, I don't wanna go yet. The party's just getting started," he asserted.

"No, Mr. Tank. This party is over. Let's go."

"Geez! Does her highness mind if I hit the can first? See, I've had a problem ever since Nam. The guys tease me, call me LBB for little bitty bladder."

"How interesting," she said flatly as he walked away.

She said a few polite good-byes to the court members, except Carol, who snubbed her. Some friends, including her neighbor, Sally, and classmates had surfaced from the crowd and she said goodbye to them as well.

Llayne waited at the door for Tank until he returned from relieving his LBB. On their way out she noted to herself that her appearance at the ball had been exactly 32 minutes long. There were other parties they were expected to attend, and she at least should stop by the VFW Hall to thank the vets. But after one long look at this man lumbering through the parking lot, whistling and shooting a pretend basketball, she knew her big night was over.

"I've dreamt of this kind of night all my life, my homecoming," she mumbled to herself, shaking her head.

"Hey, baby, whadya say?" Tank shouted in a Donald Duck voice as he dribbled the invisible ball. She looked squarely at this person. A drunk date was one thing, but a drunk Donald Duck date was something else.

"Nothing. Forget it. And don't call me baby. I want your keys. I'm driving again."

He mimed a couple of hook shots, which he apparently made because he cheered and shouted, "Two! Two!" again as a duck. "Oh boy, oh boy!" he quacked.

"The keys!" she said impatiently. She certainly wasn't about to wait for him to win this imaginary duck basketball game. He threw the keys to her with a free throw shot, hollered "Two!" in a gobble when she caught them, and continued to play.

Llayne was concentrating on the unfamiliar car door lock when she realized his game had ended and he stood close behind her, his arm up on the roof, half pinning her to the metal. She turned slightly, and he put the other arm up on the other side, trapping her.

"Whaddaya say we go to my place?" he asked. She could only guess that the grin was supposed to be sexy.

"What do you say you go to Bora Bora and stay there," she retorted.

"Ooo-oo-ooo! The lady doesn't want to go to my place? I promise it'll be a goo-ood time."

"Get in," she insisted, pointing to the passenger side of his Cutlass.

"What?" His eyebrows raised in anticipation.

"The car. Get in the car."

"Okay, okay. But no more speeding tickets. Okay?"

Within two minutes he slept and snored. Luckily she wrangled his address out of him first.

When they reached his apartment she left him in the car as she unlocked the apartment door and turned on a light in the kitchen. She was glad it was a one-story building with an outdoor entrance so she wouldn't have to drag him up a set of stairs or down a hallway. She went back for him and tried to rouse him, which proved useless. She was able to wrap his arm around her neck and help him stumble inside. It was like hauling a mammoth sack of potatoes. They shuffled through the small kitchen; then she stopped in the middle of the living room to catch her breath and get her bearings. To the left was what appeared to be a bedroom door. Bingo. Almost tumbling over as they went in, she dumped him onto the bed. Having deposited her load, she stepped back to survey the scene, a ray of streetlight working its way between the curtains, giving her just enough light to see. There he was. Her date for what was to have been one of the biggest nights of her life. Passed out cold.

Llayne contemplated at least taking his shoes off and covering him with a blanket but decided what the hell. What had he ever done for her? Besides, his bedspread was fake zebra skin. Anyone that seedy didn't deserve to be covered.

Re-entering the living room, she was struck by its bold red and black and white decor. Another phony zebra skin hung on a wall. A real sheep skin laid on the floor in front of a small, black stone fireplace. A white Naugahyde couch sat floor level, having no legs. There were exotic red and white and black and yellow pillows scattered about on the plush red carpet. And the pole lamp by the couch looked like … she turned it on … yes … a red bulb. Typical bachelor pad. An amateur porn set.

Going back through the kitchen to get to the entrance door, she did have to admit that the red-lacquered cabinets and red-and-blue-and-white-and-yellow country plaid wallpaper in that room were kind of cute. She took his keys out of the door lock, considering her dilemma. Should she take his car and call him tomorrow, or leave it and walk? If she took it, she'd have to talk to him again, which she decidedly didn't want to do. On the other hand, it didn't seem appropriate for the Homecoming Queen to walk across town by herself on homecoming night.

"Oh, to hell with it!"

She tossed the keys onto the '50s-style, chrome kitchen table covered with red laminate, stomped out, and slammed the door behind her. Bobby pins boinged in every direction as she tore the crown off her head and hung it from her arm. Hitching up her robe, she trounced across a field toward her apartment on the other side of town.

Priscilla lit a cigarette and studied her roommate. She'd felt a little sorry for herself, missing out on the fun of this big night, but at least she made a chunk of money in tips. The queen didn't even have that.

They sat in a booth at Falsetta's where Priscilla had just finished her shift. Llayne wore a wrinkled pink sweatshirt and blue jeans. The curls atop her head had been carelessly brushed out and her hair now hung in off-kilter pigtails tied in crumpled pink ribbons, and her eyes were red and puffy from crying. She looked like shit.

Priscilla said, "Tell me, if this is supposed to be the Age of Aquarius and the era of free love, how come you and me ain't gettin' any?"

That forced her friend to smile. "I don't know," Llayne said. "Maybe that's why people like that Tank and Rosie, and Peter and his women, and Mack and his women, do it so much, making up for virgins like us."

"Virgins?"

"Sure. I think after so long we're virgins again. Don't you think?"

Priscilla threw her head back to laugh, blowing smoke above her head. "Sure. Hey, I bet most guys would buy it. Have you ever noticed how many girls tell guys they're virgins, and those nimrods buy it? Did you know Sally has her new boyfriend believing it?" she asked, referring to their apartment building neighbor.

"You're kidding! What about the four guys she dated last year? Especially that one who was chasing her around the apartment the day we walked in on them?"

"Guess they were just playing an innocent little game of tag."

"Pris, they were naked!"

They laughed at the recollection.

"Yeah," Llayne said, "some guys really can be stupid, can't they?"

"Once their hormones start boiling over, yes."

"Maybe we should lie like other girls do."

"Nah. We're not the type. That's why we're dateless, stuck with each other, on homecoming night. Yea! Here's our pizza!" Hurriedly, she crushed her cigarette in the ashtray.

"Double cheese, just like you ordered!" the friendly waitress announced, and they wasted no time stuffing their mouths.

"I was too excited today to eat," Llayne excused her ravenous behavior as she held a slice above her head to slurp up a string of cheese. "Boy, that was stupid," she mumbled with her mouth full.

Priscilla nodded, swallowed a huge mouthful, but suddenly became preoccupied. "Listen," she said, leaning further over the table, "if you could screw anybody right now, who would it be?"

"Damn! I don't know!" Llayne exclaimed, dabbing at a greasy smear on her chin with her paper napkin.

"Bullshit! Who?"

"Well," she said, gulping down a big bite, "I have thought about Mack."

"What about Peter?" Priscilla asked as she scarfed down her food.

"Yeah, him, too. But he has those girls. I don't think either one would be interested in me."

"Why not?"

"I don't know. They just wouldn't. I probably don't know much about sex compared to those women they hang out with."

"Didn't Rex teach you much?"

"I didn't have time to learn much before he moved on." Her eyes gazed off. "I don't think I'll ever enjoy sex with anyone else as much as with him. He was the best."

"Now how in hell would you know?" Priscilla quipped. "You've never really had anybody to compare him with. Those two adolescents in high school and that wacko encounter with Brady Thomas don't count."

"True. But I just know. What about Benny?" Llayne asked. "Don't you feel that way about him?" Another string of cheese glopped onto her chin as she tore off a big bite and she sucked it up, wiping her chin with the napkin again.

Priscilla missed it as she stared at her plate. When she looked up her dark, smoky eyes were sad. Elaborately, she lit another cigarette. She said, "I think Benny and I were first loves. I think we could've had a good life together. But I'll never know. There's one thing I do know: He was capable of more love than anyone I've ever known. He loved me dearly, probably more than I deserve. But, because of that love, he'd want me to go on with my life. I hope I'll love somebody else someday. It'll never be the same. Not less, or worse. Just different." Calmly, she smoked.

"My god, Pris! You've really been thinking about this, haven't you?"

"Yeah, well, I haven't had a hell of a lot to do. You know, no sex or anything."

"Shoot," Llayne said, dropping her piece of pizza back onto the plate, "here I am worrying about this farce of a night and it's nothing compared to what happened to you." She reached across the table and touched her friend's hand.

Priscilla smiled and said, "Or what happened to you last summer. But don't be silly. Homecoming night, your last year of college, especially if you're the Homecoming Queen, is important. Every girl dreams her whole life long of being a queen of some kind someday. And here it is, the pits. I'd like to ring that Tank's neck!"

A few involuntary tears spilled from Llayne's eyes, dripping the last of her mascara down her cheeks. She dabbed at them with her tattered napkin, leaving red dots of sauce on her cheeks.

Linda Hughes

"I'm sorry," Priscilla apologized."I didn't mean to make you cry again."

"That's okay. I need to get it all out. I suppose Tank is a nice enough fellow. I just hate his guts. One thing for sure, I may fantasize about every guy that breathes, but I'd never go to bed with him!"

"But we'll go to bed with somebody, someday. Get married, have rug rats, all that stuff," Priscilla noted, reaching across the table with a clean napkin to wipe away the goop on her friend's face.

"I know," Llayne relented, "I guess that's what we're supposed to want. But isn't it scary? I mean, actually living with a guy and being with him every day. What if it gets boring? What if he has an affair? Lots of guys do, you know. I'm inclined to think most guys do, after what I saw at Bronco Buck's. I don't know, marriage is scary as hell. My parents seem to hate each other. I don't think I want to do it until I'm old. Like maybe 30."

Warmly trying to wheedle her friend out of her misery, Priscilla said, "Hell, the Homecoming Queen should have marriage proposals all over the place!"

"Oh, yes," Llayne grinned, "I have to beat them off with a stick. The joys of being queen." She couldn't help but think of the robe she left rumpled on the couch in their apartment and the crown plopped on the grotesque skull-shaped candle Priscilla had acquired last year during her primitive-but-peaceful ritualistic Druid cult phase, that sat unused on the shelf above the TV now that the young woman had gone back to being a Roman Catholic, albeit a rather irreverent one.

Llayne looked up from the vision that was anything but majestic and caught a boy across the way staring at her. A typical scruffy college kid, he craned his neck around the corner of his booth to look at her. Llayne pointed him out to Priscilla. When she turned to meet his glare, he quickly sought refuge in the corner of his booth where they couldn't see him.

He and the guy with him got up to leave. As they passed by, the girls couldn't help but overhear as they attempted to whisper.

The starer said, "That is her! That's the Homecoming Queen."

"Don't be absurd, asshole." The second one gave Llayne a quick once-over as they stood at the cash register paying their bill. "The Homecoming Queen would be at a hundred parties tonight." He took one more glance for reassurance. "Besides," he tried to murmur, "our queen is much cuter than that!"

Both guys gave Llayne a final scan and frowned as they passed through the door. Priscilla picked up a piece of pizza as if to throw it at their backs, but Llayne stopped her.

"Don't waste it," she advised.

To that, they settled back and finished the whole pizza. After all, they had nothing else to do.

◆ ◆ ◆ ◆ ◆ ◆ ◆ ◆

64

Her skin felt warm in the silver-mercury summer's day, then sizzled when the hot splotches of bleached sunshine escaped a stark white puff cloud with lavender-tipped wings. The water below her laid calm, at times mysteriously dark, hiding the wonder within. At other times, when a beam of sunlight struck, crystal clear aquamarine revealed a tan sand and white shell bottom. When the ray was devoured by a hungry cloud, the water once again became a murky mystery.

Twelve women stood in line on an L-shaped dock, all pretty, all in sexy bathing suits. Llayne stood on the end. The question was: Who would dive in first to test the water? Who would go, not knowing for certain all that laid below?

Two other women, named Toona and Loona Looney, who were not from the group of bathing beauties, walked up behind Llayne. They came from a beautiful, shiny aluminum ship, the Lorna Doone, anchored on the horizon. They tried to tell Llayne something, perhaps, she suspected, that she was crazy.

She dove in anyway, her heart leaping with fear upon contact with the cool liquid. What was underneath her? Grotesque, scaly carp like those she ran into once when diving off the raft out on Lake George? Sharks like the ones that newspapers reported eating people off the coasts? Monsters like Loch Ness? The fear quickly dissipated and turned into excited anticipation. The water wasn't as cold as she first thought. It was like nice, tepid bath water. She surfaced for air and a ray of mellow yellow sun struck her. She put her face back to the fluid glass and saw brightness, sand, and shells. Diving deep, she felt exhilarated with the freedom of gliding through water, feeling more at ease here than standing restlessly on the dock with all those other women wondering what to do.

Suddenly, a blanket of light fell across the bay, making visible hundreds of tiny, fluorescent orange and purple and gold and blue dancing fish, colored diamond dots sparkling as they slithered through sun-prismed water. Intuitively Llayne knew they were friends. She put out her hand and they came to her.

Delicate bubbles surfaced and she and her fish friends followed, spiraling upward, her face streaked in sunlight, the outer rays illuminating her followers. Together they formed a giant, dangling bangle with a center of turquoise spandex and flesh surrounded by bright baubles, shimmering with movement.

She reached the surface and took another deep breath. Her aquatic friends fanned patiently just below the surface. The other women still stood on the dock looking despairingly at her. Did they think she was crazy? It didn't matter anymore. They were nuts for not enjoying this wonderland of water.

But wait! She twirled while still treading water, jerking toward the horizon, and all eyes turned, including the bulging fish eyes just below the wet glaze. What was that noise? That horrible noise intruding from - screeching, screaming from - the ship, Lorna Doone. The piercing siren wouldn't stop. Her fish friends scampered away to the safety and silence of subaqueousness.

BUZZ! stop. BUZZ! stop. BUZZ! stop. BUZZ!

Who in hell was at her apartment door at ... seven a.m.? Yes, her swollen, squinting eyes could see that the little hand of the clock on the box beside her bed was on the seven and the big hand was near the 12. Her brain rummaged through its mangled cells to put meaning to that and came up with seven in the morning. Someone was ringing the buzzer at her door.

She and Priscilla hadn't come home from Falsetta's until after one in the morning. She was exhausted and still had a knot in her stomach from eating so much gooey pizza.

Stumbling as she got up, her nude body shivered against the chill. She didn't usually sleep naked, but hadn't done laundry in so long that she hadn't been able to find anything clean to wear to bed, nor had she been able to conjure up enough energy to care. She went in search of her bathrobe.

"Where is that damned thing?" she mumbled, raking through the pile of clothes at the foot of her twin bed. Priscilla flopped over on her own little bed and realized that Llayne was already up to stop the awful clamor that interrupted her sleep. Waving her hand in a "go, stop it" gesture, she rolled over and pulled the covers over her head. Her eyes never opened beyond a minuscule slit.

Llayne shuffled out of the bedroom. Finding her robe under two towels hanging on the hook on the back of the bathroom door, she covered her body, fumbling with the tie belt as she went into the living room.

A relentless finger continued to push the shrill buzzer.

It was incredible how many bits and pieces of rational and irrational thoughts tumbled around, colliding in her mushy gray matter as she staggered toward the door. Maybe their neighbor, Sally, hadn't come home last night, forgot her key, and couldn't rouse her roommate.

The fish dream. She wondered what that Dr. Lichenger, that man so stuck on analysis, would think of it. The other women: the other contestants in the homecoming election, no doubt. The water: the unknown. Or was that too simple? Not Freudian enough? Well, that's what it seemed like. The women insinuating she was crazy. Was she? Diving in, being scared, then learning that sharks and monsters weren't there, just friendly little fish. Were they the vets and the hippies? Men in general? Was her dream trying to tell her that not all men are scary like her father, that she didn't have to be afraid of them all? Who knew?

And the siren from the ship on the horizon, the buzzer still blasting: BUZZ! stop. BUZZ! stop. BU ....

The last thought to flash through her mind as she grabbed the doorknob was that this would be him, that Tank, come to apologize for being such a jerk last night. Well, to hell with him. No apologies accepted. She threw open the door.

There he was. Harold? Harold!

Had she been more alert, her defenses wouldn't have been down; but as it was, she let him trample right past her into the apartment. Standing once again in the middle of her living room, hands on thin hips, he glared at her in disgust.

"Well!" he snapped. "Wouldn't all the guys on campus who are so in love with you like to see you now? Hardly sexy, I'd say. Not even decent, for that matter. You look like shit."

"You always look like shit, Harold. What do you want?" She was too tired to muster up too much ire, but he encouraged her considerably.

"You have something that doesn't belong to you," he announced.

"I'm sure, Harold, you've never had anything that doesn't belong to you." She felt smug with what seemed at that hour like great wit.

His hair bristled. His eyes bugged. His head bolted. "I want the crown! You! You don't deserve to keep that crown! Last night I did a little digging and found out all about you. You disgusting slut!"

She panicked. Somehow he'd found out about her baby!

"You dated a professor last year!" he declared. "Students aren't supposed to date faculty members! Oh, you thought you were so secretive, but lots of people knew! You slept with a professor!"

Her exhausted brain relaxed. He only thought she'd been a stripper, was a whore, and boffed a prof. He didn't know about her pregnancy. It would have destroyed her to have this asshole degrade something as sacred as her child.

He bellowed, "You're a slut, not worthy of our crown! I want it back. Where is it?"

"What in hell are you talking about? It's mine!" Her shaken senses told her she needed to wake up to handle this. She blinked and shook her head. "You know damned well," she retorted, "they buy a new crown every year and the queen always keeps it. It's mine!" That quasi-expensive rhinestone tiara had never occupied a moment of serious thought in her mind, but now it was important to possess it because this dork didn't want her to have it.

But, as if given directions by satellite telecommunication from above, Harold turned his waxy little head and looked straight at the morbid candle skull on the shelf over the TV, upon which sat askew the infamous crown. His crooked glasses almost popped off his head when he spied it, up there above them on flagrant display. For the first time that she'd ever seen, he ripped his spectacles from his face, causing one wire temple to bend, and he marched to the shelves for closer inspection with popping bare eyes. The empty, paraffin eye sockets gawked back. It struck Llayne that the shape of Darwin's head and that of the skull were the same. Even the shade of dull gray matched. With a gasp he grabbed the shiny royal token and clutched it, along with his glasses, to his skinny, concave chest.

"How dare you?" he hissed. "You heathen!"

Llayne reached in and grappled for the crown. She almost got it away, too, but he grasped it just in time. Back and forth it went from his chest to hers as both held on like children fighting for a toy, shouting, "mine!," "no, mine!" First he pulled harder, then she did, the bramble of words indecipherable in the maelstrom.

But suddenly Harold stopped and stood cold still. His jaw dropped open and his hands, though gripping, stopped yanking. His dilated eyes moved down from Llayne's face to her body. She followed his gaze and looked down at herself.

Nude. The hastily tied belt had fallen away and her robe was open, a pink frame displaying the incarnadine, trim, buck-naked body beneath. Her rosy nipples pointed straight at the usurper, demanding his rude attention. His eyes already skimmed down to the light brown pubic hair that shone, begging, he imagined, to be touched.

"Oh!" she screamed, letting go of the crown. She grabbed clumsily for cloth, any cloth, to cover herself. Snatching up the belt from the floor, she wrapped it desperately around her waist, tying it tight over a crooked, mashed-up frock. She clutched one hand to the collar, securing its closure over her breasts, the other hand reflexively held closed the area over her crotch. It was so humiliating! Having this little twerp lay his seedy eyes on her bare body suddenly felt symbolic of her entire life - raw, exposed, unprotected. She felt lightheaded as a red hot flush of embarrassment assaulted every inch of her skin.

When she looked back up, Harold's mouth was gaped open, a dribble of drool running down his chin. He blinked his unbelieving eyes and his head shook with a nervous twitch, as if waking from a sinful fantasy - the kind respectable men didn't have. If Llayne would've had enough presence of mind to guess that Harold had never before been that close to a female's exposed body, she would've been right.

Harold sought escape. He couldn't let her, this savage, wanton creature, see the messy little bulge in his nicely pressed slacks. Spontaneously, he covered his groin with the tiara, dropping his glasses in the process. A confused step to the side placed his foot directly over them and a hundred pieces of glass ground into the carpet.

"Oh!" He looked down at the litter. "Oh!" He looked back at Llayne. "Oh, you disgusting whore!" He stumbled backward over the chair and finally made his way out through the door, the rhinestone crown in front of his little hard-on.

In his haste he left the door open. Llayne trounced over and slammed it shut. She grabbed a whisk broom and dust pan out of the kitchenette closet and stooped to clean up the broken glass. Priscilla came out of the bedroom, yawning as she scratched her hinder through her shabby flannel nightgown. "What was all the racket?" she asked. "It woke me up."

"Harold was here."

"Harold? That dinky little a-hole? What'd he want?"

"He wanted .... Oh, nothing. Well, yes, it was! He took my crown back. Men! They're always taking, taking, taking!" she admitted, dejected.

"What? No! We have to get it back!"

Llayne threw the broom down in the middle of the floor, bolstered by her friend's support. "Yes, we do!" she agreed. "But how?"

Priscilla scrunched up her face and stared at the skull candle, considering "how." "I know!" she exclaimed, as if an idea had just zapped from the skull to her brain.

"What?"

"Well, I don't know exactly what, but Mack and the guys will!"

"Mack? Oh no, we can't bother him. Not this morning."

"Why not?"

"Well, you know, he had a date last night and will probably still be busy, or something."

"You mean we might catch him in the rack with a dame? From what I've seen of Mack, he won't care. He hates Harold enough to leave his libido behind long enough to get even. Come on! Let's get dressed!"

Llayne wasn't convinced this was the best way to go about recapturing her kidnapped crown, but she didn't want to let Harold's trail get too cold. Hurriedly they dressed, dashed out to the Beetle, and sped to Mack and Neckbreaker's apartment building. They weren't sure which apartment it was, but names were listed on the mailboxes in the foyer, so they ran up the stairs and quickly found the right one. Priscilla knocked on the door.

Neckbreaker hollered from inside, "It's open. Come on in."

The smell of strong coffee stroked their nostrils the moment they opened the door. Neckbreaker, fully clothed, sat at a table reading a newspaper and sipping the coffee. The scene was so ordinary that both women stopped and stared. In turn, he was clearly flabbergasted and genuinely delighted by the unexpected visitors.

When they relayed their tale of woe he went down a short hallway and knocked on a bedroom door, giving Llayne time to study the place, Mack's place. It was a typical apartment with one living area, but unlike most college kids' residences, this one had decent furniture and lots of electronic equipment - a television, a stereo, a tape deck. Masculine and uncluttered, it was the home of grown-ups. Llayne was surprised at how neat it was.

When Neckbreaker hollered through the bedroom door, telling Mack what was going on, the door flew open and Mack, in khaki shorts, barreled out into the living room. The sight of his muscular, lean, half-bare body, and tantalizing, helter-skelter hair caused Llayne to falter and step backward. She grabbed the edge of the table for support.

That's when the woman, wrapped in a sheet, stepped part-way out of the bedroom into the hall. Llayne had to cock her head to get a good look, but was pretty sure it was a nurse from the student health center. Her long, black hair cascading over her exposed shoulders and her leg sticking out of the sheet, she said, "Mack, where're you going? Oh, hi," she said sweetly to the intruders.

"Hi," Llayne and Priscilla both managed to mumble, embarrassed.

"I'll be a minute," Mack told her, running his fingers through his hair as he smiled at his visitors. The woman disappeared and Llayne's stomach roiled at the thought of what had just gone on behind that door.

"So," Mack said, "we have to get your crown back! Neckbreaker, call a couple of the guys. We'll need four of us for this mission. The girls here will make six. That'll be just right."

Neckbreaker obeyed the command and started dialing the phone. Llayne and Priscilla sat politely on the couch while Mack went back to the bedroom to dress. Llayne pictured that woman trying to make him stay, nibbling at his mouth, licking his nipples, sticking her hand into his pants.

Mack came right back out, dressed, and they were on their way. After picking up two other veterans, who rode with Neckbreaker in the bed of Mack's red Chevy truck, they easily found Harold Hackleberry, sitting on the steps of his fraternity house. Lost in deep thought, casually twirling the crown in his hand, he didn't notice the truck stop in front of the house next door, and that was his downfall. By the time the men got to him, he had no escape. Neckbreaker easily picked him up and carried him, kicking and screaming, to the back of the truck. Mack grabbed the crown and tossed it to Llayne, who tucked it into her arms protectively. A few of Harold's fraternity brothers looked out of their windows to check out the commotion, but upon realizing it was Harold, they looked away. Nobody cared.

The military men had no intention of doing permanent physical damage to their opponent. It would've been easy, if they wanted to, but they just wanted to embarrass him. And that they did. Driving to a wooded area less than a mile away, the men stripped him, except for his black socks, and simply drove away with his clothes as Harold hysterically, hopelessly, screamed obscenities.

Llayne and Priscilla looked back as Mack drove them out of the woods and caught a glimpse of a naked Harold as he darted behind a tree. "Huh!" Priscilla harumphed. "That looked like a penis, only smaller."

Two hours later when he gave up and admitted to himself that no one was coming to rescue him, Harold hid behind garages and bushes to get home. He cursed the fall weather all the way, because it caused every clothesline to be bare. He never would've guessed that Mack had considered the wooded spot carefully, surmising that if Harold had any survivalist ability at all, which was questionable, he would be able figure out how to get home undetected.

Harold did make it home okay, with only a few girls catching a glance at his scrawny butt as he dashed into bushes, but they dismissed him as another stupid streaker. But it was arriving home that added insult to injury. When he went slinking through the back door of his fraternity house and grabbed a small kitchen towel to wrap around his waist, a fraternity brother sauntered into the kitchen and, totally unplussed at finding his brother nude except for a tiny piece of terry cloth, said, "Hey, Hackleberry. You don't need a towel that big to cover your privates, do you?" The insult scalded Harold's ears and chapped his bare little ass. His humiliation complete, he holed up in his room for hours while deciding that, after graduation the coming spring, he'd do his grad work at the University of Michigan, where cultured, respectable people got their degrees. He couldn't take this heathen tribal camp any longer!

The next day no one took credit for nor claimed the blue boxer shorts with the white polka dots which appeared at the top of the flagpole.

CHAPTER 7

Restlessly Llayne tried to watch television. The tin foil kept falling off the rabbit-ear antennas, though, causing Mary Tyler Moore, playing single career woman Mary Richards who was "going to make it after all," to skitter across the tiny black-and-white screen. She gave up and turned it off, picked up her book, and stretched out on the couch to read. But after a few pages of *Everything You Always Wanted to Know About Sex But Were Afraid to Ask*, she put it down. What was the point? She hadn't had sex in over a year and it appeared she would never have it again.

In the couple of months since homecoming, her life had become even more dull, dull, dull. She glared off into space as the tune "Raindrops Keep Falling On My Head" inexplicably repeated itself over and over in her head. "Raindrops keep fallin' on my head, and just like the guy whose feet are too big for his bed, nothin' seems to fit, those raindrops are fallin' on my head, they keep fallin' ...." Unfortunately she heard it in her own untrained voice and not the deep, mellow one of B.J. Thomas, who sang the record. Looking out the double glass doors didn't help either, with its panoramic view of the tires of the cars in the parking lot. She wondered if she'd spend the rest of her life looking at tires, going nowhere.

Priscilla blew through the front door and dumped her books on the kitchenette counter. "That geology class is the pits!" she announced as she cast off her jacket and fell into the chair. "What a drag! Never should've taken an evening class, fall asleep every time. And we've got a research paper to do by Christmas break next week. I've got so much homework I don't know if I should shit or wind my watch. Have to finish that painting, too." She pointed to a canvas sitting on the kitchenette counter, with an outline of an embracing nude couple on it.

"What you doin'?" she changed the subject.

"Oh, just getting ready for my exciting date with that millionaire I met at the country club," Llayne chided.

"Hey, I thought you did have a date tonight. With that Johnny, or Donny. What's his name?"

"Don't remember. That's how much he impressed me when we went out last week. That's why I called and canceled for tonight. Told him I have the flu."

"That's about the 12th time the past couple of months you've had the flu."

"Better than you. Can't believe you told that guy last week you couldn't kiss him because you have 'hoof and mouth disease!' Didn't you pay attention in biology? People get trench mouth; cattle get hoof and mouth."

"No. I didn't pay attention. Didn't matter; the guy was so stupid he didn't know the diff. I'm just not ready. Shouldn't have let him walk me home from work. But that's still not as bad as you, telling that one guy you couldn't go to the basketball game with him because you had a headache, then going with Sally."

"Yeah, that was bad. Out of 2000 students crammed into those bleachers, who wouldn't guessed we'd wind our way up to a seat right in front of him!"

"And he was so pissed he yelled at you in front of everybody."

"Well, I told him my headache miraculously got better."

"Right! You're the worst liar on the planet!"

"So, what're you going to do tonight? Homework?"

"Hell, no!"

"What about your paper and the painting?"

"They're not due 'til next Tuesday. I'll do it Monday night."

"Want to go to The Cabin?"

"Nah, I'm sick of The Cabin."

"Me, too. Mack hasn't even been there lately. Must be too busy with all those broads he dates."

"Speaking of broads, we could go see *Myra Breckenridge*, again," Priscilla kidded.

"Oh gag! That was the worst movie ever made!" Llayne spoke the obvious. They laughed, recalling the night recently when they'd sat dumbfounded in the Central Theater downtown, watching Raquel Welch play a transsexual schemer, Mae West play a bad caricature of herself, and Rex Reed make a complete ass out of himself.

Priscilla added, "The only thing at all worthwhile about that movie was that new actor named Tom something. Tom Seckell, or Selleck, or something. God, he's a stud! I wouldn't kick him out of bed for eating crackers!"

"Yes," Llayne agreed, "but unless Tommy-baby is coming over to ask me to marry him, wild horses couldn't drag me to that movie again."

"I know what we can do!" Priscilla exclaimed. "Some of the waitresses have being going out to the reservation to see an old Indian woman. She's supposed to be psychic. Let's go see her!"

"Psychic? Are you kidding? Do you believe in that stuff?"

"Not really. But, it might be a kick. Come on! What've we got to lose?"

Llayne looked around their drab apartment and noted, "Not a thing."

They donned their jackets and drove the seven miles to the Chippewa Indian Reservation east of Mt. Pleasant. It was obvious the minute they hit Native American soil, even though there was no sign or barrier. The land became flat and barren, the scattered clapboard houses looked poor. The night was steely gray, the land was gray, the mood turned gray, too. Two teenagers strolled down the dirt road, smoking cigarettes and hunkering into their coats to fend off the wind. Llayne stopped and asked for directions. Without a word, they pointed to a small, dingy white house with three new cars parked in front. Llayne parked between two of the five rusted-out cars strewn around the front yard, none of which appeared to be in operating order, and her rusty old Beetle looked right at home. A scrawled handwritten sign on a piece of cardboard tacked on the front door said, "Back Door." Assuming it was meant for intruders like them, they headed around the house.

In the back they looked through a glass door painted with a multitude of finger prints. There was a waiting room of sorts on a closed-in porch, so they went in. Two rusty folding chairs were occupied, two on opposite sides of the porch were empty. Musing that this place had the corner on the rust market, Llayne sat next to a man in a suit reading the *Wall Street Journal;* Priscilla sat next to a stately elderly woman who knitted badly.

A young woman emerged from a door within, turned inward and, her voice quivering with emotion, said, "Thank you, Mrs. Lacey. Thank you." She left.

A raspy voice called through the inner door. "Mr. Johnson!" The man went in and closed the door.

Priscilla joined Llayne on her side of the porch. "Mrs. Lacey?" she queried. "I thought it would be Medicine Woman or Head Healer or something."

The older woman cleared her throat in disapproval and gave them a nasty look, so they shushed and bided their time by staring at a faded picture of Jesus on the wall, fiddling with their jackets, looking out the streaked windows at scraggly trees, and trying to get a lazy, fat, calico cat to let them pet it. It totally ignored them, never moving from its spot on a rag rug near the door.

Finally the man and woman each came and went and the voice within clipped, "Next!" The two young women entered a room no bigger than a pantry. A single, small lamp with a red shade dimly lighted a card table, which was covered with a muddy-colored cloth. Dark wooden shelves, warped with age but managing to hold stacks of home canned goods, lined the back wall. The cubicle smelled like raw, dirty potatoes, although none were within sight.

"I do one person at a time," the ancient, leathery-skinned woman said from her chair behind the card table. Her age would have been impossible to guess, appearing to be anywhere from 80 to 110. Slightly overweight, with scattered white hair with ends that spiked out in random spots where it'd been carelessly caught up in black hairpins, she wore a charcoal gray housedress that'd been in style during the Depression and looked like it'd been worn everyday since then.

"We want to do it together. We don't care if we hear each other's future," Priscilla insisted.

"Fine," Mrs. Lacey snapped. "It's your life. Sit down."

Llayne sat directly across from her in a rickety folding chair. Priscilla sat on a beat-up metal trunk to the side.

"Give me your hand," the seer demanded. Llayne put her right hand on the table between them and the old, wizened woman took it. The youthful, vital woman felt a surprising warmth and comfort within the knotted knuckles. Mrs. Lacey closed her eyes for what seemed an eternity, and when she opened them Llayne was drawn into their earthy, dark brown depth.

"You will be granted a great gift," she said, her harsh voice suddenly tinged with a trace of tenderness. "The spirits will give you this gift so that you can learn. You have

73

much to learn. As so many gifts on this earth, however, yours will be cloaked in sadness. But you will survive this great sadness, even though it will seem unbearable at times. We cannot stop pain, but how much we suffer is up to us. We can learn from sadness. When we do, we appreciate the joy. You will be given the joy later. That is all I can tell you."

The old woman dropped Llayne's hand, abruptly dismissing her. Llayne was shaken for a moment, but then quickly decided this was just a bunch of gobbledygook. She rose and switched places with Priscilla. If the woman didn't tell Priscilla anything specific, either, she was just a fraud and there was no need to worry about anything she said.

It was some time before Mrs. Lacey opened her eyes and looked at Priscilla, tightening her grip on the smooth, young hand.

"The man," she whispered. "The man who went to a foreign land. He can never return. He wants you to know he loves you."

Priscilla froze.

"Don't be afraid, my child. He loves you; he always will. Even though you will not see him again on this earth, do you realize what a gift such love is? Many people never find it in a lifetime. You have it already. It will be with you always, in all you do. You must take that love with you and carry on with your life, you must marry and have children. It is very important that you have children, that this love pass down through the generations."

She closed her eyes again, and when she opened them she said, "The engagement ring. What have you done with the ring? I don't understand. You have it and you don't have it. What did you do to it?"

Both young women turned stark white.

Priscilla's voice was almost inaudible as she explained, "I took it to a jeweler last week to be remade into a ring I can wear on my right hand."

"Yes, of course. That is good," the psychic said. "That ring will keep you safe. It will give energy and love. Keep it near always. Now go. This old woman is tired." She stood up and headed for a draped door at her back, but stopped. Looking back at Llayne, her voice turning gentle, she said, "It's a child's cry that pains you. The child is at peace. God will grant you peace, too, if you will let Him." She disappeared behind the hanging, brown plaid blanket.

Each girl dropped a five dollar bill onto the plate on the table and barreled out. They drove in silence all the way home.

♦ ♦ ♦ ♦ ♦ ♦ ♦ ♦

The knock on the door startled them. Lost in a fog of concentration, they'd frantically been doing homework all evening, trying desperately to catch up before the end of the semester in three days, which would also bring them relief with Christmas break. As usual, they'd put off doing their work until the last possible minute, and were utterly exhausted. Llayne shoved her clinical psychology textbook and the bowl of stale pop-corn left over from 3 a.m. the morning before off her lap, and only fleetingly considered her appearance before going to the door. She wore a frayed, green flannel pajama-jump-suit and sloppy, red wool socks, had no makeup on, and had her hair stuck carelessly into a plastic shower cap that sat like a mushroom on the top of her head. Assuming it was Sally from next door, she opened the door.

Tommy "Tank" Tanner, looking crushingly masculine in a full-length, golden tan leather coat, stood tall and handsome at the door.

"Hi," he said sheepishly.

Llayne's mouth gaped open and Priscilla, in disbelief, jumped up and joined her roommate at the door. Her mouth formed a cavern, too.

Priscilla's head was covered in old-fashioned pin curls, for a new "do" she was experimenting with, and she wore a pink flannel nightgown under one of Benny's old Army sweatshirts and yellow handmade booties on her feet, compliments of her grand-mother. Her thick, black-rimmed reading glasses sat low on her nose.

Tank seemed dumbfounded at their appearance and hesitated for a second before gathering his composure. He said, "Oh, I'm sorry. Is this a bad time?"

Priscilla grabbed the shower cap off Llayne's head, causing dirty hair to fall in every direction, then ripped off her own glasses and said, "No. No, this is fine. Please come in." She ushered him in as Llayne poked her in the behind in reprimand. He missed Priscilla's little dance to avoid the prod as he entered the apartment, because he was busy ogling Priscilla's paintings.

His hair had grown out a little and was indeed sandy brown. His coat covered his body, but the way the garment fell from broad shoulders to a slim waist and on down to the middle of his long legs assured that there had been no change in his athletic physique. And his hazel eyes looked at them with perfect clarity.

"Wow!" he exclaimed. "These paintings are great!" He chuckled at the topless Madonna.

"Thanks," Priscilla said, shuffling her weight from foot to foot.

"Let me just get a robe," Llayne said, pointing to the bedroom.

"And let me just get lost," said Priscilla, pointing, too.

"No, please!" he insisted. "I'm just staying for a minute, and I need for both of you to hear this. I owe you both an apology. For homecoming. I know this is belated, but it's taken me two months to get up enough courage to come here. You see, I know I was an ass homecoming night. I apologize to you, Llayne, for embarrassing you and ruining your big night. And I apologize to you, Priscilla, for the concern you must have had for your friend. I know you both must hate me, and I don't blame you. I just wanted to apol-ogize anyway. I normally don't drink much, but went on a little drunken spree when I got home from Nam, and there's no excuse for what I did.

"The few times I've seen you at The Cabin I couldn't stand it. I haven't been avoid-ing you there, I've just been embarrassed. I've been avoiding going there, anyway, because I'm trying to get Rosie Saleman to leave me alone, although she seems to find me no matter where I go. Well, that's not your concern. I need to go talk to Mack, too. He has no idea how bad it was, and the few times I've seen him he keeps thanking me for representing them. I'll apologize to him, too.

"Well, that's it," he concluded, walking to the door. "Good-bye."

He opened the door and Llayne found herself saying, "Wait! Would you like a Coke, or something?"

His broad smile was quick and cute. "No thanks. I don't even deserve a Coke. Have a great holiday!" With that he was gone.

Priscilla started dancing around the room, jumping up onto the couch, hopping from leg to leg, chanting, "Llayne's gonna fuck Ta-ank! Llayne's gonna fuck Ta-ank!"

"I am not!"

"Oh yes you are! As soon as I leave for Christmas vacation! Llayne's gonna fuck Ta-ank!"

Llayne hated being so transparent, but here she was, fucking Tank. It was Priscilla's fault, actually. If she hadn't insisted they take him some of their homebaked Christmas brownies, Llayne might not have seen him again for months, if then.

Each year after their last class of the fall semester, they baked goodies to distribute to their friends to nibble on during their car trips home for the holidays. It was a daunting task as they were, as Priscilla said, food flopperoos. But it was hard to go wrong with box mixes, and it took them two hours early that afternoon to bake and arrange the treats nicely into decorated tins. One went to Sally next door, some went to Priscilla's coworkers at Falsetta's, some went to Llayne's former coworkers at the Embers restaurant, one tin went to Peter's house, one to Mack and Neckbreaker, and a couple to favorite professors, which made Llayne feel guilty because she didn't give any to her clinical psychology professor, Dr. Lichenger, whom she'd managed to avoid after class for two months. Then, upon Priscilla's insistence, a big tin went to Tank.

It took them all afternoon to distribute their offerings. Everyone was in a festive mood! Peter made them come in and eat some with everyone in his house, all of whom relished them once they got over their initial disappointment that the goodies weren't laced with pot. Mack was out but Neckbreaker offered them tea, the profs were convivial, and Tank was elated.

There had been a lovely, light snowfall the evening before. That afternoon bright sunlight made sparkling diamonds of snowdrops which fell from the bare branches of trees and gracefully twirled about in a gentle breeze. Tank casually shoveled his sidewalk as they drove up, enjoying the crisp, clear weather as much as working. His broad smile telegraphed his pleasure the moment they pulled into view. He invited them inside, offered Coke, which they accepted, and sat with them at his kitchen table and chit-chatted gaily. They really enjoyed his company and didn't leave for over an hour.

Priscilla's parents picked her up at about seven that evening to start their long journey to her grandmother's house in Florida. Llayne was staying in Mt. Pleasant for another week to help fill-in over the holidays at the Embers, the restaurant where she used to work. She was glad the manager had called, giving her an excuse not to have to go home to the strained environment of her parents' house until Christmas Eve. Half an hour after Priscilla left, Tank appeared at her apartment door. He brought a bottle of wine and the brownies to share, they drank and ate and laughed and swapped abridged versions of their life stories.

He was an only child, born of older parents, both of whom were now dead. His father, an English professor at C.M.U. for 20 years, died of a massive coronary when his son, Tommy, was only eight years old. His mom, a home economics professor for 16 years who had affectionately dubbed her beloved son "Tank" because of how he'd had a habit of barreling through the house when he was a kid, died of a heart attack when he was 21. He'd loved his parents dearly, was doted on and spoiled by his mom, he confessed, but had been blessed with a good life. Getting over their deaths had been grueling and traumatic each time, but he came out of it okay. Now he was a counselor at Mt. Pleasant High School, working on a federal program to encourage students from the Chippewa Indian Reservation to stay in school. He loved his work.

Llayne's version of her life was extremely abbreviated, and she avoided too much disclosure by noticing it was snowing again. Merrily, they took a walk around campus in a beautiful snowfall with big, fluffy flakes, playing the games that people of all ages play in such weather. Catching snowflakes on their tongues, seeing who could find the biggest one, speculating what it was like right there for Native Americans on a night like this before white men so rudely destroyed their lives. They made the obligatory snow angels in the campus park and skated on their feet down icy sidewalks in front of the Student Union, closed for the holidays. There was a perfect stillness, a calm, an overpowering beauty in it all. A fairy tale winter wonderland.

When Tank gently took Llayne in his arms and kissed her, there was an explosion inside of her, a frantic need for sexual satisfaction, a fevered desire for male companionship, a treasured hope beyond hope for true love. They walked back to her apartment and tore each other's wet clothes off the moment they stepped through the door.

And here they were fucking, as Priscilla had so crudely yet succinctly put it, on the living room floor. They hadn't even been able to wait long enough to get to her bed.

Their sexual appetites were starved, so their first round of lovemaking was a hasty meal. Slaked for the time being, they took a shower together. Then he suggested she get a few of her things together to go back to his apartment where they could build a nice warm fire in the fireplace.

On the sheepskin rug in front of the fire back at his place, they drank wine, ate cheese and crackers, and talked some more. It turned out he wasn't as big an oaf, as much a dumb athlete, or as egotistical as her first impression had warned. Here was a big, handsome, sweet, teddy bear of a man.

They made love again in his big bed with the fake Zebra skin bedspread, and this time the loving was gentle, thoughtful. Afterwards, when they lay beside each other, he said, "I sure am sorry I ever called you a witch," apologizing for his statement on homecoming night. "I was just hurt that you didn't like me. And drunk. You know, you did call me a cad. Who ever would've guessed that you'd sleep with me," he queried teasingly, "the cad?"

"Pris guessed," Llayne said. "She called this one!"

"Really? Well, tell Pris she's one smart girl." He nibbled at her belly and they wrestled in fun.

◆ ◆ ◆ ◆ ◆ ◆ ◆ ◆

The drive home to West Branch on Christmas Eve in a heavy snowfall was long and lonely. She missed Tank after days and nights of being with him every moment except when she worked at the Embers. Even then, he'd come into the Embers' bar and made friends with Kevin, the manager, who thought he was great. Kevin was in his 30s, rather attractive, and very smart. And he had a great sense of humor, which had connected him and Tank immediately. The two of them had joked with Llayne every time she went to the bar for an order.

Back in her hometown, Llayne's parents were sullen, as usual, but perked up temporarily when their brothers and sisters and nieces and nephews stopped in for holiday cheer. Her dad didn't get totally sotted until late Christmas Eve, which was a day or two later than usual.

The grueling obligatory ritual over, Llayne was happy to drive back to Mt. Pleasant two days after she'd arrived in West Branch. She'd used the excuse that the Embers needed her until school started again.

She and Tank fell into an easy routine of stopping at her apartment to pick up a book, or clothes, but staying at his. She reminded him that when Priscilla returned she'd have to stay at her own place most of the time, because she wouldn't leave her friend alone. He understood.

And that was the nature of Tommy "Tank" Tanner. Understanding, patient, friendly, fun-loving, and most of all, a hunk with an incredible body. It was probably the latter which kept Rosie Saleman on his heels. Gone for the holidays, she'd given Tank a reprieve for a couple of weeks although she called him everyday from her hometown. Consequently, he quit answering the phone. However, once she returned during the second week of January, the evening before the second semester would begin, her pursuit became aggressive again.

◆ ◆ ◆ ◆ ◆ ◆ ◆ ◆

The incident happened while Tank and Llayne were at his apartment playing charades with friends. Kevin, the manager from the Embers, and his plain-looking wife were there. So was Bob, a tall man, rotund but not fat, with black hair. He'd been a friend of Tank's since high school and was home for the holidays from Detroit where he worked at the Ford plant. He had a "thing" about shoes, which his buddies found hilarious, and on this night wore a pair of green, low-ride, leather dress boots that matched his green shirt. His lanky, stylish fiancee, Delia, accompanied him. Dale, another hometown friend who just moved back to Mt. Pleasant after flunking out of Michigan State University was there, too. He was a good-looking, fair-haired rascal of medium build. Although he was a few years younger than Tank and Bob, he'd grown up on the same street. Back then, they said, they'd considered him to be a "pest." Now, as adults, all three of the neighborhood boys had become fast friends. Dale had just started working as a field rep for the Budweiser distributorship in central Michigan and he loved it. His date was cute but hollow in the head. Priscilla was there, too, tan from her Florida vacation, and they were all having a ball madly gesturing and gyrating to act out movie titles for their teams.

Tank was laying on his back on the floor, his stomach puffed out, his face in a wild grimace. He rubbed his belly and quivered his bent legs. "Gas!" Priscilla shouted. "You've got bad gas!" Everyone laughed so hard they couldn't concentrate on what the real message might be. This was not a very serious group.

Tank grabbed a throw pillow from the couch and put it under his butt. Again, he went through the scene, then pulled the pillow out from between his legs and clasped it to his chest with an exaggerated show of affection. Llayne was laughing so hard she could hardly get the word out, sputtering, "B-birth! It's birth!"

"But what movie could that be?" Dale's date asked, holding her sides from laughing so hard.

"Birth! Birth!" Dale said, snapping his fingers as if it were on the tip of his brain.

"Birthday Party at Betty's!" Bob exclaimed.

"What in hell kind of movie is that?" Priscilla asked. "Porno?"

"Yes! Good one, too!" Bob answered, holding his hands out as if fondling two grapefruits. "Betty has these huge ..." His description trailed off as his fiancee tweaked his cheek, and everyone laughed again.

Tank frantically shook his head. No, it wasn't a porno flick! He got up and marched around the room, waving a pretend flag.

"Birth of a Flag?" "Birth March!" "Birth of a Crazy Man!" The rat-a-tat of wild guesses caused Tank to frantically shake his head.

"Birth of a Nation?" Llayne asked.

"Yes!" Tank yelled. "Too bad you're not on my team, though! You're on the other team and you just gave us a point!"

Embarrassed at her mistake, she covered her face with her hands while everyone roared. "I got so excited! I forgot!"

That's when the insistent, hard knock struck the door.

79

"Oh, no!" Tank moaned, hunching over in despair, real this time. "I'm afraid she's back." His buddies all knew about Rosie Saleman, and Dale and Bob got up to go to the door with him.

As the men walked the short distance through the kitchen to the door, Dale's date spoke the obvious, "Dale-baby says the biggest mistake of Tank's life was screwin' that Rosie. Now he can't get rid of her!" Llayne had questioned her intelligence, but the girl left no doubt that she had none.

Everyone in the living room leaned forward to try to get a look through the kitchen. Tank opened the door and there was Rosie Saleman, in a full-length, mouton fur coat and matching hat. Her long, curly, strawberry blond hair tumbled out of the hat and onto the wide shoulders of the coat. What no one but Tank could see was that the coat was unbuttoned and she wore black, high-heeled boots, black velvet hot pants, a delicate, black, see-through French bra, and nothing else.

"Hi, Tank! I'm back!" She smiled a broad smile. "Well, aren't you going to invite me in and introduce me to your friends here?" She tried to push past him to reach out to Bob and Dale, neither of whom moved, although both got a good gander at her breasts. "Well," she said, getting testy, "at least you can invite me in."

The cold from outside swooshed through the open door, invading the apartment and making everybody shiver. They didn't care, being too interested in what might happen next.

Tank said, "Rosie, we've been over this. You and I aren't dating anymore. We hardly ever did. You need to leave me alone. That guy that bartends with you - what's his name? He really likes you. Why don't you go see him?" His voice was just the right combination of empathy and firmness, making him sound like the counselor that he was.

"I don't wanna go see Fred!" Rosie whined, suddenly turning impertinent. "I wanna be with you!" She pummeled his chest with her fists and drove herself past him into the kitchen. Now she faced Dale and Bob, both of whom stood with their arms crossed like body guards. Dale had a medium build, but Bob was very big and very strong. Neither was about to let this woman get past them. Kevin joined them for reinforcement, although gawking at her chest hardly classified as help; and, the women moved to the doorway at the back of the kitchen, staring in disbelief.

"Hi, boys," Rosie said with a flirtatious smile, as if she hadn't just been beating on their friend. No one responded.

Tears flashed in the sexy gal's eyes with the sudden realization that she couldn't make this go the way she wanted, that no amount of flirting or showing off her voluptuous body would work, and before anyone had time to react, she threw herself against the wall beside the refrigerator, sliding her back down the wall until she squatted on the floor. On the way down her head hit the refrigerator and cocked her hat to one side and her coat bundled up underneath her to gape wide open.

"I lo-ove you! I love you!" she wailed, over and over. "I can't live without yoo-ou! I'll kill myself if I can't ha-ave you!"

Tank did his best to convince her to button her coat and get up, but it was no use. He was scared to take her arm to pull her up as there was no telling what she might do if he touched her.

Dale and Bob conferred with one another in whispers, then stepped in to take her by the arms to pull her up. Rosie welcomed the physical contact and clung to them, managing to rub a breast across each of their arms.

"You guys understand, don't you?" she cooed placidly, somehow managing to still look pretty after crying. "Tell him. Tell Tank he needs to let me stay."

They shoved her out the door and followed her out.

"We're taking her home," Dale said over his shoulder. "I'll drive her car. Bob'll follow. We'll be right back. Tank, why don't you see if you can get ahold of that Fred to come sit with her for awhile until she calms down."

She kicked and screamed as they held her arms and pulled her along, like cops do when arresting someone and dragging them to the slammer.

Tank stood at the door and watched with sad eyes, then went to the phone and talked with Fred in hushed tones. When he was finished, no one said anything until Dale's date spouted, "Wow! You must've done something incredible to that broad in bed! She sure does want to get into your pants again, doesn't she, Tank?"

Priscilla snapped, "There's this word, one you obviously don't know about. It's called tact.

"T-A ..." But Llayne shushed her.

Tank's friend, Dale, never dated that girl again.

CHAPTER 8

Llayne could hardly comprehend what Peter was saying. Perhaps this was some of the sadness the old Chippewa woman had spoken of.

"I'm sorry about your dad," she told him. "Is he going to be okay?"

"Oh yeah. It was a mild heart attack. Just a warning for him to slow down, I think. He's always been a workaholic," Peter said.

They sipped Cokes in the Student Union, where he asked her to meet him when he called. His new, black jeans hugged his thin, long legs and he wore his tall Chippewa moccasins. His tan, satiny, pirate shirt was open to the middle of his chest, displaying thick hair curled around a gold cross pendant which had replaced the peace sign. His hair and mustache were even trimmed, probably for his parents' sake. Flung across the chair beside him was his black cape. He just told her how and why he was leaving school immediately, only two weeks into the new semester. His dad, facing mortality for the first time, wanted to take a month-long trip to his ancestral home. He wanted his sons to escort him to Lebanon. Peter confessed that he hated traveling but would go for his dad's sake. Llayne knew he couldn't possibly mean that. The mere idea of travel was so exciting! He said that when they returned he'd finish his final semester and get his degree by taking correspondence courses and classes at Michigan State in Lansing, the university closest to his hometown.

"Furniture!" Llayne said, shaking her head. "Somehow I never would've guessed that was your family business. I can't picture you selling, like, chairs and stuff."

He chuckled. "Me either. But I did, part-time, all through high school. My great grand-dad started the company over 75 years ago when he came over from Lebanon. The Portland Furniture Store! The business does real well, even though Portland's a pretty small town. Only about 25,000 people. I've got to go home and help. My parents have always been so good to me. And, I haven't exactly been a typical son." He graced her with the huge grin she loved so much.

"Speaking of not being typical," she said, "do you think marching and taking over the ROTC Building really helped?"

He became thoughtful. "I think it helped last year when 350,000 people showed up in front of the Capitol Building in Washington. It was far out! Thousands of people in groups under banners of their states. Well, actually, I got lost and marched with Puerto Rico. It didn't matter, though. There's no way politicians could ignore us then. That damned war has to end! Here on campus we just got rid of a lot of pent-up frustration, but even that helped. It's so damned frustrating!"

"I can't imagine you not being involved in things like that," Llayne noted.

"Oh, I will be. I won't sell chairs forever. I have a younger brother who wants to do that. I don't know what I'll do, but I hope it's something that lets me keep things stirred up!"

"What about the way you live? Do you plan on keeping a commune-type house?"

"Oh, god, no! It'd give my dad another heart attack. My parents have no idea how I live here. They think I rent out rooms to other kids. I do, but in their minds it's like a boarding house. When they visit the girls even put on sweaters." They both snickered.

"I've never known anybody like you before," Llayne said. "You and the people you live with. People who, well, you know, all have sex together."

"How do you know that's what we do?"

"You mean you don't?"

He hesitated before revealing the truth. "Yeah, I've slept with all three of the women. I'll admit, it was exciting at first, like an expression of true love. Once I even slept with two of them at once." He threw her a scampish grin, she was so spellbound by his tale. "Every guy fantasizes about that, two chicks at once. Well, what I hadn't counted on was that they'd be more interested in each other than in me! I actually slid out of the bed and it was five minutes before they realized I'd left! A little blow to my ego there!" He put his hand over his heart and feigned exaggerated embarrassment. "But we all, ah, made up. After while, though, it got," he paused, searching for the right word, "exhausting. And pretty soon everybody just kinda branched out to do their own thing. But we still care about each other. It was a good environment to live in. They're all good people."

"You aren't in love with any of those girls?"

He took a sip of his 7-Up before saying, "I love them, but I'm not in love with them. I don't know if I'll ever be in love with anybody in the traditional sense."

Of course, Llayne knew that was because he just hadn't found the right woman. He'd fall in love, all right, like everybody does.

His dark eyes invaded her deepest thoughts and longings, imploring her as he murmured, "I've always fantasized that you and I would get together."

Hypnotized by the intensity of his eyes, she confessed in a conspiratorial whisper, "Me, too."

Later she would marvel at how easy it'd been in the end, after all those months of wondering what it would be like to have sex with him. He wanted them to be together. Was she the one who would satisfy him so completely he'd never need more than one woman again? Was she the one who would awaken him to true love? She thought so as she dismissed uncomfortable thoughts about Tank. It wasn't as if they were engaged or even going steady, she told herself. She walked the few blocks with Peter to his house and unashamedly shucked her clothes as she stood in his bedroom, with only a fleeting reservation about the beads covering the doorway that would render their lovemaking semi-private. They ravaged each others' bodies with no concern about yesterdays or tomorrows or the people to whom they might have obligations. For two glorious hours they had no then or when, no they or them, they only had each other.

Peter was a passionate lover, a physically beautiful lover, a skillful and inquisitive lover. He wanted to know everything, what pleased her, what didn't please her, and whether or not she liked to experiment. He led her into his bathroom and she bent over the sink, and they watched each other's flushed faces in the mirror as he took her from behind. Back in his bedroom, she sat on his dresser and opened her legs to his lust. Nestled together like spoons laying sideways on his waterbed, they did it sideways. Then he rolled her over onto her back and caressed her soft breasts as he licked her flat abdomen. A momentary flicker of fear crossed Llayne's mind when he hesitated and rubbed a spot that, upon very close examination, would reveal a thin pregnancy stretch mark. Llayne's supple, young skin had left few such minuscule lines, but Peter seemed to be upon one. Leave it to Peter, the most observant of men, to guess her secret! Then, without question, he left her belly and wandered into that pulsating place that cried for more, and any worry of being exposed fluttered away as he obliged her with his tongue and sent her into spasm after spasm of pure, unadulterated joy.

It wasn't until later, weeks later, that she realized that when he said he wanted them to be together, he meant in the Biblical sense, the sexual sense. She interpreted it to mean together together. As in ever after. Peter didn't think that far ahead and he told her so. She hadn't wanted to hear it, so gave his words her own meaning. But surely the day would come when he'd want a real relationship, even marriage, with someone. Maybe even her.

She spent many a night tossing in bed with Tank, after they had his brand of tender, gentle sex and he fell asleep, mooning about that afternoon with Peter. She revisited in her mind the impetuous savagery of their sex, and it aroused her still, even after satisfaction with her boyfriend.

The guilt became overwhelming. Guilt over laying with Tank and feeling Peter's touch, his thrust on her and in her. Guilt over having done something so hasty, so fervid, it could destroy her relationship with Tank. Guilt over wanting Peter, wanting other men, still wanting Mack.

Now Llayne knew what frightened her so much about marriage. It wasn't that she was afraid her husband would stray. It was that she was afraid she would stray, that she didn't have that good and honest quality which allows grown-ups to be faithful to the ones they love.

She tried to assuage her guilt by being the best girlfriend possible. She denied her tempestuous thoughts. She regaled herself for thinking them. She made secret vows to herself to do better in the future. She promised to whatever gods and guardian angels who would listen that next time she'd be a good girl.

She'd been a very bad girl to Tank after going back to her apartment from Peter's. When he called, she told Tank she didn't feel well and avoided him for three days. When he showed up with chicken soup to help her get better, she crumbled with the first tidal wave of guilt and let him nurse her counterfeit illness. But after a few hours of his pandering kindness, she turned moody and cranky again. He left, chalking it up to sickness and PMS.

Priscilla watched the gambit and knew her friend was in trouble, but when she asked what in hell was going on, Llayne told her to "Cease and desist!"

That elicited the terse response, "And miss this sideshow? Fat chance in hell!"

85

It wasn't until a few weeks later, when Peter didn't call or write, that Llayne realized she might be just another one of the women he loved but wasn't in love with. Then she began to soften toward Tank. She gave herself regular emotional floggings for jeopardizing his feelings toward her.

What's wrong with me? Tank's the kind of man women fight over!

Women flirted with him everywhere they went. He couldn't help it, he was so brawny and good-looking females naturally flocked to him. Even crazy Rosie Saleman still called him regularly on the phone, even though he finally threatened to call the police. He was a "babe magnet," as his friend Dale said.

I'd be insane to give him up. What more can I want?

Then on one of the few nights all semester that she went to The Cabin, she waited for Tank but she wanted more than anything to dance with Mack, who stood at the bar with his buddies. She waited for the song "Hey There Lonely Girl" to end, fearing it was too obvious, then went over when the band started Elvis's old classic "I Can't Help Falling in Love." The vets greeted her heartily and Neckbreaker grinned knowingly when she said, "Hey, Mack, I love this song. Will you dance with me?"

He followed her to the dance floor, gently pressing his fingers into the small of her back. Once again, as it had when he touched it while taking homecoming pictures, her back became an erogenous zone of its own, tingling delightfully upon contact with Mack O'Brien's hand. When she turned around he was running that hand through his wayward hair, looking at her from bottom to top. She could tell he liked her brown hot pants and silky, beige blouse. She guessed correctly that he liked the body in them, too.

Mack held out his hands and she moved into him, placing one hand on his broad shoulder and the other into his warm, outstretched palm. Slowly, they started to move, pale blue and deep blue eyes locked in a yielding embrace. They moved closer together, Llayne's soft body pressed into his hard chest. Her head tilted so that her cheek laid on his shoulder, allowing his mouth to brush lightly over her hair, sending shock waves of human electricity down hundreds of tiny shafts to tickle her scalp. His grip on her back strengthened; her hand closed over his tightly. Swaying gently in perfect rhythm to the music, they let themselves linger over each moment and languish in each heightened sensation. Mack slowly pulled his head back to look into Llayne's eyes once again, his lips parting slightly as if he were about to say something or offer a kiss.

The song ended. "Oh," he said, drawn back to reality. "Well." He was lost for words, a rare occurrence.

"Yes," she said, just as abstracted as he.

Reluctantly, they joined others as they walked off the dance floor. Tank, sauntering through the door, spied them and ambled forward, waving. "Hi, honey," he said to Llayne, with a glancing blow of a kiss to her cheek.

"Hi, Tank," she uttered in a shaky voice.

"Mack! Hey, my friend, long time no see!" he addressed his fellow vet with genuine enthusiasm.

"Hello, Tank," Mack said, and offered his hand for a shake.

"Thanks for taking care of my girl. Sorry to be so late, honey. One of my students needed a ride home to the reservation. Whoa! I love this song. Let's dance!" he said to Llayne. "Catch you in a couple of minutes, buddy," he said to Mack.

He grabbed Llayne's hand and pulled her onto the dance floor, and she strained her neck to look back at Mack. Their eyes locked, then ripped apart when she spun around as Tank twirled her by the arm. A second later when she looked Mack's way again, he'd already disappeared. She and Tank jerked and gyrated to "Momma Told Me Not to Come," the Three Dog Night song. When they finished, five songs later, Mack was nowhere in sight. Neckbreaker told them he remembered a pressing engagement.

What Mack O'Brien was doing at that moment was sitting alone in his truck at the edge of The Cabin parking lot. "You goddamned son-of-a-bitch fool!" he seethed at himself. "How in hell could you let this happen? It was that bitch, Jillie. She made you believe you couldn't have a good woman. You actually believed that shit for awhile. And in the process you gave up the best woman any man could ever want! Actually handed her over to another man. A good man, no less. You flaming idiot! Well, it's too late now, asshole! She's gone!"

But the feel of her next to him, branded into every nerve ending in his body, refused to leave him alone. Her presence lingered, it teased, it tormented. Had he read her signals wrong or had she felt the same thing that he did, at least for those few fleeting moments in his arms?

"Oh, you stupid dreamer," he said, slamming his fists into the steering wheel. He started the engine, pressed too hard on the gas, and roared out of the lot. "She's obviously in love with Mr. All-American Nice Guy Tommy Tank Tanner! For chrissakes, why couldn't you have fixed her up with anybody except Mr. Wonderful? He's a great guy. He'll be a wonderful husband and father. You could've talked to her at the beginning of the semester, as soon as you realized your mistake, but by then she was already going with him. How could you interfere with that? He's a vet, a comrade in arms. He's a friend. You can never, never try to steal a woman away from a man like that! Besides, she doesn't want to be stolen. You really are the most ignorant man alive," he cussed at himself all the way home, and way into the night, and way after that.

Llayne, on the other hand, in her usual self-deprecating manner, assumed she'd read Mack's signals wrong and that the overpowering attraction she felt while they danced had been hers alone. He never showed any indication he wanted her and never would. Yet another man she had the hots for that she couldn't have. One that gave her wet dreams, no matter how much she tried to lock him out of her mind. She'd do extra penance, on top of that for Peter, by being extra, extra attentive to Tank. Her pile of penances was starting to seem insurmountable.

♦ ♦ ♦ ♦ ♦ ♦ ♦ ♦

"Good-ness! Pammy here is a fox. Look at those pins!" Tank held up the Playboy fold-out so Llayne could see. "And she wants to be a stockbroker. Must be real smart." He looked at her sideways.

"Huh!" Llayne sniffed. "Smart women know better than to wear spiked heels to bed like that. Look at those things. They're lethal."

Tank turned the picture sideways, putting Pammy in a prone position. "Oh yeah! A little pain goes a long way."

"You men. You're all demented."

Tank snickered and put the magazine down. She left for awhile, returned with her overnight bag, and went into his bedroom. The baseball game he was watching on TV took a long while to finish, so by the time he joined her, he feared she might be mad about the pinup teasing.

She was asleep. He took off his clothes, turned out the bedstand light, and crawled into bed, reaching over to put his arm around her.

"What the hell?" he yelped, throwing the covers back and switching on the light.

Llayne turned over and posed her best Pammy pose. A red garter from her Golden Saddle Gal days surrounded one thigh, black spiked heels graced her feet. That was all she wore, along with a sly grin.

"Come here, big boy. Why not try the real thing?"

"Oh yeah. Hurt me," Tank said as he lowered himself to her and felt no pain.

◆ ◆ ◆ ◆ ◆ ◆ ◆ ◆

Good sex kept her mind from wandering. She could be faithful. Really she could, if she just kept herself occupied. She'd graduate soon; she'd be an adult. She'd have to learn to be responsible and responsible women don't fantasize about men other than their mates. She could do it, really she could, she kept telling herself.

◆ ◆ ◆ ◆ ◆ ◆ ◆ ◆

Even after weeks of self-regulating promises, Llayne found herself gravitating toward The Cabin on graduation day in early June, as if an invisible fishing line had hooked the front of her car and was reeling her in to inescapable destruction. She was looking for Mack.

She flipped the radio off as "Joy to the world, joy to the world, joy to the fishes in the deep blue sea, joy to you and me ...." came on. Radio stations had a nasty habit of over-playing new hit songs and she agreed with Priscilla, who said, "If I hear about those fuck-ing little fishes one more time I'll croak!"

Driving in silence past the stadium, Llayne was more glad then ever that she wasn't there, and she felt certain Mack wouldn't be there, either. Hundreds of kids on the unsea-sonably hot day looked sweaty and uncomfortable in their long, black gowns. The wind blustered and a number of graduates chased caps around the grounds. Yes, it'd been a wise decision to avoid that circus and have her degree sent in the mail. Poor Priscilla and her parents were somewhere in the midst of that melee.

As she drove stop-and-go through heavy graduation traffic, she wondered if each June for the rest of her life she would secretly mourn the loss of her child. She thought back over the past year: her affair with her drama professor, the stillbirth of their baby, Bronco Buck's House of Burlesque, being Homecoming Queen, having crushes on Peter and Mack, and her relationship with Tank. Who ever could have predicted that, out of all those men, she'd end up with Tommy Tanner, Tank? She'd heard that Rex Bates, that sleazeball who got her pregnant, was moving to Los Angeles to try to become a real actor. She laughed out loud. "Look out Hollywood!" she warned the smut capitol of the world. And then there was enigmatic Peter, who disappeared into Lebanon. And Mack, who thought of her as a child. A huge sigh escaped from her chest.

A wee corner of her brain sometimes shoved its way through the muck called her mind and forced her to suspect she'd been filling time, filling the void, attempting to fill her empty heart by keeping busy so she wouldn't have to think. That Dr. Lichenger, who she hadn't seen since finishing his psychology class last semester, had been the one person who wanted her to stop and think. That bit of her brain knew he might have been right. She closed her mind to let that piece sink, like a rock tossed down a well, to the depths of unconsciousness again.

Finally her Beetle made its way off campus and reached The Cabin. It surprised her how many cars were parked there in the middle of the afternoon. Apparently lots of kids opted for this graduation ceremony rather than the formal pomp and circumstance a mile down the road.

Squinting to see in the low light which contrasted the bright afternoon sunshine, Llayne saw Mack at the bar, standing beside a petite woman. The woman wore a tight halter top and even tighter jeans, and rows of gold and silver bracelets on her arms jingled as she fussed with her short, teased hair. It annoyed Llayne to no end to have to admit that the little woman was really cute. Llayne walked up behind them and said, "Hi, Mack."

He spun around and gawked. "Llayne," he said, his voice deep with emotion. "What a surprise. Haven't seen you in a moon's age!"

"Yeah, well, I've been awfully busy this semester, trying to make sure I'd graduate and all."

"I hear you. Me, too. That Master's thesis and those oral exams were real doozies! Oh, this is Naomi. Naomi, this is Llayne."

Llayne nodded and said, "Hi."

Naomi openly eyed her up and down suspiciously and said "Hello," in a rich, dulcet voice that caused a flash of envy to grip Llayne's throat. "You're the Homecoming Queen, aren't you?" the tomato asked.

"Yes," Mack interjected, "she is."

That gave Llayne the door opener she needed. "I have a little quick business I'd like to discuss with Mack. Would you mind?" she asked his companion.

Naomi opened her mouth but before she could speak Mack said, "Sure, it's okay, isn't it? Why don't you go over there to your friends' table and I'll be with you in a jiff."

Naomi didn't like that one bit and her whole body said so. "You won't be long, will you?" she complained. "This is our first date."

Mack reassured her, and she reluctantly strutted away. He and Llayne grabbed a small table. She felt it was going well so far. It took her all morning to get up enough nerve to come find him.

He ordered her a Coke and club soda with lime for himself.

"What?" Llayne asked. "No Strohs today?"

"No-oo. Not during the day anymore. I've cut back on the drinking. We just stopped here so I could say good-bye to a few of the guys. They'll be here soon." He glanced at his watch. "But I'm glad you're here," he added quickly.

"I wanted to say good-bye to you," she said.

His surprise projected onto his face. "That's so nice. Um, you and Tank are still dating aren't you?"

"Yes," she admitted. She couldn't muster up the nerve to say more, like "But I'd break up with him if you want me to!" Stupid thought, she admonished herself. *He likes older women, more experienced women. He likes tootsies like Naomi. He doesn't want any commitments and he doesn't want me. I'm just a kid to him. This is no more than a quick good-bye.*

He smiled, and it was then she noticed the absence of the ever present Camel cigarette in his mouth. Instead, he stuck a toothpick into his mouth and gnawed on it.

"Mack! No cigarette either? Did you give that up, too?"

"Yes-sir-ee! Damn near killed me, but they're gone! Cutting back on the beer was a breeze compared to giving up my smokes, you know what I mean?"

"Are you miserable?"

"Not so much anymore. Hell, I've discovered that food has taste." His smile was infectious and she smiled, too. He rolled the toothpick around between his teeth, drawing her attention, once again as so many times before, to his mouth.

"What are you going to do now?" she asked, instead of saying "Would you please run that mouth all over my body," as she wanted to say. To make matters worse, someone had put a quarter into the juke box and "Hold Me, Thrill Me, Kiss Me" bellowed tauntingly at them.

"Well, a great thing has happened," he answered innocently. "I've been bugging our congressman for months about vets' issues. The dude up and offered me a job. I'll be congressional aide to Democratic House Representative John Harrington. Is that darned impressive or what? His home office headquarters are in Lansing." His eyes twinkled and he chuckled, shaking his head. He was really happy about this. "There are too many vets like me coming home and drinking too much and thinking too little. I'll be able to work for vets' rights. I know most guys would rather just forget the whole thing, but it isn't fair what's happening. Too little appreciation, too much sweeping under the rug by the government, too much booze and dope. A lot of those guys are in trouble and I'm going to do everything I can to help them. I've learned that helps me help myself."

"Wow! What a noble cause. I'm happy for you," Llayne said.

"What about you?" he asked, not expressing his desire to have her go with him. He would never undermine his fellow vet, Tank, the man she so obviously wanted to be with, he thought.

She was embarrassed to tell him "what" about her. There was no noble cause here. "Well," she said, "I'm going to waitress at the Embers this summer, then I have a good shot at a job at the community college in Montcalm County. That's one county southeast of here so I could still live here. They need an academic counselor. Somebody to help students with their schedules and career planning."

He paused, looking surprised at her own career choice. "That's interesting," he said. "What made you decide to do that?"

Decide? she thought. There'd been no decision. She simply hadn't known what else to do. A recruiter had been on campus and Llayne interviewed, passing with "flying colors," the woman said. By doing it she wouldn't actually have to make a decision about what to do. She was terrified of being stuck in a boring job, as this promised to be, but was even more terrified of searching for something better, a search that might call for moving away alone. The most horrifying terror came with the thought of making a real decision about the direction she wanted her life to take.

"I don't know what made me decide," she replied and sucked hard on her drink. "Hey, what's Neckbreaker going to do?" she adroitly changed the subject.

"Moving back home to the family farm in Remus. He's just been hired as regional manager there for the Farm Bureau. He's getting married this summer, you know, and he's real pleased about it all." He stopped talking abruptly and stared at her.

"Well, I'd better go now," she said uneasily, sipping down the last swallow of her Coke.

"Let me walk you to your car."

Across the room Naomi practically suffered whiplash when she saw them head for the door. Mack gestured "just a minute" to her and escorted Llayne outside.

Without talking they walked to her dilapidated old bug, then turned to look at one another. He wasn't too tall, so she easily looked up into his eyes.

He jerked the toothpick out of his mouth, threw it down, and smashed it into the gravel with his heel, just like he'd always done with his cigarettes. This is it, she thought. He might kiss me. She'd take whatever she could get; platonic, chaste, probing French style with his tongue jammed down her throat.

Mack raked his fingers through his hair, then reached forward and impulsively wrapped his arms around her tight, burying his face in her long hair. "Good luck, Llayne. You're one hell of a lady. I wish you the best."

"Thanks. And thanks for everything you've done for me. You know, homecoming and all."

"It was my pleasure," he said softly into her ear.

There was a moment of stillness as they held each other close, absorbing one another's heat. When he brought his face in front of hers again, Llayne's breath caught in her windpipe. This was it. The kiss.

Mack took her head in his hands and placed upon her forehead the most searing kiss imaginable. Rubbing his thumbs over her temples, slowly he backed away.

"Hey!" Naomi hollered from the bar door, strumping her foot impatiently. "You coming back in here or what?"

In no rush to answer, Mack whispered, "You take care, kiddo."

"Yeah. You, too," Llayne said.

Stepping backwards, then sideways, he walked to the log bar. Naomi wove her arm through his and pulled him toward the door, giving Llayne a smug backwards glare. Mack hesitated for a moment and glanced back at Llayne with a look that was either concern or confusion; she couldn't tell which.

After he was out of sight, Llayne shouted, "Damn!" and kicked her car tire. "Damned men!" She stomped around, gesticulating toward the sky and swearing. Then a truck pulled around the building and halted, its inhabitants examining her as if she were an animal in the zoo.

As their truck crawled past her the driver hung his head out the open window and took a gander, then ducked back inside and said to his passenger, "Hey, that crazy girl is our Homecoming Queen!"

The other guy stretched his neck across for a better look, and said, "Nope, it ain't."

"Yes it is!"

"No!"

Their voices faded as they drove on by. Llayne got in her car and drove away.

That night Rosie Saleman threw a rock through Tank's kitchen window, while he and Llayne lay propped up on pillows on his living room floor watching *All in the Family* on television. He went outside and Fred, Rosie's fellow bartender, showed up, too. Tank stood by and Llayne peeked through the shattered window while Fred soothingly convinced the mentally ill woman that instead of killing herself, which she'd been threatening to do, she should move to Chicago to fulfill her life's dream of becoming a Playboy bunny. Eventually mollified, Rosie agreed and left with the neurotically patient man.

Relieved that Rosie would be otherwise occupied in Chicago, Tank and Llayne cleaned up the mess she left behind on the kitchen floor.

♦ ♦ ♦ ♦ ♦ ♦ ♦ ♦

The days of June blurred. Tommy Tank Tanner courted Llayne as she'd never been courted. He wrote love notes, he sent flowers, he showed up at her door with pizza, he made love to her. He affectionately nicknamed her Lela.

He teased that she didn't seem like a snob anymore, now that she slept in his bed half the time. Their sex was nice. No rising to heaven and back, no heart throbbing anticipation, no ecstasy beyond belief, no "Oh, baby, I love you." Just nice.

But Llayne was realizing that nice could be good. With him she learned to relax, to ask for what she wanted, to be the aggressor when she felt like it. Experience, finally, taught her that sex had nothing to do with the unobtainable dichotomies of pretending to be a nice girl while posing like the women in Playboy. Sex between two people could be whatever they wanted it to be.

Never, however, did they mention love. Tank never talked to her about Vietnam, either.

Not since the day she asked, "Do you ever think about Nam?"

He said, "As little as possible."

"Do you believe in that war?"

"I believe I didn't want to come home in a casket." It was one of the few times he was ever short with her.

Llayne's beliefs remained strong but, sensing it would do no good anyway, she never discussed it with him. Once she overheard him tell Dale about some of the unusual and funny times, but saying nothing about the actual killing or his philosophy about the validity of the conflict. He told Dale about being stationed in Plei Ku near the north perimeter and how he had a relatively safe job charting troop movements. He was almost killed once, however, when one of the men in his own barracks got so high on drugs he shot up the place while everyone slept. Before being pinned down by three soldiers, the guy put a bullet through Tank's mattress within inches of his groin. Dale groaned and automatically grabbed his fly. Tank talked about vile Charlie and how many, many American soldiers smoked dope or did drugs to make it through the incomprehensible hell. They played trivia over walkie-talkies during endless hours of otherwise mind-numbing, boring guard duty. Sports and women's anatomy were the favorite categories. They talked a lot about the women back home and knew every detail of each other's sex lives.

Once Tank and another guy followed two Vietnamese girls who advertised their availability by holding up their skirts and revealing their nakedness as Americans drove by. Tank laughed as he told Dale how he and his cohort brought their Jeep to a screeching halt, hurling a cloud of dust at the whores. Undaunted, the women - gooks, some soldiers call them, Tank said - led them to a shanty not far from the road. Inside on the dirt floor were pieces of filthy, blood-stained cardboard upon which they were to perpetrate the act of fornication. The men ran out, sick, with the dusty girls badgering them from close behind. Racing back to the safety of their base, the soldiers knew some of their fellows partook of such sex, any sex. Some of them ended up in the "Hanoi Hotel," as prisoners of war, or died when the woman they were screwing happened to be a Charlie who set them up. Dale sadly shook his head as his friend confided in him.

Tank did talk openly with Llayne about feeling different since the war. Emotionally, that was expected. But he was different physically, too. He was slower moving, his former athletic agility hampered. His LBB, little bitty bladder, was a joke but also a nuisance. Doctors couldn't find anything wrong. He didn't talk about it too much, though, being more interested in having a good time.

♦ ♦ ♦ ♦ ♦ ♦ ♦ ♦

He grabbed a carrot out of the grocery sack on her kitchenette counter and held it like a microphone. "What's your name...?" he shoo-bopped, dancing and striking a singer's pose. "Is it Mary or-r Sue? What's your name? Do I stand a chance with you...?" He flung the carrot across the room and jumped on her, devouring her neck.

"No, no!" she squealed. "If you can't remember my name you can't have sex with me."

"Are you kidding? How could I ever forget you, Charlene?"

"Oh, okay. Come on, Carl."

They played Charlene and Carl all afternoon.

♦ ♦ ♦ ♦ ♦ ♦ ♦ ♦

"He may be ugly," Priscilla said as she appraised the man walking by them at The Cabin, "but have I heard things about him!"

"Like what?" Llayne wanted to know as she, Tank, and Dale leaned across the table with interest.

"Sally said he's hung like a horse!" Priscilla's eyes gleamed with mischief.

"Oh, fine," was all Dale could retort as he inhaled a gulp of beer.

Tank said, "Now, Pris, you know what guys like Dale and I always say: Which would you rather have, a guy put his thumb in your ear and just let it sit there, or have him put his little finger in your ear and move it around?"

When they stopped laughing, Priscilla asked, "Is it possible for a girl to get both?"

Dale snorted into his beer.

♦ ♦ ♦ ♦ ♦ ♦ ♦ ♦

"Tank, what's this mask?" Llayne asked, holding up to her face the triangular, bowl-like, plastic mask with the little holes all over it.

Suddenly Tank was on the floor howling and she didn't have a clue as to why.

Finally he said, "It's called a cup."

"A what?" she wanted to know. He was laughing so much she couldn't understand what he said.

"A cup. A guy wears it here." He rolled onto his back and formed a triangle with his fingers, placing it over his private parts. "It's to protect a man's jewels while he plays sports."

Slowly Llayne lowered it from her face, held it out with two fingers, and dropped it to the floor, vowing never again to pick up anything she found lying around on that man's bathroom floor.

♦ ♦ ♦ ♦ ♦ ♦ ♦ ♦

"I don't know, Lela," Tank said. "Whadaya think of the old proverbial air strips?"

"What air strips? When did they build them?" She didn't even know Mt. Pleasant was getting an airport. The nearest one was Tri-City more than 30 miles away.

"They've been under construction for a long time," he said, pulling the rearview mirror over to look at himself while managing to keep an eye on the road as he drove. He whistled like a jet taking off as he raced his fingers over the two strips of slightly receding hairline on either side of his skull, exposing shiny, taut skin. "On quiet nights I sit and listen to my hair fall out. But, whadaya say? Does it make me sexy, like Yul Brynner?"

"More like a bald duck," she teased.

As expected, his response was in Donald Duck speech. "Oh yeah?" he quacked. "I'll tell ya what, lady, ya wanna fuck a duck?" He grabbed her knee and she playfully slapped him away. "Oh, come on! You ain't lived 'til you've fucked a duck."

So, they went to his apartment and did what ducks do when their tail feathers get in a fluff.

♦ ♦ ♦ ♦ ♦ ♦ ♦ ♦

Fun. That was what their relationship was all about. Nothing too serious. Nothing too threatening. Just fun, until Llayne could figure out what in hell she wanted to do with her life.

At least that's what she thought until the day in early July when Priscilla moved out of the apartment to go to Grand Rapids, where a high school job as an art teacher awaited her. It wasn't until her junior high friend moved 180 miles away that Llayne was finally forced to face reality. It was time to make some grown-up decisions. Most of her college classmates had in fact already made those decisions.

Was she going to take the academic counselor's job that had been offered to her at the community college? Where would she live? With whom? Was this it? Where was the travel and excitement she longed for? Why was she too much of a coward to go find it?

Tank asked Llayne to marry him the very night Priscilla left. He wanted to settle down. He wanted a family. He wanted it with her. And he wanted it all right away.

Chapter 9

Tank was uncharacteristically serious. Nervously, he bit his lower lip. This wasn't easy for him. A bead of perspiration formed on one side of his forehead and dripped down his temple. Whether it was due to his emotional discomfort or the summer heat in their apartment, which had never known air conditioning, was hard to guess.

Llayne sat quietly on the couch, her chin on her knees and her arms wrapped around her bare calves, patiently waiting for him to gather the courage to say whatever it was he wanted to say. Perhaps he changed his mind about getting married tomorrow, although she doubted it. Maybe he felt a cathartic urge to confess rampant sexual affairs with thousands of women. Maybe he was still having one.

The sight of his hazel eyes drowning in tears caused her to go to him where he sat in his new black, Naugahyde, easy chair and sit on the red carpet at his feet with her head in his lap, stroking his arm. She looked up into his handsome, square-jawed face and saw nothing there but tender-hearted affection. So, he wasn't going to call off the wedding. His tears subsided as he found comfort in stroking her hair, and he said, "I have something important to tell you," repeating his statement of moments before.

"Okay," she reassured him.

"There's something you need to know." His voice cracked and he cleared his throat. "Something that happened when I was on R&R in Saigon. I met a girl - it's stupid. But, I really fell for her. I know, they warn soldiers about being lonely and falling in love in a foreign land. She really was a nice girl, though. That was the problem. She was just a girl, only 17."

"Do you feel like you want to go get her?" Llayne asked, shocked at the depth of her sudden jealousy.

He considered the question. "No," he answered. "That's impossible. She has her world; I have mine. But I feel so terrible knowing she's stuck there, in that horrible country, and I have all of this." He swept his arm to indicate all that was his life. "But she wouldn't be any more comfortable here than I was there. It was terrible for her, though. Her mom was dead and her dad had sold her to a brothel."

"Wait a minute! You went to a brothel?" That didn't sound like him.

"Yeah, well, I hadn't had much experience with sex and I was horny and scared and at least they were supposed to be healthy, no diseases."

"You didn't have much experience with sex? Come on!"

"No, it's true. Oh, there were a number of clumsy attempts in college, but nothing special. And almost nothing in high school. No decent girl would even look at me then, I was so chubby."

"You? Fat? You're gorgeous!"

He couldn't suppress a prideful grin. "That didn't happen until college. I was a real late bloomer. Anyway, I thought you should know about her."

His candor endeared him to her and she crawled up into his lap, putting her arm around his neck. They kissed, deeply.

When their lips finally parted she said, "You really cared for her, didn't you?"

"I thought I was in love," he stated honestly. "One week with a girl. I know it's stupid. She was a virgin, I think that was part of it. I felt so responsible for her. I spent every dime I had to stay the week."

"Oh, sweetie, isn't that like an old trick? For a whorehouse to claim a girl's a virgin and charge more?

"Yeah, but she bled like virgins are supposed to. I," he paused, shaking his head, "I have to confess I started out using rubbers - they drill that into us in the army - but when I ran out I just went ahead. I got checked out by the doc as soon as I got back to base, though, and she didn't give me anything. So, I really think she was inexperienced.

"She thought she fell in love with me, too. She couldn't be a whore. So, I took her to her aunt's house at the end of the week. The madam was so pissed! But her aunt promised to take care of her."

Llayne's heart went out to him. He was such an innocent. "What was her name?" she asked.

"Soon Lee Francois. Her grandfather had been a French soldier."

"Was she pretty?" she asked, masochistically feeding another stab of jealousy in her gut.

"Yes. Here." He struggled to tug his billfold out of his back pocket, and pulled out a picture of himself and a petite girl with glorious, long, black hair. The girl was truly beautiful.

"If we stay together, are you going to keep that picture in your pocket forever?" Llayne tried to lighten the mood by lightening her voice.

"No. I promise," he said, nuzzling her neck. "I'll put it deep in my safe deposit box and never look at it. I just wanted you to know I was in love one time before."

It was time to tell him about her past, too. About her affair with Professor Rex Bates, the stillbirth of their baby, the men she had sex with, the men she loved, or thought she loved, all the heartbreaks. This dear, sweet man, who would take a vow tomorrow to love her forever, had just opened his heart to her, exposing with utter trust his deepest feelings. It was her cue that it was her turn to do the same.

She said nothing. Not because she was ashamed, but because to do so would be to reveal her true self to a man for the first time. She'd been friends with men, she'd slept with men and even bore the child of one, she'd had enormous crushes on lots of men and she'd rambled on to men about her life without talking about herself. But she never revealed her soul to a man and she wasn't about to start now. If ever she could, it would be with this man. But not yet. The prospect was still too frightening. If she really let him get to know her, he might doubt her as much as she doubted herself.

After cuddling in his chair for a while longer, they moved to the bedroom and made love, yielding to one another's needs, healing each other's wounds.

♦ ♦ ♦ ♦ ♦ ♦ ♦ ♦

The next day 23 people gathered for the August wedding in the cedar campus chapel with tall, impressionistic, stained glass windows. Llayne's parents; Priscilla and her parents; Dale and his new girlfriend; Bob and his betrothed, Delia; Kevin and his wife; a few teachers who worked at Mt. Pleasant High School with Tank; a couple of Chippewas; and a few other long-time hometown friends of Tank's were there. Most of Llayne's college friends had graduated and moved away, so her side of the chapel remained sparsely occupied.

It was a lovely, temperate day. Llayne wore a feminine, white, full-length, organza sundress with a halter top which allowed her hair to graze her tan, bare back. Her wide-brimmed, white straw hat had a hot pink band with flowers, and her belt and stacked-soled sandals were also hot pink. She looked good!

Priscilla, as maid of honor, wore a hot pink and lavender flowered sundress and a straw hat, and Dale, as best man, and Tank wore black tuxedoes with lavender cummerbunds and pink carnations on their lapels. The chapel was decorated in pink, lavender, and white flowers. It was a touching ceremony. Simple and short, just the way the bride and groom wanted it.

After a brief, fun reception in a party room at the Embers restaurant, which Llayne's former boss, Kevin, took great pride in organizing, the newlyweds left for their honeymoon. The bride changed into a hot pink, velveteen outfit which consisted of a halter top and hip-hugger, bell-bottomed pants, which left her tan, tight midriff exposed. The groom wore shorts and a short-sleeved golf shirt. They spent the weekend up north in Traverse City on Lake Michigan, and could have stayed longer, as he had the summer off from his counseling job at the high school and she didn't start her new job as an academic counselor at the community college for another two weeks, but Tank was anxious to get home and settle into a nice, comfortable married life. To live happily ever after until death did them part.

♦ ♦ ♦ ♦ ♦ ♦ ♦ ♦

Comfort was anathema to Llayne. Bored on one Saturday afternoon while Tank played basketball with his buddies, she idly flipped through the *Sears & Roebuck Fall and Winter Catalog* as she lay sprawled out on the living room floor, propped against one of the big floor pillows. Janis Joplin's bawdy drawl blared from the stereo as the singer lamented about Bobby McGee. A *Penney's Catalog*, a *McCall's* magazine, a *Mt. Pleasant High School Continuing Education Schedule of Evening Classes*, some pencils, and a bottle of Coke were spread out to her right side. She grabbed the frosty bottle and took a long draw. Then a dress in the catalog caught her eye, a long-sleeved, periwinkle blue, cotton number which buttoned down the front and had two sets of patch pockets, one set on the chest and one below the waist, and it had a matching tie belt. She found the order form in the middle of the book, tore it out, and started filling it out. She need-ed new clothes for her new job. Boring clothes for a boring job. Just two weeks of help-ing students plan their college schedules had already taught her that.

She sighed. After one month, married life was already starting to close in on her. Oh, yes, she adored her husband. In fact, she doubted there could be a better husband on this earth. But the marriage routine was already promising to promote the doldrums at an alarming rate. The excitement she always longed for was nowhere in sight.

At least she'd been able to talk Tank out of buying a house and having children as soon as possible. Instead, they would stay in the apartment for another year and save money for a big vacation next summer. They both had summers off, so would have lots of traveling time. They toyed with the idea of camping throughout the West. There was a Blackfoot Indian reservation in Montana that Tank wanted to visit, and Glacier National Park up there, too. Then they could go down through Yellowstone Park and the Tetons, to the Grand Canyon, and then to Mesa Verde, the ancient pueblos carved into the side of a cliff that once housed the Anasazi Indians. They could cap the trip with a national powwow that was being held in Santa Fe, where the Pueblo Indians, descendants of the Anasazi, were indigenous to the area. It wasn't what Llayne would have picked for her first big trip if she were on her own, but it did sound terribly exciting. If she could just last until next summer.

Janis moved on to "Half Moon" as Llayne finished the Sears order form and picked up the schedule of evening classes. Knitting class. Fat chance! Beginning macramé. No way! Belly dancing. Hm-m, she thought, this might be interesting. "Learn how to perform this exciting, ancient dance," she read aloud. She went to the phone and called to regis-ter.

◆ ◆ ◆ ◆ ◆ ◆ ◆ ◆

Kerina was a voluptuous, 45-year-old, Turkish beauty. The class of 32, rather ordinary-looking, American women, dressed mostly in jeans and sweatshirts, watched in amaze-ment as the instructor, who had informed them she had given birth to four children, moved her resplendent body to the exotic Middle Eastern music. She looked like a sen-suous, dark-haired angel. Her arms flowed like delicate wings as she twirled her aqua, chiffon veil above her head, her large breasts shook within her coin-covered bikini top, her flat abdomen rolled rhythmically above the coin-covered belt that rode low on her hips, and her shapely legs peeked out from beneath her diaphanous, aqua, chiffon skirt which had a slit all the way up one side.

"Hip lift, hip lift, hip lift, belly ro-o-o-ll!" she called out the names of her moves. "Hip, hip, hip, fi-gure eight!" Her students gawked as she made the ancient dance look easy. "Now, here's a backbend." Kerina dropped to her knees, arched her back until her head met the floor, draped the veil across her face, and fluttered her arms above her. Slowly she rose, waved the veil triumphantly, and bowed just as the music ended. Applause filled the small gymnasium. Kerina bowed again, and in a thick accent, said, "That's what you will know how to do by the end of this eight-week class. And although we've been relegated to this ridiculous elementary school gymnasium, we'll just have to imagine ourselves in a richly appointed harem room."

Llayne instantly liked this Kerina. The woman knew how to pretend. Just what Llayne needed.

During the two-hour class, Kerina taught her pupils about the history of belly dancing. The folk art form most likely began, she said, with primitive African tribes' fertility rites and moved up the Nile to countries surrounding the eastern Mediterranean Sea. *Bedouins,* Arab nomads, turned it into a birthing ritual called *belidi,* where women rolled their bellies and breathed in cadence to the *dumbek* drums their men played outside the tent, as they helped facilitate the birth for a woman in labor. It was essentially an early form of La Maze, a popular method used in America to teach women how to breathe during labor. In belidi, the dancers never let their feet kick too high from the ground, signifying the connection of humans to the earth and the new baby's connection to it, too. The toes on one foot may slowly drag across the floor, but never leave that surface for more than a step. The dance didn't become sensual by modern standards until it moved into the harems of Arab sheiks. Many women, sometimes hundreds of women, all vying for the favor of the same master, spent endless hours conniving ways to outdo one another. That's when sexy costumes came into the picture. Then in 1893 America got ahold of the idea when "Little Egypt" and her dancers were a sensation at the Chicago World's Fair. Audiences were shocked! So, of course, strippers and movies soon mimicked the dance form. That brought an end to any semblance of authenticity. In the early 1900s, Theda Bera, the first actress to be known as a "vamp," emblazoned the genre with her own brand of naughtiness in movies like *Cleopatra.* Kerina reassured her class that they would learn an authentic version of the folk art form, not a cheap Hollywood knockoff.

She gave the women suggestions for making costumes to wear to class, to help them "get in the mood." They could wear their bikini bathing suits and make chiffon circle skirts to wear over them. Everyone needed a chiffon veil, and the more they wanted to elaborate with jewelry, the better. She introduced them to George Abdo's and Mohammed El-Bakkar's records of Middle Eastern music, which she could order for them. Then they stretched their bodies with yoga movements, and finally learned three basic belly dance steps: the walk, the hip lift and the figure eight. Kerina told them to practice at home and come back the next week in costume, ready to learn more moves.

◆ ◆ ◆ ◆ ◆ ◆ ◆ ◆

"Hey, what's that?" Tank asked as he barreled into the living room. His gray tee-shirt and sweatpants were sweaty, and he held a basketball at one hip.

101

"My costume for belly dancing class," Llayne answered from where she sat on the floor, cutting on a huge piece of red chiffon. She flicked a piece of the fabric at his face and he flinched, swatting at it as if it were a bug. "Remember?" she jarred his memory. "I told you I'd need it for tonight, because I'm going to an advanced class at the instructor's house. She says I'm good."

He grinned. "Of course you're good. Anything that involves moving that hard little body ..." He lost his train of thought as he bent to tickle her ribs, accidentally dropping his ball in the middle of her soon-to-be belly dancing skirt.

"Hey! Watch it!" she admonished, whacking the ball aside. "This thing's all dirty!"

"Yeah, but we won!" he bragged, picking up the ball and twirling it on top of his index finger.

"So, you're saying you're good, too?" she teased.

"Sure," he said, grinning. "Wanna see?"

She followed him into the bedroom to "see."

That evening, when she first arrived at Kerina's house, she thought it ordinary. It was a typical ranch style on a typical neighborhood street. A friendly, nice-looking man answered the door; a bunch of kids sat in the living room watching TV; and, although the home was richly decorated in exquisite ivory, gold, and pale blue wall coverings and fabrics, none of that could have prepared a visitor for the lush decor, for the exotic world, that laid below in the basement. The man, who introduced himself as Kerina's husband, ushered Llayne to the basement door, and the moment he closed it behind her she knew this was the kind of experience she'd been longing for.

She was looking down half a flight of stairs at a wall covered by a mirror in thick, carved gold frame. The stairwell was dark except for a variety of lighted candles on a fancy golden table in front of the mirror, and glimmers of light from a depth further below to the left. Strains of a soft, exotic song wafted up to titillate her ears. Slowly, she descended, her footfalls producing no sound on the steps covered in plush, lavender carpet. Looking down into the mirror, she watched her legs in her jeans, then her torso in her suede jacket, then her face as she came into full view. Turning, she viewed the scene at the end of the stairs.

A multitude of candles of every shape and size, in every type of candleholder, surrounded the room. There was no other light. Four women, including Kerina, in a colorful array of costumes, danced slowly to the music. They were so engrossed in what they were doing, they didn't notice Llayne standing at the foot of the stairs, so she had time to take it all in.

They danced barefoot upon an exquisite Persian rug made in a delicate ivory, gold, peach, aqua and lavender pattern. Panels of silk and chiffon fabric in colors matching the rug were draped about the sides of the room and drawn back with huge, silk tassels. Big, fat, pastel, velvet pillows bordered in satin rope were cast about the sides of the room on the floor. Mirrors covered three walls, reflecting the flickering candlelight, the enchanting textured colors and the women lost in the dance. *Belly dance*, Llayne's heart pitter pattered. She didn't know where it would lead, and that was part of the excitement!

The song ended. The dancers came out of their trances and noticed Llayne.

"There you are!" Kerina greeted her. She introduced her to the others and showed her to the dressing room beneath the stairs. Llayne took her old, red, flowered, bikini bathing suit and new, red, chiffon, hip-hugging, full-length, circle skirt out of the paper bag she brought and changed her clothes. When she joined the others, they were working on their belly rolls. Llayne readily joined in and was soon as lost in the music as her new partners in dance.

They danced fast, slowly, wildly, humorously and sensuously. Totally exhausted after two hours, they collapsed onto the floor pillows, dabbing at their perspiration with thick towels and drinking water from delicate crystal wine glasses that Kerina passed around. Kerina dried her own glistening throat with a pink towel, sipped a glass of water, then smiled grandly as she emptied her hands. Walking to the center of the room, she clapped twice. She said, "Okay, my little harem girls, what do you think? Should we initiate a new storyteller?"

The women laughed and hollered, "Yes!" Llayne had no idea what Kerina was talking about.

"Okay! Okay!" Kerina agreed, throwing her head back to laugh. She came closer to Llayne and said, "This in not just a class. This is a group called Scheherazade." The name trilled off her tongue. "You remember Scheherazade, don't you?" Llayne shook her head. She'd never heard of this sha-hair-a-thing. Kerina continued, "Scheherazade was a beautiful temptress in one of the stories in *Arabian Nights*. That is a collection of over 200 stories, the most famous work of Arabic literature. In her story, Scheherazade saved her own life and the lives of many other young maidens by being a master storyteller. King Shahriyar had discovered that his wife had been unfaithful, so he had her killed. Then, out of fury, he vowed to marry a new maiden each day and have her killed the next morning. When he married Scheherazade, that evening she told him a story. He was so entertained by it that he let her live the next day, so that he could hear more that evening. One story let to another, night after night, for 1001 nights. By then the king had fallen in love with her and was over his killing rampage.

"We are like Scheherazade. But we tell our stories with our bodies, with belly dancing. We would like to initiate you into our group.

"There is one catch, however. We go to Detroit one weekend a month to dance at the Cedars, a Middle Eastern club in Greek Town. And we don't tell our husbands what we're doing. They, poor souls, think we go to take lessons and shop."

Kerina quit talking and she and the others examined Llayne, waiting for her response. The novice was taken aback. It would be fun. It would be exciting. It would be weird and unusual. But she couldn't lie to Tank. Could she?

"I'll do it!" she said.

♦ ♦ ♦ ♦ ♦ ♦ ♦ ♦

Tank stood in the middle of the tiny, stark living room at Chief Jackson's house on the Chippewa reservation, looking huge and fair compared to the residents. About 30 Chippewas of all ages, and Llayne, sat around the room. Llayne felt overdressed in her short, print dress and knee-high, patent leather boots. She even curled her long hair, something she rarely did, and it hung in feminine ringlets about her shoulders. She wanted to make a good impression on her husband's associates, the people with whom he spent so much time as a counselor working with Indian high school kids. Well, she'd gone too far, she brooded. Her getup was definitely overkill and maybe even insulting to their hosts. It screamed, "I'm white and you're not!" and she would have given anything to be wearing jeans like they did.

Although all eyes were on Tank, she could feel herself being evaluated with sideways glances. They were judging whether or not she was good enough for their beloved Mr. Tanner.

Tank, looking exceptionally handsome, wore a pale blue, cardigan sweater and pale blue jeans. He just finished inviting a teenaged girl to stand up and make her announcement.

"Oh, Mr. Tanner," the girl said shyly, "you do it. You go ahead and tell them. I'm embarrassed." She hugged the wide-eyed baby girl sitting on her lap.

"Well, you shouldn't be embarrassed, Sue," Tank addressed her. "You should be proud! I came here tonight," he continued, addressing everyone, "to help Sue announce that she will have acquired enough credits to graduate from high school at the end of this winter semester. Although she'll be done at the end of December, she can walk across the stage at graduation next spring and get her diploma, just like everyone else!"

There were shouts of joy, and Sue timidly hung her head over the baby, although she couldn't keep a large smile from cracking across her mouth.

"She's the first Jackson to graduate from high school!" the chief, her grandfather, declared proudly.

"And she's the last of my eleven children, so she was our last hope!" Sue's mother revealed.

"This is wonderful! You've accomplished so much!" The older woman went over and hugged her daughter and her granddaughter.

Tank continued, "Considering the conditions under which she's accomplished this ..." He rethought his words as it occurred to him that what he just said might have sounded insulting. He was still getting used to Chippewa customs. They wouldn't call their lifestyle "conditions.""Ah," he said, "I mean, given that she has so many other things going on in her life, it's amazing she finds time to do all that homework. You've really done a great job, Sue. I'm proud of you, too." He went over and shook her hand, then rubbed the top of her baby's head.

Sue said, "Thank you, Mr. Tanner. I couldn't have done it without your help."

The room broke out in applause. Those people loved Mr. Tommy Tanner.

Suddenly Llayne felt like a shallow blob of inert substance. Compared to her husband's life, hers was inane. Oh, she helped kids plan their classes at the community college in her job as an academic counselor, but they could all figure it out themselves if they used their brains for two minutes. She didn't make a real impact on people's lives like this. And Tank's goal was to become vice principal or principal someday, and to have even more of an influence on young lives. She was enormously proud of the man she married. And a little in awe. He was so sincere, so gentle and sweetly optimistic. She doubted she could ever be that good a person.

Everyone stood and milled around, eating snacks and chatting. People were very polite to her, but she knew they could never revere her like they did Tank. She did learn that Mrs. Lacey, the palm reader she and Priscilla had once visited, had died recently at 102 years of age. Llayne's first thought was that the wizened, old woman had finally joined the people she'd been talking to anyway. She'd have to tell Priscilla during their weekly Sunday evening phone call. She'd also tell her about the remarkable young Chippewa woman who was graduating even though she had a baby.

In the car on the way home, she said, "It's amazing Sue did this with a baby."

Tank grinned and answered, "Three babies. And a husband."

"Three kids! Oh my god! You mean that baby was just her youngest?"

"Yeah. She's had one a year for the last three years. Got married when she was 14. She's only 16 now."

"No!" Llayne couldn't believe it.

Tank rubbed his wife's knee and said, "Yes. But, her husband is very supportive of her education. He's a whopping 17. Quit school when they got married. Works at a gas station downtown. Sue is brilliant. Could have a real future in front of her, if she wanted it."

"Will she go to college?"

He shook his head sadly. "I'm trying, but we haven't gotten that far yet. If I can convince her to go, I'm sure I could get her a scholarship, her grades are so good. We'll wait and see."

He smiled warmly at her, and Llayne's heart flew out to him. "They love you so much," she whispered. "So do I."

"And I love you, Lela," he replied.

It was one of those moments that inexplicably binds a couple together in their souls. A moment that, once spent, can never be retrieved or undone, a moment that changes everything forever. "I have something to tell you, honey," she confessed rashly.

"Shoot."

She started to tell him what her belly dancing group would really be doing in Detroit the coming weekend, but a moment of reflection stopped her. He might insist she not go. And she was going. "I love you so much it hurts," she said.

He pulled up to their apartment, turned off the engine, put his seat all the way back, and pulled her over to sit on top of him, facing him, with a knee on either side of his hips. "God, you look beautiful tonight," he said between kisses as he ran his hand up the short skirt of her dress and tugged at her silky panties.

"Tank, you want to ... right here?"

"Yeah. Here. Now. Nobody'll see us under this big, old tree. It's as dark as Hades tonight anyway." He already dispensed of her panties and released the bulge beneath his fly. Roughly, uncharacteristically for him, he took her quickly.

♦ ♦ ♦ ♦ ♦ ♦ ♦ ♦

Llayne looked out the back seat window of Kerina's long, yellow Cadillac and thought about two nights ago when her husband had ravaged her in his car. She smiled at the passing trees as the memory caused a stirring in her groin as she felt herself become aroused. Maybe this belly dancing thing in Detroit wasn't such a good idea after all, because she wouldn't be able to have sex with Tank tonight.

"What did you tell your husband we were going to do in Detroit?" Kerina asked over her shoulder as she drove.

"I told him we're taking a belly dancing class from one of the top dancers in the country, who lives in Detroit," Llayne replied dutifully.

"True," Kerina said.

"And," Llayne continued, "we're going to eat at a Middle Eastern club in Greek Town tonight. Then we'll stay at your relatives' house."

"True," all of the others chimed in.

"And, we're shopping at the Eastern Market tomorrow morning, and stopping by the Novi Mall on the way home, and we'll be back by seven tomorrow night."

"True!" they exclaimed. Kerina added, "We will do all of that. But, we'll also be dancing on stage! You didn't tell him, did you?"

"No," Llayne said, feeling guilty. Tank had hated to see her leave for the weekend and had relented only after Dale suggested they take in the CMU football game together.

It was clear that none of the other women, the members of Scheherazade, felt guilty about not telling their husbands what they really did in Detroit. Llayne was learning a lot about each of them on the three-hour trip. One was a 40-year-old, divorced bank clerk; one was 30 and married to a teacher; and another, Jean, was an attractive, 36-year-old brunette who was married to a prominent Mt. Pleasant physician.

Kerina was from a very wealthy family in Turkey. She lived there until she turned 18. Headstrong and determined to move to America, she used her college fund to attend the University of Michigan, which made her parents extremely unhappy. Always having found their only daughter to be a trial, especially when she took up belly dancing, which she learned from the servants, they had hoped she'd get the U.S.A. out of her system and come home after college. So, they were even more outraged when she married an American man, a construction contractor, and settled in a small town, Mt. Pleasant, in the frigid northern part of the country. They had disinherited her and she hadn't seen them since. Most distressing to them, Kerina said, was that she become a Roman Catholic and was raising her children as such, after having been raised Moslem. What her parents didn't know was that her oldest brother funneled family money to her as often as he could, and he reassured her that when their parents were dead and gone he would see to it that she received her share of the inheritance, which would be considerable. In the meantime, she could always come to him in an emergency. He couldn't stand the thought of his beloved little sister ever wanting for anything.

Llayne couldn't imagine such a thing. Family money. Money of any consequence. The concept was as foreign to her as Kerina.

She also learned that Kerina was a horrific driver. Although she'd been to her great-aunt and -uncle's home in Detroit many times, and had in fact rendezvoused with her brother there on several occasions when he visited the States, she couldn't find the place and got lost in a horrible part of the city. Llayne had never seen anything like it: street after street of slum houses.

"Wow," Llayne said. "I never knew so many poor people existed."

"Haven't you ever been in a city before?" Kerina asked.

"Sure. Once when I was in eighth grade a friend invited me to come down with her and her parents to a Tigers' game. We didn't stay overnight, though. But, I've been to Houghton Lake and Saginaw a lot," getting off the topic of poor people to defend her lack of travel experience, doing her best to sound worldly, although neither place was more than an hour away from Mt. Pleasant. "My last year of high school and my first couple of years in college, my friend, Priscilla, and I used to go to the Music Box in the summertime in Houghton Lake. Great place to dance for kids under 21. It's like a big outdoor dancing patio. We met Sonny and Cher there before they became a hit. They weren't very good, though, so I didn't think they'd ever make it big! The next year they did 'I Got You, Babe.' Who would've guessed? And we used to go to Saginaw to a place called Daniel's Den to see Bob Seger and the Silver Bullets. They were always great, even before they made it big! I just knew they'd make it. So, I've met some real famous singers. Oh yeah, and once in college a bunch of us came to the Vest Pocket Theater here in Detroit to see *Hair*. That was great! We got up on stage at the end and danced with the cast."

"Hey," Jean asked, "isn't that where they'd invite people up on stage to dance naked?"

Llayne laughed. "They were naked. We weren't."

"Oh. What a shame," Jean said, and everyone laughed.

Finally, Kerina pulled onto a highway and declared she knew the way from there. Thirty minutes and four more wrong turns later, they arrived in Dearborn Heights, an exclusive neighborhood, eons away form the one where they'd been lost. The house they were staying in turned out to be a mansion and Llayne couldn't believe the opulence. She didn't even want to dance that evening. She just wanted to amble about that incredible place.

But dance they did at the Cedars, a small but very nice Middle Eastern club in the part of downtown Detroit known as Greek Town, where the atmosphere was actually homey. The Cedars served good Arabic food including grape leaves stuffed with lamb, rice and yogurt; tabbouleh salad; kofte, ground lamb patties grilled to perfection; shish kebabs, marinated in dry white wine; pilaf, baked rice surrounded by a bed of fresh-cooked peas; and baklava, the heavenly desert made with layers of thin pastry, finely chopped walnuts, and honey. It was no wonder so many families, as long as everyone was over 21, ate there together. Although "nice" Arab girls still didn't belly dance, American Middle Easterners seemed more relaxed in their beliefs and treated the dancers with nothing but playful respect. It was a bit of their culture and they were proud of it, enjoying it immensely.

Llayne had been granted the "Dance of the Seven Veils," where she began swathed in layers of silk and chiffon veils, then unwrapped and discarded them one-by-one. Fast, then slowly, then fast again, she danced to "Ya Habiba," which meant "my love," played by the three-piece orchestra sitting at the side of the stage. Although nervous because it was her first public performance, she knew she did well. She could feel it in her body. Ending with a triumphant backbend, she rose and twirled in lieu of a bow and flittered off the stage. A quick, backward glance as she neared the dressing room to the side of the bar, reassured her that Jean was scraping up the tips which had been thrown onto the stage floor for her.

"Yowwee!" Jean cried as she entered the dressing room, spreading the bills out in her hands. "Look at this! Two 100s. Three 50s. And a zillion 20s and 10s. You did great for your first time, Llayne! Oh, sorry, forgot your stage name is Leila." She handed the cash over to Llayne.

"Wait a minute," Llayne said hesitantly, holding the bills out like they might be infected. "This can't be right. These people must be drunk. Surely they didn't know they were throwing such big bills. I mean, I don't make this much in a week at the community college."

The rest of Scheherazade laughed. "It's okay, honey," Kerina reassured the rookie. "They know what they're doing. This is good food and music and entertainment to them, and they love it. Besides, they can afford it! Don't worry about it. You did great!"

The owner of the club, a striking American man of obvious Arabic heritage, in his 60s and a snazzy dresser, knocked on the dressing room door. When they invited him to enter he complimented them profusely, giving them a dish of Turkish Delight candy. "It's going beautifully!" he commented. "Our customers are having a great time! Everyone is loving it. Just don't let that one kid get you down, the one sitting alone in the right-hand corner. He came in last week and tried to harass the dancers. I caught him reaching out to grab the derriere of one girl when she walked by him, but he says that wasn't what he was doing and she said she never felt anything. He hasn't done anything yet tonight so

I can throw him out, but I will the minute he bothers you. We don't like his kind in here."
With that warning, he left.

No one was dancing at the moment and the band played a soft, breezy tune. The members of Scheherazade couldn't resist peeking out of the dressing room door and spying on the perpetrator in question.

"Geez!" Llayne said disgustedly as she chomped on a piece of the super sweet, pistachio nut candy. "He reminds me something of this twerp in college. A wimp named Harold Hackleberry. I mean, this guy's fat and Harold was skinny, but there's something about the wimpiness that's the same." Unlike Harold, this man was overweight and had a mop of brown hair. Llayne briefly told her friends about Harold and what the vets had done to him. They enjoyed the tale, and then Kerina acquired a look of pure mischief.

"Let's invite this jerk back into the dressing room," she said. "Jean, go get him." Jean obeyed and left. "Now," Kerina continued, "when he gets here, just follow my lead."

"What?" Llayne tried to protest, but her leader shushed her with a finger to her lips.

The young man followed Jean like a slobbering puppy. Kerina invited him to stand in the middle of the room and the women surrounded him.

"You know," Kerina addressed him, "we couldn't help but notice you out there all by yourself. Maybe you'd like some company."

"Sure!" he admitted, his eyes wide.

"You like dancers, don't you?" she asked. He nodded his big head vigorously. "You like to think about dancers and imagine what you could do with them." He nodded again. "You've been out there fantasizing which one of us you'd like to be with. Which one do you want?" The women lined up in mock display.

Llayne hung back, not knowing how to take all of this.

"G-gosh," he stammered, "it's hard to pick."

"Maybe you could have us all," Kerina mocked. "Which one would you like to start with?"

"Um-m-m," he hemmed and hawed, working his pudgy jowls nervously, delirious over his good luck. "I could start with you," he said to Kerina.

"You could, could you?" she said. He nodded once again. "Well, that's what you think!" she yelled, whacking him across the top of his head, like a mother cat does to a misbehaving kitten. A flash of confusion crossed his stupid face. "How old are you?" she demanded to know, thrusting her face into his and angrily stamping her fists onto her hips. He didn't answer. "How old?" she asked through clenched teeth.

"Ah, 22," he said, looking at the door for escape. Her demeanor had changed so drastically, he just wanted out. But, the dancers tightened their circle around him and he couldn't get past them without shoving somebody out of the way. And he doubted he'd be successful at doing that.

"Twenty-two my ass!" Kerina exclaimed. "You've got I.D. or you couldn't get it. I bet it's fake, isn't it? Isn't it?"

"No, no, I promise," he submitted, "I'm really 22."

"Well, what in hell is a 22-year-old, young man doing alone in a club at night, drooling over older women? I'm old enough to be your mother, for goodness sake! Oh, if you were with your family or friends and wanted to enjoy some good food and entertainment, that would be fine. But that's not what you're doing is it? Is it?"

"Um-m. Um-m-m..." His brain had died from fright.

"Now, here's what you need to do," Kerina instructed. "Go home. Tomorrow morning get your fat ass up out of bed and go jogging. Get some of the lead out. Meet a nice young girl. Treat her like a queen. Go live a real life and stop fantasizing about the one you wish you had. And leave us dancers alone! You got that?"

He stood mute, staring at the floor.

"You got that?" she asked again, whacking him once more across the top of the head.

"Y-yes, m'am," he relented.

"Now, get out of here and don't come back," Kerina laid down the law.

He fled from the room as the women rolled their eyes and shook their heads.

Jean noted, "One thing about Kerina is you never have to wonder what she thinks. She'll tell you! And that kid will never be the same!"

The owner came back and told Jean it was her turn to dance. After that, Kerina capped the show. They made even more money than Llayne. It was a whole new world to Llayne, one with money in it.

♦ ♦ ♦ ♦ ♦ ♦ ♦ ♦

"Honey, I have to tell you about this thing we did in Detroit last night." Llayne sat on the couch with Tank, munching on popcorn together as they watched TV.

"Is everything okay?" he asked, suddenly concerned.

"Oh, yes. It's just that we did more than take a belly dancing lesson and shop and eat at the Middle Eastern club in Greek Town. It turns out we belly danced there."

"At the club?" he asked. She nodded. "You mean they found out you guys have a dance group and invited you to dance, on the spot?"

She swallowed hard and said, "Yes." It was only a small lie, she told herself.

He wanted to know what kind of club it was and she described it to him. It really was a nice place.

He asked, "Didn't it feel like that strip joint you used to work at? The one you hated?"

The comparison had never occurred to her. "No," she said thoughtfully. "This is just so different. It really does feel more like folk dance, like clean, ethnic fun. And we don't strip, for goodness sake!"

"But you did get up on stage and dance in that costume you made?" She'd made a new costume with a gold-coined bra and hip belt, and a red skirt interwoven with a gold thread, and all of the veils.

"Yes," she confessed. There, she said it. She simply hadn't been able to keep it from him. It he weren't so honest she could have, but he was so she couldn't. She heaved a heavy sigh. That would be it, he'd get mad now. She'd never seen him angry before, and he was so big the prospect was profoundly frightening.

Tank stood up from the couch and ran his hand over his thinning hair, turning away from her. Every muscle in her body involuntarily tensed, preparing for the onslaught of abusive words.

He turned back to her, knelt at her side, and took her hand. "Lela," he said gently, using his pet name for her, "that scares me. I know it might be a nice club, and Greek Town's a nice area, but it's still downtown Detroit. It's a big city and it's dangerous. And dancing like that, you never know what kind of weirdo might be watching and what he might decide to do. I don't want you to go again."

She let out a long sigh. Could this possibly be his real response? Maybe he was playing tricks on her. When she was growing up and her dad had been mad, especially if he were drunk, which was often, he always flung nasty names and dirty words at her. Tank's response was totally new to her. Instead of being upset, he seemed concerned.

"I made 412 dollars in tips," she said.

His eyes widened as he turned that revelation over in his mind. "Well," he finally said, sitting down beside her again and patting her hand, "maybe it'll be okay if I come and make sure you're safe. It is only one Saturday a month. I can stay at Bob's if you wanna stay with the girls. I won't get in the way. I promise. I'll just kinda, um, guard you. All of you."

She didn't bother telling him that with Kerina they didn't need to worry about being guarded. That woman was one tough cookie and could take care of them.

But, it would be reassuring to have Tank there as backup. She never knew a man like this in her life! Llayne threw her arms around her husband and crushed him with happy kisses, a gesture which spilled the bowl of popcorn all over the place.

♦ ♦ ♦ ♦ ♦ ♦ ♦ ♦

It never happened before and it was as exhilarating as it was frightening. Why it was happening on that fall day, a day seemingly like all other fall days, she didn't know. Everything was the same as usual. And everything was different.

During the 50-mile drive home from work, Llayne was in a mellifluous mood, feeling more alive than she had since when she'd been a carefree little girl. She was gripped with a sensation of wholeness, a feeling of being a real woman.

Maybe it was a combination of things, like that drive, her dancing, and her marriage, all intertwining within her to make her feel renewed. Although the drive had become such a habit after eight weeks that she hardly noticed the time or distance anymore, it was fantastically beautiful Michigan farmland. She thought of it as her land and her private time. If another vehicle did design to enter her narrow road, it was a lazy tractor, wad-

111

dling a short distance before plodding off into a field. That country route offered hypnotic solace after a day of humdrum work at the community college.

And her dancing had made her aware of her body in a new way; it's connection to the earth, it's ability to express feelings, and to simply feel good itself. Kerina had taken home movies of the group rehearsing in her basement one night, and Llayne was amazed at how good she looked on film. She never saw herself that way before.

Her marriage to that marvelous man was still a wonder to her, too. Tommy Tank Tanner was like a great big teddy bear of a man, cuddly and kind.

It was as if all of those things had caused a stubborn, rusty, old door to open and reveal to her a whole new way to live. It made her feel so alive!

In no hurry to leave her private Eden, she let her Beetle amble along while she enjoyed the splendor of the gently rolling hills, a creek meandering through a field, trees and more trees, old farms and animals, like the young buck which gracefully glided across the road up ahead. It all seemed placed on earth for her solitary pleasure.

More mesmerized than ever before by the warm autumn scene splashed with the golden glow of approaching dusk, Llayne was suddenly overtaken by an ice cold fear! It startled her so completely she slammed on the brakes of her car. Her foot shook so hard she could hardly press the gas peddle, so she slowly pulled over. The gravel on the side of the road crunched and the machine stopped. She got out of the car. Standing at the side of the country road she saw - what?

"Nothing," she said aloud, amidst the quiet.

Cautiously, she surveyed every detail of what was around her, expecting an omen or a sign. A breeze whipped up and a few neon leaves left the flashing orange branches of the electric trees from which they had been zapped of their last bit of energy. The dying vegetation lifted gently then fell in slow motion, painlessly alighting on the pavement in front of her. The leaves seemed to be saying something to her as they danced delicately on the tar surface, and then they were inert as the breeze subsided, only to pirouette merrily with one last breath of wind. Finally, they laid still.

From where she stood she could see about half a mile of lolling Tarmac in either direction. Old farms were scattered along each side of the road with fields backed by brilliantly colored woods. Not far away was a tattered, once-red barn about to tumble down. Rolled haystacks slept in toasted brown fields. Hills traipsed into red, gold and green corridors of trees, their vivid hues enhanced by the day's final rays of sun. The magical artistry of the scene took Llayne's breath away. All was perfectly still in still perfection.

Having received no insight through her investigation, she turned to re-enter the car. As she grabbed for the handle, she was shocked by the touch of slick, cold metal compared with the warmth of the raw world she just examined. Then, with a force that caused a blow to her gut that almost knocked her down, her comprehension caught up and she knew what she'd been sensing. It had at last revealed itself to her.

"Oh my god!" she screamed. "No-o-o!"

She reached toward the patch of pavement scattered with dead leaves and time froze as the picture became clear: The big head of a man, lifelessly pale, on a stiff white pillow, a starched white sheet drawn up to his slack chin. And then hands, sad hands, reaching down and pulling the sheet up and over the big, inanimate head.

"Tank! No!" The words caught in her throat as she gasped for air. Her beloved husband was dead. She was certain. She felt the breath leave his body as it had just left her own, just as the leaves had fallen from their life. His spirit was calling out to her.

Tank was dead! Probably in a car accident in town. Now he was on a hospital gurney, "expired." The pieces fell together at last and formed a clear message. That was why that day, of all days, she'd had such heightened senses. She was being sent a message. The image of the dead head became incised on her inner sight.

She forced a feeble smile. "This is stupid!" she admonished herself. "You've really let your imagination run away with you!"

The rouse didn't work. The terror of horrid realization stuck. The shaking in her limbs seemed to be in a foreign body, yet it overtook her. She clung to the side of the Beetle for support. The crying seemed to come from another, yet tears were wet on her face. She used her jacket sleeve to dry them. She lost control and a great badgering power had taken over.

"I've got to collect myself," she said, embarrassed when a lone truck came over the hill and the driver saw her talking to herself.

The battered-up, muddy truck slowly pulled up beside her, and an old farmer in overalls stuck his arm and head out the window. "Evening, miss. Is there anything I can help you with?" he asked kindly.

"Oh no. I just stopped to look at how pretty it is out here," she lied poorly.

His bright eyes, framed in a helter-skelter network of wrinkles, took her in and telegraphed their knowledge of her deceit. "Yes, it is pretty out here," he responded. "Peaceful. You just take your time and enjoy it, but be careful on your way into town. This time of night there are plenty of deer running across the road."

"I'll be careful," she promised. "Thanks."

He cocked his head in a gesture of farewell and drove away, his truck lumbering over the hill.

Llayne forced herself to take a couple of long, deep breaths and get into her car. Her fingers were so stiff she could hardly turn the key, but eventually her bug moved toward town. She needed to get home. She had to be there when they called to tell her about Tank's accident. She wondered who "they" would be. Police? A minister? Who in hell has the atrocious job of telling people their loved ones have been smashed to smithereens? She didn't know.

She drove on, believing she would soon find out.

The empty space where Tank usually parked his Cutlass glared at her as she approached the apartment building. But, of course, she told herself, his car was destroyed. No longer in shock, a fact which in itself shocked her, she became over-

113

wrought with sadness, knowing that gone forever was the security she felt upon arriving home and having Tank there. Normally, he was home first at the end of a work day.

The click of the latch echoed into emptiness as she unlocked the door and opened it to dead silence. Her new home, Tank's apartment, her comfort at the end of a long work day, her retreat from the pressures of the outside world, now felt barren. Entering with trepidation, she moved through the blood red kitchen to the middle of the living room, seeing that "home" in a new light. That place had betrayed them, that sanctuary could not save them from the hell of death.

She stood not knowing what to do next. She looked from the black phone on the glass end table to the black fireplace to the blank TV back to the black phone and then to blank, black nothingness. Death was everywhere.

Indeterminable time passed as she stood mute as a granite cemetery stone and tried to calculate all that had just been. The road, the leaves, the wind.

Eerily, astute consciousness crept back into her being as she became keenly aware of something. It was a presence. A spirit.

Her senses alert to the uncanny sign, a chill trickled down her back, prickling her spine. Her newly discovered sensitivity told her that her husband's ghost had just come home. The supernatural apparition could be perceived as surely as if another living being were in the empty space behind her. Fearing the spook was angry because he died and she got to live, her terrified instincts told her to stand perfectly still so as not to alarm it. Only her skittish eyes moved as she fearfully looked behind ...

"Boo!" Tank hollered.

She jumped so hard and screamed so loudly it frightened him and he bolted backward, falling over the couch.

"Good lord, Lela!" His eyes glared bewilderment as he clumsily scrambled to his feet. "I meant to scare you," his voice softened to a chuckle as his usual good nature returned, "but you scared the living shit right out of me!"

Now he was laughing. For the second time that day Llayne's brain couldn't keep up.

"Hey, Lela honey," he said, "you left your key in the door, and it was wide open." He threw her keys on the end table and the chinking sound startled her. "Oh, yeah," he went on, "Dale and his new girlfriend want us to go out to eat with them tonight. Okay?"

Only then did she truly see him. He was really there. Right in front of her. Talking as he nonchalantly took an earth-toned, plaid, flannel shirt off his mortal body while he walked as a bipedal being into the bathroom. As if nothing had happened. He shouted from the bathroom, "Okay, honey?"

When she didn't answer he poked his half-clad body around the corner, wiping his just-washed, square jaw with a fluffy, white towel. His animated head was very much alive.

"Lela, what's wrong?" He lowered the towel and studied her with inquisitive, hazel eyes. "You look like you've seen a ghost."

"I'm, I'm fine," she stuttered.

Convinced, he said, "Well, good. Come on then. We've gotta get a move-on if we're gonna meet them on time. Hut to!" He chuckled as he went into the bedroom, enjoying the use of his old army lingo.

Llayne went to the window, drew the new, sheer, white curtain aside, and looked out into the driveway. In its usual spot was his Cutlass, gleaming gold from a new washing. Now she laughed. She did know that ghosts didn't drive cars. How could she have been so certain he was dead? There he was right in the next room - big, vital, handsome, jovial, warm, teddy bear Tank.

She rushed to the bedroom where he was putting on a fresh sweatshirt and pinned him to the mirrored closet door with her much smaller frame, reaching up to anchor his head by running her fingers through his thinning but wavy hair. She gave him the biggest kiss she could muster. All to his delight. Putting his hands up in mock surrender, he inhaled deeply and said, "I don't know what that's for, but I'll take it." His big hands fell to surround her waist for one of his abundant hugs.

Filled with giddy relief as he held her, Llayne considered trying to explain, but knew she couldn't. What would she say? "By the way, I saw you dead today?" She released him and walked to the closet to change.

Tank followed his wife's movements with his eyes as she walked away from him, considering whether or not he should be concerned over her strangeness, but decided she must have had a weird day at work.

A wave of relief swept through Llayne as she walked to the bathroom to touchup her makeup. In the space between the bedroom and the bathroom she decided that what she experienced on the road was no more than a tired brain that went haywire for a few minutes. It'd been nothing but a silly, stupid, short circuit in her imagination.

She swept it from her mind. To erase her private, inner embarrassment at having been so ridiculous, she busied herself with getting ready to go out to dinner.

"You ready yet?" he asked after about three minutes.

"Almost!" she hollered from under a sweater that she was pulling over her head.

"Almost only counts in horseshoes and grenades. Let's go!"

She hustled out the door with him and shut off the last light, hopefully shutting out her fear.

115

Chapter 10

Dinner with Dale and his new girlfriend was fun. Llayne couldn't remember the names of Dale's dates and didn't even try anymore. They came and went too fast. But that one wasn't as much of a numskull as most of them, and the evening really was enjoyable.

But that night in bed before falling asleep, Llayne's mind had time to return to the events of the afternoon. Unable to sleep, she shook Tank's shoulder as he softly snored.

"You asleep, honey?" she asked rhetorically.

He started. "Huh? Oh, yeah, I'm wide awake. What is it?"

"You learned all kinds of psychological theories for your Master's degree in counseling, didn't you?"

He rolled over in the dark, shook his head to clear it, and looked up at the ceiling, placing both hands behind his neck. The glimmer of light from the streetlamp outside filtered through the window and tinged his bare, bulging biceps in steely blue. "Sure," he answered. "We learned about guys like Sigmund Freud and Carl Jung and Fritz Perls. Boring old geezers, if you ask me."

"Were most of your classes about theories?"

"Nah. Mostly they were what was called 'sensitivity training' and 't-groups' where we all sat around and expressed our feelings and watched the instructors make passes at the girls. A waste of my time, but it gave me the degree I needed. Why? What's going on?"

"Oh, I just thought maybe you'd learned what it means when somebody all of a sudden has an irrational fear, like a fear of death."

"Honey," he said, rolling over to put a strong arm around her waist, "are you suddenly afraid of death?"

"Yeah. Stupid, isn't it?"

"Nothing's stupid if it bothers you. Let's see now. Old Siggy," he said in a bad German accent, "would probably say your fear is of a sexual nature. Everything was of a sexual nature for Siggy. I, however," he went on, reverting back to his own hardy voice, "think you might be afraid that all of this might end, because you've never been so happy before. Or so you claim." He nuzzled her neck. "But just in case Siggy's right, maybe we should have sex to get rid of your fear."

"Oo-oo," she cooed, "you are one good counselor!"

While they romped, her fear subsided. When they were finished, however, it plagued her again, like a monster hiding under the bed, rearing its ugly head just when she wanted to fall asleep. They started discussing it in the dark and ended up spending two hours in the middle of the night talking, crying and laughing about death, confiding to one another stories about every fear, every ghost story from their childhoods, every ghastly nightmare, every neurotic guilt trip, every euphemistic religious dictum and every scary movie that had ever frightened them.

Tank told her, "When I was a kid I heard about a maniac who shot people at random at a baseball game. I loved playing little league ball but was scared to death, certain the nut would find my ballpark in Mt. Pleasant, Michigan, and start shooting! I was always on the lookout while I played."

"Yeah, well," Llayne said, "I had nightmares about having my head cut off with a page from a book, like you can cut your finger on a piece of paper. The book was blue and had a silver seven on the cover with a circle around it." She shivered upon remembering the petrifying, recurrent dream of so long ago where she would always wake just as her head was chopped.

"I saw a movie called *Village of the Damned*," Tank said, "about kids from outer space who were demons. Their eyes would laser devilish deeds, and their parents were unsuspecting at first because they'd been born like normal kids. Dale's little sister was born right after that and she was kinda cross-eyed. I was absolutely certain she was one of them. I didn't know how to break the news to my friend." He laughed at the recollection. "She did grow up to be a devil, too."

"I was afraid to finish my prayers," Llayne told him. "I didn't want to ask God to take my soul 'if I should die before I wake.' I wanted to ask Him to just make sure I woke. Then I was afraid we were all just part of a giant's dream, and when the giant woke up, it would all be over. Zippo!"

They were on a roll and the memories snowballed for both of them. He continued, "My buddies and I used to dare each other to roam the cemetery at night. One night there was a newly dug, empty grave. We shoved each other toward it until dorky Ernest fell in. He started screaming as though he were being buried alive. It terrified us so much we all screamed and ran like hell. Nobody stayed to help pull the poor kid out. I always felt just awful about that, especially since Ernest did end up in therapy for about nine years."

"My friend Linda Lake," Llayne told, "had an attic trap door in the ceiling of her room, where we slept at her p.j. parties. I was 16 before I stopped being afraid 'the blob' would drop out on us while we were sleeping."

"Yeah," he chuckled. "The good ole days. The innocence of youth they call it. Hell! When I was a teenager I already knew for certain I was going to hell when I died. My grandmother belonged to a fundamentalist church and had me totally convinced I'd go straight to hell if I so much as touched a girl before marrying her. Shit! Dale set me up on a blind date when I was 15 with Libby Matinowski. Je-e-sus! She was a dog but she was stacked! When you're 15 and the girl's 16 and stacked, it's a big deal, especially for a chubby kid like I was. I was so nervous, I just knew I was gonna wet my pants before the night was over. I was sure I was gonna wanna touch them and that, of course, I couldn't. You know - hell. Well! Ugly, but stacked, Libby gets me in the back seat of her car and starts neckin'. All this stuff I'd never dared think about for fear Satan would reach right up out of hell and grab me as I stood. Libby's kissin' and runnin' her hands up and down my thighs. Man, I had sensations I never knew existed. Next thing I know she's unbuttoned her blouse and has 'em

118

pulled right outta her bra," he said, illustrating breasts at his chest with his hands rounded, "and they're just sitting up there under her chin staring at me like two lost, pink-nosed puppies begging to be petted. God almighty! I knew it was already too late. Satan was well on his way. So, I might as well enjoy a bit of heaven before having to go to hell. I touched them. Here I am, in bliss, right? I think this fondling stuff is the greatest. But not Libby. She grabs my head and shoves it right in there between 'em! Now I know I'm gonna die 'cuz I can't breathe!" Llayne was laughing as hard as he was. "But ya know what the worst part was? Ya wanna know?" He shook his head in mock dismay as Llayne shook hers in ascent. "That was it! I thought I'd done the most blissfully sinful thing a person could ever do, playin' with Libby's lusty tits like that. She wanted to do more but I'd already come in my pants and had to go home. My one and only opportunity for sex in high school and I blew it!

"I dreamt about that night for a year. Then - this is really the worst part - then I found out my Catholic buddies had been going all the way with Libby for two years. And all they had to do was confess, do penance, and they were clean to do it again. I just didn't understand how that could be! Why did they get to stay out of hell and I have to go?"

They laughed spastically. On and on they talked, and finally their fears and funny stories were spent, and they curled into each other like spoons to fall into a peaceful sleep.

♦ ♦ ♦ ♦ ♦ ♦ ♦ ♦

"May I talk to Mr. Tanner?" Llayne asked in a camouflaged voice.

The school secretary asked, "May I tell him who's calling?"

"No."

The woman hesitated then rang through.

"Mr. Tanner here," he answered.

"Is this the Mr. Tanner who ravages women and sends them into fits of ecstasy?" a southern voice droned.

"Who is this?" he hissed. His irritation at the harassment was obvious. All he needed was for another Rosie Saleman to intrude upon his happiness.

"This is a woman who wants to be ravaged."

"Lela, is that you? That better be you!"

Her giggles couldn't wait. It was good enough that she got by the secretary, who knew her well, but now her own husband wasn't sure it was her. In her own voice, she said, "Yes! And I want to be ravaged!"

"I can handle that! When? Where?" Relief reverberated in his voice.

"Tonight. Our house. By the fire."

"I'll be there!"

After sweet good-byes, they hung up and Llayne got down to the business of fixing a special meal. It would be a day-early Thanksgiving feast and would take a lot of preparation, as pots and pans and food were a combination with which she seldom complicated her life. For this evening she decided to use her grandmother's recipes in a seductive setting. Grandma wouldn't mind. They would be having roasted turkey, mashed potatoes, homemade noodles with sinkers, green beans, bread homemade at the bakery and apple pie, all accompanied by a good Rhine Bear Liebfraumilch wine. They would sit at a romantic little table she specially set in front of the fireplace. She was just like an old-fashioned housewife and Tank would come home to her after a hard day at work. Thank goodness the community college had more extra days off around the holidays than the high school did, giving her time to do this!

Quickly and quietly she worked, not letting a television or radio interrupt the intense concentration this cooking thing demanded. Barring an always possible culinary catastrophe, all would be ready at the precise moment.

Tank tore into the heap of food on his plate. "This is great!" he complimented his wife, his high forehead glistening and his sandy brown hair shimmering in the light of the fire. Llayne sipped on her wine and with impish eyes looked over the sparkling glass at her husband.

"What?" he asked, grinning. "You look so mischievous! What's on your mind?"

"Oh, it can wait."

"Really? So," he said, chomping on a turkey leg, "something is up. Well, let me tell you first how ravishing you look this evening." It was true. He thought he'd never seen her look more beautiful, in a pink, scoop-necked, silky nightgown, which advertised her nakedness underneath. Her hair fell about her shoulders in loose curls that danced in the glow of the fire.

A single taper candle burned on the table, and soft classical music played in the background. He brought her flowers that sat in a vase on the mantle and smelled wonderful. It was the most romantic meal they ever shared.

After making pleasant small talk throughout the dinner, which included seconds for Tank that rivaled the size of his first go-around, Llayne served the pie. She'd finished her sliver and he was working on his second piece when she said, "I've been thinking about something ever since last month when I had that spell of being afraid of death. I want to bring life into the world. I'd like for us to try to get pregnant this spring. I know I said I wanted to wait until next fall, but that seems so far away, I don't want to wait anymore. If I go off the pill early in the year, a few months from now, then we try in the spring, we should have a child late next year or early the following year. And I won't even be very pregnant for our vacation next summer. Traveling will be fine. I'll have to look for a new job to be closer to the baby, but with the experience I have now, maybe I can find something at Central."

Tank had put down his fork and hung on her every word. When she finished, he looked from her to the fire and back to her. "Are you sure this is what you want?" he asked gently.

"Yes."

With a grace that was uncommon for the big man, he rose from his chair and knelt at his wife's side, burying his head into her belly. "Oh, Lela," he whispered, "this makes me so happy!" When he raised his head to gaze into her eyes, there were tears in his. She wiped the teardrops away and they kissed deeply. Then Tank gently lifted her up and laid her down onto the sheepskin rug directly in front of the fire. As if unwrapping a delicate gift, he methodically gathered her gown in his big paws and pulled it off over her head. She lay flat, stretching her arms up onto the floor above her head and provocatively rubbed her knees together, allowing her pretty, naked body to be her offering to him. It was an absolutely exquisite gesture, especially in the low light of the fire. Without taking his eyes off of her for one second, he stood and took off his clothes, the mere sight of his wife arousing him more and more with each passing moment of anticipation. When he lowered himself upon her to take her, it was with a wild, intoxicating passion like none either of them had ever known. He lived up to that reputation she teased him about earlier, that of being a ravager who sends a woman into fits of ecstasy.

At four the next morning, Llayne's eyes flew open as she suddenly awoke from deep slumber. A dream had been telling her something. She lay there for what seemed an eternity with a trillion thoughts racing through her head when the one that had been escaping her was finally captured: The time had come for her to grow up. That was part of what facing death had been about, that was what bringing another life into the world was about. She couldn't avoid it any longer.

Uncertain if she was up to the task, she lay restlessly at her husband's side for over an hour, then decided it was too much to think about all at once, and rolled over and went back to sleep.

♦ ♦ ♦ ♦ ♦ ♦ ♦

"Hey! No Rice Krispies?" Tank shook the box as he looked at the half dozen or so little crisps in the bottom of his bowl. "How's a man supposed to play a decent game of basketball without Rice Krispies in his veins?" he teased. He was in a gay mood. The guy always woke up happy and, in Llayne's estimation, there was something wrong with that, but ever since a few nights before when she told him she wanted to have a baby, he'd been absolutely jubilant. As soon as he awoke the next day he asked her what she thought of naming a girl Tanya or a boy Tate. "Good names to go with Tanner," he said. He'd obviously given it more thought than she had. But now, his attention was diverted by breakfast and the absence of his favorite cereal in his bowl.

"The road to the store runs for both of us, Mr. Muscle," she answered good-naturedly, sitting at the kitchen table in her old, white bathrobe, nibbling on a granola bar. "If you want Krispies, go get them. Besides, I thought Wheaties was the breakfast of champions."

"Only for wieners who need proverbial help. Us real champions only need little crispies! Well, I'll leave the box out so whoever goes to the store next won't forget to get some." He placed the box in the center of the kitchen counter and said, "Guess I'll have to stop at Robaire's Bakery to get some morning chow."

She offered him a bite of her granola bar and he wrinkled up his nose. He liked making fun of the healthy foods she sometimes ate. After a quick kiss, he asked, "Do you know how much I love you?"

"Yes. As much as I love you."

"Okay, as long as you understand. Ya *biet*?" He liked using the phrase he learned in Vietnam.

"I *biet*. I understand," she said, smiling.

He winked playfully as he grabbed a basketball out of the red wire bin by the door, then whistled his way out the door. Llayne recalled homecoming night and his drunken, pretend, duck basketball game. She never saw him drunk like that again, although he did lapse into duck squeak on occasion.

She picked up the cereal box and threw it away. It would be a long day before he came home. He and Dale and some other guys, teachers from the high school, would play a few games at the school gym, then go for lunch at Falsetta's, and then go back to the gym for a few more games. They'd cap off the day with a beer at The Cabin or The Bird. It would be late afternoon before he came home.

There was so much she needed to do, but most of it involved housework, so she dismissed it. Rambling through the apartment, she took her time getting dressed. After pulling a C.M.U. sweatshirt over her head, she watched out the window as big, fat snowflakes twirled to the ground in a merry jig. It was late November, the time when it usually started to snow in Michigan, the precursor to a long winter. She turned her attention back inside the apartment and decided to play records.

Tom Jones filled her home with, "She's a lady, whoa, whoa, whoa, she's a lady ... talkin' about the little lady, and the lady is mine ...." He was such a sexy man! She heard that women actually threw their underpants at him onstage. She turned up the stereo full blast and wondered if everyone does that as soon as they're alone. And, as people do when alone, she danced, gleefully, seductively. Lately, she hadn't been much of a lady with her husband, and he loved it!

The ring of the phone jarred her. She answered it reluctantly.

"Llayne, it's Dale," she heard. "You've got to come to the hospital. Don't worry. It's okay. But Tank fell on the basketball court."

"Oh no! Did he break his leg?"

"No," Dale said, seeming confused. "We don't know what's wrong. He said his leg went numb after a terrible pain shot through it. He can't walk."

"I'll be right there."

She slammed down the phone, grabbed her coat, and ran to her car. Her Beetle sped all the way to Central Hospital.

Tank was already checked into a hospital room when she arrived. He refused to get into the bed, so sat on top of it. Dale and a couple of the other basketball players milled about the room.

"It's only a pulled muscle," Tank insisted. "It already feels better. I'm sure I can walk just fine. I'm ready to go home."

A strange-looking, balding doctor who appeared to be in his 50s, Samuel Klickensteiner he said his name was, came in and politely asked the other men to leave. He took off his wire-rimmed glasses and rubbed the bridge of his nose as he informed the young married couple that his preliminary examination had found a hardness in Tank's stomach. "I don't know what it is, and we need to find out. We don't usually run tests on the weekend, but I don't want to wait on this. We'll prep you tonight," he said, looking intently at Tank, "and do the testing tomorrow. We'll talk tomorrow about what treatment might be necessary." When he left, Tank's buddies came back in and they all spent the afternoon watching sports on TV.

At suppertime a hefty nurse, Miss Brundage her nameplate said, shooed the men away and gave Tank a bland meal on a tray. As he ate, he complained about the food with every bite until the tray was empty. Then Llayne spent a couple of quiet moments alone with her husband before she, too, was banned from the premises by the formidable Miss Brundage.

Llayne stood on the front steps of Central Hospital, the early winter wind cutting her face.

It felt good, like an awakening slap. Everyone, including Tank, was putting up a good front, but she knew her husband was going to die. She'd already seen him dead. Looking up at the sky, where a million brilliant stars spoke to her, she knew that God had given her a warning in her premonition. That Entity understood her vulnerability, her inability to cope, her fears, and had tried to prepare her for the tragedy to follow. As if a missive from that mysterious God electrified her soul, Llayne knew with instant clarity that there was one person here on earth who could help her. He had, in fact, been there all the while, waiting, and Llayne had ignored his existence.

She never had real help in her life, not from her parents as she grew up, and she had a hard time accepting it from her husband because it made her feel like a child taking it from someone with whom she was supposed to be an equal. She didn't know how to ask for nor yield to it. But now she must.

Carefully guiding her rusty, white bug through snow-clad streets, she drove to the other side of town. Strangely, a few weeks earlier she looked up the address in the phone book and driven by with no purpose. Now she had a purpose.

Terrified, understanding that she stood on the precipice of a whole new life which loomed before her, Llayne parked in front of the elegantly rejuvenated, white, Victorian house. It was a lovely, old place. A single light shone above a beautifully carved oak door with a beveled glass window.

Tentatively, yet with more determination than ever before in her 22 years, she walked up the brick sidewalk to the house. A snowman that someone had attempted to build in the front yard caught her attention. There wasn't quite enough snow yet, so it was a short, crooked, little guy who made her smile. She trod up the few steps to the wraparound porch. Pushing the brass button on the antique doorbell, she heard a pleasant thrum inside. The door flew open.

"Hello, dear," a lively woman with dyed, red hair exclaimed. Fixing the collar of a fake tigerskin coat she apparently just donned and buttoning it over her big bosom, she looked at the visitor with warm eyes that were decorated with makeup and laugh lines.

"Oh! Hi," Llayne said nervously, quite certain she was at the wrong house. "Is this where Dr. Lichenger lives?"

"Why, yes. Please come in." The woman, whom Llayne guessed to be in her 40s, stood aside and motioned the guest into a wide, warm hallway, the smell of what must have been a good supper loitering about in the air. "I'm Ruth Lichenger, Ray's wife," she said, holding out her hand.

Llayne had seldom shaken hands and hers felt limp in the woman's firm grip. "I'm Llayne Robertson, a former student of your husband's," she said by way of explanation.

"Ray dear!" Mrs. Lichenger hollered toward the back of the hall. "You have company."

A faint, "I'll be right out," echoed back.

"Please excuse me, Llayne. I have to pick up our son from a friend's." Ruth Lichenger patted Llayne's arm, flashed a radiant, red-lipsticked smile, and said, "Good-bye." She bounded out and closed the front door behind her.

Llayne stood alone in the oak paneled hall, stunned. Staid, boring Dr. Lichenger was married to that animated woman? And he was "Ray dear?" When he shuffled down the hall in his usual brown suit, minus his usual bow tie, and with fake tigerskin slippers on his feet, Llayne's impression of him turned full circle. There was more to this man than she'd suspected. She couldn't believe she ever considered him shallow enough to be sexually attracted to her. She could, unfortunately, believe she'd been shallow enough to harbor that suspicion. And she suspected this family single-handedly, and footedly, kept some fake tigerskin salesman in business.

Surprise rose and fell on the psychotherapist's face as he approached her, replaced by a friendly expression. He held out his hand to shake and she did better this time. "Hello, Llayne," he said in his New York accent. "It's good to see you. Come into my office." He led her down the hall and caught her glancing at his slippers. "A gift from my wife," he explained, grinning.

"So I figured," she said, grinning back.

They entered the room from which he'd emerged, and he closed the door behind them. A Tiffany-style lamp on his desk, with a design that looked like a cluster of pebbles, which she felt certain he must have brought from New York, cast a golden glow about the room. He turned on a floor lamp with a frosted globe and the room brightened with more soft light. Unlike his campus office, here the books and papers were neatly arranged on shelves except for a few on his dark wood desk. The furniture was good antique and, although there didn't seem to be a color scheme, everything was rich-toned and solid. Safe and assuring. The psychotherapist motioned for her to sit in one of two cushy, brown leather chairs facing each other; he sat in the other.

His mustache had a touch of gray which she hadn't noticed a year earlier. He stroked it but once, seeming to have almost broken the habit.

"We did have another meeting," he said, "but I hadn't thought it would be a year late." There was no malice in his voice. "What can I do for you?"

The tears let loose, and he handed her Kleenex and remained silent until she could talk. "I'm so mixed up," she sobbed. "My husband, Tank, Tommy Tanner, is dying. I love him dearly, but we didn't start out madly in love like most couples and that seems odd. But, god! I don't want him to die! I saw him dead already, in a kind of vision thing. It was weird! An old Indian woman told me once that something bad would happen. And I had a baby the summer before my senior year. I got pregnant by Rex Bates, the drama professor. He didn't care, and the baby was born dead, anyway. But it was so awful! I'm going crazy!"

She took a breath, realizing her disjointed story made no sense. This was so different from the time when she wouldn't talk to this man, or anyone, about her problems. Now she had no choice. Her world was crumbling down and she couldn't hold herself up alone any longer.

The kindness in his big, brown eyes washed over her and seeped into her heart. Why hadn't she seen that kindness before? Because, she realized, she never really saw anything before.

He leaned slightly forward, his forearms resting on his thighs. Taking his time in responding, he said, "Let's take this one issue at a time. First, you aren't crazy. Crazy people don't know they need help, and here you are getting help."

"Does that mean I was crazy when I wouldn't let you help?"

He smiled slightly. "No, it means you weren't ready yet, and now you are. Besides, sometimes it's normal to be a little crazy when so many strange things happen in our world. R.D. Laing, the British psychologist - do you remember learning about him in class? - he once asked who was craziest: someone in a crazy society who adjusts to that society or someone inside a mental institution who refuses to?" Llayne smiled. More seriously, he added, "Now, let's deal first with what happened first, your child. Then we'll talk about your feelings about your husband and his illness a little later, as these things all seem to be connected for you. Tell me about the birth and death of your baby."

She told the entire sorry story; he took a few notes; they heard his wife and son come home in the middle of it. When she finished, he told her that ethically and legally, he could not repeat outside of those walls anything that was told to him by a patient. However, he wanted to report Professor Rex Bates, without using Llayne's name, in case the man ever tried to get a reference from the college for another teaching job. She readily agreed.

125

He said, "It was horrible of Rex Bates to make no attempt to help you through your ordeal. And even though you say you weren't ready for a child, it sounds as though you feel enormous loss over the stillbirth."

Her tears let loose again, and she said, "Yes. Even though I knew I couldn't keep the baby, I still thought about how healthy and happy it could be with a loving, adoptive family. Oh, at the last minute I thought I wanted to keep it, but I had nothing, nothing to give a child."

He summarized what she said with, "Your loss was so final, it ripped your heart out."

"Yes!" she wailed. It felt so good to talk to a grownup who understood.

He gave her time to calm down, then gently prodded with, "And now your husband may be dying. It sounds like the fear of another loss is overwhelming for you. I want to hear about what's happening to him, but first let's talk about your feelings toward him. You said you didn't start out madly in love."

"No, we started out on the wrong foot. We hated each other at first, but we didn't really know each other. Then we became friends. The very best of friends. When he asked me to marry him, I knew I could never find a better husband. But I wasn't ga-ga over him, like most women are with their boyfriends. I've grown to love him more and more since we've been married. But that seems like a weird way for it to happen."

He said, "It only seems weird when you compare it to the American myth that lustful attraction is the one and only way for a relationship to begin. That myth is everywhere in this country, in the movies, in novels, in magazines. But not all cultures believe that to be true. Many believe that friendship is the best way to begin a marriage."

She grinned, saying, "So, I'm weird in America, but in some foreign tribe I'm cool?"

He matched her mirthful tone and said, "Well, yes, something like that. I'm asking you to be more broadminded about what's 'cool.' If it works, it's cool." They looked at each other for a moment, then he added, "Do you think you could tolerate one more short lecture from your old professor here? I know we don't lecture in therapy, but we haven't officially started therapy yet, so I want to take a little leeway."

"Shoot," she permitted. Actually, with his dry wit and vast knowledge, his lectures had always been quite interesting.

"It doesn't matter whether or not two people are 'ga-ga' over each other at the beginning of a relationship," he began. "What matters is where the relationship ends up, in a state of true love. True love and lustful infatuation are not the same thing and, this is where Americans get confused, you don't need lustful infatuation to get to true love. It sounds like that's what you did, and there's absolutely nothing wrong with that.

"Listen," he said, becoming even more intent, "lust is nothing but a primitive, physical response in our bodies. Primitive people weren't intelligent enough to know they needed to procreate to keep the species going, so the human body learned to play a trick. It works like this: A cave man would see a woman across a crowded cave," he wove his tale as Llayne smiled at the analogy, "and the moment his pea-brain recognized her as being of the sex and age to procreate with, his body would become alert. Hormones would flow that would cause him to become aroused. The same thing would happen to the women."

She interjected, "You mean they got horny."

"Yes, they got horny. They had sex, made babies, and the species survived. Now, humans have supposedly evolved, although we all know someone we wonder about. I have an Uncle Bert in Brooklyn! *Oy vey!*" Llayne was giggling out loud, just as she often did in his classes. He continued, "We know better intellectually, but our bodies are still primitive and respond by being sexually attracted, by feeling lustful infatuation toward others we could procreate with. In fact, this response is so automatic in the body, it's really not all that big a deal. We'll all be attracted to many people throughout our lives. It may be interesting and fun, but we're intelligent enough to know that doesn't mean we have to sleep with that person, or even say hello to that person. And we're intelligent enough to know that such feelings certainly don't constitute real love."

"Yeah," she interrupted, "but I bet you were really attracted to your wife right off, weren't you?"

She didn't miss the flicker of lustful memory that crossed his face. He said, "In all honestly, yes, I was. But the fact that it's grown into real love is the greatest blessing of my life.

"But here's the most important part of this lecture: the lust, because it depends on temperamental and unreliable hormones, always dies. It always dies eventually. It may take six months or four years or seven years, but it always wanes. If that's all you've got, you've got nothing when it's over."

"Wait a minute," she said questioningly. "Do you mean the passion always dies? That's sad."

"No! That's the good part! If you truly love one another the passion becomes greater! It may be different, more often thoughtful than hasty, more often giving than selfish, but it's much better. That's what lasts. Lust doesn't. In lust you're responding to your own fantasies of how you think that person is, because you've got these wild hormones botching up your brain. In true love you've taken the time to get to know that real person. The real person is almost always more complicated, deeper and more rewarding to know than any fantasy you ever could have had. Fantasies are too easy, too shallow to build a real life on. The real person may be a disappointment in some ways, like he doesn't pick up his socks, but he's always more intricate in other ways, like he loves classical music and you hadn't known that.

"Oh, yes, sometimes someone gets to know a person and learns that their fantasy was way off the mark. Rather than being more intricate or more interesting than imagined, the object of their lust is just an abusive jerk. That's why I condone divorce sometimes.

"But far too many couples run to divorce court, and Ruthie sees them all the time as a lawyer," he said, shaking his head, "much too quickly. They're at the point where the lust has died, as it always will, and they don't know how to get to real love. So they call it quits. They don't even know they're standing on the threshold of the most exciting time in their marriage, a time to grow, to learn, to explore. Too many people go back and do the lust thing over and over, with different people, or with each other. How sad. They miss the best part of being together.

Linda Hughes

"So, you see, Llayne, you and Tank are on the right track. Don't worry that it's not the way most other people do it. Most of them don't know what they're missing."

She said, "You have no idea how much better that makes me feel. I was afraid I'd cheated Tank out of something he should've had. It feels like a weight's been lifted off my shoulders!

"Shouldn't that be required learning for college kids before they go off and get married? How come they don't teach stuff like that in college?"

"Oh, my, no. It's much too practical. We have to make sure we tangle your web as much as possible before you go out to weave your way through the world," he responded, as she grinned at his intended irony.

"The thing is," he continued, "it sounds as though now you're afraid you and Tank won't have much time to enjoy your love. Tell me about what's happening to him."

"Well, he's in the hospital and they're doing tests tomorrow. But I don't need tests. I know. I saw it, and the psychic Indian woman told me. He's dying."

"They haven't done tests yet? So, you don't know for sure?"

"No, but yes, I know."

He considered that before responding. "I'm not denying the power of the premonition you had, or that of a woman who may be psychic, but why not take one thing at a time? You have so much to deal with. Let's deal with the possibility of Tank's death if and when it's a reality. It's possible you're projecting your experience with your child onto what's happening to your husband. Let's take this very, very slowly. If we're going to work together, we can't do everything at once."

"I'm sorry I waited so long," she said. "I apologize for skipping out on our last appointment."

"And I apologize for handling it badly back then. You'll get more out of therapy now, because you'll be paying for it." There was a twinkle in his eye.

Llayne grinned. "Of course. How much will I be paying?"

"Sixty dollars per session. People put more value into what they must pay for. I don't do free counseling anymore. We'll do the same thing we did back then, but now you'll pay attention and work harder to make certain you get your money's worth."

He looked at his watch. Realizing how much of his Saturday evening she'd stolen, she offered to make her first payment. He told her that would begin the next time, and they set appointments for the following Wednesday and Friday evenings, and Mondays and Wednesdays after that. They agreed that twice a week would be best. He walked her down the hall; she heard laughter from what must have been the kitchen; he held the front door for her. A backward glance as she waved caught the empathy expressed on his face, and Llayne knew that this time they would work things out.

◆ ◆ ◆ ◆ ◆ ◆ ◆ ◆

"Hey, honey," Llayne greeted Tank early the next morning. "Are you ready for your tests?"

128

"I sure as hell better be," he grumbled. "Do you know what they do to a nice guy like me around here? First, I had to have an enema! Haven't had one of those since I was a kid and ate too many cheese balls left over from my parents' party, and I got constipated. Gave me a nice visit from one of the Rrhea sisters, I'm telling you."

"Who?"

"You know, Dia Rrhea. As they say, better to get a visit from her than her sister Gono."

"Okay, I get it. Diarrhea and gonorrhea. Ha, ha." She kissed his head at his receding hairline and sat down on the bed beside him.

"And," he continued to whine, sounding very much like the little kid he just talked about having once been, "they made me drink some white, chalky stuff. Yuck! Now they won't give me any breakfast. I'm starving!"

"Want me to go get some fresh donuts from Robaire's and have them ready when you get done?" she asked, knowing she sounded like a placating mother.

"Yeah! Get lots of those glazed donut holes. And some jelly doo-dups!" he said, using his nickname for donuts.

A nurse came and took him away in a wheelchair, which he found ridiculous, and Llayne was told he'd be done in about two hours. So, she walked the few blocks through fluffy snow and sunshine to Robaire's Bakery, went in, and sat at the counter. She bought a box of a dozen glazed donut holes and ate eight of them with orange juice. Robaire's donuts were unlike any she ever had, perfectly fluffy, perfectly tasty, and just plain perfectly good. She savored letting them melt in her mouth. Then she bought a dozen more, adding three big, fat, jelly donuts.

When she got back to the hospital, Tank wasn't ready yet, so she ate four more delicious donut holes, licking her fingers when she was done, while sitting in the waiting room reading rumpled-up, old magazines. Finally she saw him being wheeled back to his room.

"Doo-dups! Doo-dups!" he cheered. He downed the whole box of pastries like an alligator, and before long lunch was brought in and he inhaled that, too.

The phone rang just as Dale came in with a grocery sack. It was Bob, in Detroit, and Tank had quite a time convincing him he didn't have to come to Mt. Pleasant, as Dale had suggested to him earlier on the phone.

Dale, in the meantime, seemed to be moving in. Having surveyed the hallway to make certain no one was spying on them, he pulled a six-pack of Budweiser beer out of the sack, scavenged in his pocket for an opener, and opened one each for Tank and himself. He opened the window and put the rest of the pack on the ledge in the snow. He took a cold bottle of Coke out of the bag and opened it for Llayne. Then the cornucopia of a sack produced a big bag of pretzels, a bigger bag of Lay's potato chips and a jumbo container of French onion dip. The small cadre of friends settled in to watch Michigan play Notre Dame on TV.

"Mis-sus Tanner!" Miss Brundage, the stoic nurse, yelled as she stormed into the room. "You cannot sit on the bed! And you," she turned on Dale, "get your feet down! That is not sanitary!" Dale, sitting in an arm chair, dropped his feet off the foot of the bed, but Llayne didn't budge from her husband's side. Miss Brundage glared at her. "Well!" she seethed, realizing that nothing short of a fist-a-cuffs could make this insolent young woman behave. "I'll have to tell the doctor about this!" With a huge "humph!" she blasted out of the room. Thankfully, she'd been so upset about Llayne sitting on top of the bed, she hadn't noticed the guys stuffing beer and junk food under it.

An hour later, Dr. Klickensteiner came in with an x-ray under his arm. He was quicker than the nurse and glimpsed the brown bottles of brew as the guys hid them, again. Only a flicker of response crossed the physician's face, and he said to Tank and Llayne, "I have the test results and need to discuss them with you." Nodding at Dale, he said, "You'll need to step outside."

"He can stay," Tank asserted. "He's cool. This is Dale LaBlanc. Dale, Dr. Klickensteiner." The two men shook hands.

The doctor ran his big hand over his bald head, a gesture which indicated this wasn't easy for him, but he didn't mince words. He said, "There's a growth of some kind in your abdomen. I don't know what it is, exactly, and would like to do surgery tomorrow morning to find out. Here, look at this," he instructed, holding the x-ray up to the window. A large, black hand of many fingers reached out through the lower trunk of Tank's body.

The three younger people went over to the window and stood mute, gawking at the bewildering shadow-picture. Finally, Tank said, "Give it to me straight, doc. Do you think it's cancer?"

Dr. Klickensteiner sighed. "I'm afraid that's what it looks like. We'll know for certain after surgery. We'll run lab tests on a sample, and take out as much as we can. But with some kinds of cancer, it's not good to remove it. That just aggravates it. So, it's a judgment call once I get in there and look at it. There's always a possibility it's a benign tumor that won't cause any trouble except for the need to be removed." Even with that last hopeful sentence, the man looked burdened and sad.

"Don't worry, doc," Tank said, lightening the mood. "I know you'll do your best. Hey, I survived Nam. I'll survive this, too."

The physician looked at the handsome, athletic, young man and marveled at his positive attitude. "I hope so, son," he said. "I hope so." He started to leave, then turned around with an after-thought. "Oh, after supper, no more food today. Someone will be in later to prep you for surgery. And definitely no more beer." A slight grin escaped from his lips. "Miss Brundage is quite upset enough as it is."

They watched more TV until Dale's parents came to visit, then Bob showed up at suppertime with a large Domino's pizza. Dale had called him again to tell him about the surgery and he "hauled ass," as he said, to get to Mt. Pleasant from Detroit. He offered comic relief with his red tennis shoes, and Tank razzed the huge man unmercifully, asking him if he were the new dainty Dorothy in the *Wizard of Oz*.

At eight o'clock all of the visitors were kicked out by a scowling Miss Brundage.

Chapter 11

"Mrs. Tanner," Dr. Klickensteiner said, arousing Llayne from the stupor she fell into in the waiting room. It was noon, the surgery had begun at seven. "Your husband is out of surgery and doing fine in the recovery room. May I talk to you?" He motioned down the hall.

"Sure," she said. "Can Dale and Bob come?" The doctor nodded assent.

Dale's mom, also waiting with them, hugged her son, Bob, and Llayne, then the three young adults followed the doctor down the long hall. He ushered them into a small filing room and shut the door. They found folding chairs while he sat on the edge of a messy desk. He took the green, surgical skull cap off of his bare head, then looked at Llayne.

"I'm afraid it doesn't look good," he said. "It is cancer. Lymphoma. Cancer of the lymph glands, a network of tube-like structures that cleanse the entire body. That means the cancer cells could have traveled anywhere. It could be everywhere, or it could be nowhere. We just won't know unless it shows up someplace else in his body." Llayne admired this man's bluntness. He could be trusted. He went on, "The tumor in his abdomen infected his spleen and we had to remove it. A person can live, however, without a spleen. And the tumor was pressing on a major artery that would have caused the pain in his leg. We've relieved a lot of the pressure, but couldn't remove the whole tumor. He'll begin chemotherapy, drug therapy and radiation treatments to shrink what's left. So, the bad news is that it's cancer. The good news is that he's young and healthy and new discoveries about cancer cures are being made everyday. Whether or not there will be a cure in time for him, I honestly don't know. His chances are 50-50."

None of his listeners said anything as the doctor's words torpedoed them.

"Tell us what to do to help him," Bob finally said.

"We'll do anything," Dale added.

The response was, "You're doing it. You're being his friends."

Later, when Tank aroused to a slightly somnolent state and was back in his room, Dr. Klickensteiner repeated directly to the patient the results of the surgery.

That's when Llayne went into action, becoming a mother lioness protecting her cub. She lectured her groggy husband on the importance of a positive attitude. She fluffed his pillows. She told him he must eat right, stay healthy and exercise. He must not let the treatments get him down. He must survive!

♦ ♦ ♦ ♦ ♦ ♦ ♦ ♦

The next afternoon when everyone was hanging out in Tank's room, Miss Brundage rushed in with clean bandages. Stiffly, she lifted the covers, peered down at Tank's abdomen, and said in a curt voice, "That's not as long as I thought it would be."

"Why, Miss Brundage," Tank said with a slick smirk, "I do hope you're referring to my scar."

The old battle-ax huffed and puffed, dutifully changed the long bandage, then huffed and puffed again as she fled the diabolical room. Everyone broke into laughter as soon as she was gone.

Bob would be returning to Detroit, and work, the next morning, so he treated everyone to more Domino's pizza that evening. The patient had quickly regained his appetite and ate half of a large all by himself. Llayne was elated that her dear husband was doing so well!

At their second appointment, Llayne and Dr. Lichenger concentrated on her feelings regarding the birth of her dead child, her perception of a lack of options in the situation, and the absence of family support for this or any emotional event in her life. She hadn't even told her parents yet about Tank's illness. It would just be a hassle, having to deal with her mom's passivity and her dad's drunkenness on top of everything else.

She could sense Dr. Lichenger's style right away. He wasn't going to let her get away with whining about her parents. He was going to encourage her to accept the fact that they were as they were, to learn from that, and to move on with her life.

"And now," he said, with 15 minutes left to their session, "let's talk about your husband's illness. The surgery went okay and the test results are in?"

"Yes. And although he has lymphoma, cancer, he's doing just great!"

"I see. What does his doctor say?"

"Dr. Klickensteiner says his chances are 50-50. But he's obviously in the 50 percent that'll make it. He feels fine, he's eating like a horse, and he had his first chemotherapy treatment and it didn't bother him at all. They told him to expect an upset stomach, but as soon as it was done, he ate a whole plateful of homemade brownies a friend had brought." She smiled over the marvel that was her husband.

"And what do you think now about the premonition you had?"

"That was so stupid! I can't believe I let it bother me! And some crazy, old, Indian woman telling me bad things would happen. Pfft!" She shook her head in dismissal.

Dr. Lichenger thoughtfully leaned forward, placing his elbows on his knees, and allowed silence to hang in the air as he considered what his patient had just said. He told her, "There's something I'm going to ask you to do, Llayne. This is important. It would be good if you could do it before our next session. There's a woman named Dr. Elizabeth Kubler-Ross. She researches death and dying. Go to the library and find any one of her books, and read as much of it as you can before we meet again. Don't worry, it'll be pretty fast reading. Dr. Ross believes that when death is imminent, people who are dying and their loved ones go through three stages: denial, anger and acceptance. Although most start with denial, no one seems to glide nicely through the stages. A person can be in

132

denial at nine in the morning, accepting at noon, and furious by three in the afternoon. It's a real roller-coaster ride. And there's no way to stop it. But understanding it, anticipating it, can help. I'd like to see what you think about her work. Will you read it?"

"Sure," she said to placate him. She knew she didn't really need to read it because Tank's death was not "imminent."

She beat a hasty retreat to Kerina's house, where she still had time to catch the last half of Scheherazade rehearsal. There she danced all of her cares away.

♦ ♦ ♦ ♦ ♦ ♦ ♦ ♦

"Hey, Doc K, I'm all better," Tank reassured Dr. Klickensteiner. "I can do this chemo stuff as an outpatient, can't I? I'm ready to go home!"

The conscientious physician reminded him that he had a major operation just five days earlier and there might be an accumulative effect of the treatments. He might get sick yet. He needed to stay for one more day, at least.

Tank pouted like a kid. "Ah, geez! It's so boring in here!"

Dr. Klickensteiner lowered his glasses on his nose and looked over them at his petulant patient. "It seems to me you've been having a pretty good time. What with the beer you keep on the ledge outside the window, and the assortment of people who constantly stream in and out, and climbing out the window last night and leaving for awhile."

Now Tank looked like a little boy with his hand caught in the cookie jar. Llayne asked, "Where'd you go?"

He confessed, "You were out belly dancin', so Dale and I just went down the street to shoot a few hoops in the park."

Llayne was incredulous. "In the snow?"

"It was a real nice night. Hardly even cold. We're having a warm spell, don't you think?"

Dr. Klickensteiner said, "Let's not get off track here. Your treatments are very important. You need to stay healthy. No colds, no flu, no sniffles would help. Take it easy, my friend." Even though he reprimanded his patient, it was obvious the doctor liked Tank. Maybe he even envied Tank's childlike bent for fun and wished he himself could relax long enough to do something spontaneous and crazy. He turned to leave, then had another thought. "Oh, by the way, some of the nurses have asked that you tell the Indian medicine man not to burn his 'magic' sticks in here. They think they stink up the place."

"Sure, Doc K, whatever you say. Hey! By the way, I've decided if my hair falls out, more than it already is, like everybody keeps telling me it will, I'm just gonna shave it all off and call it the Klickensteiner Cut. I wanna be cool like you!" Tank ran his hand over his head like the physician sometimes did.

The doctor let go of a rare, genuine smile, which gave a whole new look to his face. "All right!" he said. "Cool like me," he said in disbelief. "That's one way I've never thought of myself." He let go of a huge smile again as he left the room.

The moment he was gone, Tank returned to the persuasive argument he'd been delivering to his wife when the doctor had come in. "Come on, honey," Tank entreated, pulling on his wife's arm as she lay on his hospital bed, where she plopped down the moment they were alone again. He was up and raring to go, and she was tired. She danced until almost midnight at Kerina's house the night before. "No one will know!" he reassured her. His energy amazed her. He'd been poked and prodded and perforated, and she was exhausted.

"What if Miss Brundage comes in?" she asked to stall him, so she could rest.

"Want me to ask her to join us?" He laughed heartily at his own sick joke, then said, "Nah, her shift doesn't start for another hour. Believe me, I've got the routine down: seven a.m., putrid breakfast brought by perky, volunteer candy-striper with tight buns; eight a.m., you show up with real food from Robaire's; nine o'clock, tests run by mean vampire technician who loves my blood; nine-thirty, chemo, boring, boring, boring, with drugs dripping into my arm in a room with no TV where I'd go berserk if you weren't with me; eleven-thirty, putrid lunch brought by same perky, volunteer candy-striper with the good buns." She playfully gave him a slap across his thigh. "Ha!" he laughed, "but her buns aren't as good as yours, of course." He reached underneath her and pinched her behind, and she slapped his hand away. "Then," he continued his recitation, "early in the afternoon, Doc K comes in to check on me. See, that's done. Then nothing happens until three when Miss Brundage comes on duty and I have to think up ways to annoy her. So, no one will bother us. Come on, Lela!" he coaxed, nibbling at her neck. "It's been almost a week!"

She couldn't resist him. "Okay," she relented, "but we're going to be very, very careful of your surgery scar."

"Sure, sure," he agreed, leading her by the hand into the small, white, sterile bathroom to the side of his bed.

Once inside, with the door securely closed, they made love with Llayne bent over the sink, silently vowing to herself that she would never, never, let this man know that having intercourse with him now frightened her, that she harbored an irrational fear that his cancer would spill from his body into her own. And if his cancer didn't get her, maybe all of those strong drugs would. She closed her eyes and forced her fear into a dark recess of her mind, allowing her to concentrate on the decision she made the day she learned he had cancer. On that day she stopped taking her birth control pills.

Afterward, she wanted to take a nap, but he needed more exercise, he said. "Let's take a walk around the hospital. I need to burn off some energy!"

Llayne plodded behind as he jogged, bounced, shadow boxed, skipped an imaginary rope and was a general nuisance in the long, pale halls. Many a nurse shot a reprimanding look at him, but no one told him to stop. It was obvious that, except for Miss Brundage, he'd become a favorite.

"Hey, Nurse Sarah," he winked at a 200-pound nurse, "ya wanna jog with me?"

"I ain't goin' nowhere with the likes of you," Nurse Sarah laughed, wagging a finger at him. She went on to her next patient with a smile on her chubby cheeks.

"Hello, Vampire John," Tank shot a forefinger at a technician.

The guy, pushing a cart covered with instruments and needles and vials, grinned at him and said, "Hey, blood man. I'll be back for more tomorrow."

"Yeah," Tank, the blood man, said, "and you're gonna go drain some other poor victim right now, aren't ya?"

"You bet!" the technician said, acting like a vampire, pushing his exposed teeth into an overbite and clawing his hand, before disappearing into a room.

Tank laughed as he led Llayne into the emergency exit stairwell. She was thankful for a place to sit, on a landing, while he ran up and down, up and down, taking two steps at a time.

"Hey, Lela, look at this!" he urged. Just as she glanced up half a flight, he jerked open his robe and flashed his naked body. At that very moment a candy-striper, who appeared to Llayne to be the one with the tight buns, barged through the door behind Llayne, putting the girl at eye level with Tank's lively boner. Totally shocked, the cutie screamed and dropped the tray she'd been carrying. The pills, in small paper cups, bounced every-which-way down the stairs.

"Oh! I'm so sorry!" Tank tried to apologize, but the girl had already disappeared back through the door. "Geez! I didn't mean to scare her," he moaned, coming to sit by his wife, with his robe wrapped tightly around him.

"Honey," she reassured him, "this is a hospital. She sees naked men all the time. If she doesn't, she's not doing her job."

His grin was huge and very sly. "Well, then, I guess she's just never seen one as good as this!"

They went back to his bathroom and made love again.

The next day Miss Brundage checked him out, almost throwing him out of the hospital. He gave most of the flowers which had been sent to him to the children's ward, with one big bouquet of pastel carnations going to the nurse's station, and a bouquet of red roses for Llayne to take home. Many of the staff made a point of saying good-bye and wishing him well.

As the next few weeks passed, the young couple fell into a routine of going back to work and fitting his treatments into their schedule after work. Sometimes Llayne couldn't get home in time and he went alone. But, he said that didn't bother him at all.

Indeed, he went back to watching and participating in sports as much as he had before. And, she went back to dancing at Kerina's once a week. Tank encouraged her to do the things she liked and not worry about him. She also continued to see Dr. Lichenger, but she didn't like it so much anymore and cut her appointments down to once a week. They were getting to be a hassle. After all, there was no longer any urgency, because Tank was doing just great.

Christmastime approached and Llayne asked Dr. Lichenger if he wanted to skip the holiday week. He explained that Hanukkah wasn't all that big a religious holiday for Jews. She hadn't known that Jews didn't celebrate Christmas and tried to mask her ignorance. They met two days before Christmas.

She never got around to reading that Dr. Ross' work on death and dying. He asked her about it again. "No, I don't really think it applies to us," she said. "Tank isn't dying. He's doing fine."

Dr. Lichenger pondered that statement, then replied, "Llayne, I know I told you in the beginning not to worry until you had all the facts about your husband's illness. Now you have the facts. This is a deadly kind of cancer. It is possible, even probable, that your husband will die from it. Remember when I said that denial is the first stage people go through? I think you and Tank are both in denial. You both need to face the facts and prepare. Make legal arrangements, financial arrangements. Does he have a will? He should have. Then you can put those kinds of worries behind you and concentrate on keeping him as well as possible for as long as possible. And if he lives to be an old man and you prove me wrong, so be it. But you could end up in an awful mess, financially and otherwise, by not being ready for any eventuality. You're both preoccupied and just not thinking about those kinds of things now. But, if he thought about it, I bet your husband would want to do whatever he could to make sure you'd be okay if he does die."

She liked this man immensely during that first evening that Tank was in the hospital when she so badly needed someone to talk to. Now he was annoying her again, just like the old days. "I can't come for the next couple of weeks," she said abruptly. "We have to go to the University of Michigan Hospital. They have some new drugs for Tank's kind of cancer and they're going to try them out on him."

He asked if she'd like to make an appointment for the following week.

"Well, I'll call you," she lied. "I don't know exactly how long we'll be gone."

He resisted, but she insisted. Her desire not to talk about all of this bullshit anymore was just too strong.

When she drove away she saw him looking out of a window at her with dark, limpid eyes.

◆ ◆ ◆ ◆ ◆ ◆ ◆ ◆

They'd had a fun Christmas, surrounded by friends, and now New Year's Eve was even better! James Brown shouted from the stereo, there was food and booze aplenty, and about 30 people were crammed into their tiny apartment. There was Dale and his date, who paid little attention to one another; Bob, in blue, low-ride boots which matched his blue shirt, and his betrothed, Delia; Kevin and his wife; Priscilla and Stan, her handsome, blond, new boyfriend, a 30-year-old real estate agent of Dutch heritage from Grand Rapids; a few teachers who Tank worked with and their spouses; Kerina and the rest of Scheherazade, and their husbands; and, some other friends and acquaintances.

"Okay, okay, everybody!" Dale stood in the middle of the living room and shouted. No one paid a bit of attention. He stuck two fingers in his mouth and let out a shrill whistle. That caught a little bit of attention, so he did it again, and more people looked his way. "I have something to say!" he screamed.

"Oo-ooo! Quiet down everybody!" Tank commanded, turning down the stereo. "The man here has *something to say!*"

Many others mocked Dale's sudden, uncharacteristic seriousness with oo's and ah's. He stood on a footstool and yelled, "I've got something important to read!"

Bob piped up, "You can read?" That elicited a lot of laughs.

"Yeah," Dale razzed his childhood buddy, "something you know nothing about! Okay. Now!" He cleared his throat nervously and pulled a crib sheet out of his pocket, glanced at it, and said, "As we all know, our friend Bob is getting married on Valentine's Day. Well, the Saturday night before, Tank and I are hosting the bachelor party to beat all bachelor parties! Seven-thirty, meet at The Bird downtown. And every man in here is invited!" That garnered a lot of male cheers, especially from guys who just met Bob for the first time that night. "What you girls are gonna do that night, we don't know, and we don't care!" he said, laughing. "We, however, are going to have dancers like you've never seen before!"

"Oh, yeah?" Kerina asserted. "Honey, boy, you've never even seen real dancing!" Good naturedly, she started to sway her hips and belly roll right in front of Dale, and his jaw dropped to his knees. Tank turned up the music and she let loose, her long, red dress and jangling jewelry accentuating her sexy moves. The men cheered wildly! Not one to be left out, however, although totally untrained, Priscilla jumped in and joined her. Tank, of course, couldn't be ignored, either, so he pulled up his shirt and had his friends in stitches with his exaggerated belly thrusts. Everyone joined in and the room went wild with frenzied, primitive dancing, until Tank noticed the clock and started handing out glasses of champagne to celebrate midnight.

At the stroke of 12 he shouted, "It's 1972! Happy New Year!" He and Llayne drew on a long kiss, then looked into one another's eyes and promised that 1972 would be the year they'd bring a new life into the world.

◆ ◆ ◆ ◆ ◆ ◆ ◆ ◆

137

Tank slept like a baby in the backseat of the Cutlass, cuddling his pillow and blankie. Llayne glanced back and was glad he conked out before seeing how bad Highway 23 had become. When they had left Mt. Pleasant three hours earlier, there had just been a light snowfall. Now they were in the middle of a full-blown blizzard.

"Damn" she whispered to herself. "I can't see a thing!" She tried wiping the inside of the front window with her gloved hand, but to no avail. It was a frozen, white waterfall coming at her from outside, and visibility was almost zero. At a snail's pace, she let state highway signs show her where the road was, even though she couldn't see the green things until she was right on top of them. And none of them could be deciphered. They were too covered with ice and snow. Just little bits of the corners peeked out to guide her way.

But there was no way was she going to let this damned storm stop her from reaching the University of Michigan Hospital in Ann Arbor. They had new drugs there. Drugs that Tank needed. And, by god, she would make certain he got there!

The car skidded on ice and she carefully moved the steering wheel in the direction of the spin. The vehicle corrected its course and once again crawled straight down the road. Thank goodness there hadn't been any oncoming cars! Most drivers had wisely decided to stay indoors, so traffic was light. There were a few cars scattered around, stuck in the snow on the sides of the road. Wreckers and police cruisers were often nearby, but pretty soon they wouldn't be able to get through either.

She squinted to try to see past the windshield wipers, flapping away like icy, shaggy wings. But, without them, the pane would instantly be covered with a sheet of ice. It was one of those "white knuckle" trips; she clung so hard to the wheel her knuckles were undoubtedly white under her thick gloves.

Thank goodness they had left at seven a.m., even though it was usually a two-and-a-half-hour drive and their appointment wasn't until one in the afternoon. At the rate they were going, they'd just make it.

Finally, the exit sign for Ann Arbor loomed ahead! Enough snow had blown away that she could read *-nn Arb—*. Then, suddenly, about a quarter of a mile from the exit, the Cutlass died. It just died, dead, kaput. Slowly, she coasted to the side of the road, seething under her breath. "You goddamned motherfucker! Don't you dare die on me now!"

"Honey, did you say something?" Tank asked innocently, having been roused in the backseat.

"Oh, well, sweetie," she said, mustering up every bit of calmness she could, "the car just stopped. The engine seems dead. See?" She tried to start it. Nothing. Tank pulled himself up and watched as she tried again. Nothing.

"Geez!" he exclaimed. "This sucker's deader than a doornail!"

She tried intermittently for 10 minutes, but it wasn't going anywhere. "Listen, sweetheart," she said soothingly, "I'm going to have to walk to the gas station that's at the end of this exit."

"Damn! It's snowed a lot!" he said, concerned. "How can you tell there's a station down there? I can't see a thing."

"There was a sign for it back a ways," she lied. She had to take a chance there would be a station. She had to try to get help because help wasn't coming to them, of that she felt certain. Every wrecker or police car was by now either occupied or stuck themselves. "It isn't far," she reassured him.

"I don't know, Lela," he stalled. "I don't want you out there. It looks treacherous. Let's just wait until a police car comes by."

"Honey, we can't wait that long. We'll freeze to death first. Look, I've got warm clothes on. Boots, coat, scarf, hat, gloves. I'll be fine. I'll be back in no time."

He glared outside and was appalled at what he saw. "God, I'm sorry. You're going through all this hell for me. Listen, let me go. I'm feeling much better. I'll do it."

"No! You've had that wretched flu ever since New Year's Day, and you were in pain this morning and took one of those strong pain pills. There's no way I'm going to let you go out there and pass out in a snow bank. Absolutely not!"

"I'm so sorry," he moaned. "I hate this. I just hate it!"

"Hey, no problem," she said, stretching around to kiss him. "I love you."

"I love you, too," he said, dismayed as she got out of the car in a hurry, closing the door quickly so not too much of a Canadian blast would blast him. She wrapped her scarf tightly around her neck and mouth, and turned to wave. He waved back, his broad face looking sad and helpless through the frozen glass.

The moment her back was to him her demeanor changed. "That goddamned useless piece of shit Cutlass!" she seethed, her voice muffled though her thick scarf. "I hate its frigging guts. Nothing but a pile of trash! Leave my husband out there to freeze to death. No way! And You! God! Where in hell are You? How could You let a good man like this go through all this shit? Why don't You go pick on some damned ax murderer or something? We've got plenty of them around. And they seem to be healthy enough to kill and kill over and over again. Where are You? You Bastard! I hate You! Do You hear me? I hate You!" Her tears froze the moment they fell from her eyes, her lashes hung with globules of ice, the tiny hairs inside her nose had frozen, making each breath feel like a freight train moving through her nostrils, snow fell into the sides of her boots and each step felt like she was lugging lead boots. Trouncing through snow banks, sometimes three feet tall, she cussed and cried all the way across the field that appeared to be a shortcut between the Cutlass and what should be the end of the exit ramp.

Twenty minutes passed, and the young gas station attendant looked up in surprise when she entered his Shell station. He hadn't seen a car drive up. "Why, hello, m'am," he said politely. "My gosh! Here, let me help you!" He took the crying snowwoman by the elbow and led her around the counter to the back of the small station, where an old man sat by the fire of a Franklin stove. The old guy immediately gave up his chair and Llayne plopped down. The young man said, "M'am, we have coffee and hot chocolate. Would you like a cup?"

"Cho ... Chocolate," she said, her sobs finally subsiding. "But, I can't stay here. I have to get help to my husband. Our car is dead out on the highway and he has to get to the hospital right away!"

"Okay," the older one said, taking over. "You stay right here by the fire. Get out of your wet coat and boots and things while I call the police. Won't do any good to call a wrecker, but the police will answer. Now, you get dry and warm or you'll catch your death of pneumonia." He went to the phone and dialed while the other guy got her hot chocolate.

She took off her gloves and hat and scarf and coat and laid them out on a stack of tires by the stove. Then she took off her boots and turned toward an oily patch of cement to empty them of snow and water. She left on her thick, wet socks as she stuck her toes up to the toasty, warm fire and ran her fingers through her soaked, matted hair to encourage it to dry. The heat was bliss. Slowly, she began to thaw as she wolfed down the hot chocolate. The young man brought her another.

"The police want to talk to you," the old man said, handing her the phone.

They wanted to know if her husband's illness was contagious. "God, I hope not," she said. "It's cancer."

Within five minutes a police cruiser with big snow chains on its tires pulled into the station to pick her up. It was miserable putting on her damp outer garments and leaving that fire to go back out into the cold, but she was relieved to be getting back to Tank.

They drove backward up the ramp, which didn't matter as no traffic was moving in either direction, and turned the cruiser around beside the Cutlass. Tank was so exhausted that one of the two officers had to help him into the back of the police car, beside Llayne. A wrecker that one of the officers had called showed up to take the car to the station to be fixed. The police drove them to the front entrance of the University of Michigan Hospital, and again one of the policemen helped Tank as he shuffled inside the building.

It wasn't until later that Llayne realized she hadn't thanked the station attendants nor the police. It was inexcusable, but she didn't have the energy to worry about it.

After a half-hour examination of Tank, a Dr. Germaine came out to the waiting room to talk to Llayne. No one else was there, so he didn't hesitate to say, "Mrs. Tanner, I'm so sorry, but your husband's condition has deteriorated rapidly. I found a lump today on his neck, which means the cancer has developed into lymphosarcoma, a much more aggressive cancer than what they've seen in him to this point. That's why he's had these flu-like symptoms. He was in pain again, so I gave him another strong pain pill. He'll be out most of the afternoon. The experimental drugs that Dr. Klickensteiner wanted me to try on him won't do any good now. The cancer is too far gone. The drugs wouldn't do anything but make him sick. I'm so sorry. The prognosis has changed." When she didn't say anything and just stared at a bland abstract painting on the wall, he added, "Mrs. Tanner, do you understand what I'm saying?"

Her vapid eyes moved to him and dully she said, "I understand." With that she dismissed the useless physician by putting on her soggy coat. She went to get her groggy husband.

They were back in the hospital lobby, coming upon the two gas station attendants waiting for them there, before she gave the Cutlass another thought. The young man, taking Tank's arm, as he obviously needed help standing up, said, "We've fixed it m'am. It had a dead battery, but there's a bran' spankin' new one in there now. It'll be fine."

The old man asked, "Do you need help finding a place to stay tonight?"

At the same moment, Llayne and Tank looked out through the big glass doors, their attention caught by intense sunlight, blinding as it reflected off of snow and ice. "Wow! Look how pretty it is outside," Tank slurred with a grin. "It looks all better out. I'm so sleepy! I sure would like to go home to sleep in my own bed tonight."

"Oh, no!" both attendants protested at the same time.

The older one continued, "The snow clouds have passed over and the sun's out, but the roads will be impassable for days."

Llayne didn't give it a moment's consideration. Her husband wanted to sleep in his own bed, and so he would. "Thanks," she said, "but we already have a place to stay."

The men both nodded, and it was then she remembered she needed to pay them. They absolutely refused to let her give them money. At least she remembered to thank them this time.

She settled Tank into the back of the car and took off toward home. This time it was a fairy tale journey in a wonderland of crystal and white. She wondered if it was possible that the same vengeful God, who had made the first trip such hell, had given her this one as a gift. Although a few cars were splayed about on the highway like tinker toys buried in sparkling sugar, the Cutlass was the only vehicle in motion, blazing a trail through thick snow that parted to reveal a mirror of ice underneath. Surely it was the hand of God which nudged the machine in the right direction. Icicles hung heavily from snow-laden trees and power lines, glistening in the sun. Even those lines that were down and criss-crossing one another on the sides of the road, added an element of tangled glory. It was like journeying through a web of wonder. Millions of diamonds, droplets of melting ice, twinkled everywhere.

About 40 miles from Mt. Pleasant, a snowplow joined her, so she fell in a hundred feet behind it to make the drive easier. At seven that evening, just as the stars were starting their tour of the night sky, she pulled up at the apartment. Tank bestirred long enough to look up at the sky and comment on its beauty. Then he went inside and slept in his own bed, just like he wanted.

Utterly exhausted, Llayne built a fire and drank more hot chocolate in front of it, cozy and warm in her comfy robe. Her eyes refused to close for sleep.

CHAPTER 12

"If you die, I want to die, too," Llayne rolled over in bed and faced her husband. "I can't live without you." The comment came out of nowhere. They had never discussed the trip to Ann Arbor two weeks earlier, nor the prognosis that had come from it.

"Don't talk like that," he soothed, stroking her cheek. "That's ridiculous. If one of us has to die, the other needs to live. Live for both of us. Get married again, have children, enjoy life. That's what I want you to do. That's what I would do."

She thought he might cry but instead, he made love to her. He tired quickly and she pushed aside her fears to provide most of the effort, so that it was a kindhearted, gratifying sharing for them both.

♦ ♦ ♦ ♦ ♦ ♦ ♦ ♦

By mid-January, they both gave up trying to go to work. Oh, she attempted to go to the community college a few days a week to fulfill her obligation as an academic counselor, but the dean of her department had suggested she take a leave of absence. That offer had come on the day he arrived at work at eight in the morning and Llayne had already been there for three hours. Her sleep each night, and Tank's, was so often interrupted with his pain and with getting up to give him medication, that she lost track of time that night. Thinking it was six-thirty, her usual time for getting up, she'd arisen at three-thirty, dressed for work, driven the fifty miles, and not realized her error until seeing the empty parking lot. It'd been pitch black outside, but it was always dark during her morning drive. The sun didn't come up in the winter in Michigan until about the hour she arrived at work. The night janitor had been shocked when she came in at five. He'd hung around, worriedly keeping an eye on her, to tell the dean, who had in turn suggested she stay home for awhile. She readily accepted the offer and at 11 that morning had driven home, so dog-tired she was hardly able to make the trip.

Worn-out and depleted, they stayed home for the next couple of weeks. Lots of people came to visit. Chief Jackson and his granddaughter, Sue, stopped by regularly with the tribe's medicine man, who burned the "magic" sticks that made the house smell like springtime, which Tank loved. Teacher friends came over. The high school principal dropped in one evening, looking haggard and bereft. A thoughtful woman who worked with Llayne drove 60 miles one Saturday afternoon to bring them a loaf of homebaked bread and to ask if she could do anything for them. Of course, there was nothing she could do. And a professor at the community college called to tell Llayne that Tank had been included in his church's prayers. Kerina, unusually somber, came over to bring them a beautifully crafted, gold cross, an antique from her homeland. She offered to hang it on the wall opposite the bed where Tank could see it and he agreed, which surprised Llayne. He never gave a hint of being religious. But he genuinely appreciated the gift. Priscilla and Stan visited from Grand Rapids, and Priscilla spent a day cleaning the apartment while she sent a willing Stan out to do the laundry. Their living conditions had become a little ratty, but neither Llayne nor Tank had noticed, let alone cared. Kevin and his wife visited, and Dr. Klickensteiner called to check on them. Dale's parents came over, and Dale came almost everyday for an hour after work. Bob came on weekends, with Delia, from Detroit.

It was on the third weekend in January when the weird incident took place. Tank, Llayne, Bob, Delia and Dale were watching the news on TV. The newscaster said, "It appears that President Nixon may soon be ending the war in Vietnam. He continues to cut back troops. Some analysts speculate that it may all be over by next year."

Llayne said, "It's about time. There's never been any reason for us to be there anyway."

It was true, she reflected later, that it had been a terribly callous and insensitive remark. But still, Tank's punch rocketed through the air so fast there was no way she could have anticipated nor escaped it, had he not changed its direction at the last instant, and landed his boulder of a fist into the wall instead of her jaw. Even though he hadn't touched her, she reflexively tumbled backward off her chair and onto the floor at the same moment Tank's left hook blew a hole in the plaster beside where her head had been.

They all sat as frozen as arctic glaciers. Tank most of all. Then, quaking in terror over the depth of his repudiated anger, he started to cry. He reached pathetically toward his wife, only to recoil, as if not trusting himself to touch her.

It was Bob who responded first. He said, "Delia, take Llayne for a ride. Leave now." Llayne was in such a state of profound shock, she didn't question the mandate. The women put on their coats and left.

When they came back an hour later, Tank was in bed, lost in a deep sleep. Bob and Dale were quietly fixing the wall, while each nursed a Bud. Llayne never asked them what they did to calm Tank down, and they never offered an explanation. All she knew was that from that day forward, her husband was his old self; the most gentle, teddy bear man alive.

And she knew that she could never again mention Vietnam to him. He wasted a year of his short life there. It was cruel to say it was a waste. Of course, she realized that wasn't the only source of his anger. The real source, the one that ran deeper than any wound that any word or even any weapon of war could make, was the anger that Dr. Lichenger had told her about. The one a person feels when death is "imminent."

In the week that followed, with his bolt of frustrated fury unleashed and spent, Tank gathered a tad more energy and went outside the front door each day to fill the bird feeder. She'd been doing it for him, but he enjoyed doing it again himself and would stand in the snow, watching the excited, small creatures come to feed. Many times he reminded Llayne that the feeder must be kept full because the birds had come to depend on it and had not flown south because of it. Without its seed, they would die in the barren winter.

Then, as the flu-like symptoms set in again and refused to depart, Tank wanted to be left alone in their bed more and more often, with easy listening music on the radio. His body was so achy, he thrashed about trying to get comfortable. Still affectionate, he hugged her, kissed her, and held her hand when he was awake. But once in bed, his body couldn't tolerate much cuddling.

Somewhere in the deepest, darkest corner of her soul, Llayne felt relief at his desire to be left alone, an abatement her conscious mind dare not recognize for fear of guilt, tumultuous guilt over being afraid of the cancer that devoured his torn body, afraid that she might "catch" it, afraid of making love for fear that the deadly chemicals from the intense treatments or the dreaded disease itself might spill with the semen from his thinning body into the core of her own, afraid of the ugly surgery scar that cut his once handsome body from waist to groin, afraid his dying breath would be breathed into her during a kiss, afraid of life without him, afraid of missing him so much she would wither away and die herself, afraid ....

Routinely, she sat beside their bed and silently stroked his head as he fell asleep, then got up to watch television alone for an hour or two, then crawled in beside him and wrapped her arms around his ravaged body. It wasn't long, though, before he sloughed her off in discomfort.

◆ ◆ ◆ ◆ ◆ ◆ ◆ ◆

"Lela! Lela! Wake up!" Tank shouted.

He stood at the side of their bed, jiggling her shoulder. In utter confusion, she squinted her eyes open and looked at the bedroom window. It was still dark outside, the middle of the night. What was he doing up and alert at that hour?

"Come in the kitchen! Those people are in there!" He was as gleeful as a child at Christmas.

My god, she thought, *we're being robbed and he's too doped up to realize it*. She grabbed the phone to call the police.

"What're you doing?" Tank wanted to know.

"Calling the police!"

"No! The police won't understand! They might hurt them, and they're really nice. They took my hands and we danced around the kitchen. They're happy 'cuz I'm gonna come be with them soon! Them and my mommy and daddy! They said I get to see my mommy and daddy real soon!"

A flash of fear seized her chest, then Llayne realized he was hallucinating because of the drugs. She hung up the phone.

"Wanna come meet them?" he asked, excited.

145

"That's okay, honey," she consoled him. "They're gone now." She spoke as gently as possible to the exhilarated child.

"No-oo-o!" Like a six-year-old wanting to show a new friend to mom, Tank took her by the hand and led her into the kitchen. "Oh, they're gone." His disappointment was obvious as they entered the dim room, lighted only by silver-blue moonrays slinking through the window over the sink. "Oh well," he decided brightly, "they said they'll be back!"

He led her to the couch, where he lay down and drew her down with her back to him. Pulling off the boxers he slept in, and lifting off the nightgown she slept in, he gently made love to his wife. It was a rapturous tenderness, a slow burning lust, a deep-seeded desire that gave them the energy to join their bodies in love. It was a sharing so complete that neither of them would ever exist again for one moment of their lives without the other as a part of them.

Afterward he slept peacefully, with his arms wrapped around her, covered by an afghan on the couch. She lay with her eyes open, in awe and fear and, yet, thankful to "them" for coming to give her beloved husband strength and comfort and peace, and for visiting from the other side to prepare him for his upcoming journey. She hoped they were right, that he would be with his parents soon. As much as she knew she would miss him, she knew she couldn't comprehend how happy they would be to see their son again. Squeezing her eyes tightly closed, she silently prayed to God to let it be so.

◆ ◆ ◆ ◆ ◆ ◆ ◆ ◆

"Lela sweetheart, I need your help," he whispered in a hoarse voice.

Her eyes squinted open and saw darkness. Having been awake most of the night she was confused about time. The red and black art deco clock on the fireplace mantel told her it was six o'clock. The sun wasn't up yet.

"What, sweetie? What's wrong?" she asked, stretching forward from beneath the afghan to wrap her arms around his waist as he sat naked on the edge of the couch.

With eyes bleak and yellow from sickness, he looked at her intently. "I want you to help me," he said, his voice soft gravel, "take all the pills. Go get me the pills, honey. I want to take them and get this over with."

She was struck dumb as he fondled her hair, pleading with his sad, sick eyes. She said, "Oh, Tank. I can't do that."

"I wouldn't ask you if I could find them. I know you hide 'em 'cuz you're afraid I'll forget how many I've taken and take too many. Please go get 'em." Suddenly he gasped for breath and doubled over in pain.

"Oh, sweetie! Does it hurt?" She scrambled nearer and wrapped her bare body around him from behind, with her arms around his chest and her legs around his waist, in a wistful hope that such a gesture might transfer strength.

146

"Yes, it's starting to hurt real bad all the time now. I can't stand living like this. This isn't life. Help me end it."

"We can't do that," she repeated, not because she felt it was morally wrong, but because she was a coward.

Humped over in weakness, he sloughed her off. Sitting alone on the end of the couch he looked like a shell of the masculine man he once was, his sallow skin hanging loose on his still broad frame. He'd finally given up. "Well, then," he said determinedly, "take me to the hospital. I wanna go see Doc K."

Llayne was stunned. It never occurred to her that he would want to be anywhere but home if he were dying. The explosion of separation and loss almost annihilated her. Struggling to stay afoot, she fumbled around to hurry up and get dressed. She went outside to scrape snow and ice off the Cutlass and turned it on to warm it up for the short trip to the hospital. Back in the kitchen she called the emergency room to tell them they were coming. When she went back into the bedroom she was amazed to find him dressed and ready to go, with his coat, hat, gloves and boots on, slumped over on the side of the bed.

"Come on, honey. Let's go." She held out her hand to help him up, but instead of rising, he took her hand and held it to his chest.

"Please, Lela," he begged, his eyes pleading into hers.

"Come on," she said softly. "Let's go."

He hung his head in abject despair.

In the car she panicked when she thought he died as he slouched and lost consciousness. But, he came to and she was able to breathe once more.

At the emergency room door a nurse helped them inside. Dr. Klickensteiner, "Doc K," as Tank had come to affectionately call him, was already there. He quickly examined his patient and had him whisked to a room.

The physician looked like a defeated warrior, Llayne thought, as he approached her in the hall. He motioned to a bench and she sat down. Running his hand over his wan, bare head, he dropped down to sit beside her. He examined both of his hands as they moved to and covered his knees, hands that had saved many lives but would not save this one.

Taking a deep breath first, he spoke in a low voice. "I'm sorry. There's not much time. What would you like us to do?"

For an instant she wondered if he was alluding to some sort of life support system, IVs and all that stuff, but let the thought pass as she wouldn't consider anything so ridiculous. This needed to end. Tank wanted for it to end. "Just get rid of the pain," she said.

He looked at her for the first time since sitting down and said, "We'll do the best we can." Slowly, like an old man who had just gathered a hundred years within his being, or the weight of the life of another being, he rose and trudged away to give directions to the attending staff.

147

Llayne joined Tank in his room and watched as the first shot of morphine sent him into an infant's sleep, curled in a fetal ball, his belly rising and falling with each unperturbed breath. A contented smile sat on his lips.

When he awoke he complained of his legs being cold, so she rubbed them through the sheets. He told her that felt good before falling back into deep sleep.

The next time he woke up he asked for another pain shot and a nurse administered it unquestioningly. Before falling asleep, he gripped Llayne's hand, which brought her to full attention because his hand had been limp in hers for most of the day. He moved his lips and she bent down to hear.

"What, honey?" she asked.

"It was wrong."

"What, honey? What was wrong?"

He gasped for breath and whispered, "The Vietnam War. War, any war, is always wrong. And it was wrong of me to get mad at you about it. I'm ... I'm so sorry." Llayne clasped his hand as tears brimmed her eyes.

Hours later as the sun set outside the window, she asked Dale, whom she called about noon, to pray with her. They stood on opposite sides of the bed, one of Tank's hands in each of theirs as they held each other's hands at Tank's chest.

Squeezing her eyes shut in concentration while she tried to remember what prayers sounded like from her youth, she said, "Dear God, You know and I know I haven't been the most faithful churchgoer all these years. In fact, we both know I haven't been since I was about 10. But, that's because I don't believe You would limit Yourself to such small places. I believe You are everywhere, You are with us now. I know I've expressed my, um, displeasure with You lately. Okay, I've told You I hate You. But what I'm asking You now isn't for me, it's for Tank. So, please don't hold what I've said against him. He's such a good, dear, sweet man, Lord. There couldn't be a better person on this earth. Please help him. Please help him come into Your arms. Let him see his parents. Let him be at peace." The words stuck in her throat and she couldn't go on. Lowering her head to Tank's chest, she cried. She and Dale continued to clasp hands as he, too, wept.

A short while later, instinctively understanding that he should, Dale left the room, leaving the young couple alone. She sat up on the bed, holding her husband's head in her lap, stroking the two wonderful strips of slick skin where his hair receded from his forehead. Tank roused and looked up into her eyes. For the first time in days, his hazel eyes were luminous, seeing her perfectly clearly. He smiled broadly and his masculine jaw squared itself off. He looked profoundly handsome.

"I love you, Lela," he said, his voice strong and husky. "Thank you for being my wife."

Pressing her lips so gently to his forehead that it could have been a kiss from an angel, she smiled and whispered, "You're welcome. Thank you for being my husband. I love you and will always love you."

148

"I know," he replied, a broad grin lighting up his beautiful face. "And my love will always be with you." Snuggling his head deeper into her lap and turning to kiss her hand, Tommy "Tank" Tanner closed his eyes and died.

Cradling his head to her chest and stroking his forehead, Llayne sobbed uncontrollably.

♦ ♦ ♦ ♦ ♦ ♦ ♦ ♦

Dr. Klickensteiner fell hopelessly into the chair next to Llayne in the hospital hallway. He apologized for something that wasn't his fault, his patient's death, and his pain over that loss was evident.

"He liked you so much," Llayne told him. "Thank you for taking such good care of him."

The physician devotedly asked if they could do an autopsy, reminding her that anything that could be learned might be helpful to others. He said total respect is kept in dealing with the body; indeed he spoke of the human body as if it were sacred.

Llayne had never given that any thought, but instantly knew that Tank would want to help others. She agreed to the autopsy, after which they would cremate the remains.

He asked if she wanted to see the body one last time. She declined, wanting to remember her husband as he'd been when she last saw him alive.

"Is there anything else I can do for you?" the doctor asked. "We could get you a cold compress to put on your eyes."

She actually chuckled. Her eyes, red, swollen and sore from crying, hadn't even crossed her mind. "No," she declined. "They'll be okay."

"Well, try to get some sleep," the ever-mindful physician advised.

"Sure," she said to appease him. "I'll do my best."

Methodically, he rubbed his knees with his big hands, and eventually said, "His wedding ring. Would you like to have it or do you want it left with him?"

"Oh, I'd like to have it!"

"I'll get it for you," he said, rising.

She asked, "What happens to the clothes he wore in here?"

"We can get them for you."

"Yes, I'd like them, please. I'm going to give his clothes to the Salvation Army. He'd like his warm things to go to people in need."

He nodded agreement and said, "I'll go get his ring." Relieved to have an assignment, a tangible task to perform, he disappeared down the hall. Five minutes later he came back with the ring.

Handing it to her, he said, "They'll have his clothes for you in a few minutes. Goodbye, Mrs. Tanner." They shook hands, then, not knowing what else to say or do, he briskly disappeared.

Tank's gold band burned Llayne's palm. Had it really been on her live husband's finger as recently as yesterday? How could something as useless as a ring survive, but not him? She unhooked the gold chain she always wore around her neck, slipped the wedding band onto it and put it back on. The feel of Tank's ring on her throat gave her comfort.

She stood up, waiting motionlessly in the long, bland hall and wondering at all the whiteness. A nurse entered through a door at the far end. They were the only people in the usually crowded, bleached, corridor tube.

As the woman walked toward her, Llayne couldn't tell what she had in her hand. She was all white with the first bright rays of morning light illuminating her as it streamed in clear prismed beams through the glass in a double door behind her. The light moved in crystal clear rays as she moved, suspending her in air as she flowed gracefully down the long, milky hall. The glow cast an ethereal halo about her head, distorting her features into those of an angelic alien. Only the bulk of what she was carrying seemed out of sync. The glare of light made it hard to tell what it was, but it was black. So much white, and a ball of black. There had been so much white in Llayne's and Tank's life together - the white of her homecoming gown, her white wedding dress, the white snow, white hospitals. Why, she wondered, does life have to be black or white? As the other woman drew nearer she could see the object better ... it was ... a garbage bag.

With her final step the nurse transpired the stream of light and stood before Llayne. The two women stared into one another. It was Miss Brundage, and for the first time, Llayne saw the tenderness beneath her tough exterior.

Embarrassed, the nurse handed the wife the garbage bag. "I'm sorry," she said, "this is all I could find to put his clothes in."

"That's all right." Llayne took the bulky bag of heavy winter clothes.

"I'm sorry," Miss Brundage said again. This time she didn't mean the bag.

"So am I."

With matching misty eyes they looked at one another for a moment too long as people do in discomfort, then turned and forever walked their separate ways.

Who would have predicted that a scant six months after a wedding there would be a memorial service for the groom? Five hundred people crammed into the Central Michigan University Chapel. The reverend's dulcet voice rose over the crowd. Sun shone through the opulently colored windows. Soft human skin touched sublime hard wood. But nothing brought joy. Sadness ate into every soul; sadness devoured the air; sadness painted the house of God a dull coat of gruesome grief.

Llayne didn't cry. She supposed it was expected of her and didn't know why she didn't. There simply were no more tears inside of her. There was nothing inside of her.

"Llayne, there's something you need to know."

Llayne recognized the woman speaking as Ann Harris, who'd been in Tank's Mt. Pleasant High School graduating class and who recently moved back to town after a divorce. She looked like so many women who were popular in high school but didn't move on in life, becoming has-beens before they've really been. Her hair was bleached and teased, out of style, and her tight dress clung to a lumpy body. Has-been Ann had obviously lost track of her 7&7s.

They stood amidst the lovely burnt orange and brown decor of the basement banquet room at the Embers Restaurant, where Kevin had arranged a gathering after the memorial service. A bar with a white uniformed bartender provided libations.

"Listen," Anne said conspiratorially, "you know the Big T and I were long-time chums. I mean, I knew him long before you ever came to town." She took a slug of booze from her cocktail glass. "We were friends in high school, and when I saw how he filled-out at college I would've grabbed him in a minute if he would've let me. He wouldn't give me a tumble then because I was preggers and hitched. Well! I just think you should know. A few months ago I tried again to get the Big T to give me a roll in the hay. You know, I was so lonely after my divorce and all. Told him a bunch of us old buddies were meeting, then I was there all by my little lonesome. Well! He wouldn't do it. Said he was married to you, and that was that!" Her arms swung open to emphasize her story and a splash of alcohol spilled on her wrist. She licked it off, then tapped a flimsy finger at Llayne's sternum. Llayne remembered the incident well, because he asked her to go and she declined, telling him she'd be in the way as he reminisced with his old friends. "Well!" Ann slurred. "I wanted you to know your husband was faithful to you." Raising her glass in a lone toast, she gulped.

"Ann, I already knew that. I wouldn't have been married to him otherwise." The drunk looked bewildered for a moment, until remembering which way to the bar.

Llayne wandered through the obstacles she recognized as people. A teacher named Steve Robbins, who worked with Tank at the high school, consoled a group of teachers. When Llayne walked by he gave his condolences and handed her a poem he wrote. He left her alone to read:

Ode to a Friend

We walked among the poplar and pine
Looking for a hopeful sign.
The future held no earthly plan
For this man I called my friend
The whimpering wind with sorrowful sighing
Mourned with me - my friend was dying.

While he lives upon this earth,
He cherishes life and knows its worth.

He stands before all - tall and strong -
He understands his time's not long.
His death he faces with no crying.
"The price," he says, "of life is dying."

The hour has come - draw the veil.
No word of comfort should prevail.
I mourn not his physical death
For his spirit spans the breadth
Of any earthly chasm or goal.
So silence the bell - it need not toll.

Save its sound for those who die
Without knowing a morning sky,
Or sleeping on the earth's good land,
Or sensing the feel in a child's hand.
These are his - so silence the bell.
These are his - he knows them well....

"Llayne!" the neighbor woman she barely knew interrupted just as Priscilla walked up and was about to speak too, but the intruder was so intense both younger women turned to listen. The old woman with a mass of silver hair sprayed into a helmet took Llayne's hand. Llayne marveled at how often her hand had been grasped on this day. It annoyed her, having people touch her as though her husband's death made her body public property. The neighbor woman leaned close, her spicy perfume hitting like a bomb, to give her condolences, as had so many.

"I know just how you feel, darling," she said. "It's so difficult, losing a loved one. Nothing can replace what you've had together. I know! Last year my dear Amos died, and my life hasn't been the same since."

Priscilla asked, "Was Amos your husband?"

"Oh dear no! Ole Charlie, my husband, kicked the bucket years ago. Amos was my sweet fox terrier and he was one of the family. It was a great loss."

Priscilla recovered from shock first and grabbed her friend's arm, pulling her away. They landed directly in front of a vaguely familiar couple who reminded Llayne that she was young and would remarry. Priscilla pulled her away before they both started slugging their way out.

"Let me get you a Coke," Priscilla offered, depositing Llayne in a secluded, fern-strewn alcove. Llayne watched her friend walk away and thought she'd never seen her look so sophisticated, in her plain, navy blue suit, with her thick, auburn hair falling straight to her shoulders. Llayne surveyed the rest of the room. There were professors and college administrators who'd been friends of Tank's parents; school teachers; business people; Chippewas; strangers. There were Dale and Bob talking to Stan, Priscilla's nice boyfriend, who was as blond and tall and handsome as ever. Dale looked totally bereft. Bob was terribly subdued, even wearing plain, black, dress shoes with his neat, black suit. Then there was Kevin, running around to make certain the food and drink service was good. Kerina, elegantly dressed in a brown Chanel suit that matched her eyes, with black piping that matched her hair, which was up in a French twist, and wearing simple pearl-and-diamond jewels, looked like royalty as she talked quietly with townspeople whom she knew. So many people. So many words. Words, words, words. They couldn't bring Tank back.

"There you are!" Kerina said, joining her in her corner. "You okay?"

"No," Llayne replied, relieved to be able to be honest with her friend.

"No kidding! Geez! Americans should drink less and dance more," the Turkish woman noted, looking out at the crowd. "You know, we need a mourning dance ritual for funerals. Help us all express our grief, and get it out. Americans are so uptight about emotions!

"It would help you, too, honey," she suggested, hugging Llayne around the waist. "Come back and dance with us as soon as you can."

"I will," Llayne promised.

Suddenly Rosie Saleman, the sexy ex-consort of Tank's, appeared before them. Both women's eyes popped as they quickly appraised the willowy, six-foot-tall dazzler from head to foot. Kerina, not knowing who she was but catching the jitters in the lulu's eyes, said, "I'll leave you two alone to talk. Llayne, honey, I'll be right over here if you need me."

"Oh! Okay," Llayne said after her friend, briefly tearing her gaze away from Rosie to see Kerina walk away. Her eyes, however, shot back to the intruder, like a bullet to a target. Llayne didn't know what to say to the Playboy Bunny, who just stood there, so they leered at each other uncomfortably. Then a bolt out of the blue image of Rosie dancing wildly with Tank at The Cabin came uninvited into Llayne's head and offered a carefree moment of relief that almost made her laugh. That memory was very different from the woman standing in front of her now. Rosie had found a style that made her more sexy than ever. Rather than boldly advertising her voluptuous body like she used to, now her blatant sexuality hovered beneath a demure, black chemise dress. A small, ruby-studded, gold broach was her only accessory, her abundant strawberry-blond hair was pulled into a wispy chignon at the nape of her neck, pinkish, curly tendrils around her face emphasized her perfect porcelain skin. She was drop-dead gorgeous and it was impossible at that moment for Llayne to believe that any red-blooded, American male would have given up this creature for her. With a body like that, what did it matter that the dame was totally whacko?

"I, ah, hate to bother you," Rosie finally began, haltingly, "but last year I gave Tank a necklace with the Playboy rabbit. I just thought maybe he kept it, and if so, I wanted to ask for it back before it got thrown out or something." She was quite nervous, but seemed to be relatively sane for the time being. The agony of lost love shone in her gold-flecked brown eyes. She had loved him in her own mad way, maybe she still did.

Llayne remembered well the tacky bauble which sat in his jewelry box, never worn. She asked about it once and he vaguely responded that it was nothing.

"Yes, Rosie. It's still at the apartment. Why don't you stop by tomorrow and pick it up?"

"Oh, thank you! I won't stay or anything. I'll just pick it up and let you be. We have to get back to Chicago, anyway ..." her voice trailed off as a big, salt-and-pepper-haired brute of a man in an expensive, black suit, a stereotypical gangster type, came up and took Rosie by the arm and led her away.

Had it been another time, another occasion, Llayne would have liked to have asked Rosie what it was like to be a Playboy Bunny. After all, she'd once been a Golden Saddle Gal herself. Of course, it seemed like that had been a thousand years ago.

After eons, after she felt as ancient as an Egyptian mummy and as zestless as a Caribbean zombie, and as ugly as the two combined, the reception ended. Her best friends went to her apartment with her and everyone seemed obsessed with trying to make her eat some of the barrels of food that people kept bringing to her door. She fixed a plate to get them to leave her alone, set it down out of sight, and went back to sipping a Coke. That was the only thing that tasted good to her.

She sipped on a frosty Coke, looking out the window at the snow on the ground. Something had escaped her mind, a thought that had blown in and vanished just as quickly when she'd been interrupted by Rosie Saleman and her gangster escort. They stopped by for the Playboy Bunny necklace. When they pulled up Llayne had just remembered something she was supposed to do and now, 10 minutes later, she couldn't remember what it was. It was driving her to distraction!

Everything had been so hectic for the last week, yet, at the same time it felt like her life had stopped moving. Dale had come over often; Priscilla had stayed with her for four days after Tank's death; Kerina had slept over one night; and, Bob and Delia had just left after spending the weekend so they could attend the memorial service. As much as she loved her friends, and as thoughtful and difficult as it must have been for them to stay over, she was glad to finally be alone. Alone with her thoughts about Tank.

It hit her! The birds! They hadn't been fed in a week! Rushing out, expecting to find little, dead, birdie bodies littering the ground under the tree where the feeder hung, she was relieved to see that there was still a bit of feed left. Tank had apparently filled it to overflowing the last time he went out there. Wondering if he knew she'd forget, she went back inside to get the feed bag. Birds started gathering the moment they saw her head toward the tree with the bag in her hand. *Smart little buggers,* she thought. She scooped out plenty, and they wasted no time in enjoying the feast. Smiling as she watched one tiny fellow peck at the overflow that was scattered about on the hard-packed snow, her expression suddenly changed. She bent down to inspect the snow.

With the precision of a robot, she turned her head back and forth to scan a path from the tree to the apartment and back, discovering a pattern of a man's footprints. Tank's footprints, from the last time he came out to feed the birds. The snow had been soft on that day and his steps had left distinct imprints. Then the weather had turned colder and frozen them. There had been no new snow, so they were as clear as if he stepped out there just 30 seconds earlier.

She dropped to her knees and touched one of the impressions her husband's big feet had left in the snow, the last mark of a footfall he left on this earth. It seemed like the last indication that he'd ever been there at all, and such a transient one.

It felt like just a few moments later when she heard a teenaged boy say in a cracking voice, "Mrs. Tanner, are you okay?"

Then she heard a younger boy hollering, "Mom! Come quick! The woman who's husband croaked, she's stuck in the snow!"

Her mind jerked back to the present - exactly where it'd been she couldn't say - and she recognized the two kids who lived with their mother at the far end of the apartment complex. The older one was frantically waving the younger one away, regaling him for his insensitivity, as their mother came out and slowly approached her.

"Mrs. Tanner," she said kindly, stooping down beside Llayne, "you need to get up out of the snow. Here, let me help you." She reached out to offer a hand. Having been on her knees for so long the joints were frozen stiff, Llayne took the extended hand.

Before rising, though, she said, "His footprints are here in the snow. See?"

The neighbor woman looked down and said, "So they are. But he wouldn't want you to sit out here with no coat on and catch cold, now, would he?"

"No," she admitted. The woman straightened up and pulled on Llayne's hand until she was up, too. "Thanks," Llayne said, and she walked into her apartment without looking back. The woman and her children watched her go, shaking their heads in pity.

She wasn't pregnant. The blood in her panties broke her heart. It'd been doubtful, as she hadn't had time to go off the pill early enough, but she'd still been so hopeful. It was one more heartache, in a world full of them.

Chapter 13

"Mrs. Tanner," the grocery store manager nodded as he greeted her. The name still caused Llayne to turn around and look for Tank's dead mother. The manager continued, "Listen, I haven't run into you here since your husband died last month. I want you to know how sorry I am. I didn't know him well, just saw you two in here, but he seemed like a hellava guy."

"Well, I appreciate that," Llayne said.

He nodded again and walked toward the meat counter.

That had gone pretty well. Usually people didn't know what to say; consequently, all kinds of strange things came out of their mouths.

She rolled her cart around a corner to begin the chore of buying food, something she hadn't even thought about until now. She'd lost weight even though friends and neighbors were constantly trying to feed her. That morning her jeans had fallen down over her hips after she zipped and buttoned them. It wasn't until then that she realized she needed to eat to stay alive. Right now the jeans were gathered around her waist with a tight belt.

Nothing on the aisle struck her fancy so she turned the corner to the produce counter, only to run into Ann Harris, the has-been from Tank's high school days.

"Llayne! Hi! Oh, it's so good to see you. Well! Don't you look great. That sweater new? I heard you've been doing just fine." Her voice lowered in mock sincerity. "Went right back to work and everything, according to the grapevine. Well! Everybody's just talking about how marvelously you've pulled through and how quickly you bounced back. I told them we'd never have to worry about you. Couldn't imagine you sitting around in black for a year any more than Scarlett O'Hara." Her attempt at fake humor was nauseating.

That was the kind of dumb stuff people actually said. Llayne had already ascertained that Ann was an underhandedly malicious person. Many who made cruel remarks did so out of ignorance, but hers were intentional and Llayne couldn't take any more from that cow.

"Ann," she said, picking up a big, fat, ripe tomato, "stuff this in your mouth, or up your ass, and get out of my way." She aimed the soft vegetable at Ann's face and relished the look of dread, then pitched it at the groceries in the sow's cart and watched her jaw go unattractively slack as the robust blob struck, burst open and splattered juicy red goo and slimy little seeds across boxes and cans and jars that had carefully been selected for purchase.

Llayne wheeled away without looking back. She expected a tomato to strike the back of her head, but none was forthcoming.

Forcing herself to dismiss the bitch from her mind, she attempted to concentrate on the food thing. But it felt strange being in a grocery store. It was a routine of normal life that she forgot during an abnormal period in her life.

Bread. She needed bread. She always bought bread. Oh, not the big one, she realized. A small loaf would be enough. She placed the unfamiliar little package in her basket and wheeled on.

Frozen foods. Orange juice. One, two, three, four cans into the basket. Oh no. A couple would do. One, two back in the freezer. Her cart continued.

Ice cream. The freezer door opened automatically revealing Chocolate Fudge. But, she suddenly recalled that it had been his favorite. She didn't eat ice cream. A swirl of frost escaped into the aisle as she stared into the enormous freezer, its icy tentacles reaching into her throat and frostbiting each breath as she tried to inhale. She couldn't remember what to do next. Oh! The door needed to be closed. It closed.

She scurried to another aisle. It was becoming a bizarre place. She didn't recall it being like that before.

Boxes. So many baffling boxes on shelves. She didn't know what she needed. She couldn't even remember why she'd come to that strange place.

Round boxes of oats ... little boxes of snack bars ... littler boxes of raisins ... bigger boxes of cereal. She recollected eating cereal. Raisin Bran ... Frosted Flakes ... Corn Flakes ... Wheaties ... Cheerios ... Rice Krispies ...

Rice Krispies. Out of habit she reached for them. The box was in her hand before she recollected there was an unopened box in the cupboard at home. It had been there a month ago, and no one had opened the cupboard door since then, so it must still be in there. The box needed to go back on the shelf.

The box of cereal stuck to her hand, lifted in suspension, her hand quaking as the dreaded box took control. It would not return to its allotted spot. Her arm became heavy, a giant syringe in the sky sucking all substance out of it. Box ... awareness ... s-u-c-k ... paralyzed. She couldn't make the box go back. Fear tremored through her body, an emotional earthquake. Like a mocking Statue of Liberty she stood with one hand stiff above her head. Sweat dripped down her arm, not from her hand she thought, but from the evil box.

A small boy skipped merrily toward her, took one look, stopped dead in his happy tracks, then ran the other way. An eternity elapsed and then, as if dropped down from heaven, the store manager was at her side. Gently he took the sinister box from her hand and put it back into its hole on the shelf. Her arm collapsed and fell to her side, the spell broken.

"It's okay, Mrs. Tanner," he reassured her. "Here, I'll help you." He gently guided her as he pushed her cart down the aisle. She felt exhausted and her arm was numb, but she could move.

"Just tell me what else you need and I'll get it for you," he, her savior, said. The skinny, homely, little man had exorcised the evil monster from the box that had devoured control of her life. And he wasn't afraid of her. She didn't need to be embarrassed with him, although something told her she was supposed to be.

"No," she told him, her voice frail. "Nothing else. I want to go home now."

He went to a closed check-out counter, rang up her few items himself, took out her money when she handed him her wallet, and counted out the correct change. He took them - those foreign objects in brown paper sacks - to her car for her. Llayne never even noticed Ann Harris gawking at her insidiously, a wry smirk on her face, from behind the newspaper stand out front.

"You sure you're okay to drive?" the store manager asked after Llayne got into her car. "I'd be more than happy to drive you home. One of the bag boys can follow in the truck and bring me back. No trouble at all. The kids love an excuse to leave the premises."

"Thanks. No. I'm okay," she said through the open window. She started the engine, remembered something, opened her mouth to speak, but forgot what it was. "Thanks again," was all she could think of.

Through her rearview mirror she noticed him standing alone in the middle of the parking lot watching her drive away. *Thank God for people like him*, she thought. *They balanced out the ones like Ann Harris.*

She would never know him well enough to know that 10 years earlier his wife had died and that he experienced the same thing the first time back grocery shopping. The hoopla surrounding the funeral, the hundreds of condolence cards, dealing with all those annoying insurance forms, paying staggering medical bills, all of that paled in comparison to confronting the mendacity of sustaining life with food. His wife had died so long ago, yet he remembered all too well how the little things had gotten to him. He ached for young Mrs. Tanner. He knew it wasn't over for her yet, and it wouldn't be for a long time to come.

They annoyed her, those things in the sacks. She couldn't remember why she bought them or what she was supposed to do with them now that they sat on the kitchen counter staring at her.

A mite of ding dong dust flicked away in her brain, revealing a cogent thought: she used to put those things inside of the wooden doors hanging on the walls glaring at her day-after-day. She opened the doors, not knowing what to expect.

Surely it had been in a different lifetime when she had been connected to any of this. White dishes. Red glasses. Little tin things. Too confusing to figure out what they were. Another opened door revealed boxes. So many damned boxes again! Powdered milk (had she used it to cook with?), granola bars (had she cared about her health?), macaroni and cheese (no, she hadn't cared too much!), rice, Bisquick, corn meal and Rice Krispies.

There it was again: the evil, sinister box, tormenting her in her guilt and anguish. It knew it'd been bought for Tank and so it boldly taunted her, wanting her to feel the pain and shame of her feeble attempt at being his wife. Just like that wretched Ann bitch, it was the most cruel demon on earth and she couldn't let it go on harassing her. She had to destroy it!

♦ ♦ ♦ ♦ ♦ ♦ ♦ ♦

Crazy. She realized she'd gone crazy. Crouched on the floor in a safe corner she understood that was what had happened.

It was dark. Waking up was difficult, as if she'd passed out rather than had fallen asleep. She was cold, her face burned from crusty, dried tears, and her body hurt from being wadded into a ball for so long.

How long? she wondered. *Where am I?* She looked around as her swollen eyes attempted to adjust to the darkness. A sixth sense told her it was the room where "they" had come to dance with Tank in the night. Terror struck as she fretted that they would come for her that very moment. She had to find out what time it was so she knew how long she'd been in that condition. Her befuddled brain recalled there was a clock some- where in there - the room which she now recognized as the kitchen - so she scanned the dark. The glowing, numbered moon on the wall said it was two minutes after three. In the morning. It was black outside the window so it had to be the middle of the night. And it was time to get up off the hard, frigid linoleum.

Her body resisted movement, aching as she rose and stretched its limbs. Her eyes searched for a switch and she turned on the muted stove light. There! Maybe "they" wouldn't come with the light on.

When she turned and saw the room, she was shocked to see what she'd done. There were Rice Krispies everywhere, in the stove burners, on the counter, scattered across the floor, in the plants, in her hair. Shreds of the box were strewn about the room like con- fetti. The rest of the new groceries had been heaved in every direction. The empty bread package hung lopsidedly over the edge of the sink, crouton-sized pieces of bread laid around waiting, it seemed, to feed the birds. The red kitchen phone laid on the floor off the hook.

Llayne had become a lunatic, tearing first at the taunting cereal box, and then at the other substances of life that mocked death. She tore and bit and threw and wailed and destroyed, finally falling helplessly bereft and fatigued onto the floor where, on its barren, cold surface, she found solace in the corner and fell into a coma-like sleep, hud- dled into a lump.

Now she needed to clean up the mess, to get rid of the evidence of her insanity. Obsessed with returning to normalcy, she meticulously picked at the litter, cleaning every morsel out of crevices, corners, plants and burners. She had to clear it all away before she could rest.

When she was done she went to the bathroom and brushed crunchy bits of cereal out of her hair, fresh tears falling all the while. The sight of herself in the mirror terrified her. The person looking back at her was someone she didn't know. That person looked truly insane. Blotchy and swollen and ugly and insane.

When her hair was free of the demons, she went into the living room and collapsed onto the couch. She couldn't sleep in the bed. Tank had slept in that bed.

At 10 in the morning she jerked awake, bolting up as she realized she'd missed work. But what she was supposed to do and what she could do wouldn't mesh. She couldn't go. She didn't have the strength to go there and pretend to be a normal human being. She couldn't let anyone see her like that, a lunatic.

The dean was understanding on the phone when she finally got up the energy to get up and call. He'd been trying to reach her but apparently her phone had been off the hook, he said, and he was about to call someone in Mt. Pleasant to go over to check on her. He asked if she wanted help. She told him no.

At eight o'clock that night, after a day of laying on the couch and staring off into space, she finally gathered enough courage to go to the phone and make the call she knew she must make. Contrite, she asked Dr. Lichenger if he would consider taking her on as a patient again.

He agreed to see her in his office in his home at eight the next evening. For 24 hours Llayne sat on her couch and waited.

◆ ◆ ◆ ◆ ◆ ◆ ◆ ◆

A sense of peace bathed her. Being in that room again, sitting in the comfortable, worn leather chair that cradled her like a mother's caress, brought a feeling of security she hadn't felt in a long time. She recognized it as the temporary reprieve that it was, but welcomed it all the same.

"What can I do for you, Llayne?" Dr. Lichenger got straight to the point as he leaned forward in his chair with his elbows on his knees.

"Well, first of all, thank you for the sympathy card," she began. "I got so many. Yours was nice because it wasn't too sappy or anything. And thank you for seeing me again. I suppose you want to use me as a poster child for denial. I know I was a terrible patient last time. I'll try to do better this time."

"You don't need to please me," he said. "You need to do whatever it takes to get well."

"Get well. You make it sound like I'm sick."

"You are, in a way. There's a Yiddish proverb, *an aynredenish iz erger vi a krenk* - a delusion is worse than a disease. Mental illness is every bit as serious as physical illness, only the signs are harder to read. So we tend to ignore them until the illness is well established."

"Am I mentally ill?" She could hardly speak the words and, yet, hearing a tangible label offered a morbid sense of relief.

"You are, I believe, very disturbed. Tragedy has found your door many times throughout your young life, and not only with the recent death of your husband. I'm glad you've come back for help.

"But, we must set some ground rules this time. I want you to agree to work with me for six months. We can't possibly accomplish anything in less time. No skipping out when it gets tough, no more denial. We're going to face these demons of yours and work through them. The only way to the other side, Llayne, the good side, is straight through the bad side. It'll be hard and painful and you'll probably hate me sometimes."

She grinned. "I've already done that."

"Good. Maybe that's over. What specifically brought you back now?"

"Well, I think I was waiting for you to feel sorry for me and come save me. Or for anybody to save me. Nobody came. Oh, there were always lots of people around. But no one could save me."

"That's a common fantasy, especially for women who were raised with princess fairy tales, that someone will save them. As you will realize, you must save yourself. That's why I couldn't come to you, as much as I may have wanted to."

She sucked in a deep breath. "You wanted to come?"

"Well, let me say the parent in me wanted to save you, as it has with others at times, but the professional in me knew that wouldn't work. It would only complicate your recovery. It would keep you from learning how to save yourself. My role is to help you learn that for yourself.

"If I don't let a person take the first step to come here and seek help, they won't take the next step, or the next, and will stay stuck in the same place, the same illness, forever. That's why I'm so glad you took the initiative to come back. Now we have the potential of really accomplishing something."

She gravitated toward the sound of optimism in his voice. "Part of what brought me back," she told him, "was the pain. You say we'll have to work through pain. Couldn't be any worse than what I've already felt." He nodded understanding. "Figured if I'm going to be miserable anyway, I may as well do it where there might be some hope." She told him about her grocery store episode and the devastation in her kitchen.

"As you remember," he said, "we talked before about the common stages of grief. You're right, you could have been a poster child for denial. But you've felt uncontrollable anger, too, which your kitchen witnessed, and now you're getting to acceptance."

"Why didn't you tell me how stuck I was in denial?" she asked.

"I did. You denied it." His dry wit tugged a slight grin out of the corners of her mouth.

"Tank went through all of those stages," she reflected. "By the end, he'd accepted death."

He said, "And that's what we'll work on for you. Acceptance of all of the tragedies in your life. The neglect of your parents, the loss of your child, the death of your husband. Everyone experiences tragedy but you've had a lot while young. You haven't had the necessary skills for dealing with difficulty, the skill to be able to learn from such experiences. Some people go through their whole lives never learning how to turn the bad into good. Your coming here tells me you've had enough of that. You're ready to learn."

"Yes," she agreed. "I feel so stupid. Like there's a secret code to life that everyone else knows but I don't for some reason. Like I've been left out because I'm not worthy, or something."

"There is a secret code of sorts, and some people do learn it from loving, supportive parents when they're children. You never had anyone to teach you. That's why I'm here. To teach those like you who missed out."

The way he said that caused her to ask an impertinent question. "Did you miss out, too, when you were a kid?"

The look in his eyes said it all, but he added, "More than you could ever know. But I got help and now I'm a very contented man. My belief is that if I can do it, so can you, and so can anyone else who truly wants to."

Llayne suddenly realized that Dr. Lichenger was a person, just like her. He'd been a boy, perhaps an unhappy boy, who apparently had experienced problems and had risen above them to live a happy life. Llayne wanted desperately to learn every clue he knew to solving the mystery of life. She concentrated on his every word. She wrote what he said in a notebook as soon as she got home. She took his suggestion that she join a Widows' Support Group that met on campus. She never would have considered that before, believing that she wasn't really a widow because widows were old, non-sexual women who would have nothing in common with her.

But now she was ready to open her mind. She had to or she wasn't going to make it.

♦ ♦ ♦ ♦ ♦ ♦ ♦ ♦

The first meeting of the Widows' Support Group, the WSG, dispelled any misconceptions Llayne may have had about the members being old, self-suffering, non-sexual women. The moment she entered the classroom where they met, she could see that she was the third youngest. There were 11 other women, one ancient, two in their 50s or 60s, six in their 30s or 40s, and two who looked 16 but were actually, she later learned, 17 and 20. The youngest women's husbands had died in accidents. A number of the others had lost their spouses to illness, mostly heart disease and cancer.

Cheryl, the county social worker who facilitated the group, was like an earth-mother hippy with long, straight, dark brown hair, with no makeup on her plain face, and wearing patched jeans and a hand-knit sweater. She introduced the meeting by teaching the group about "grandiose individuality." She wrote it on the blackboard and said, "This is what psychologists call it when a person feels like a victim, and believes that when something bad happens to them, it's worse for them than it is for anyone else. Even though millions of people, all over the world, may have experienced the same tragedy, we each have a tendency to think, 'It's worse for me than its ever been for anyone else before." That's why this kind of meeting is so important, to help you put the trauma you've been through into perspective. Of course, being widowed is a horrible thing to have happen to you. And of course, everyone handles it in their own way, some better than others. And although feeling sorry for yourself is common and maybe even helpful in the beginning, the time comes when you need to get past self-pity and start putting your life back together. That's what we're doing here.

"Essentially, you have two choices: you can feel sorry for yourself for the rest of your life and be miserable, or you can accept your relationship for what it was - good, bad or indifferent - thank the "powers that be" that you've had this chance to learn so much, and go on with your life. That last one is the only choice that makes any sense to me." Then she invited the women to talk, to tell stories about what had been difficult for them.

"I went crazy a lot," one woman told the group. "The first time I went crazy after my husband died was when I stopped at the cleaners and the girl gave me some shirts of his that'd been there for months. Well, I went off the deep end! Screaming at the girl, shaking shirts in her face, like it was her fault he died and couldn't pick up his own damned shirts. That poor girl. I took the shirts and stuffed them in the trash can and roared away. It was so childish."

Another said, "For me it was right after he died when the lawyer told me he hadn't left a will or anything. No insurance, nothing! All those years I just assumed he'd always take care of me like he always had, even in death. Huh! I felt so stupid! Still feel stupid!"

"Yeah," Llayne joined in. "My husband only had a small insurance policy, but that's already gone to pay medical bills that weren't covered by insurance. I had no idea that so many new drugs and treatments aren't covered, and I'm sure he didn't either. His boss, the principal at the school, told me he tried to get more life insurance, but it was too late. He already had cancer and no company would touch him. And he didn't have a will, so if I need to sell his car I can't until it's probated, because it was in his name alone. That'll take months. I don't qualify for any kind of benefits, but at least the Veteran's Administration gave me 500 dollars toward his funeral, because he was a vet. That at least covered the cost of his cremation. But, I know he had no idea how much debt he was leaving behind."

"Mine didn't have much insurance either," an Hispanic woman named Maria said. "And me with two little kids to raise. I hated his guts right then and took it out on his best friend, telling him if he'd been a real friend he would've made sure John had taken care of things. He yelled right back that I was an irresponsible wife for not doing that myself. What really made me mad was he was right."

"That's not so bad. I seduced my husband's best friend," a plump, fortyish lady said, looking more like a Cub Scout den mother than a seducer. "Right after the funeral. Saddest part is, his wife is, was, my best friend. I was so damned hurt, and angry, and vulnerable. I just wasn't thinking straight. Like if I could have sex with a man, any man, it would prove I was alive. I was desirable. My husband's death made me feel so rejected."

"Yeah, what better way to prove you're not going to die like your husband did than to have sex. Right?" Cheryl, the facilitator, hit the nail on the head, evidenced by all the nods.

"The last thing I want is sex," a hard-looking woman in her mid-50s said, taking a drag on her cigarette. "I hated it with my husband for all those years and I sure as hell don't want more now that I'm finally free. And if that ain't good for a barrel of guilt I don't know what in hell is!" She sucked hard on the paper stick.

"People think old folks don't have sex," an elderly, gray-haired, wrinkled woman said. "Well, we don't have it often, but when we do it's worth remembering. I miss my husband's closeness, just touching. The little conversations. His feet wrapped around mine in bed. And I miss the sex. Clarence was good!" They all chuckled.

"I haven't thought about actually having sex yet," Llayne said, taken aback by her new insight. "I've been too busy going crazy." She told them about the groceries, and it felt wonderful that in that room with those people she was as normal as nails.

"What about the ghosts?" a woman named Carla asked.

"Ghosts?" Cheryl, the facilitator, inquired.

"Yeah," Carla said. "You know, afraid your husband's ghost will come to haunt you, or get mad when you finally move the furniture where you want it instead of where he wanted it, or watch when you have sex with someone else."

"Yes! I've been afraid of that," someone chimed in.

"Me, too," another agreed.

A quick survey revealed that most either feared or welcomed their husbands' ghosts, but they did believe in the ghosts. And, if not their husbands', then other ghosts referred to as "them."

"My husband was with me for one month after he died," Carla said. "Watching, protecting; then when he realized I was okay, he left. I told my therapist and she said it's normal to feel the presence of the person for some time after they die simply because we're so used to having them there. I agreed with her just to shut her up, because she obviously didn't understand. He was there!"

Cheryl stood up to the blackboard, writing as she cited statistics that shocked most of the group. They learned that, in the U.S.A. in 1970, one-and-a-half-million widows were under the age of 45 and one in every six women over the age of 21 was widowed.

"Although we may not like the evidence," Cheryl said, "the fact is most women are and will be widowed in their lifetime. That means it makes sense for married women, of all ages, to prepare for that fact. Just like a man should, too, in case his wife dies. Wills, insurance, child guardianship, future plans, should all be discussed and arranged as soon as a couple marries, in case either spouse dies. If you love someone, it makes sense to get all that business out of the way and settled, allowing for more time and energy to enjoy being together. It's a matter of education. Young people think it won't happen to them at all and old people think it won't happen to them yet. As you all know too well, it does happen.

"Please, teach your kids, your sisters, mothers, and friends to take care of this business before it's too late. Say 'I love you' to those you love every day. You don't know if that person will walk through the door again. You wouldn't want anyone you know to be as unprepared as some of you, would you?" Heads shook. "Then teach them, and take care if you marry again. By the way, statistics also tell us you will marry again."

Most looked interested in that fact, but the hard-looking woman said, "Not me!" To that she and the others laughed.

Cheryl drew a jagged line on the board, like the ones in films showing annual growth on corporate charts. The line started at the bottom on the left and worked in jags up to the top on the right. "This," she said, pointing to her drawing, "is what recovery from this process of dealing with death looks like. You start down here," she pointed to the low end of the line on the left, "and hopefully end up here," she said, pointing to the high end of the line on the right. "But, notice what's in between isn't an easy road. You'll feel better some days, only to fall into a valley again. You'll work your way out of that rut and rise further than before, but will fall again. You don't, however, fall as far down as you have before and you rise a little higher each time you do. Your lows get higher and your highs get higher, and finally you come to full acceptance."

"But I don't wanna git outta my rut. I like bein' stuck right where I am," the sweet 17-year-old, Tammy, said. She'd been so quiet throughout the meeting everyone shushed and hung on her words. Tammy was a pretty, thin blonde who looked the picture of a damsel in distress in her frayed, checkered dress with its tattered collar.

Cheryl pulled her chair over and sat next to the teenager, leaning close. "How are you stuck?" she inquired.

"Well, I ain't told nobody. It ain't jus' that it's embarrassin', it's like tellin'll mean I'll hafta do somethin' 'bout it, and I don't wanna. I don't never wanna 'nother man in my life. There cain't never be nobody but Ernie. I'll never make love to nobody but him. We've only bin married fer a year. Our anniversary was last week. I runned away with him when I was 15. My parents was so-o-o furious! But we jus' knew we was meant to be together ferever."

"When did he die?" Cheryl asked.

"Six months ago. In a train accident. He works fer the railroad and got crushed 'tween two cars. But, I'm still married to him ferever. He's my man!" Her translucent skin crinkled around her eyes as she attempted to sew a pattern in her mind without a thread of intelligence.

Every other woman in the room was aware that she used present tense when speaking of Ernie, who was long gone.

"You still feel connected to him," Cheryl reflected.

"Course! I ache to have him touch me, to hear his voice. He still does those things, but it ain't the same. We have wonderful talks at supper. I still make two suppers ever' night and its like he's right there 'cross the table from me." Impervious to the malediction in her words, she continued, "But best of all, I take out his dirty tee-shirts and stuff. I ain't never washed 'em. I touch 'em and smell 'em. What could be closer to a man than his skivvies?" Her fragile attempt at a smile looked delicate enough to break.

No one moved, grasping the gravity of the situation.

"Tammy," Cheryl asked carefully, "are all of his things still in your house?"

"Course. Where else would they be?" Tammy looked up with eyes as innocent as a fawn's.

"It's normal to want to be near your husband's things for awhile," Cheryl said. "In fact, smelling his unwashed underwear is more common than not, but the time comes when you need to move on with your life. You need to get out of the rut. One way to begin doing that is to start getting his things out of the house. For example, the Salvation Army always needs clothes for the poor. Maybe Ernie would have liked the idea of someone else having his clothes, someone who really needs them."

"Oh, yes, m'am, Ernie likes that. He's so kind," Tammy said.

Cheryl reminded her in a gentle voice, "He was kind. He's gone now. May I come to your place this weekend and help you sort through his things?"

"Okay," was the simple reply, said in the acquiescent tone of a lost child.

Cheryl took Tammy's hand and they sat like mother and child throughout the rest of the meeting. Eventually it was over, and everyone agreed it'd been productive. They laughed, cried, and hugged, taking special care to hug the oldest woman who needed to be touched and Tammy who needed all the help she could get. Finally only Carla, Maria, and Llayne were left.

"Let's go to Falsetta's and get a beer," Carla suggested.

"I'm good for a Coke," Llayne said.

"Beer for me!" Maria announced.

"They'll never publish this!" Carla announced, louder than normal. "We've just combined two taboos, sex and death!"

"Sure they will, girlie," Maria reassured, snapping her fingers at the waitress for another round. Coke and long-neck Schlitz bottles rimmed the table. Stacked in the middle of the table were scads of bar napkins. Written upon them were notes for their "article" on widows and sex. It seemed like a good idea when they started it. They concentrated as best they could on organizing the smattered story and eventually seemed satisfied the pieces were properly in order.

Carla picked up a napkin, turned it to the light and said, "I'll read these as best I can and fill in the rest. Okay. Suggestions about sex for widows. Number one, don't return your Coke bottles." They giggled.

She continued, "Number two, practice solo sex. You will not go blind.

"Number three, seek counseling. Do not, however, seduce the therapist, not to be confused with 'the rapist.' Their couches aren't comfortable, anyway.

"Four! Sneak into a sleazy movie house and buy a vibrator ..."

Llayne halted the rendition by asking, "They really sell those vibrator things in those triple X movie places in Detroit?"

"Yes," Carla affirmed, winking over her beer bottle as she raised it for a long guzzle.

"Do you have one?" Maria asked her.

"Yes, I do." Carla wiped her mouth with the back of her hand.

"What's it like?" Maria couldn't be quieted.

"Get your own and find out!" Carla teased as she pieced together a torn note napkin. "Now, where was I? Okay, number five, share sex with a single friend who understands your bereavement. Do this only with assurance that no one else would be hurt, like a wife or lover or children. Be sedate at any rate. This is not an ego trip to be flaunted, the look-at-how-fast-I-can-get-another-man-syndrome, it's an honest sharing of physical needs between two grown people.

"Number six, find a new friend, one whom you trust. Relate on a here-and-now basis. If it becomes appropriate later to share all that you've been through, it'll happen. In the meantime, this is a new and much needed happening. Let it be.

"Seven. Yes, the one-night stand. Find someone decent and single. Seduce him. Enjoy it. Supply the rubbers yourself.

"Number eight, take out some of your frustration by keeping a journal, diary or by writing an article. Like this one.

"Number nine, travel. Expand your mind and/or take a survey to determine if Latinos and cowboys really are better lovers!

"Ten, read dirty novels and take cold showers.

"Eleven, consider the benefits of abstinence. And if you find any, let us know. Ha! We know, 'If nuns can do it ...' Seriously, many people, not necessarily us, would suggest the merits of abstaining during this period of change.

"Conclusion: Whatever you do, remember that your first sexual encounter after the death of your mate may be a great comfort emotionally as well as physically. But be aware of your potential vulnerability. You've been scared and lonely, damn it! It may feel like true love. It may very well be. And it may very well just feel like it. Above all, be gentle with yourself. You don't need to feel guilty for what you do as a reaction to this situation, as we don't always make the most appropriate first choices. But, there are always more options.... Man, this is heavy shit!" Carla ad libbed.

"Come on," Maria goaded her. "Go on. This is my part, the best part."

"Okay, okay," Carla relented. "Allow yourself time to grow and to love again. Because of all that you've experienced and learned, from the smallest aspect of your own personality to the nature of the universe and the interrelationship therein, you will be able to love with more breadth than ever before. You have been given the opportunity to understand the fragile beauty of life, to know that love is life, to sense that the love of the one who is now gone from you will be with you always, so that you will one day love again.

"There!" she announced, wadding up a couple of the napkins and tossing them over her shoulder. Llayne and Maria considered the gesture for a second, then did the same.

Carla stood up and exclaimed, "Let's move on!"

She did want sex. It was hard to admit, but she did. The problem was she wanted it with her husband. The thought of sex with another man repelled her, and she wasn't anywhere near a sleazy porn house in Detroit where she could buy one of those vibrator things, so she chose number two on the list of options. But, she had to set it up in a way that would make it a totally new experience. It couldn't remind her of Tank, if it did it couldn't possibly measure up to him and wouldn't be gratifying.

She decided to put on her new album, "El Hombre - the 50 Guitars of Tommy Garrett." The album cover promise to "take you to the heart of Mexico" offered a welcome respite from her familiar and depressing life. The guitars begged to blare, so she turned the volume up as high as she dared.

Stretching out on the couch in her bathrobe and closing her eyes, she followed the songs and did a merry Mexican shuffle and a lively hat dance in her mind, where she wore a brightly colored, gored Mexican skirt with white, ruffly petticoats, a white off-the-shoulder blouse and red cowgirl boots. A red rose bloomed from her hair. Then, in her fantasy, a rugged, dark-haired gaucho came to her. He took her hand and they danced, the feel of his muscular, sweaty body excruciatingly stimulating as he pressed against her. His deep-set eyes beseeched her to want him, and he kissed her roughly, his mustache and stubble of a beard scraping her soft skin. His intensity excited her maddeningly. Finally, he led her out of the barn, where the musicians played and others danced, and took her to a pile of fresh hay in a field under the stars. There, to the rhythm of the guitars in the distance, he made passionate love to her. Llayne let her fingers play his part to great physical satisfaction.

"It was amazing, Dr. Lichenger!" Llayne couldn't sit still. She roamed around his office, looked out the window through maple tree branches to the garden in the backyard, meandered back to the desk, then scanned the bookshelves.

"Tell me about it," he said.

"Do you say that to all your patients?" She was amused by him tonight.

"Do you think I do?"

"Do you always answer a question with a question?"

"Why shouldn't I?"

They laughed together then got back on track. She forced herself to sit.

"We talked all evening," she told him about the Widows' Support Group. "We had so many of the same experiences. I'm not the only one who went crazy!"

"Really?" He widened his eyes in mock surprise.

169

She'd grown to like this Dr. Lichenger very much, now that she was over hating him. "Yeah," she said, "one woman still smells her husband's dirty underwear. I liked smelling Tank's shirts from the hamper for a little while, but this woman's husband's been dead for six months!"

"Is she from around here?" he said, concern infiltrating his dark features.

"Oh, don't worry, the social worker who led the meeting is going to help her get rid of his stuff."

"That's a good start," he said, relaxing.

"You know, I don't feel guilty any more. That woman, she's so young and uneducated. She loved so unrealistically. Tank and I were real, and in real love. I feel lots of things, but guilt over what I didn't do, what we might have missed, isn't one of them anymore.

"You know what though?" She continued candidly, "I still feel sorry for myself sometimes because my marriage was ripped away from me. I can't totally turn that self-pity off all at once. But the Widows' Support Group taught me to go easy on myself. Tank was such a great gift to me, of course I miss him! And, of course, I wish I could have kept that gift with me forever. But I don't feel so panicked anymore, so terrified that without him I won't make it. In fact, I'm certain I will. Someday, soon hopefully, I'll even stop feeling sorry for myself altogether and will feel nothing but eternally grateful that I ever had that gift at all. Sometimes it doesn't seem fair, though. Because of Tank's death I've learned about life, and might love someone else someday with more awareness than I ever could have otherwise."

"Life isn't always fair," he stated.

"You know, in the beginning I just wanted him to save me. I had no idea where that would lead. That I would grow up so much."

Dr. Lichenger thoughtfully reflected, then said, "Your parents couldn't help you much in growing up because no one helped them. Your marriage has taught you a lot, a lot that can help you break that old family cycle that's probably gone on for generations. You have a chance to be a better parent, someday. To be the kind of parent you've always wished you had."

Those last words warmed her insides. She liked the notion of having more children someday and knowing what to do to care for them well. In fact, one of her favorite fantasies was that her first child had survived, and that the doctor told her it was dead to make it easier for her to give it up, and that it lived happily somewhere with a loving adoptive family, which meant she had done what was best for her first baby.

The discussion about families and destructive family cycles - why it's so easy to get caught up in them, why "cutting the tangled umbilical cord" is so difficult, and how to chart your own course in life instead of staying tethered to debilitating family ways - ran until the end of the hour, and for many sessions to come.

◆◆◆◆◆◆◆◆

Dr. Lichenger said, "We've talked a lot about you as a daughter, you as a wife, and you as a widow. Now let's talk about you. Just you. Let's look at the 'you' that is there regardless of anyone or anything else. Because life goes haywire sometimes, as you know, you need to have a clear picture of yourself, so that no matter what's going on outside of you, you know what you have to draw on inside of you to handle it.

"Imagine this: a small airplane picks you up, takes you out over the ocean, and drops you off on a small, tropical island. And the airplane flies away. You don't know if it's ever coming back; you don't know if anyone is ever coming to get you. In other words, no one is coming to save you. You have to save yourself. What would be true of you, alone, on that island? What qualities do you have that you'd have no matter what, qualities that you have regardless of whose daughter you are, or who you are or aren't married to, or what job you have? What's inside of the true you?"

The lush, green island with its sandy beach already loomed in front of Llayne's mind's eye. Getting away from it all in a place like that sounded great! She considered the question and said, "I'd still be me. I'd still look like me, although I'd probably get healthier without Coke to drink. But I'd still have light hair and blue eyes and my basic build."

"Good. What else?"

"Um, I'd still be smart! I'd have to use my brain in different ways, but I'd still have it." She stopped, thinking.

"Ah, ha," he encouraged.

"I'd still like people and there wouldn't be any, so I'd have to make friends with the animals." She smiled, pleased with the idea. "That would be fun, and I'd still like to have fun! A monkey or two, a parrot. I'd like that!"

"What other survival skills would you have? Your body, your brain, an ability to relate to other creatures, a desire to have fun, and ...?"

"Well, I always survive, no matter what. If I'm dead broke, or pregnant, or if I've made a stupid decision, I always pull through. I would on the island, too. I'd watch what the animals eat and try it, too. I'd follow them to a source of fresh water; they have to have it, too, and would know where it is. I'd figure out how to fish. Yuck! But I'd do it if I had to. I'm strong enough to build some kind of shelter for myself. Maybe look for a cave to stay in during storms."

"Just like you're doing here, in my office," he noted.

"Yes! Just like here. I'd use every resource available to survive."

"Good! So, you know you can do it. If a plane showed up two years later, there you'd be, healthy and happy, waiting for them on the beach. And if the plane didn't show up for 20 years, the same would be true. And if the plane didn't show up for a hundred years and all they found were bones on the beach, you still would have been a healthy and contented woman." She shrugged her shoulders and nodded yes. "That's the attitude I want you to remember, to carry with you everywhere you go! You've been doing it, but I

171

want you to be conscious of your ability to do it. It'll help you be less afraid of new things."

"Funny you should say that," she said, pointing her finger into space at some floating idea, "because I've been thinking of something new and it scares me to death. You just made me feel like maybe I need to look at it differently."

"What's that?" he asked.

"Well, I hate my job - you know that - and I have to find a new career. Not just a job, but something I really want to do. Maybe this is stupid." He lowered his head and looked at her through heavy lashes in a gesture of mild disapproval. "Oh, right," she said, getting the message. "It's not stupid because I shouldn't put myself and my ideas down like that. It's just a new idea. Okay, here it is: I saw myself in Kerina's home movies when she filmed us at belly dancing practice one night. It was the first time I ever saw myself in a movie. I was surprised at how, um, interesting I looked. I can't say I'm drop-dead beautiful, because I know I'm not, but I have a look on film that's engaging. Interesting, is the word that keeps coming to mind. I think I could be one of those news reporters or weather people on TV. Now, I don't have any idea how people get those jobs, but I looked into it and Michigan State has a new Master's program in communications, and television broadcast is one of the areas you can do. I know, State is famous for being an agricultural college and the kids call it Moo U, but that program is supposed to be excellent.

"It's just all so foreign to me. Lansing seems like such a big town, being the capitol and all, and Michigan State is a lot bigger than Central, and I don't know if I can cut a Master's program. I've never even known anyone who does that kind of work - television. In West Branch everybody's a farmer or a teacher or an office worker or a clerk in a store. But, that's what I really want to do! I figure I could work at some small, local station, like Bay City maybe, and if I don't make it on TV I could at least work behind the scenes. That couldn't possibly be any worse or any more boring than what I'm doing now."

He steepled his hands underneath his chin, considered her new idea, and said, "You've really given this a lot of thought. I think you're right, you should do what you really want to do. It'll be more work, and more time, but you've accomplished that before. You can do it again. And if it gets you to where you want to be, it'll be worth it.

"I've always thought that one of the greatest sadnesses of life would be to be to be 80, 90, 100 years old someday, lying on your deathbed wondering what it would've been like if you would've tried something you really wanted to do. But you didn't have the nerve or the survival skills to do it, so you just lay there wondering, disappointed. If you give it a shot and you fail, so be it. You'll always know you did your best."

He became thoughtful again and added, "But I suspect you won't fail at this. It sounds like a good match with your skills. You know, those people who have those jobs aren't born with them. They don't come out of their mother's wombs spouting the news or with little pointers and a weather map." She giggled as he continued, "They learn those skills, and you can too!"

She beamed with pleasure. The idea had been blooming in her head for months and it was a relief to know someone else agreed with her that it wasn't totally ridiculous. His feedback was invaluable in encouraging her. In the core of her being, she knew she could overcome her fears and do it!

Their sessions together started moving toward planning her new life rather than trying to fix her old one. It was a refreshing change, as if she stood at a corner, looking down a new road at new possibilities.

But before she could make that turn and travel that path, from which she knew there would be no return, there was one piece of her old life which needed to be taken care of, a closure which would open the way for her to take the first step down that new road.

CHAPTER 14

Llayne dug her toes into the sand. Facing due west, clutching a small box, she let the warm spring breeze coming off of Traverse Bay whip up her hair. Yes, this was the spot. An image of Tank's solid, bare bottom diving into a wave tickled her inner eye.

"This is it! This is where we skinny dipped during our honeymoon," she hollered to Priscilla, who trotted toward her as best she could, being huge with child as she was.

"Wow!" Priscilla huffed, sticking her hands into her overalls to support her protruding stomach. "This is so pretty!" she exclaimed, looking out from the isolated spot just south of Mission Point where the old lighthouse stood. Plump, white clouds skated gracefully through the sky, ice blue at its zenith and deepening to true blue where it met the horizon of the dark blue water, which stretched in front of them to the other side of the bay, beyond which laid Lake Michigan. Here in the sheltered inlet, gentle waves licked at the tan sand beach.

"Yeah," Llayne agreed, "I love it here! It's so pure, so raw. It sure is cold up here in the winter, though! The road that comes through the woods to this beach was closed most of the winter. I thought it would be forever before everything thawed enough for us to come out here. But it sure is nice today. Here, let's sit." They plopped onto the sand, Llayne continuing to hold the six-inch-square, navy blue, cardboard box to her chest.

Llayne looked at her friend's belly, and the paint-stained coveralls. "What're you painting now?" she asked.

Priscilla took a little ball of gum out of her mouth and threw it into the sand. She stopped smoking cigarettes and started chewing gum the moment she learned she was pregnant, and always seemed to have a wad in her mouth. Gracing the horizon with a wide smile, she looked at Llayne sideways. "I'm painting Noah and his ark. A mural on the wall in the baby's room. Can you imagine me painting baby stuff? It's turning out even better than I expected. We can never move and leave it!" she chuckled.

"Hey, come on," Priscilla changed the subject. "How're we gonna do this? You want me to do it, and you watch? Or do you wanna do it? Do you want me to watch or should I go back to the car and leave you alone?"

"I want us to do it together. For the men we've lost. For the baby I lost. For the baby to come." She smiled at her friend's big belly. "For every woman on earth who's ever loved and lost, and survived to love again." Llayne looked out over the water. Priscilla followed her gaze.

"You can see him, can't you?" Priscilla asked.

"How did you know?"

"Because I saw Benny for a long time, in places where we had fun. Happy places. I think that's where they come back to. Not to where they felt pain, but where they felt joy. Actually, places where they screwed their brains out. I bet during your honeymoon you two did it 'til he tickled your tonsils, right here on this beach! So, of course he'd be here. This is where he had one of the best times of his life!"

Llayne guffawed, shaking her head. "No, Miss Nosy, you're wrong! We didn't do it on this beach. It was out there," she confessed, waving her hand at the bay, "in the water."

"Oo-oo, sounds nice and kinky to me. Hey! You ever think that maybe that's the only reason we come to earth in these bodies?"

"What? Just to screw?"

"Sure!" Priscilla said. "Why not? It's the best reason I can think of to be here. Preachers think it's to do good; psychologists think it's to fulfill our potential; our mothers think it's to make them happy. My new highbrow mother-in-law thinks that about her son, and she's mighty unhappy that her thoroughbred eloped with white trash like me." She giggled and rubbed her tummy. "But, maybe all that stuff is bull. Maybe we can do all of that up there in heaven. But maybe every thousand years or so every angel says, 'You know, it's been too long since I've had a good screw, and I'd like to go down to earth in a body and get me some. Okay, God?' And God says, 'Right on!'"

Llayne playfully slapped her friend's knee and said, "You are so bad!"

"Yeah. And so are you. You love sex as much as I do. I hope you get to have some again some day," Priscilla chided.

"Ha! I hope so, too. I'm nowhere near ready, though. And with this letter," Llayne noted, setting the box close beside her in the sand and, becoming serious, pulling a letter out from her jeans' pocket, "it'll be a long time before I even have time to think of being with another man." The incredible, shocking letter had arrived that morning and she already thought of it as "the miracle letter." Glancing over it for the hundredth time, she said, "This would have made him so happy! Tank, honey!" she called, her face to the sky. "Come look at this!" She held up the pale blue piece of paper and it waved in the wind.

"Hey, Tank!" Priscilla joined the allusion, pointing to the letter. "This one's for you, sweetheart!"

They smiled together. Llayne lowered the precious missive and they huddled heads, reading it yet again.

Llayne patted the top of the box and said, "I think he knows, Pris."

"I know he does."

"Here, you guard this," Llayne said, handing the paper over to her trustworthy friend, who carefully folded it and placed it deep into her pocket. "You stay here and rest while I build us a fire. Can't be on the beach without a fire!" She walked along the back of the 40-foot-deep beach and brought back stones, one at a time, each about the size of a loaf of bread, making a circle with them near where Priscilla sat in the sand. Then she disappeared into the trees behind the beach and reappeared with an armload of wood. "There!" she said, arranging it within the circle of stones, in good Girl Scout fashion. Taking matches from her pocket, she lit the pine cone kindling on the bottom, and in no time they had a good fire.

Priscilla heaved her bulky body up and almost tottered over, until Llayne grabbed her hand to pull her up. Like a capricious child, the pregnant woman dragged her toes in the cool, wet sand as she walked to the fire. Automatically, she put her hands up to warm them over the flames. "It's nice out today," she noted, "but a fire still always feels good."

"Yeah, it sure does," Llayne agreed, with her hands over the fire, too. Finally, she said, "Well, it's time." She picked up the square box, walked to the water's edge, and carefully attempted to take the fitted top off the box. It wouldn't budge. "Darned thing," she said, frustrated as she tried to pry the jammed top with her fingernails.

"What?" Priscilla yelled from behind her.

"He doesn't want out," Llayne hollered back, just as the top flew off and a few pieces of the box's contents tumbled out. Surprised, Llayne peered into the container. "Hey, Pris! Come here and look at this!"

Priscilla went to her friend. She, too, stared into the box.

"Well, I'll be damned!" Priscilla said. "When they say 'ashes' I thought that meant, you know, ashes. These are little ..." Her hand involuntarily reached toward a piece but quickly withdrew.

"Yeah," Llayne agreed. "They're like little pieces of bone. Or, shells. That's it! They look like shells. Can't even tell them from the shells in the sand." Llayne stooped and picked up a shell from the beach, then reached into the box for a piece. The young women glared at the white shell and the white piece of bone in Llayne's hand. They were identical.

Llayne held the opened box high above her head, a waft of minuscule particles blowing out and into the sky like magician's smoke. "Ashes to ashes, dust to dust, shell to shell!" she said in a voice that rang loud and clear over the water, punctuated by the splashing of the waves. "Rest well, my dear, sweet man! And don't worry, I will take care of everything!" She tossed the rest of Tank's cremated bone fragments into the water, and they spewed in a skyward arch that hung suspended midair for a fraction of a moment before falling in a cadenced chain into the bay. "I will love you always!" she bid farewell to Tank's gentle, malingering spirit.

Priscilla waved and added, "Say hello to Benny for me! Tell him I love him, too!"

Together they stared out over the water for a long, long time, then finally turned to go back to the fire. Llayne flung the box into the flames and they watched it burn until every shred had been incinerated. They threw sand on the fire to put it out. The ceremony was over.

Wrapping their arms around one another's waists, the two young women walked up the shore and through the woods to the car. They drove away knowing they would be forever friends, in life and in death.

◆ ◆ ◆ ◆ ◆ ◆ ◆ ◆

For the next two months Llayne prepared for her new life, the one that the miracle letter had portended. Knowing she couldn't mess up now, she outlined every detail, every aspect of what needed to be done. Coming home from work at the community college each evening, she had not a moment to relax. Two evenings a week were spent in therapy in Dr. Lichenger's office, one was spent dancing in Kerina's basement, and every other free moment went into planning and tying up loose ends.

Finally, the momentous day arrived.

♦ ♦ ♦ ♦ ♦ ♦ ♦ ♦

The colorful patchwork pattern below was fringed with vivid green trees, sequined with sparkling blue lakes, embroidered with bright red barns and white farm houses, and braided with prosaic brown trails and gray roads. The earth became a giant, homespun, Americana quilt of square-acre fields and various other designs of rural life.

The United Boeing 707 rose above the scene surrounding the Indianapolis Airport and entered billowing, white clouds with pink-tinged edges. The little girl's wide, hazel eyes glared out the window, half fascinated and half afraid. They occupied two of the three seats alone, as no one sat beside them. Llayne held the two-and-a-half-year-old tightly in her lap and the little one responded by grasping the front of her new mother's ruffled, pink blouse.

Mother. The awesome phrase had been used to describe Llayne a week earlier in court, for the first time in her life. The judge had said, "Congratulations, Mrs. Tanner, on becoming a mother," when the official proceedings were completed.

Llayne watched her daughter's heavy, dark eyelashes flutter, then close. Her tummy rose and fell gently as she snoozed, and Llayne swept a black wisp of hair off her cheek. The new mother knew she had never before held anything so precious.

Like her child, she too was fascinated but frightened by this new adventure they were taking together, this new life for each of them. Her daughter presented an enormous responsibility, but this time would be different from the first time when Llayne had wistfully thought she wanted to be a parent, because this time she intended to fulfill the needs of her child rather than merely expecting the child to fulfill her own needs.

The lustrous eyelashes flickered and opened, and the little girl examined Llayne's face with inquisitive eyes, still not totally comfortable with this new woman who was taking care of her now for some reason she couldn't comprehend. "Sto-wee?" she said shyly, in her child's tongue. Llayne had told her the "story" the night before at bedtime in the hotel room and she seemed enthralled with it.

"Okay, sweetheart," Llayne agreed, patting the front of her daughter's pink-flowered, cotton jumper. Using her best story-telling voice, Llayne began, "Well, once upon a time there was a strong, handsome, American soldier named Tommy Tanner who went to Vietnam to fight so a long war could end, so nice people wouldn't get hurt anymore. This handsome soldier met a beautiful young woman named Soon Lee Francois."

"Soon Lee Francois?" the wee one mimicked, picking out the few words which sounded familiar.

"Yes, the name Soon Lee is Vietnamese and the name Francois is French because her grandfather had been a French soldier. Now, beautiful Soon Lee and the handsome American soldier fell in love. But, the American Army told Tommy, who everybody called Tank, the Army told him it was time for him to go home all the way across the ocean, so he did, and Soon Lee couldn't go with him. When he got home he married Llayne. That's me," she said, pointing at herself. Mesmerized and mystified, the child watched Llayne's mouth, trying to comprehend words beyond her grasp. She didn't understand them but felt comfort in the tone of voice. "So, Tommy Tanner never even knew that he and Soon Lee had a daughter, or that Soon Lee died, and that their daughter was raised by a great aunt. Then, sadly, before anybody could write and tell him that he had a child, he got sick and died, too. He went to Heaven, to be with Soon Lee," she added in an abrupt improvisation.

"Then I got a letter from the American Red Cross. The letter told me about my husband's daughter, about Ken Yoon Francois. You!" She tickled the little belly and the girl giggled. "Well, I was so-o-o excited because, you see, I don't have any children. Then, they sent you to me. You came on that big military airplane all the way across that bi-i-ig ocean with all those other women and children. Remember?"

The child realized she'd been asked a question and her eyes searched the air to her upper left for meaning and memory. She wasn't certain, but nodded.

"Last week I went to court to make you my daughter and changed your name to Kenyon Francois Tanner, so you can have your daddy's last name. Then I flew to Indianapolis to pick you up, because that's where that nice Red Cross lady lives and she took you with her. Wasn't that nice of her?" Kenyon searched Llayne's face in wonderment. "Now," Llayne continued, "we're flying into an airport called Tri-City, then we're getting into your daddy's car, it's called a Cutlass, and we're going home to Mt. Pleasant. But, it won't be our home for long. We're starting a new life." As she expected, the little eyes closed again and Kenyon fell fast asleep. It'd been a long, exhausting, confusing journey for her.

Llayne thought of the letter, which was at home in the safe deposit box with the picture that Tank had kept of Kenyon's mother. It truly was a miracle letter, telling of the child's existence, which no one on this side of the Pacific Ocean had previously had any knowledge of, and about the child's mother, Soon Lee, the young Vietnamese woman Tank had told her about, the one he fell in love with. Soon Lee had been a mere 15-year-old when she'd been sold by her father to the whorehouse. Tank had thought her 17, and too young at that. He'd taken her to her great aunt, having no idea he impregnated her. Llayne wondered if he ever considered that possibility and worried about it. Soon Lee had died in childbirth and the aunt had raised the baby. Then the old woman had died of tuberculosis.

179

Ruth Lichenger, who served as Llayne's lawyer, had insisted on checking the records. There was as much certainty as possible that she was Tommy Tanner's child. The birth certificate, a rare commodity in war-torn Saigon, listed Tank Tanner, U.S.A., as the father. The baptism record - thank God the old aunt had been Catholic or there wouldn't have been corroborating evidence - also noted him as the father.

But once she laid eyes on the girl, Llayne didn't need official documents. Kenyon was not a typical, delicate Asian girl. She had her mother's black, lush hair and sensually shaped eyes, but the crystal blue-green, hazel hue of those eyes matched Tank's perfectly. And the square jaw, the lean but muscular body, the broad lips sheltering perfect white teeth, and the voice, which was already husky for one so young, were feminine versions of Tommy Tanner.

The letter explained that when the little Amerasian girl showed up in an orphanage, someone took special notice because of the information on the birth certificate and baptism record, and called the American Red Cross. It really was a miracle that anyone had called and that the Red Cross had seen fit to write to the father of the child, finding instead his widow.

She looked out the window into the clouds and knew that Tank's spirit hovered nearby and that he was happy to finally know that he had, after all, been a father. He would absolutely adore this little girl.

Studying her sleeping daughter, Llayne felt an odd pang of guilt over the thought, which felt disloyal, that this baby would help heal the hole in her heart over the loss of her own flesh-and-blood. But the guilt waned as quickly as it'd come. Although Kenyon would help her get over the sorrow of her losses, that of her baby and that of her husband, she suddenly understood how a mother can love each of her children equally. One child could never take the place of another; each had their own special place in a mother's heart. If a child was lost to a mother, that child's spot stayed in her heart forever, no matter how many other spots were happily occupied. A mother never forgets.

She wondered if it could be the same with husbands. The love for one would be in her heart always, opening rather than closing that heart to accept another man.

Kenyon let out a huge sigh in her sleep, tasted her tongue a few times, then fell still again.

Llayne smiled and stroked her hair, feeling consummately blessed. Looking out at the clouds below, she felt a thrill at traveling toward a new life. It made her chuckle when she realized that this round-trip flight to Indianapolis was her first time on an airplane and the furthest she'd ever been from home, but that her two-and-a-half-year-old daughter was already much more traveled and more worldly than her 23-year-old mother!

She held tight to her sleeping child and gazed out the window at the amazing, shimmering, cloud-cast sky. With absolute certainly she felt Tank's presence. *He is here. He knows. This makes him very happy.* "Don't worry, honey," she whispered. "I'll take care of her with every bit of wisdom, strength, and love I can possibly muster. I'll do it for you, and for her, and for me. And I promise to teach her about you and about your love." Love for him and for his daughter, now her daughter, too, swelled within her breast.

♦ ♦ ♦ ♦ ♦ ♦ ♦ ♦

The surprise homecoming bash her friends threw to welcome Kenyon was overwhelming. The little girl's eyes were huge orbs, taking in all of the people and food and gifts. Everyone Llayne and Tank had ever known seemed to be in the Ember's party room, and the stack of gifts for Kenyon made Llayne cry in appreciation. She was dead broke and had no way of buying anything. Every toy, every item of clothing and every necessity seemed to be provided by those big-hearted people.

Still quite shy, but clearly pleased by all of the attention, Kenyon clung to her mother's skirt as she met Uncle Dale; Aunt Priscilla, whose enormous tummy looked like it was about to explode; and Uncle Bob. It started to go on-and-on, but Uncle Dale suggested they forget introductions and open presents. Kenyon liked that a lot! Still wadding a corner of her mother's skirt into her fist, with the other hand she fondled each gift as a grown-up unwrapped it. She especially liked the miniature dancing veil that Miss Kerina gave her, with sparkles on the edges. Then they opened Uncle Bob's gift. Dapper, as usual, in orange and white leather shoes that matched his orange and white Hawaiian shirt, which he acquired recently during their honeymoon on Maui, he and Delia gave Kenyon a pair of sequined tennis shoes. For the first time the little girl let go of her mother's skirt, and with both hands she grabbed the shoes out of the box and wanted them on right away! And she wasn't about to take them off. It was a week before Llayne could convince her not to sleep in them.

♦ ♦ ♦ ♦ ♦ ♦ ♦ ♦

Llayne pulled up to the beautiful Victorian house and sat for a moment in the car, just looking at it. She would miss the place. Kenyon, who'd been crunched over snoozing in the roomy passenger seat of the Cutlass, stirred and popped her head up to look out the window. Another new place, another new adventure.

No sooner had they exited the car and started up the brick walk when Ruth Lichenger, with her husband close behind, flurried out of the front door and down the steps to greet them. "Here she is!" she exclaimed, holding out her hands to Kenyon. Ruth wore a plaid, sleeveless dress in pink and yellow and purple tones, with a number of colored bracelets chiming from her wrists. Of course, she had on lots of makeup and had her red hair nicely coifed. Kenyon apparently liked what she saw, because she flung her arms up to be picked up. "Oh my!" Ruth said, happily lifting her up. "Aren't you a dear!" Kenyon grabbed at her earring and Ruth had to hold the little hand away.

"Hello, Llayne," Dr. Lichenger said, shaking her hand.

"Oh, yes, hello, Llayne," his wife said, laughing, reaching out to give Llayne's hand a squeeze. "Didn't mean to ignore you. Come on in!

"Now," Ruth directed, "you two go back to the office and finish your business. Kenyon and I will be just fine!" She whisked the little girl through the living room and they disappeared behind the kitchen door.

"She'll feed her," Dr. Lichenger explained as he and Llayne walked down the hall. "She feeds everybody."

They went into his office, closed the door, and sat in their usual chairs. She felt sad and ecstatic at the same time, and both emotions crossed her face.

He understood her mood. "It's hard to believe this is our last session," he said. "It's August, seven months since your husband died."

"I can't believe it, either," Llayne replied. "It seems like everything has happened so fast, at the same time it's taken forever."

He smiled. She liked his smile and his black mustache with its touch of gray. "We've accomplished a lot in a short time," he said. "And now you have a new life. An extraordinary new life."

She couldn't help but beam with pleasure at that thought, and stood up and went to the window, remembering the time just after she'd been elected Homecoming Queen when she wanted to escape out of the window of his campus office. Now she wasn't sure she wanted to leave his safe haven. She'd been more of her true self in this room than anywhere else on earth, vulnerable, terrified, capable, incompetent, petulant, funny, angry, womanly, childish, self-assured, ignorant, a genius. So many aspects of her personality, her mind, her very soul, had been revealed right here. Once in awhile she felt a stab of fear that if she left the security of this place, she might lose some of those parts of herself and not be able to handle the "extraordinary new life" that awaited her.

But, usually she felt ready. It was time. They had discussed that at great length, too, for the past two and a half months, ever since the letter about Kenyon had arrived, the letter that had changed her life so drastically, forever.

She leaned on the window sill, unaware that the broad green leaves of the maple tree outside blew softly to form an impressionistic frame around her flowery, yellow, sundressed body. Dr. Lichenger thought her quite a pretty woman. Someday, if she filled out a little like his Ruthie, he thought she might even be a very pretty woman.

They discussed her new life, her fears and mostly her excitement. She'd been accepted into the Communications Master's Degree Program at Michigan State University, which felt like she was walking into a new country, the whole television business was so foreign to her. But that was part of its appeal!

There was the little hang-up of being dead broke. Tank's meager life insurance policy had paid off the last of the medical bills that hadn't been covered by his health insurance, and their vacation savings had paid for the adoption and Kenyon's transportation to the United States, which meant there was nary a sou in the coffer. But, Llayne's job experience at the community college had helped her secure a part-time job advising students in the Financial Aid Office at State. She surmised that it would be a real yawner, but determined that she could handle it as long as it was temporary. As a part-time employee of the college, she qualified to take Kenyon to the school's child care center while she worked and went to class. She'd learned that Kenyon was very sociable, having a ball playing with Kerina's children, even though they were older and spoke to her in English, which she didn't yet understand, while Llayne did one final dance session with Scheherazade. Kenyon would get along great with the other kids in child care, which helped assuage Llayne's guilt over having to take her there. To help matters even more, as long as she took at least 12 hours each semester, Llayne would qualify for a student loan. She'd make it, somehow.

She and Dr. Lichenger chatted amicably, making certain her plans were well set, with her asking a few questions and him interjecting spurts of wise advice, until finally an hour was up.

"Ruthie's probably filled your daughter to the gills," he said, motioning toward the kitchen. "She hasn't had a young one to feed this week. Our son is visiting his grandmother. We'd better go save your child."

Llayne said, "She's so neat, isn't she? Ruth, your wife."

"Neat?" he repeated, smiling broadly. "I never quite thought of Ruthie as 'neat,' but indeed she is!"

"You adore her, don't you?"

"Yes, I do," he admitted, opening up to his personal life since it was their final session.

"I hope I have that someday. The kind of marriage you two have."

"Well, then, you'll have to work for it like we have. We don't take each other for granted; we listen to one another; we understand that true love is much more than physical attraction, although that's nice, too! We've learned to negotiate our disagreements, which we didn't know how to do at first. Especially the ones about our son. And Ruthie has learned to totally ignore my mother during her annual one-week visit when she complains incessantly about the way Ruthie dresses and about our messy house."

"I love the way your wife dresses! It's so unique! And your house isn't messy. It's homey, lived in. Nice."

"We think so. But my mother is of another opinion." He laughed about his mother, so Llayne felt free to do so, also. Then he rose from his chair and Llayne left her perch on the window sill, suddenly feeling deflated that their appointed time had come to an end.

Standing together, facing one another, he said, "There's a Yiddish blessing: *got zol aykh shoymer un matzil zayn* - may God protect and deliver you. That is my parting blessing to you and your child."

"Thank you," she said softly. "Thank you for everything." Awkwardly, because she knew he would never breech professional etiquette and do so, she reached up and hugged her mentor's neck. He hugged, too. When she backed away, she saw a glint of a tear in his eye to match her own.

They went into the kitchen where Ruth, having put a white apron on herself and having tied a blue one around Kenyon's neck, was feeding the little one chocolate cake. Kenyon was in bliss, with cake all over her face. "Oh! There you are!" Ruth addressed Llayne and her husband with a big, bright pink smile. "Now, you two sit for some cake. If this is going to be a going away party, then let's party!"

After she stuffed herself with the best cake she'd ever eaten, and they all stood out on the sidewalk, Llayne said to Ruth, "Thank you so much!"

"My pleasure, dear. Now you keep in touch, okay?" the vivacious woman said, hugging Llayne and then Kenyon one last time.

"I will," Llayne promised, taking Kenyon by the hand. "And thank you," she said for a final time to Dr. Lichenger. Just then Kenyon broke from her grasp and ran to the psychotherapist, grabbed him around his knees and squeezed. He stooped down, quite wobbly with his legs in a vice grip, and she let go to thrust her arms around his neck. Gently, he put his arms around her and embraced her. Satisfied that she hugged everyone, Kenyon trotted back to her mother.

Dr. Lichenger beamed as he waved goodbye. Ruth blew kisses. And Kenyon, seeing that for the first time and thinking it great fun, blew kisses back to them all the way down the street until their car had turned a corner and the Lichenger's disappeared from sight.

◆ ◆ ◆ ◆ ◆ ◆ ◆ ◆

Llayne was learning a lot about her daughter. The kid loved chocolate. She adored music, with James Brown seeming to be her favorite. She liked to dance, dragging the little veil with the sparkles that Kerina had given her around everywhere, and insisted on wearing her sequined shoes from Uncle Bob during every waking hour. She was extremely sociable. In other words, Llayne mused, she was her father's child! And, she was picking up English very quickly. Llayne had to start watching her own language, ever since the day she hung up the phone after talking to Priscilla, and Kenyon had said, "Hell, mommy, shit, hell!" Once in awhile she'd rattle off a sentence or two in Vietnamese, stop, wrinkle her nose in thought, then continue in broken English, instinctively understanding that people there couldn't understand the words she already knew.

As they packed for their move to Lansing, Kenyon brought out the photographs of Soon Lee and Tank in the double frame, and said, "Mommy?" pointing to Soon Lee.

"Yes," Llayne said. "Mommy."

"Mommy?" the child said again, this time pointing to Llayne.

"Yes," Llayne reassured her, pointing to the picture and to herself, then holding up two fingers. "You have two mommies."

Kenyon nodded understanding, then studied the photograph of Tank, a picture of him in his college baseball uniform. "Huh?" Kenyon questioned, pointing to him.

"He's your daddy. Remember? We talked about him before. He's Kenyon's daddy."

"Oh!" Kenyon exclaimed. "Daddy!" She kissed the photo, leaving a messy smudge on the glass, then did the same to Soon Lee's picture. Llayne decided never to clean that glass.

♦ ♦ ♦ ♦ ♦ ♦ ♦

She laid on the floor in the dark, thinking about the move that was coming up in two days. Everything was done. The Beetle had been sold to a junk dealer for the price of hauling it away. In two days the lease was up on the apartment and a new lease started on a one-room efficiency in Lansing. Her last check from the community college had arrived, meaning they would be able to eat until her first check came from her new job. Llayne was thankful she had the foresight to get paid over 12 months, even though she had the summer off. Packed boxes were piled everywhere, turning the place into an obstacle course, and she and Kenyon were living with bare essentials. There was just one last visit to be made.

The phone rang and she almost didn't answer it. It was such a peaceful evening. Kenyon was asleep in the bedroom and Llayne was stretched out on the living room floor with the sliding glass door open, the soft evening breeze billowing the long, white, sheer curtain into the room, causing it to look like a levitating angel. A cacophony of summer night sounds from the field behind the apartment complex, crickets and frogs, and a train in the distance, bathed over her body and relaxed her. But something - maybe that angel - caused her to pick up the pealing black thing. She said hello and the voice on the other end made her heart to skip a beat.

"Hello, Llayne," Mack O'Brien's full-bodied voice resonated over the line. "It's Mack. Mack O'Brien." His explanation was redundant; she'd known instantly who it was. "How are you?"

"Mack, what a surprise. I'm okay. How about you?"

"Oh, I'm doing good. Are you really okay?" he asked again, lowering his voice with genuine concern.

"Yeah," she reassured him, "I'm really okay. I wasn't for awhile, but I am now."

"Good" he said, then paused. A moment of silence hung in the air. "Listen, I, um, just read about Tank's death in *Centralight*. You know, the alumni magazine that goes out twice a year. I haven't kept in touch with anybody in Mt. Pleasant and didn't know what had happened until reading about it today. It was such a shock! I called to tell you how sorry I am. I'm just so damned sorry you had to go through that. Is there anything I can do for you?"

Funny you should ask, she thought. "Well," she said, "there's more to the story." She told him about Kenyon and he was delighted. That relaxed the mood and they caught up on everything. First, he wanted to know more about what had happened to Tank, and it was a relief for her to discuss it freely, without tears for a change.

Then she asked what he'd been up to, and he told her that he still worked for the Congressman but was planning a political career of his own. Half of his time was spent in Lansing, the state capitol but also his employer's home district, and the other half in Washington, D.C. He said he liked Lansing better and wanted to concentrate on an elected position within the state. He still talked to Neckbreaker regularly on the phone. And, surprisingly, he and "that old hippy" Peter Smith had become quite good friends, even working on a couple of political issues together. Portland, where Peter lived, was only about 20 miles from Lansing. Peter, it turned out, had become mayor of his hometown, the youngest mayor in the state.

"Are you still working at the community college?" he asked.

"Well, that's another story," she said. "I'm moving to Lansing." Another long silence ensued when he didn't respond. He had to be holding the phone tight, she thought, for her to hear his breathing so clearly. "I'm working part-time at State and getting a Master's in Communications."

"Whew," he said, "right here in Lansing! Let me take you two girls out to dinner when you get here."

Her heart plumb stopped in her chest, turning off the switch that sent electricity to her brain. When it started up again, her noggin churned a few gears before gathering a coherent thought. She couldn't do it. She just wasn't ready to be with a man she'd once been attracted, very attracted, to. Her hesitation had already told him what he needed to know.

"Llayne, I don't want to intrude," he said. "You've got a lot on your plate. I can wait and call after you've had time to settle into your new place. Do you have that phone number yet?" She gave it to him, relieved not to have to make a decision yet about eating some food together.

"Mack, are you married?" she finally got up the nerve to ask.

"Nah. I was engaged, but it didn't work out."

"Oh. I just wondered. Well, thanks so much for calling. Talk to you later."

"Sure. And if you need anything - anything - give me a call. I know just about everybody around here who could help with, you know, anything." He was nervous again, like he'd been at the beginning of the conversation, and she found that endearing.

"Thanks," she said. "Bye."

"Bye, Llayne."

She hung up the phone and lay there on the floor, her mind a swirl of half-baked thoughts. No, she finally decided, she just couldn't handle seeing him right now, if ever. Her life was chaotic enough.

◆ ◆ ◆ ◆ ◆ ◆ ◆ ◆

"Hurry, honey!" Llayne beckoned.

Kenyon pranced into the bedroom to get her veil. She had to have it with her in the car. They were scurrying out the door for their final visit before moving when the phone rang. Llayne dashed to pick it up. "Hello!" she said, short of breath.

"Hey, Llayne!"

"Peter? Peter Smith!"

"Right on! How are you, you good-looking thing?"

"I, I'm fine," she stammered, a flashback of their afternoon of sex projecting his exquisite naked body in front of her mind's eye. Instantly, she became aroused. Flustered, she managed to say, "Things have changed a lot around here."

"Yeah, I just read about what happened in *Centralight*. Do you believe I read that thing? But, I'm glad I did. I had no idea! Tell me how you're doing."

In 10 minutes she gave him an abbreviated version of the story of her life in the last year. He seemed genuinely sorry about Tank, but equally pleased that she and Kenyon would be in Lansing.

Dispensing with formality, she asked, "Are you married?"

"Llayne, Llayne, Llayne!" he playfully admonished. "You know me better than that!"

"Yeah," she chuckled, "I guess I do. You never did do anything the traditional way, did you?"

He let loose with a bellow of a laugh. "No, guess I haven't! Hey, what do you need in the way of furniture?"

"Oh, nothing. Really, we're okay. I don't have any money for anything, anyway."

"I'm in the furniture business! Remember? Now, what do you need? Do you have a child's bed for your daughter yet?"

She confessed she didn't, and thought of how much Kenyon's little legs thrashed around in their bed every night. He insisted on sending a small bed to her apartment in Lansing.

Flummoxed over his generosity, she promised to call him when they got to Lansing, and started to bid him a hasty goodbye, with lots of thanks thrown in, when she remembered something. "Oh! Congratulations on being mayor! Mack called last night, and he told me. The youngest one in the state. Wow! What did you do? Go totally capitalist? You know, short hair, suit and tie?" she teased.

"Hell, no! The hair's pulled back in a ponytail, and I wear Maverick ties with my suits. Remember Maverick on TV? He wore a little ribbon tie. That's what I do. Just couldn't force myself to do the typical thing. And people love it. They call me 'a character.'" He chuckled.

"They're right!" she laughed with him. They said goodbye, and she hung up and squeezed her eyes shut, vowing not to give a moment's thought to that afternoon so long ago. She didn't have time to even think about, let alone actually have, sex. Oh god, though, when she closed her eyes she could picture him in the buff so clearly. That beautiful hair in a ponytail.That broad chest with its curly black hair.That slim waist.That flat stomach.That ...

"Mommy!"

Her eyes flew open and there was Kenyon standing at the door looking cute as could be in her red jumpsuit, a gift from the homecoming party, her sequined tennis shoes, and her veil trailing from her hand. Mommy had told her to hurry and then she had to wait. She was ready to go!

Llayne scooped her up and they took off on their last visit.

When the Cutlass peaked over the hill on Highway 30 and Llayne looked down into the valley below at the old-fashioned, gray, barrel water tower with "West Branch" painted in black cursive lettering on the side, her stomach did a nervous rumba.That small town laid out before her, her hometown, seemed so removed from her life now. It was so remote, so far up in the boonies in the middle of a huge, thick forest which ambled up and down gentle hills. It looked benign, yet it had been the source of her sorrow and her joy as she grew up.Those and other memories flooded her mind as she drove into the valley, turned right onto Houghton Avenue at the Court House and Jail, past the Catholic Church, beyond Rau's Tavern, and turned right onto the little side street that cut across at the old train station to South Fourth Street.

When they reached the third house on the second block, a white clapboard house that was over a hundred years old, as were all of the houses on the street, her mom ran out to greet them, wiping her hands on the hem of her apron. Used to the routine of being greeting by strangers, Kenyon threw her arms into the air to be picked up and fawned over. Llayne's mom was ecstatic to meet her new granddaughter!

Llayne said,"Honey, this is your grandma. But in our family we call her Mo Mo. Can you say Mo Mo?"

Kenyon understood the question of being asked to repeat a word, she'd been asked it so many times lately."Mo Mo," she said dutifully, ready to go into the house to see what kind of food was awaiting them.There was always food for them when they went to see people.

Chocolate chip cookies, just out of the oven and still warm, awaited. Kenyon dug in.

"We're having supper in two hours, so I won't let her have too many," Mo Mo said.

"Yeah," Llayne said,"try to get them away from her!"

The three females continued to snack at the kitchen table, while the two older ones chatted. Llayne's mom wanted to know every detail about the child.

Then, half an hour earlier than usual, Llayne's dad walked through the door in the same kind of blue, workman's uniform he always wore, dusty from the day's work as a tree trimmer for the county, with his lunch bucket in his hand. He somehow looked thinner and even younger than before, his graying but thick hair still tinged with red. He grinned hesitantly at Llayne and nodded hello, but had no choice other than to drop the lunch pail and sweep Kenyon into his arms. She stood up in her chair and practically threw herself at him. She gave him a huge, chocolate-covered kiss on the cheek while he got dust all over her clothes. They both smiled grandly.

"This is your Po Po," Llayne told Kenyon.

The child said, "Po Po."

"Listen," Llayne's mom said, "why don't the three of you walk down to the IGA and get some ice cream to go with our cookies after supper? That'll give me time to finish what I have to do here to get everything ready so we can eat!"

Her dad excused himself to spend five minutes cleaning up, while Llayne cleaned Kenyon's face, and then they left for the store. As soon as they were outside, Llayne's dad picked up Kenyon and set her on his shoulders. She seemed totally at home with him and loved the view from so high.

No one spoke as they walked the block and a half to the store, and it occurred to Llayne that her dad and her daughter were a good match. He'd never been much of a talker, except for that one fateful day of drunken rambling so many years ago, and Kenyon was probably sick of being asked to repeat everything. All three of them enjoyed the silence as they sauntered down the sidewalk under big, long-standing trees. They walked past the two houses that completed their block, across the street, past the veterinarian's ramshackle barn, over the railroad tracks, and by the Victorian-style train station, which was a small, bright green building and now housed Hazel's Barbershop. Kenyon pointed to the station and exclaimed, "Huh!"

Both adults uttered, "Ye-ah," to acknowledge her liking of the interesting building, and they walked on in silence.

The little girl's eyes widened as they approached Houghton Avenue, the main street, and she clung to her Po Po's hair. She was a little intimidated by the road that was bigger than the others, even though only two cars passed by, slowly at that, and there was but one traffic light, one block east to their right, where one black, '59 Ford truck waited for the light to change. West Branch had never been what anyone would call a hub of activity. They stood on the corner for a moment while all three of them took in the town.

Llayne loved the place in an odd, conflicting way. It really was a wonderful, quaint town, originated by a lumbering community in the early 1800s. Someday, if she ever got over the memories of her troubled childhood, she'd probably unabashedly love it.

She scanned the block to her right which harbored the Model Restaurant and Bar, the primary place to eat in town, and the West Branch Jewelry Store, which had been the source of her childhood fantasies about growing up to be rich someday so she could buy some of those baubles, statuettes or knickknacks. The block further down held Linton's Dress Shop, with dresses that most females in town could afford, but not the ones in her family. Her mom had made most of her clothing and had taken her and her brother to Robert Hall's in Bay City, 60 miles south on Lake Huron, every other year before school to buy snow clothes, coats, hats, mittens, snow pants, and Kickerino snow boots. The outer garments were necessary, as the kids walked a mile to and from school each day.

Beyond Linton's sat the Dime Store, with its squeaky, slat-wood floor, which had every item anyone could possibly ever need, and the Midstate Theater. Across Houghton Avenue down at the end of that block was the Mill End Store, with its magical upstairs where every sort of junk could be found for a nickel, and behind that, not visible from her vantage point but she knew it was there, stood the volunteer Fire Station, with its wide doors open when weather permitted, revealing the big, red fire truck at the ready. Her eyes traveled back down the block across the street in the direction in which they stood, and she took in the Kimball Glass Company, with its door ajar so passersby could peer in to see windows being cut, and Gould's Drug Store, which had a soda fountain where she often bought a Coke after school.

Behind that block, running parallel to the stores, was an alley that she couldn't see but knew by heart. Behind the alley were a few out buildings, once stables, and behind that was the west branch of the Rifle River, the one the town was named for. As a kid Llayne had followed the stream to school each day, which was much more fun than walking on the sidewalks through town. Only once had she slipped in mud in the springtime and fallen into the water, which merely required the drying of her shoes in the sun before her mom got home from her job as a secretary at the doctor's office. And only once had she lost a mitten in the winter when she threw a snowball into the freezing water and the thing had stuck to the frosty ball rather than staying on her hand. There had been no way to rectify that one and she'd been punished by having to go to her room without supper. But, winter was far too cruel to expect a child to go without mittens, so her grandmother, her Mo Mo, had knitted her new ones. All-in-all, a pretty good record of staying out of mischief, Llayne thought, not able to repress a grin.

Having surveyed the entire whistle-stop, her eyes returned to her dad and Kenyon, and suddenly she was struck by the image of him carrying the black-haired child with the big, almond-shaped eyes, the very kind of child who haunted him for so many years in his nightmares. Kenyon seemed to bring him peace.

Robert, "Red," Robertson turned and smiled his most glorious smile at his daughter, then turned to his left to walk the few steps into the IGA. She held back, savoring the startling moment.

On the way back to the house, after buying vanilla ice cream, he said, "Llayne, I want you to know something. It may not make a difference to you, and I would understand if it doesn't, but I know I'm an alcoholic. I'm in AA now and I don't drink anymore."

She didn't know what to say. One big smile hadn't made her trust him, and he was right, his sobriety didn't make a difference to her. Was it supposed to excuse the horror she lived through as a child? She believed he'd stopped drinking for good like she believed the Titanic hadn't taken on water, or the Russians had quit spying, or Casa Nova hadn't lied to women.

He went on. "I know this doesn't excuse anything, but I just thought you should know. So you can trust me and your mom with Kenyon."

"How long have you been in AA?" she asked.

"Fourteen months. I haven't had a drink in 14 months."

Llayne was shocked. Her dad had been sober for over a year and she hadn't known. It made her realize that she didn't really know him, any more than he knew her. The question on her mind was: Did she want to know him? She couldn't, in all honesty, answer that one yet.

But for Kenyon there was no question. She loved the people called Mo Mo and Po Po. When supper was over and it was time to take the hour-and-a-half drive back to Mt. Pleasant, she wailed and grabbed for her grandparents.

It was inconceivable to Llayne that, after so many years of trying to separate herself from her parents and their negative influence, they might become a part of her life again because of her daughter. And they might be a positive influence. The difference now for Llayne was that she knew how to be her own person, no matter what they did.

During the drive home, they listened to the Bay City radio station. Llayne hoped it would distract Kenyon from her agony over having to leave Mo Mo and Po Po and, eventually, it did. After about 10 miles, they both hummed along, as best they could manage with Kenyon's off-key warbling, to hit songs like "Candy Man," "Too Late to Turn Back Now," and "Alone Again, Naturally."

No kidding! Llayne thought. *So many people in my life, and yet I'm so alone again in one regard.* She ached, literally ached, for Tank. Every time she thought of him it was as if the devil thrust his thorny hand into her chest to wrench her heart, squeezing and twisting it with all his beastly mite. In the Widow's Support Group, she learned to expect it to get worse before it got better, and it had. She missed him so much!

She thought of the phone calls from Mack and Peter and wondered if she could still possibly be attracted to one of them or even both of them when she did finally see them again. Fantasy was one thing, real life was quite another. Maybe she wouldn't have any desire once she saw them. But, what if she did? Which one would she want first? The moth-eaten thought, as moldy as her Homecoming Queen cape, made her laugh out loud, and Kenyon giggled, too.

191

CHAPTER 15

Making love again was as if it had always been meant to be. He was a rapturous lover. And she was starved for him. But, it'd taken them months to get to that night in February when they'd finally grabbed each other in a frenzy of desire.

She put off seeing him for three weeks after she and Kenyon had moved to Lansing in early September the preceding fall, giving him one excuse after another on the phone for why he shouldn't come over. But then he showed up at the apartment one night, six-pack of Coke in hand as a house-warming gift, insisting that he just stopped by and wouldn't stay long.

Kenyon had stared at him with wide eyes, precociously measuring him up, finally deciding he was okay. After all, he brought something good to drink. Plus, he complimented her on her sequined shoes.

He stayed about 10 minutes and then, true to his word, he left. It'd been a good thing, too, because the moment she laid eyes on him again, Llayne knew she was in trouble.

Time and time again she vowed to herself that she wouldn't complicate her life with him, or with any man. *I need to concentrate on Kenyon, I'm too busy, I'm not ready,* she'd chanted within her head like a mantra.

But he just kept on stopping over, about once a week in October and November, never staying long, sensing Llayne's need for independence and not wanting to pressure her. Intuitively, he understood her desire to do things on her own and to succeed at being a single mother. She wanted to unpack her own boxes, paint her own walls, and hang her own pictures. She wanted to take good care of her child, handle her new job and do well in school. She wanted to plan her own destiny and open her own jars. After all, she depended on a man once before, and he died on her. He grasped the exigency of her knowing she could go it alone if she had to, and once she knew that inexorably, perhaps she would choose not to anymore. Perhaps then she would be ready to let him into her life. So he took it very, very slowly.

It was December before he started stopping over at her place twice a week, and one of those evenings he brought nominal gifts for Christmas, for which he was invited to stay for dinner. It was January before he couldn't contain himself any longer and went over almost every day. She didn't tell him to go away, which encouraged him mightily.

From her point of view, he was making it more and more difficult for her to keep her vow of celibacy. She did everything within her power to deny her feelings, but they just refused to cease and desist! *And I used to be so good at denial,* she mused.

Kenyon adored him, too, as he did her, calling him their "man-friend." She liked it when they went to his farmhouse aways from town, 'cuz he had lots of rooms and a yard to run around in. But she liked it best of all when he came to their place at night to read her bedtime stories. He knew about her daddy, the Tank daddy in the picture by her bed, and sometimes he told her stories about how her daddy had been a baseball player, and a hero, and a very nice man. But that Tank daddy was gone to Heaven with Soon Lee mommy. They were the same stories her mommy told her, but she liked it even better when he told them to her. Kenyon wished their man-friend could be her daddy.

Llayne relished it that he and her daughter hit it off so well and that he had become her own best friend. That was, until early February, a year to the day after Tank's death. On that evening he became her lover.

That day began when Llayne woke up with a start at four in the morning, recalling with absolute clarity the dream she'd just had. Or, perhaps it hadn't been a dream.

Tank had come to her in her sleep. It filled her with joy to see him again. He'd looked so beautiful, standing before her, a look of absolute peace on his face and an aura of ideal patience about him. He would wait for as long as it took ...

As soon as she awoke she knew what he was waiting for; he was waiting for her to move on with her life. He'd been gently, lovingly prodding her, telling her without words that it was time for her to stop measuring her life in terms of how long it'd been since he died. She needed to go forward, for herself and for Kenyon. He was very, very pleased about Kenyon.

Arising quietly, so as not to awake Kenyon, who slept on the other side of the hanging, flowered sheet which separated their beds in the one-room apartment, Llayne let the moonlight that filtered in through the window light her way as she went to her jewelry box and opened it. The gesture caused the ruby inset in the delicate, gold ring on the third finger of her left hand to glint in the low light. The band, her wedding ring, was a replica of a Victorian wedding ring. She'd thought she would never take it off. Yet, her husband, her former husband, had just told her it was time. Slipping it off her finger, she kissed it, and reverently placed it into the box next to his wedding band, the one she wore on a chain around her neck for so long. Now the circles, the rings, seemed complete, belonging together. Someday they would belong to Kenyon.

It was hard for her to go to her mundane, part-time job in the Financial Aid Office at eight a.m. after such a momentous event in the wee hours of the morning, but life moved on. She went to class in the early afternoon, then picked Kenyon up from child care and went home as usual. But things were different. It was the night she would have her first real date with their man-friend. He invited Llayne out to dinner, just the two of them. On occasion they had accompanied one another to after-work functions, but had never had what could be called a real date. It was the first time.

A neighbor, a Brazilian woman, had offered to sit with Kenyon. So, Llayne had a babysitter and she even had the next morning off from work. She had no excuses left for not going out with him. Besides, Tank had come to her, leaving no barriers whatsoever.

Kenyon watched in wonder when her mommy took a lingering shower in the late afternoon. She always took a fast one in the morning. Usually when her mommy picked her up from the play place, they came home or went to the park and played some more. But today mommy was too busy. She was going to dinner with their man-friend, and Kenyon didn't get to go.

Llayne finished her shower, towel dried her body and her hair, wrapped the towel around her body and securely tucked in the tip, then put her hair up in rollers, something the child had never seen before. Usually she just let it dry naturally. Kenyon wanted rollers in her hair too, and Llayne managed to get a couple to stay in the silky mane. Then Llayne stuck her head under what looked to Kenyon like a big balloon hat attached to a hose. She said it was to dry her hair. Now Kenyon thought the whole thing was really getting ridiculous. How long could someone spend getting ready just to go eat? It was so boring!

Still, the little one stood by and stared as her mommy finished taking the rollers out of her hair and combed it. Then she put lotion all over her body. Of course Kenyon wanted some on, too, so her mommy put some on her arms. Then mommy painted red nail polish on her own fingers and toes. Kenyon didn't get any polish, though, 'cuz she was too little. She was too little for makeup, too, which her mommy spent a lot of time putting on her own face. "Besides," mommy said, kissing the tip of her nose, "your little face doesn't need makeup because it's perfectly beautiful just the way it is."

By the time Llayne dropped the short, red shift of a dress over her head, Kenyon had long since left the bathroom to go play with her toys. She was happy when the neighbor woman, who had a solid build and long, curly black hair, and was dressed in jeans and a sweatshirt, came over and whisked her away. Finally, she'd have somebody to play with! She gave her mommy, who was acting so strangely, a quick kiss and then flitted out the door in her special shoes, with rollers in her hair, and dragging her veil behind her.

As soon as the door closed behind her daughter, Llayne felt a stab of abandonment, as if her security blanket had vanished. She would be all alone with him. She wouldn't be a mommy, or a student or a buddy. She would be a woman.

And I've known for months that this night would come. I just wouldn't admit it!

With that revelation spotlighted in her mind, she conceded that the time had come for total self-disclosure. The unqualified, unadulterated truth was that she wanted him and she wanted to do everything within her power to make certain he wanted her. That's what all of the fuss was about. It wasn't about to be a casual date. She wanted everything about herself to be compelling, enticing.

Bending over to put on her new, black, dressy shoes, she allowed her hands to massage each foot first. The sensation was luscious. Desiring more, she ran her fingers up her slim calves and up under her skirt to trace her long, soft thighs. In the absence of underpants, she allowed her fingertips to brush the curly hair hiding at the juncture of her legs. *This is what it will feel like to him!* That knowledge thrilled her. She put her skirt back down and caressed each unbound breast through her dress, just like he would, causing her nipples to turn into hardened beads. Suddenly her legs buckled with excitement and she almost tumbled backward.

195

Leaning against the wall, she looked in the mirror and told herself to slow down. Maybe he wouldn't touch her. *Maybe this is all I'm going to get tonight.* The thought made her laugh a deep, throaty laugh out loud. *No, I'll get this from him. And more. He wants me as much as I want him.* He made that clear with every visit, every gesture, every look, every word, every silence.

Taking a deep breath to compose herself, she put on the silky, red sweater with the delicate, black edging that matched her dress. She spent a week's pay splurging on the outfit at K-mart, an outlandish expenditure for her, but one she delighted in making.

Realizing he'd be there any minute and she needed to stop dallying if she wanted the real thing rather than her fantasies, she daubed Shalimar toilet water behind her ears, on her neck and behind her knees. Scuttling out of the bathroom, she went to the dresser beside her bed and opened her jewelry box, examining its meager contents. A quick scan determined that she didn't have anything to wear with her outfit. She started to flip down the lid when a sparkle from the corner of the box caught her eye. She fondled the two wedding bands, then closed the lid.

Back in the bathroom, she glanced in the mirror for a final appraisal and liked what she saw. She was a little thinner than she'd been in college, having gained back some of the weight she'd lost after Tank died, when she became far too thin, but not all of it, so she was still thinner than before. Her jaw angled with the loss of baby fat and her ash blond hair, which fell in loose waves almost down to her waist, only held a hint of the bleached streak that had once so boldly striped one side. She wore her make-up in more natural tones now, except for the red lipstick she had on tonight to match her dress. But most of all she looked more grown-up. She'd grown from a girl into a woman. Her deep-blue eyes radiated confidence and insightfulness, qualities they hadn't held when she was in college. And now those big, beautiful eyes also radiated mischief. It made her smile. She was ready for him!

Right on cue, there was a knock at the door. With calculated steps she walked to the door and opened it.

Mack O'Brien stood there, running one hand through his wavy, dark brown hair and holding a dozen red roses in the other. He grinned sheepishly at her, his washed-denim blue eyes taking her in from head to toe and back again.

Although she'd never tell should he decide to dispense with the posies from there-on-in, it was the thick hair and that screwy grin which did it. She took his hand in hers and pulled him inside. They gazed into one another's eyes for only a brief moment before falling into a passionate kiss.

The flowers were forgotten and dropped to the floor, the dinner reservation was ignored, and nothing else in the world mattered. Months, actually years, of mutual sexual attraction exploded into wildly erotic coupling.

Still standing just inside of the front door to her small apartment, the intensity was so great it felt like they might detonate to self-destruction. Their mouths sought every morsel, every angle on one another's faces. They kissed hungrily, licked lavishly and sucked gently. She ruffled her fingers through his hair, as she longed to do for what seemed like an eternity, the scent of his Old Spice intoxicating her.

Casting her sweater aside, he ran his hands all over her willing, supple body, up and down her bare arms, around her luscious breasts to finger her nipples through the thin fabric, encircling her small waist, across her curved hips, and clutching her solid buttocks in both big hands. He lifted her off the ground and her legs automatically went up around his hips, causing the short skirt of her dress to gather in her lap. Gazing down, he saw the nakedness there and moaned like a lion in heat.

With every ounce of control he could manage, Mack gently nudged her away and stood her in front of him. In total supplication, she let him look at her.

After sloughing off his suit jacket, he picked her up so carefully it was as if she were the most priceless package imaginable, with one hand across her back and the other beneath her knees, while she hung onto his neck. He carried her to the big bed on the other side of the room and gently laid her down. Staring at her, he stood at the side of the bed as if in a hypnotic dream. She lifted herself up and stared back. Having already undressed one another with their eyes, he took one dainty foot in each hand to yank off her shoes. Then he kicked off his own leather loafers and bent down to tug off his socks. When he stood up again, she reached up and untied his blue-patterned, silk tie, pulled it off and flung it away. He wove his fingers through her sumptuous hair. She unbuckled his leather belt, slipped it out of its loops, and playfully pretended to whip him before dropping it. He grabbed the hem of her skirt and finagled it up around her squirming hips to run his hands over her bare, smooth legs, delicately tracing with his fingertips every inch of solid muscle, while he let the anticipation of what laid beneath that rumpled skirt swell inside of him. She reached up and unbuttoned his pale blue shirt, tearing it off of his body. Her eyes widened with pleasure as she ran her fingers through the spirals of hair on his hard, muscle-bound chest, and wended her way down to the button on his pants. It flipped open easily and she fingered the zipper, feeling the rock-hard bulge beneath. That did it. All control dissolved and he tore her new, red dress off over her head. She jerked the zipper open and shoved his pants down. They fell to the floor, followed by his pristine white Jockey shorts.

The pupils of Llayne's eyes involuntarily expanded at the sight of him fully naked. He was all lean muscle, he was magnificently endowed, he was gorgeous. He was irresistible.

Mack's eyes glazed over in bliss as they roamed from her firm breasts rising and falling with excited breaths, to her slim torso which collapsed into a concave pleasure bowl with a cute belly-button in its center, then down to the mound between her legs, protected by a light brown nest of curly hair, moving up and down in primeval thrusts. It was an invitation he couldn't resist any longer. He dropped onto her and finally the sublime moment arrived. He entered her and she plunged into that netherworld between rapacious consciousness and primitive unconsciousness, that world where nothing mattered but sexual gratification, nothing except his thrusting himself in and out of her, harder and faster, gorging her groin with a need so great.... Soaring higher,

higher, higher, she reached her peak and let out a scream. Her delight made it impossible for him to hold back any longer; he moaned with sheer rapture as he, too, reached the ultimate satisfaction. Clinging to each other, they lay there for a long time, gently stroking one another's bodies.

When her desire began to grow again, she reached down to find some of the milk he'd left inside of her. Swabbing her lower lips, she came up with a thick, juicy fingerfull. She showed it to him, then in a spontaneous gesture, stuck it into her mouth to taste his cream. Slowly she pulled her finger out of her mouth and rasped, "You're delicious."

"Oh, yeah? Well, we have to be fair here. It's my turn to taste you." He raised the middle finger he used to explore her furrow. "Smell it," he said, and they hovered together to take in the scent. "Your love balm is still there." He put the finger to his mouth, she put her face next to his, and they each licked the finger with their tongues, intermingling those tongues as they did so. "Um, you taste good, too," he whispered.

"Oh, yeah?"

"You little animal," he interrupted, "you want more, don't you?"

She bent her arms up over her head and lowered her eyelids to look at him mischievously. "How did you guess?" she teased, rocking her hips to meet his. "O-oh! I see you want more, too," she noted, lowering an arm to wrap her hand around the object of that insight.

"Gee, how did you guess?" he asked rhetorically.

This time their lovemaking became more than mere physical coupling. This time their bodies joined together to serve as a bridge for the joining of two souls.

Being with Mack almost felt like she was making love for the first time because she was a new woman, emotionally and spiritually. Never before had she had that kind of heady liberty, that kind of confidence, nor that kind of erotic creative freedom to offer to a man. Never before had she been that comfortable with her body and her mind. Never before had she been that much of a woman. With love overflowing in her heart, she knew that everything that had happened to her in her life to that point had made her the woman who could love this man like she never loved before. She was immensely grateful.

Memories of screwing with Rex, the sleazy professor, were erased; her former dalliance with the young hippy, Peter, was a wisp of an amusing flashback; the remembrance of making love with gentle Tank became a cherished, treasured primer. Now she couldn't imagine ever wanting to make love with anyone but this man. With Mack O'Brien.

"You know," he said, breaking into her thoughts as they lay at rest, "I went back to Mt. Pleasant the summer after graduation to try to find you. I found out you were marrying Tank, though, so I left."

"Why did you want to find me?" she queried.

"To ask you to marry me," he confessed boldly. She stared at the ceiling in silence. "Well, don't you have anything to say?" he wanted to know.

"Sure," she said, looking over at him in the now darkened room. "I'll say 'yes' as soon as you ask me. You haven't asked me yet."

His smile was enormous as he turned over onto his stomach and locked his hands as if pleading. "Llayne Robertson Tanner, will you marry me?"

Tenderly she stroked his cheek. "Yes," she said.

After a deep, celebratory kiss, she said, "You've changed the ritual of proposing marriage. It's supposed to be on one knee, after a nice dinner or something, with clothes on. You're buck naked and on your belly, after screwing my brains out."

"Well," he chuckled, "I didn't want to do the same old thing everybody else does. Actually, I had the whole ritual planned quite nicely. We were going to have a romantic dinner, then I was going to take your hand, and give you ... Oh my god! I was going to give you ..." he said as he jumped up and rummaged through his pants' pocket. "This!" he declared, bouncing back onto the bed and holding up a ring. A glint of diamond sparkled in the dark as he put the ring on her finger.

Mack O'Brien held his betrothed as she wept with joy into his broad, bare shoulder.

Eneida Estacio, the Brazilian neighbor woman, was no fool. She saw the gorgeous hunk of a man come to the apartment next door day after day, and every one of those days she saw him leave a horny man. Yet, sexual electricity sizzled between him and Kenyon's beautiful young mother. As far as she could tell, it was the first time the two adults had been alone. It was time for some sparks to fly! So, it was no surprise to her when he drove up that night, went into that apartment and never came out. His shiny, new, black truck never moved from its parking spot.

Ah, how Eneida swooned over the idea of true love. At age 41, she doubted it would ever happen to her. Her job as a housekeeper at the Harley Hotel, which had excited her upon her arrival to the United States two years earlier, had grown dull and tedious. And she missed her Brazilian *tele-novellas,* short-series soap operas on television. Although more crudely produced, they were much bolder, sexier and more fun than mundane American soaps. The goings on next door were proving to be a good replacement, though.

That's why, when Llayne called at 11 o'clock that night, just like she promised she would, to come and get Kenyon, Eneida put her off, insisting that the child was so sound asleep on the couch there was no need to wake her until morning. Llayne hesitated, said something to the man, and finally agreed. "I'll pay you extra," she said.

"Oh, no, don't even think about it," Eneida said. "It's been such a pleasure." She didn't mention that the pleasure wasn't just being with the child, it was entertaining herself by snooping and speculating.

◆ ◆ ◆ ◆ ◆ ◆ ◆ ◆

Kenyon awoke to delicious smells of cooking food. She was a little confused at first, but quickly remembered that her mommy was right next door. And she was happy that she'd been allowed to sleep in her sequined shoes. Holding one hand out to admire the bright pink polish Miss Eneida had painted on her nails while clutching her veil with the other hand, she galloped to the kitchenette area to check out breakfast. It looked very promising. Her mommy just fixed cold cereal in the morning, because they were always in a hurry.

"*Bom dia,* Kenyon!" Miss Eneida, standing at the stove flipping over a round, flat thing in a pan, cheerfully greeted her.

"*Bom dia,* Miss Eneida!" Kenyon mimicked, hopping up into a chair at the table.

"Very good! *Muito bom!* We may as well get you speaking proper Portugues as soon as possible," she chuckled. "Now, would you like some bacon for breakfast?"

Although quite certain she never had any of that before, Kenyon said, "Yes, please."

"That's '*sim, por favor.*'"

"*Sim, por favor.*"

"*Muito bom!* Oh, you and I are going to have so much fun!"

Miss Eneida showed Kenyon how to pour syrup all over the *panquecas*, and let her drink coffee. Kenyon didn't like that stuff, but it was fun to drink out of a big person's cup. Gobbling down the chow, she thought that maybe she better come over there every night, but then realized she'd start missing her pink princess bed, the one Uncle Peter had given her. Maybe she could just come over for *panquecas* and coffee every morning!

As that idea took shape in the little girl's mind, Mack and Llayne were next door scrambling to get him showered, dressed, and out of there before Kenyon came home. It didn't help when he pulled Llayne into the shower with him, where the level of steam rose even higher.

Once she was out of the shower, with a towel wrapped around her body, she suddenly remembered the roses which had spent the night on the floor and rushed to put them in a vase. They held up well, looking healthy and smelling wonderful. She set them on the kitchenette counter.

In the meantime, Mack, naked as a jaybird, was sorting through all the clothes that had been cast about the room and came up with Llayne's new, red dress. "Oh my god!" he croaked. "I ripped it right off of you! Oh, I'm so sorry, honey. You didn't even get to wear it out. I'll get you a new one." He held up the shredded garment.

She laughed. "That's okay. That dress served its purpose. Wearing it out wasn't the idea."

"Oh, yeah?" he questioned, dropping the dress and going over to nibble on her neck, unwrapping her towel and throwing it to the floor. "Are you saying I was set up?"

"Um, do you object?" she cooed, turning around to wrap her arms around his neck so they could feel the breadth of one another's clean, Ivory-Soap-smelling, bare bodies. "I don't object," she said, "considering that's what you've been doing to me for the last four months. Admit it. You've been setting me up to get to this, haven't you?"

"What I've been doing is falling even more and more in love with you," he admitted, bending his head to tenderly kiss her left nipple as he cupped that breast in his hand. "And, setting you up so we could have sex," he admitted. Two inches from her face, his broad smile lit up his handsome face, then he cupped and kissed her other breast.

Llayne let her head drop back as she ran her hands through his hair while he tantalized her ductile nipples with his tongue. Her knees became weak, yet again. "Honey," she uttered, "we have time for one more quick one before Kenyon comes home." Her hands moved down to caress him.

"Are you sure?" he asked, already anointing his fingers within her. A groan answered, so he quickly turned her around and she bent over the kitchenette counter. Reaching around to continue to fondle her irresistible, pliant boobies, he entered her determinedly and it was just a matter of seconds before each of them moaned with culminated pleasure. Wrapping his arms around her, they slumped over the counter together and started to laugh.

"We can't do this all day!" he noted. "I have to go to work."

"Quit!" she suggested.

"Well, I want to make money to take care of my new family," he offered as they stood up and she turned around, which caused him to hold her out at arm's length. "It really would be best if I didn't get fired right now."

"Oh, damn. I guess we'll have to wait until you get off at five before we can make love again. I don't know if I can stand it!"

Mack guffawed all the way back to the shower, where he stepped in for a quick rinse, after which he quickly dressed. Giving her a big good-bye smack on the lips, he said, "See you at five!" and left.

Llayne, still nude and holding a towel up to her body, watched through the window as he drove away. "Oh, Mack O'Brien," she said, " you have no idea what you've got yourself into! We're going to do this a lot!" She laughed heartily.

♦ ♦ ♦ ♦ ♦ ♦ ♦ ♦

And so they did, time and time again, with Kenyon visiting her new Brazilian friend. It was getting to be more and more entertaining for Eneida Estacio. She didn't miss her tele-novellas so much anymore.

The woman wouldn't have given her sexy soaps one more thought if she could have seen what was going on next door. It was far more ribald than anything she could have imagined!

Although Mack never again stayed all night, he came over every day after work, and sometimes Miss Eneida would take Kenyon for half an hour before supper. And, once a week, every Saturday evening, the couple planned an entire evening alone until eleven when Kenyon came home, which meant that once a week they had hours to ravage each others' bodies. Sometimes their lovemaking was tender, sometimes funny, sometimes rough, and always satisfying.

◆ ◆ ◆ ◆ ◆ ◆ ◆ ◆

She made him get naked and sit on a pillow on the floor. Her apartment was dark except for a bunch of lit candles. Exotic music played from the stereo. He felt ridiculous. But then she surprised him by coming out of the bathroom in her Dance of the Seven Veils costume. She'd told him about her belly dancing, but he had no idea how good she was! Her body movements were eye-popping to watch, each motion exciting him to distraction. Gracefully, she unwrapped the top sheer veil, a pink one, and wrapped it around his neck. He'd never had such a delicate, soft fabric on his hard body before, and it prickled his skin with pleasure. Her jasmine aroma lingered in the air to heighten the sensation. Eventually all seven veils, each a different soft color, had been unwrapped from her body and loosely swathed around his. She danced before him stark naked, having foregone the usual costume underneath the veils, and he was aroused beyond repair. They made love in a sea of pastel chiffon, transported to a foreign land of eroticism.

◆ ◆ ◆ ◆ ◆ ◆ ◆ ◆

Having delighted in plotting to bring to life a fantasy he confessed to her, she went to the government building that housed political offices, marched unannounced into his neat room, and closed and locked the door behind her. Mack looked up from a Veterans' Administration report he'd been studying, and it only took one glance of her in the rain coat and high heels before he guessed what was about to happen. Chucking the report and leaning back in his chair with his hands behind his head, he prepared himself to enjoy the show. As anticipated, she flung off the coat to reveal her nudity underneath. Mack started to shake his head and giggle. Never in his life had he expected that fantasy to come true! As her giggling mingled with his, he decided, what the hell, they may as well complete the fantasy. With one giant sweep of his arm he got rid of everything on top of his desk, papers and pens and do-dads flying, and picked her up to set her on top of the bare wood. There, in the middle of an ordinary work day, on top of his work desk, they went to work on each other.

◆ ◆ ◆ ◆ ◆ ◆ ◆ ◆

One of Llayne's fantasies didn't quite work out. Ever since the afternoon Mack had taken Kenyon and her for a walk in the woods outside of Lansing, and they'd run across a small, swinging bridge over a secluded creek, she thought of making love on that pliable bridge. So, one night Mack took Llayne back out there to make her dream come true. In her imagination, however, the bridge swung to and fro in a gentle, swaying motion. In reality, however, it bopped up and down, and the boards clapped together to pinch her butt. Bellowing with pain, she shoved Mack off of her, sending him through the side ropes to fall over the side of the bridge!

Fortunately, the agile ex-Green Beret snatched at a rope and landed safely, right-side-up, standing in the cold water. Then he screamed! Once they got back to his truck, and she helped him dry off, and he kissed her "butt boo-boos," they laughed uproariously at their own stupidity. Then they realized they'd never done it in his new truck, so they forgot about the bridge and initiated the virgin vehicle, right then and there.

◆ ◆ ◆ ◆ ◆ ◆ ◆ ◆

Llayne's mind was lost in a fog of lust as she parked in front of the campus child care center and got Kenyon out of the car. Mack had been unbelievable the Saturday night before in his truck out by that bridge! She couldn't wait to see what the next Saturday would bring!

"Llayne! Hey, Llayne!" a young woman hollered from amidst a crowd of students scurrying to class.

"Hi, Cindy," she greeted her classmate, stopping to talk.

"I need to ask a favor," the woman said, pathetically wrinkling her brow. "I skipped class last Friday and need to borrow some notes. You got any I could take until class time today?"

"Sure," Llayne said, dropping Kenyon's hand and shuffling through her notebook. She liked Cindy and wanted to help. "Now, where are they? I know I took some, although I have to admit it was pretty boring and my mind kept wandering." She didn't add, "to sex.""Ah! Here they are!" She ripped out two pages and handed them to Cindy, then automatically dropped her hand down to take Kenyon's hand off her coat. The child always grasped an item of clothing when a hand wasn't available. But, there was no small hand holding on to her coat.

Llayne flung around to look. Kenyon was gone. "Kenyon! Kenyon!" she yelled at the top of her lungs, instantly frantic.

"Oh my god!" Cindy said, putting her hand to her mouth.

"You go that way," Llayne ordered, pointing at the mass of people in one direction, "and I'll go this way. We'll meet back here."

"Okay!" Cindy said, taking off.

"Have you seen a little girl?" Llayne immediately started asking as she hurled through the crowd. She was greeted with lots of negatives, a few grunts and a dozen offers to help her look. Students scattered in every direction, quizzing other students and looking everywhere.

Llayne ran to the car, thinking Kenyon may have gone back for something, but the car was empty. Then she ran into the child care center, hoping she'd gone in on her own, but none of the teachers had seen her and they, too, became alarmed.

Suddenly is occurred to Llayne that Kenyon may have strayed just a little way, so she returned to the spot where she'd been talking to Cindy. Two students along the way reported that they hadn't found her little girl yet, but they solicited more help. "Don't worry," she was reassured, "we'll find her!"

Suddenly a campus policeman came to her and said, "Are you the lady who lost her little girl?"

His phrasing pained her, and she had to admit, "Yes."

"Somebody just flagged me down to tell me. I radioed for help. We'll do our best to find her," he said, making Llayne feel like he was saying, "Seeing that you're not capable of keeping track of her yourself." "Is this where you lost her?" he asked.

"Yes," was all she could manage to say.

"Okay. You stay right here, in case she comes back here. Let us look. Would she possibly have gone back to your car?"

Llayne pointed to the Cutlass, parked not 50 feet away. "I looked. She's not there. I checked the child care center, too, and she's not in there."

Another officer arrived. "Listen, Harry," the first one said, "why don't you check the child care center out real good. If she's familiar with it, she might be hiding in there. You know, playing a game."

"Check," said Harry, and he took off.

"Now, don't move," the first policeman said as he left.

The sense of loss that overcame Llayne hit like a hurricane. She started to sob, and a female professor stopped to offer support. "Help me! Help me!" Llayne began screaming at the students walking past, no longer able to stand idly by. "Help me find my little girl!" Her intensity garnered the attention of more young people and before long the professor had sent huge groups of them out in quickly organized search parties.

"Help," Llayne continued to sob, even as scores of people were now searching.

Then there was a rumble of cheerful voices coming from the direction of a building on the other side of the parking lot, and a student ran up to shout, "We found her!"

Llayne ran through the lot toward the group of searchers, and the sea of coats parted to reveal an Asian man holding Kenyon. The child was smiling broadly.

"I'm so sorry," the man said in a southern drawl, handing over the little girl. "I didn't even notice her following me until I reached my classroom door and someone pointed her out. I had no idea how long she'd been behind me, or where she came from. I stood there in the hall with her, thinking maybe her parent was right there somewhere."

Llayne clutched Kenyon to her breast, and said to him, "Oh, thank you! Thank you so much! Thanks to all of you!" she said to the crowd, swiping at her tears with one hand while she clung to her daughter with the other. Mystified, Kenyon helped her dry her tears.

The students and others congratulated themselves for a job well done, and started to scatter.

"You know," the Asian-looking man said, "she kept talking to me in Chinese or something."

"She's Vietnamese," Llayne explained.

"Oh, of course. Well, I see why she thought she could talk to me. I'm sorry I couldn't understand her, though. You see, I was born and raised in Knoxville, Tennessee. Third generation Thai. I know nothing of any foreign language, unless you count Tennessee southern." That actually got a thin smile out of Llayne. "Well, you take care now," he said as he started to walk away. "And you, you little sweetie," he said, patting Kenyon's hand, "you stay with your mom."

"Thanks again," Llayne said as he waved and became lost in the shuffle of people.

"Well," the policeman said, frightening her as he appeared behind her, "I see everything is okay. You keep better tabs on her from now on," he scolded.

"I will," Llayne promised. "Thank you."

Later that afternoon, when she sat over coffee with Eneida Estacio and told her what had happened, the warm Brazilian woman reassured her that even the best of parents lose a child once. "But only once," she said, "because it scares you so much you'll never let it happen again."

"No I won't! But, geez! She's my daughter and I feel like she's safer with you than with me! You've never lost her."

Eneida patted her hand and said, "But Llayne, I've been baby-sitting for 25 years, with thousands of nieces and nephews in Brazil, which, if I recall correctly, is one of the reasons I moved here. So, I've had lots of experience. Now you have more experience, too, and you know to be more careful. And you will be!"

Llayne loved the dear woman for being so kind.

But later that evening she told Mack and explained that when Kenyon got lost that, as well as being distracted by her classmate, she'd been preoccupied with thinking about having sex with him and, therefore, they couldn't have sex anymore.

He said, "Never?"

She said, "Never!"

"But, don't you think that not having sex will preoccupy your mind more than having it, and therefore, we'd better have it to free your mind to concentrate on taking care of Kenyon?"

"Oh, you are good," she admitted. "Very, very good."

"I know," he said with a crooked grin.

Llayne crawled into her bed that night vowing to be a better parent. Never again did she want to experience that devastating sense of loss. Losing Tank had been bad enough; she would never, never let herself lose his child. She learned a parenting lesson the hard way: do not ever let go of that little hand!

◆ ◆ ◆ ◆ ◆ ◆ ◆ ◆

Her vow to never have sex again lasted for five days, until Mack confessed to having repeated fantasies of dancing with her again. He never forgot that time at The Cabin when they held each other close. She never forgot it either, of course, so it was the perfect way to ease her back into closeness. On Saturday evening at his place, he put on the song they danced to on that night so long ago, Elvis Presley's "I Can't Help Falling in Love," and once again they melted into one another's arms.

Their lovemaking that night was so gentle and tender Llayne thought she might float away into a weightless, spacious, star-sparkled sky. As long as Mack came with her, she didn't care where this relationship sent her.

♦♦♦♦♦♦♦♦

Sometimes he was tender and sometimes he was a wild man, liking his sex slightly on the dangerous side, which surprised Llayne considered he just announced his candidacy for the State Legislature. He wanted to represent the Lansing district and had the endorsement of the Democratic incumbent who was retiring after 20 years on the floor. Mack's present boss, Congressman John Harrington, also gave his blessing. So, it would seem it was time for him to be careful.

Apparently, that thought never crossed his mind. They were at the campus library so she could study. Spring semester mid-terms were coming up and it was important that she prepare. So far her grades had been great and she didn't want to slack off. She even achieved a measure of notoriety in her Soap Opera Production class, where class members produced, wrote, directed and acted in a semester-long soap opera that was aired daily across campus. "Gone With the Breeze" had become a student favorite. And she was the head writer and star actor. Miss Eneida had given her some great ideas for storylines, taken from Brazilian *tele-novellas,* and Llayne loved playing the part of Harlett O'Hara, the irreputable, long-lost cousin of that other O'Hara woman. Every day her face glared out from TV sets all over campus, so she was readily recognized everywhere she went at Michigan State. Already that evening three students had commented to her about it: "Hey, Harlett O'Hara! Groovy, man!" "Miss Harlett! Is it really you?" and "Ain't you that broad on TV?"

That was what got Mack going. She was innocently trying to study when he said, "Miss Harlett, let's go into the janitor's closet!"

"Why, Mr. O'Brien! What kind of girl do you think I am?" she mocked in her exaggerated southern accent.

"I know what kind of girl you are. That's why I want to go into the closet with you!" he razzed.

"Now, Mr. O'Brien, you wild Irish rogue, you promised that if I brought you to the library you'd be quiet so I could study," she admonished, wagging a finger at him.

"We can be quiet in the closet. In fact, we'll have to be, unless we want to get arrested."

That did it. She couldn't resist the challenge and he knew it. They never tried making love without making noise before.

He got up first and went across the hall to slide behind the door marked "Janitor's Closet." She waited a minute, making certain no one was watching, then followed. They discovered that they could make love without a peep.

♦ ♦ ♦ ♦ ♦ ♦ ♦ ♦

The clackity-clack of the train wheels and the farmland scenes whisking by outside the window excited her. She'd never been on a train before, and she'd never been to Chicago before.

He couldn't believe she'd never been outside of Michigan, except for that one quick trip to Indianapolis to pick up Kenyon. It thrilled him to be able to introduce her to the fabulous Windy City. They'd peruse the Field Museum, see the sights from the Sears Tower, stroll down Lake Shore Drive to take in the view of Lake Michigan, window shop along the Miracle Mile of Michigan Avenue, eat at Mulligans Public House on Roscoe Street, dance at the Rush Up on Rush Street and make love in their room at the Clarion Hotel. He had the perfect weekend planned.

Sitting shoulder-to-shoulder in the wide, clean Amtrak seats, they didn't bother to talk, being totally comfortable just to be in one another's presence as they trekked toward their fun destination. It was just a matter of time, however, before their sexual energy started to feed on itself, magnifying and careening off of the confining walls of their bodies like an ion in an atom splitter.

"I can't wait to get to our hotel room," her saucy voice intrigued him as she turned away from the window and nudged his neck with her nose.

"Why wait?" he asked, grinning his sly, cockeyed grin. Her eyes became full moons at the suggestion. Pulling his jacket over on top of her lap and checking around to make certain no one was moving about or coming into their unpopulated corner of the train, he turned his back to the aisle to shield her from anyone walking by, slipped his hand under the jacket, glided it beneath her short skirt, and adeptly pulled aside her panties. Plunging into her with his fingers, he gave her a shock that sent her head into a tailspin. Her eyes closed to become languid quarter moons as she relinquished all common sense and surrendered her body to Mack's ministrations. "Now," he whispered into her ear, "you must be very, very quiet. I know you can be quiet." He was interrupted by wave upon wave of silent spasm in her lower body as she dug her nails into his arm.

When her flesh finally became tranquilized from satisfaction and her head laid contentedly on his shoulder, she looked up into his eyes and said, "That wasn't fair. All for me. None for you."

He replied, "Believe me, that was for me, too. But if it bothers you," he chuckled, "I'll let you do one just for me when we get to our room."

And so she did.

CHAPTER 16

Waylon Jennings and Willie Nelson soothed Mack's nerves as he sped away from his office, their mellow voices emanating from the radio, "Sometimes heaven, sometimes hell, sometimes it's hard to tell ..." Mack had been partial to country-western music ever since Nam and at the moment he needed his songster buddies to calm him down. The disastrous meeting he just had with his new political advisor had really pissed him off. After one brief consultation, he fired the guy's sorry ass.

Running the meeting over in his mind, he stewed over what the dickhead had said. First, he wanted to know everything about Llayne so he could ascertain whether she'd be an asset or a hindrance in Mack's campaign for the State Legislature. Mack had ended up telling the guy he didn't give a fuck what he thought. He was marrying Llayne in June and that was that.

The stiff, conservative man had frowned and tried to give him a stern lecture about the importance of disclosure so he wouldn't be hit with any surprises in the middle of the campaign. He already knew that the candidate's fiancee had been a belly dancer and found that disturbing.

He said, "And worse yet, she plays a harlot on campus television. We must advise her to quit the show."

"It's a class," Mack had corrected him, "and she's not quitting. Besides, it's funny as hell. The students love it."

"Maybe so, Mr. O'Brien," the man had quipped, "but these students can't help you. Most of them are too young to vote. And the ones who can vote are such hippies they don't care."

The asshole had had the balls to insult his fiancee and his constituents, and suddenly Mack had found pleasure in thinking of how the guy would shit bricks if he knew Llayne had once worked in a strip club, let alone that she gave birth to an illegitimate baby. But those things, which she confided to him in trusting confidence, would never be known, not if he had anything to do with it. They couldn't drag that information out of him with thumb screws. So much of what that advisor interrogated him about was nobody's business and had nothing to do with the campaign or his ability to lead.

Besides, Mack was too savvy not to have an alternate plan in mind. Should that information ever become public, he'd use a novel approach for politics. He'd tell the truth. She'd been a desperate college kid who'd been taken advantage of by an older professor. He'd bank his career on being able to turn that into voter sympathy. But hopefully, it would never come to that.

"Now," the advisor had said, "we already anticipate trouble from your former fiancee, Senator White's daughter. She's promised to go public with how badly she believes you treated her. Her most recent quote is, 'He dumped me like yesterday's trash the minute that trashy dame came along." She's a real loose cannon. Can't you do something to mollify her?"

Mack had sat there, not answering, thinking of Sarah Jane White, so beautiful and yet so vacant. He'd long since realized he'd become engaged to her because he yearned to settle down and have a family, not because he'd loved her. It'd been a mistake he realized the moment he read about Tank's unfortunate death and had fallen all over himself to get to the phone to call Llayne, who still had no idea he broke his former engagement after seeing her again, not before. Sarah Jane had been an irate viper about it.

"No," Mack had said to the advisor, "there's nothing that can be done about Sarah. We'll work around her."

"She would've been the perfect politician's wife," the fool had made the mistake of saying. That's when Mack had kicked the piss-ass punk out of his office and stormed outdoors to seek refuge in his truck, and in the singing cowboys.

Dust flew as he raced down the country road with the windows open, whipping his tie off as he drove and unbuttoning the top three buttons of his shirt so he could get some air. Four miles out of town and past his own stone farmhouse, he continued a mile further, turned onto another dirt road, drove another mile and came to a small, field-stone Presbyterian Church. He pulled up in front, turned off the engine and sat in his truck admiring the place in silence, letting its peacefulness wash over him. Just looking at it calmed his frazzled nerves.

It was a charming, aged house of God, well over a hundred years old. Each of the side walls contained three stained glass windows of aqua, gold, purple, pink, white and clear shards of glass soldered into simple, spiral flower designs. They would have been much less expensive than the traditional religious stained glass windows depicting Bible scenes, but were equally inspiring, in Mack's opinion, contrasting beautifully with the gray stone walls. The original congregation built the church with their own hands, but must have pooled their meager resources to purchase the windows, which would have been brought in from a city, probably Detroit, by horse-drawn wagon. What a precarious trip that must have been!

He took a long, deep breath, felt rejuvenated and considered that before him was a typical farm community church like so many that dotted the Michigan countryside. A piece of history that he adored. He genuinely loved the state of his birth and had made it his personal quest to serve it and its people, finding in that mission the excitement he'd sought all of his life. He even aspired to become governor someday. No one knew that except Llayne. She seemed to be the only one who understood his deep feelings toward that patch of the earth, the left-hand mitten of the lower peninsula and the upside-down lady's boot of the upper peninsula that made up Michigan. The name itself was an Algonquian word meaning *great water.* Great water certainly surrounded it, all right, with shores on four of the five Great Lakes.

Every time he thought about it he was amazed at how the state had become settled. Of course, there had been the Native Americans first - Algonquian tribes like the

Chippewas, Menominees, Ottawas, and Potawatomis; and the Iroquois tribe, the Wyandots - all of whom had been sorely mistreated by the government, in Mack's opinion. He wanted to help them, at least what was left of them. Then the French fur traders and missionaries had come, then the "English," who actually consisted mostly of Irish, Scots-Irish, Dutch, German, and Polish immigrants who'd been encouraged to move west by elite East Coast officials, most of British heritage at that time, who didn't want such "rubble" in their cosmopolitan coastal cities. In the late 18th and early 19th centuries, those immigrant farmers had toiled with mules and crude tools to clear the land of forests filled with pine, maple, oak, and white birch trees, and of the gray stones so common in the area. Melting glaciers that had deposited the rocks and carved out the Great Lakes on their journeys southward in prehistoric times. Once the fields were tillable, the farmers had been practical, using the wood in the interiors and the stones for the exteriors of their farmhouses, out buildings and churches.

During the present time, a church like the one in front of him seemed remote, but back then it would have been the central gathering place in the area. No more than a dozen farm families would have been needed to fill the place. No one would have been able to travel to town, anyway, in the oppressive winter weather. Mack was amazed and proud that those pioneers had succeeded in supporting one another as they eked sustenance out of that tough ground in tough northern weather. No wonder their church had been so important to them.

He shook his head, recalling how that obnoxious political advisor had recommended that he start attending church regularly because it would look good to the public. He scoffed! Going to church was something that one did because of a call from the soul, not because of how it would appear to others.

He got out of his truck and stood there taking in the soothing holy place. A large lawn rambled around the building to meet a cemetery with eroded, mossy headstones that stretched to the woods in back. The church and yard were in good repair, still having a small congregation, with the minister from Lansing coming out each Sunday for an early service before he returned to the big Presbyterian Church for a later service.

Mack went to the plainly carved, oak, double doors and found them unlocked. People around there still trusted one another. Inside it was cool and musty smelling, with muted rays of afternoon light filtering through the antique windows. The back wall, behind a small, wood alter which supported a two-foot-tall wooden cross, also contained a stained glass window like those on the side walls, and the cross cast a majestic shadow in front of the tinted prism of floral light.

There was one chair on each side of the alter with its back to a side wall. One was an old parlor chair made from a kind of wood he couldn't determine, and the other no more than an old, intricately carved, oak kitchen chair. To the left of the alter area against the side wall stood a rickety upright piano painted white. There were 10 pews down each side, each simply yet sturdily handmade of maple. He walked about halfway up the aisle, the pine floor welcoming each footstep with a salutary creak, and sat down, reverently running his hand along the back of the pew in front of him. More than a century ago someone's hands, probably a farmer's, had painstakingly made that pew.

He put his hands together and lowered his head in prayer. "Dear God," he began, clearing his throat, "I know I haven't talked to You in a long time. That's why I think it's time for me to make amends. I don't know if You remember me from Nam, but I took Your name in vain a lot. I also prayed to You a lot, but I'm pretty sure You didn't hear me.

"Anyway, I haven't been in touch since, and I want You to know how much I appreciate the blessings You've given me recently. This woman and this child you've put in my care are the greatest gifts I've ever known.

"And, Tank, if you're up there, and I have no doubt you are, I want to thank you, too. I don't know if it was Divine intervention or my own stupidity that put you and Llayne together, but you were so good to her. You know, I put off my feelings for her in college, telling myself she was too young for me and wasn't ready for a man like me. Now I know how well I lied to myself. I wasn't ready for her. But I am now. I want you to know that. Those two females have given me new energy, new life, new purpose! I promise to take care of them with everything that's in me!"

Bathed in absolute peace, slowly he raised his head. A bright beam of light pulsated through the colored glass window behind the alter as Mack O'Brien's face took on a aura of awe, reflecting the surge of renewed faith he felt that there was a God.

Fifteen minutes later, after allowing himself to sit still and assimilate what seemed to him like generations of love and support emanating from the old place of worship, he went out to his truck, took one last look around, and grinned. "Oh, by the way, God, Tank," he said with his face to the sky, that political advisor rudely invading his thoughts, "if either one of you fellows can help me learn patience, I'd appreciate it. It'd be good if I didn't lose my temper and beat the living shit out of some ignorant asshole during my campaign." He gave them a two-fingered salute and hopped into his truck to drive home.

Sunlight continued to illuminate the little country church.

It was a glorious, sunny, June day when the wedding took place in the little country church. Friends and family members from all over the state, co-workers, and even a few well-known politicians, all crammed into the nave. In the front row on one side were Llayne's mom; Llayne's brother, whom she hadn't seen in years and who showed up unexpectedly on leave from Germany looking handsome in his army dress uniform; and Priscilla's husband, Stan, who held their adorable, towheaded, nine-month-old son. Mack's elderly parents, all the way down from Escanaba in the upper peninsula, a major journey for them, and Mack's two older brothers, their wives, and a couple of teenagers, sat in the front row on the other side of the church. One look at Mack's siblings and

Llayne could see how her soon-to-be-husband got so scrappy. He grew up having to defend himself from those two swarthy guys.

The groom beamed. At his side, his enormous best man, Neckbreaker, stood busting out of his tux as the ceremony began. The pianist played "Here Comes the Bride" as Kenyon, the flower girl, walked down the aisle in a pastel peach-and-blue-and-white flowered dress with white lace trim and a white lace petticoat underneath, and scattered white rose petals from the basket she carried. She had a hard time concentrating, though, because it was so exciting having all those people together!

"Uncle Dale!" she whispered excitedly, stopping in her tracks. "I'm awful hungry! You got any gum?" She knew he always did. All eyes were on her and the crowd tittered as Dale quickly unwrapped a stick of Juicy Fruit and hastily crammed it into her mouth. Three more steps down the aisle and she halted again. "Uncle Bob! See my new shoes?" She twisted her foot from side-to-side to show off her white footwear. "See the teensy bows on top?" After he agreed that they were cool shoes, she continued her trek. Noticing the Lichengers and giving them an enthusiastic wave, then spinning around for Miss Eneida and Miss Kerina to show them her dress, she finally managed to throw a few white rose petals into the aisle. But, there was one last interruption.

"Hey, Uncle Peter!" she hollered, giving up trying to whisper as she enjoyed the limelight. Reaching across the woman on the aisle, she grabbed the edge of his suit jacket and yanked. "Did you know yesterday we put my pink princess bed in my own room at Mack's farmhouse? 'Cept I can call him daddy now!"

"Yes, princess," Uncle Peter said, grinning from ear-to-ear. "Now you'd better get on up to the altar."

"Oh, yeah," she agreed, suddenly remembering the rehearsal the evening before and that she wasn't supposed to be talking. She was supposed to be throwing the rose petals onto the floor. So, she decided to get her part over with as quickly as possible and turned her basket upside down to dump the last of the petals into a pile in the aisle. The whole room was in stitches by the time she finally reached the side of the altar.

Then Priscilla, as maid of honor, walked down the aisle in a beautiful, light coral suit, carrying white roses. Stan and their little boy waved at her, and the baby suddenly shrieked with glee and clapped. Everyone laughed again, and Priscilla's shoulders shook with mirth.

Mack's eyes riveted toward Llayne when she appeared at the door on her father's arm. In an elegant off-white suit, with her hair gathered up under a lovely hat with a puff of veil around it, she looked stunning. The solitaire diamond earrings he gave her the night before as a wedding gift and her diamond engagement ring were her only jewels. A hush fell over the crowd, and the piano vibrated with a more rousing version of the wedding song as the bride and her dad walked to the altar.

Llayne Robertson Tanner and Mack O'Brien took their wedding vows and solemnly swore to love one another forever. And they meant it.

♦ ♦ ♦ ♦ ♦ ♦ ♦ ♦

Mack whisked his bride away for a week-long honeymoon on St. Martin's island in the Caribbean. His fellow politicians admonished him for leaving in the middle of a campaign. His new campaign manager fretted when Mack wouldn't give him a phone number to call in case of emergency. But he didn't care. It was their honeymoon and the first real vacation of Llayne's life.

For one fantastic week they stretched out their scantily clad bodies in the sun; drank silly, colored drinks in tall glasses with umbrellas stuck in them; strolled up and down the ocean beach; and even read a couple of good books. And, they savored each other's bodies in ways they never imagined possible. Never, never, it seemed, would they get too much of one another.

♦ ♦ ♦ ♦ ♦ ♦ ♦ ♦

"You damned son-of-a-bitch!" Llayne seethed at her husband.

Totally unglued and sweating profusely, Mack looked at the doctor for help. "It's okay," the obstetrician reassured him. "She'll hate your guts until it's over, then she'll love you again. Trust me; I've seen it a thousand times. Now! Let's get back to work!"

Swallowing hard, Mack bent over his wife and softly spoke into her ear. "Push, honey," he advised, just like he learned to do in that La Maze class.

"You push, damn it!" she hissed at him. All that lovemaking had brought her to this moment of excruciating pain and, if she didn't love him so much, she would hate Mack O'Brien's frigging guts! She didn't remember it hurting like this the first time and felt certain he'd purposely done something to make it hurt more! She screamed again and grabbed his hand, crushing his knuckles together in a vise grip that Mack would have sworn was that of a 400-pound wrestler named The Crusher. He grimaced and bit his lower lip to try to keep from shrieking himself.

In the hospital waiting room, four-year-old Kenyon was bored. That baby business was taking much longer than she expected. Where was that kid, anyway?

She took a nap in the big chair, but now she was awake and needed something to do! If that baby would hurry up and get there they could play together.

Po Po snoozed beside her in another chair, his head tilted to one side and a newspaper open in his lap. Mo Mo had been there, too, when Kenyon had fallen asleep, but she was gone now. *Pro'bly getting coffee,* Kenyon thought. She was always getting coffee and wouldn't even let her drink any like Miss Eneida did.

Fiddling with a button on her overalls, she stiffened her knees to look at her shoes. Yup, she looked nifty! Her Mo Mo had let her dress herself that morning. She had on her yellow blouse with the ruffled collar, her Oshkosh overalls, her green socks and her shiny, red shoes. Mo Mo had even tied Kenyon's favorite purple and orange ribbon around her ponytail.

Opening her mouth to finger a new molar, she thought about how nervous her daddy had been when the baby started to come. He was in there with mommy now and Kenyon was glad a doctor was in there to take care of him.

Her thoughts ping-ponged around, and she remembered the time when she went with mommy to that big building with the round top, the Cap-tall, where daddy went to work. Mommy had taken her way upstairs to look down on a big room with lots of men sitting at desks. They were awfully noisy! It had seemed like it might be fun when the man in front hit his desk with a hammer and shouted, but then, all they did was talk and talk and talk and it got so-o-o boring. Her mommy had kept telling her to stop fidgeting, but finally took her down the street to a diner to get a chocolate malt. She loved the diner! They got to sit at a counter on stools that twisted around. It was too bad her daddy didn't work there. That would be a lot more fun than being a boring leggy-slater.

Maybe she'd work at the diner when she grew up. Or maybe she'd be on television like her mommy. Mommy wasn't on TV anymore, but she was going to be pretty soon. It was her new job. She was going to tell people what was new every morning.

Kenyon's mind dismissed that bit of information and flitted back to chocolate. She sure would like a chocolate malt now! Leaning over the arm of her chair, she stuck her face two inches from her Po Po's, then thought better of it and cowered back into her own chair. It might be "rude" to wake him up. So many things were "rude," according to her mommy. Thinking hard, she tried to figure out if Po Po would care if she woke him up. He didn't seem to think anything was rude. He was so much fun!

She heard her Mo Mo talking to another lady once and she said that Po Po was different now 'cuz he didn't drink anymore. *How silly!* Kenyon thought. *He has to drink or he'll get too thirsty. 'Sides, he's always been 'xactly the same. He's funny and reads stories and walks on his hands. That's just great, 'cuz pennies fall out of his pockets and he lets me scoop them up to keep.*

Making a decision, she hopped down from her chair and happily jumped up into Po Po's lap, crushing the newspaper. He awoke with a smile and they giggled together as she hugged his neck.

"Are you awake?" she asked.

"Why, yes, I'm wide awake," he said, blinking his eyes. "At least, I am now. Hey, would you like to go get some chocolate milk?"

"Yeah! Chocolate milk is groo-oo-vy!"

He held her small hand as they walked down the long white hall, seeking out the world of groovy chocolate milk.

◆ ◆ ◆ ◆ ◆ ◆ ◆ ◆

Kenyon peered over the rail of the hospital bed, disappointed. That baby in her mommy's arms was awfully tiny. He didn't seem to like to do anything but sleep.

"Here, how about if you hold him?" her daddy suggested. He picked her up and sat her in a chair, then picked up the baby. With wide eyes, she took the small bundle from his arms into her own and held on tight, determined not to drop it on the floor.

Llayne and Mack, along with her parents, beamed as they watched the children together. Mack bent over his wife, freshly scrubbed with her hair straight back in a pony-tail causing her to look 16, and they shared a long, proud kiss.

Crouching over the baby, Kenyon studied his sleeping, chubby, red face and abundant, curly, red hair. Almost whispering, she said, "Wake up, little red Zachary! God brought you to us to love! But first you have to wake up, so we can show you how much we love you!"

Llayne clasped Mack's hand, her eyes sparkling with joyful tears, as she realized how true those innocent words were. *We all have to wake up, so that we can accept love.*

That was the best homecoming of all!